SASSY LOVE
LOVE IN THE CITY SERIES

ALEXANDRA BANKS

Copyright © 2025 by Alexandra Banks.

All rights reserved. No part of this book may be used or reproduced in any form whatsoever without written permission except in the case of brief quotations in critical articles or reviews.

This book is a work of fiction. Names, characters, businesses, organizations, places, events, and incidents either are the product of the author's imagination or are used fictitiously. Any resemblance to actual persons, living or dead, events, or locales is entirely coincidental.

For more information, or to book an event, contact:

alexandrabanksauthor@gmail.com

Book design by Alexandra Banks

Cover design by Alexandra Banks & Yondette Dungca

First Edition: October 2025

ISBN – eBook – 978-1-7637728-8-5

ISBN – Paperback – 978-1-7641949-6-9

ISBN – Hardcover – 978-1-7641949-7-6

ALSO BY ALEXANDRA BANKS

Rosewood Ranch Series
Tough Love
Heart & Hope
Saving Grace
True North

Fire Island Series
Tender Heart
Fire Heart

Love in the City Series

Sassy Love
Burning Love
Tangled Love

To the women who barely survive but deserve to thrive:
We see you. We see your enduring strength and the effort it takes to make
it through the day.

This book is a dedication to you.

Even if, we as readers, only make 1% of a difference . . . we're committed
to helping-starting with this book.

TOO MUCH
DOVE CAMERON

GET IT DONE
GUY SEBASTIAN

LOOK WHAT YOU
MADE ME DO
TAYLOR SWIFT

TRAINING
SEASON
DUA LIPA

WE CAN'T BE
FRIENDS
ARIANA GRANDE

KISS ME
DERMOT KENNEDY

SPIN YOU
AROUND
MORGAN WALLEN

LOVE IN SLOW
MOTION
ED SHEERAN

ALL OF ME
JOHN LEGEND

COVER ME IN
SUNSHINE
PINK &
WILLOW SAGE HART

AUTHOR'S NOTE

TW –

This book contains difficult scenes and recounts, including displacement and domestic violence. For the full list of trigger warnings please visit - https://www.alexandra-banks.com/ebook

The location, topographies and personas of the places and characters in this story have been fictionalized. They may not accurately represent actual location and terrain.

<u>*PSA - Love in the City Series*</u>

This series is my way of paying it forward. All eBook and Kindle Unlimited profits from this series go to charities that help women around the world. The information for this is at the back of the book!

You can access the playlist here!
https://open.spotify.com/playlist/7ASUXJ3Lkpj50EyRKL8z6v

SASSY LOVE

CHAPTER 1
CARLIE

"For fuck's sake."

Acid twists in my stomach and anxiety peaks through my veins with every thunderous heartbeat. How the hell did this happen? Same old bullshit, different idiot at the wheel. My hands are creeping through my hair, my stilettos pinching my feet at the wee hour of eight a.m.

Letting my eyes fall shut, I block out my own reflection along with the city view from the foyer outside the corner office I worked years to finally inhabit. The brown eyes staring back at me may be mine, but I can't bear the penetrating stare of my own stupidity.

Papers shuffle behind me, a tentative throat clearing. "This wasn't your fault, love. I am sure the board will understand?" Her voice is too high. She doesn't believe a word she said.

I have known her long enough to know her tells. The slightly elevated pitch of that saccharine statement is a dead giveaway.

Sorry, Millie.

Exhaling, I spin to face her, the heel of my stiletto grinding into the luxury carpet.

Millicent DeLuca hands me my morning coffee, as she's done for the last seven years, and settles into the one piece of furniture she requested in her office that marks the barrier between the rest of the company and my own office. Her late father's polished chair creaks with her descent, and she closes her eyes, taking the first sip.

I lean against her desk and sip my coffee. The heat scorches my tongue. Caramel latte with oat milk and a dash of cinnamon.

She never forgets.

"How did this simple account turn into such a shitstorm? I mean, how hard is it to attend a press conference and not screw it up! The one time I wasn't there. Christ, Mills, the board is going to have a field day with this. They were unimpressed I took the week off for personal leave as it was, and then this happens—with one of our biggest clients. I am so done for."

"You cannot be responsible for the actions of a grown man, my girl. Surely, they will see that?"

I shake my head and return my gaze to the floor-to-ceiling windows that surround both our offices.

If I lose my job, so does Millie.

I pinch the bridge of my nose and try to squash the sick feeling curling its way up my insides. Millie is here because she was living in poverty for years before anyone found out. After her husband passed, her ingrate children sold her house, and she moved to a condo. *Not* rent controlled.

She lived on food stamps and a government pension to pay the utilities . . . until that ran out, too. When we met, she was living out of a bus shelter.

At the spritely age of seventy-five, she is one hell of a secretary, taking no slack from those asshole board members. Apparently, public relations remains submissive to finance and every other department who thinks their gender gives them precedence over my agenda and priorities. But Mills hands out reality checks to each one of them daily.

And I love her for it.

The phone rings and we both jump, exchanging a wary look. Millie moves to her desk and picks up the receiver.

"Miss Lamont's office, Millicent speaking."

Always so formal, Mills.

"Ah, yes sir, she will be there in a few minutes."

The phone returns to the cradle with a clunk, and her face tightens.

I run a hand through my hair. "That was Cole, wasn't it."

No need to panic. The head of the board summons people on a regular basis, right? I tighten my grip on the cardboard cup in my hands.

"Whatever happens, you stand your ground. If they were so worried about client behavior, they should have sent a replacement to that event for you."

She's right. This isn't all on me.

I down the last of my coffee and duck into my office to grab my tablet and phone. The screen lights up. One hundred and seventy-nine emails. *Urgh.* I suppress the urge to toss it out the open window I don't have, instead straightening my navy pencil skirt and checking my red silk blouse in my mirror behind the door before reapplying my lipstick.

Never hurts to look your best, especially if you're about to have your cage rattled. At least I can save face, somewhat, by keeping up appearances. Something my mother taught me after Dad walked out on us when I was eight.

The one and only thing my mother bothered to give me—a tough outer shell.

Millie holds the door for me, giving me a reassuring smile. I inhale, nod, and stalk my way down the hallway to the elevator. Two floors up, I step out onto marbled floors. As if even the floor is more superior up here.

"Mr. Carlson is waiting for you, Carlie," Nerada says. At least she is always kind. But her gaze darts away quickly and she busies herself with shuffling items on her desk.

Shit.

Outside his door, I shove my shoulders back and swallow past the lump in my throat. I knock lighter than I intend to.

"Come." The older man's voice is brusque and low.

I open the door and walk toward his . . . gigantic marble desk. I guess the furniture was jealous of the floor.

Every inch of my body vibrates as I hold Cole's gaze. His grey eyes—flanked by sun-kissed, creased skin—burn into mine. His mouth is a thin line as he smooths down his tie. He nods to the chair in front of his desk, and I sit.

A heartbeat later, the door opens behind me, and three suits walk in. Damage control in the form of legal and finance, I suppose.

"What the hell exactly were you thinking letting your highest-paying client fend for himself in the biggest press release of his career, Miss Lamont?" Carlson snaps.

Not trusting myself to respond right away, I try to channel my inner Millie. "With all due respect, Cole, my leave was cleared by HR, and my client is a grown man. His actions are his own responsibility."

"I was anticipating that answer. Yet we assure our clients when they sign up with our firm that we will be there to guide them in situations like this, so that they are not left to fend off the paparazzi wolves alone."

"Why wasn't someone sent in my place?"

"That, we are not sure of. Perhaps a lapse in your planning?" a low voice says as I turn to find the guy from legal, his smug over-round face puckering as if just being in the same room has him sour.

The other two suits stand on either side of him.

Finance and . . . HR?

I snap my gaze back to Carlson.

"My planning was and is adequate. One of the other PR reps had been assigned to cover my clients for the short time I took leave."

"You are blaming this on a junior?" the next guy says. Obviously from finance with that shiny silver tie and gelled-down parted blond hair that looks like his mother's been styling it since he was in diapers.

"No, I—"

"It appears clients of this caliber are above your head, Miss Lamont. Effective immediately, you are demoted to smaller accounts, nothing over the monetary value of two hundred thousand. You will report to the department below yours tomorrow morning for a rundown and allocation of accounts. If this isn't going to work for you, we will require your resignation in no more than two weeks. Is that understood?" Carlson's grey eyes have darkened.

I open my mouth to reply but words slam against the rock blocking my airways.

I look at the three men in the room, still standing.

Ambush.

This was a fucking ambush. Fire seeps through my limbs,

flooding my neck and face. The third man in the room hasn't taken his focus off me the entire time. Conflict laces his dark blue eyes, his jaw tight. I think I saw his picture in a monthly blast. The new HR guy.

He hasn't say a single word.

This was an ambush, and a premeditated one, by the looks of it. I turn back to face Cole. If I lose my job, so does Millie. So it's a no-brainer; I have to stay.

"That will be fine, Mr. Carlson. I won't let you down again."

HR guy flinches a little and drops his gaze to the marble floor.

I rise and hold my tablet and phone to my chest. "I will start clearing out my office." I make for the door faster than stilettos are meant to travel.

"Oh, and Miss Lamont," Cole grunts.

I turn back.

"You won't be requiring your secretary. You will be letting that old fossil go. That's not negotiable and effective immediately."

The gasp that leaves my mouth sends a prickle behind my eyes. I straighten and meet the HR guy's gaze. His face is now stone, the dark hair that was neat before is now slightly tussled. He must have run a hand through it as I was walking out.

I stalk to Carlson's desk and press my fists, one almost cracking the screens of my devices, to the edge. I lean closer as I grind out, "I quit."

My palms turn sweaty while I extricate myself from the ambush, making a beeline for the rest room. I slam my tablet and phone on the vanity, head lighter than a hot fart in Alaska.

I lose my stomach to the sink, knuckles white around the porcelain.

God, how am I supposed to tell Millie she doesn't have a job?

I rise, leaning closer to the mirror, and grab paper towel to fix my smudged lipstick and drool-lined chin. Mostly respectable, I push through the restroom door and make my way to the elevator.

The finance and legal guys wait in front of it.

Just fucking great.

I walk to where they stand and force a smile. The guy from legal runs an eye from my stilettos to my gaze and smirks as the elevator dings and the doors swing open. He swaggers into the small space, and I screw up my face at his back. The finance guy catches the gesture and his brows lower.

I wait for the doors to close before hitting the button for my floor, then tapping my tablet to wake it up. Scrolling through emails so I have somewhere other to look than their arrogant faces, my gaze snags on an email from Millie.

YOU OKAY?
M.

She never texts, but email is okay with her. I smile at her sweet ways, swiping the app closed before my conscience has the chance to respond and tell her she is jobless and it's all my fault.

"Guess someone more deserving will get that big office of yours now, Carla?" legal guy says, victory twisting his stupid mouth into a smirk.

Ass.

His pale, sweaty hands cling to his laptop and notepad at his waist. The guy from finance gives him a sideways look. If I am not mistaken, it's a warning. One that goes unnoticed.

"I suppose." I shrug. That is the least of my worries right now.

"You didn't really think you could worm your way to the top by looking pretty and wearing those spikes, did you?" he says.

Finance guy shifts on his feet, fixing his gaze to the opposite wall.

"Oh, I don't know, they have worked pretty well so far. But I guess you wouldn't know anything about that, since the last titty you sucked was your mother's."

His jaw drops, eyes tight with something like horror scrambled with embarrassment.

Finance guy struggles to hold a straight face, his shoulders wobbling. Legal guy's face turns red.

The elevator slows and stops, binging over muffled laughter.

"See you around, Mary," I say, pinning legal guy with a glare, and step out.

"Mary?" he chokes.

Finance guy clears his throat. "She just called you a virgin."

The doors close and howls of laughter fade below the floor as the elevator descends. Finance guy, at least, has a sense of humor. I walk down the corridor toward my office. The blurred vision of Millie pacing in front of her desk through the opaque glass stops me short before the door.

Closing my eyes, I draw in a long, ragged breath. The door swishes open, and I open my eyes to see a frantic Millie, wringing her hands at her chest, eyes wide.

I shake my head. "I'm so sorry, Mills."

CHAPTER 2
LAWSON

The day I took the job for Cole Carlson, I knew I'd traded my soul for money. Today was the first time I actually saw evidence of that unfold in real time. And I stood there . . . not saying a damn word. I push the iron up for another rep. Fire burns through my shoulders and biceps.

I hold the weight, letting it burn every fiber in my arms.

Good, I deserve it.

I chose Human Resources to help people get a fair chance, and there was *nothing* fair about today. After years slogging away at a double major, being the only son of four to head to college instead of staying home on the ranch or signing up for the army, I was desperate to prove myself.

So, a business degree with management and human resource electives was my choice. Fat lot of good that did in Carlson's office today. Fairness didn't even have a chance to raise her timid head in that stifling, toxic room that may as well have resembled a tundra of marble and chauvinistic ego.

"Someone's quiet tonight." Miles throws me a sideways

glance as he settles onto the machine to my left. His bulky size from working out for his day job as kitten rescuer means he's wedged into the machine. We started college together, but hitting the books made him restless. Running into burning buildings is apparently more his style.

"Shit day," I utter.

He raises an eyebrow.

"Yeah, yeah. I know. Nothing life or death. Only the justice of the world and my conscience battling."

He chuckles before settling into his first rep. Shoulder press. Probably lifting my entire body weight, let's be honest.

"Hey, I have the easy job. Follow orders, save the day. Don't die. You, my friend, dance with the devil. That will always have you trapped in here." He points to his temple and lifts another rep.

His square jaw clenches. His biceps and shoulders strain with the weight, but the cheek in his brown eyes doesn't waiver as he blows me a kiss.

"Fuck off, Milo."

I lift another rep.

He eyes my form before starting his reps again. "You know, if you ever get sick of dancing with Satan, the FDNY would take you on."

I chuckle at him now. "Yeah, sure, bud. I think I'll leave you to the hero work."

His machine returns to base, and his hands fall from the grips, his gaze squaring with mine. "You don't think HR is important?"

"Of course I do. But my ability to help people is . . . limited. At least it is in Carlson's particular realm of hell. And what am

I doing for the big picture, you know? Celebrities don't exactly need more people on their side."

"I'll bet the people that have to work for them do, though."

I hang my head.

Yeah, they do.

And I failed them miserably today.

When I joined the business world, my father told me that careers were built on the backs of others. I'd always assumed that meant leaders paving the way for their teams. In the last few hours, I have come to realize that he meant men like my greed-driven boss standing on the backs of others, crushing souls and breaking bones to build his bank balance and his reputation as the biggest shark in town.

Or city. New York City. We're not in Kansas now.

It will never sink in that I'm not the naive young guy who left Montana. At almost thirty-eight, I have an Upper East Side apartment, a career I love and, up until today, have been proud of and worked my ass off for. It's a far cry from ranching. That's always been my brothers' thing, not mine.

Besides, I look better in a suit.

My arms fail. The gym machine whines, then the plates crash down, and the guy on the leg machine to my left slides an annoyed look my way.

Yeah, me and you both, bud.

Fuck today.

Six ways to fucking Sunday, as my brothers would say.

"Let's finish up, hey," I say to Miles. He wipes his brow and neck, tossing his towel onto his shoulder.

"I just hope Lamont opens and responds to the email I sent her." I sigh, wiping the sweat from my face. I'm not worried about Carlson pinning me for holding him and his gutter tactics accountable. I can find another job if I have to. Hell, I've had more than my share of fresh starts in this city that never sleeps. From wanting to escape questionable bosses to needing a pay raise to keep my apartment. I can adapt to almost anything. A trait I share with my father.

"She'll be fine, I'm sure. Anyone who can earn the corner office in Carlson's world can handle themselves." Milo gives me the 'you know I'm right' look.

"Guess so."

I do three more reps and wipe down the machine in the small gym before walking out into the night air, two blocks from my apartment. Miles falls in beside me, looking around, always aware of his surroundings. Should have been a cop.

"Grabbing takeout tonight? The game's on, if you're up for it?" I ask.

"Nah, up early. Shift tomorrow."

One of his twenty-four-hour shifts. Don't know how they do that shit.

"All good, bud. Catch you on the flip side." I raise a fist, and he smashes his to mine.

"Night, Laws." His wide smile brightens his face, as it always does. "Don't stress over it, hey? It'll work itself out."

Always the optimist, my best friend. Of the three guys that make up my circle, Miles is always the one to lift us up when things go sideways. It's no small wonder he's FDNY's bravest.

Me, I'll be at war with my version of injustice into the middle of the night, no doubt.

If the position wasn't keeping me in my apartment and I didn't have barely a month in this job under my belt, I'd move on.

Then someone else could ignore the rules, bend the business institutional codes for Carlson's wicked ways. I'm sure their bottom line would be better off without me.

Because the second Lamont opens that email, she'll have all she needs to hand the old man his own ass on a silver platter on the grounds of blatant sexism, unfair dismissal, inequality, not to mention the loss of her assistant.

That was a curveball not even I saw coming.

That office has always had an executive assistant, if the company records are correct. And Carlson had no grounds to terminate her position, either.

Ageism.

Oh, and the list keeps getting longer . . .

I hope she makes use of the legal recommendations I made. For women everywhere, she should.

I make my building and push through the door after entering the code. Traipsing up the three flights of stairs to my apartment, I am lost in my head when the squeals reach my ears. Gripping my gym bag, I look up just as wild brown eyes and blonde hair fly at me. Then, a megawatt smile topped with the prettiest damn freckles and curly brown hair falls in beside her, and I'm smothered by two of my favorite people in the whole world.

Exactly what I need right now.

"Laws!" Ruby hugs me so damn tight, I choke out a laugh as Addy dots a kiss to my cheek.

But someone's missing . . .

"Where's Gracie?"

"Mack wouldn't let her drive with us. Apparently, her condition means she flies in style. I'll pop over and pick her up in a few hours." Ruby holds me at arm's length. Her brows fall.

Adds tilts her head, a hand gravitating to her hip. "Laws, what's wrong?"

"Long day is all." It's then I notice their bags by my door.

Ruby gives me her best 'stop with the bullshit' look.

"Come on. Let's get you two inside." I shove the key into my door and open it. I toss my bag inside and pluck up theirs. They follow me in, making themselves at home like they always do. And, damn, I'm so grateful for them today.

"I didn't know you guys were coming," I say, placing their bags in my room. I'll take the sofa, as always.

Adds turns back, frowning. "It's been planned for three months, Laws. This new job is consuming you. Need to talk about it?"

Fuck.

How did I forget three of my favorite people were coming?

Carlson really is messing with my head.

"You know what you need?" Ruby pulls her jacket off and leans into my shoulder.

"What, Rubes?" I say with a laugh.

"Wine—or whiskey, in your case—and a good laugh."

She's not wrong.

"Let me shower first, okay?"

"Sure thing, then we're watching something hilarious. Feel free to get drunk." Rubes winks at me.

I roll my eyes at the woman who turned my little brother's life around. My little brother who, in return, gave her the family she's been missing all those years.

"I'll make you a snack. Go, go!" Adds wanders into the kitchen. With a daughter of her own now, she's almost as bad as Ma. But you'll never hear me complain about either woman.

"Thanks," I breathe.

I wander to the bedroom and into the en suite. The din of laughter, clinking glasses, and kitchen noises fills my home. Well, apartment.

It's never really been a home.

The sound of my family here bolsters my spirits like it always does.

I shower quickly and throw on a T-shirt and sweats, not worried about impressing the girls; they'll no doubt be in their PJs the second Gracie lands. I can't wait to see her.

I choke up, thinking about what she and Mack went through to find each other.

Fuck this mood.

I suck in a long, bursting lungful of air.

Nope. Shut this bullshit down, Lawson.

I'm not letting Carlson get to me. Every single person who's ever had to fight for the right to be safe and happy is why I took this stupid fucking job in the first place. I may have been misguided, too focused on not becoming financially ruined while trying to hang onto this apartment.

Maybe it's time for a change.

I pad to the kitchen to find the girls on the sofa, wine in hand, Netflix on the oversized flat-screen TV. I grab a beer from the fridge and plop between them with a sigh. It's a happier sigh than before. I let my head fall back on the headrest of the sofa and close my eyes.

"Okay, what are we workshopping?" Rubes whispers in one ear.

"Who do I need to bury under one of Harry's fence posts?" Adds whispers in the other.

The hearty chuckle that rattles my Adam's apple earns a poky finger into my ribs. "Ugh, I don't know . . ."

"Yes, you do. Give it to us," Ruby demands.

I crack my right eye to meet her brown eyes, the fire lining them currently lit up for me. Luckiest fucking brother-in-law in the world. Brother. We don't consider these girls in any way removed from our family. They are Rawlinses, through and through.

These are my sisters.

Hell, they fight for our family like they were damn well born into it.

"Laws . . ." Adds says softly. "We worry about you."

I crack the other eye, and worried browns find my gaze.

I sit up, brows dropping. "No, Adds." I'm shaking my head. "Don't feel sorry for me. I'm the problem."

She tilts her head. "Wha—"

The doorbell rings.

"Shoot! What time is it?" Rubes flies up off the sofa.

I glance at the minimalist silver clock I bought with my first apartment. Seven oh five.

I push off the sofa as Rubes checks her phone, madly swiping through her messages as she mutters something under her breath.

I swing the door open.

The smile that splits my face earns the prettiest grin from the woman in the hallway.

"Hello, Gracie."

Her face scrunches, and she falls into my chest. "Oh, Laws, I *missed* you."

I splay a hand over her messy bun of light brown hair, hugging her petite frame to my chest. Her protruding belly presses into my stomach, reminding me why she didn't drive with the girls. My brother's wife, his baby mama, and fucking salvation.

She pushes from my hold and studies my face.

Her bottom lip worries through her teeth and she shifts on her feet as she rubs a thumb over my brows. "What's got you all wound up, hey now?"

These fucking women. I swallow past the stone in my throat and make a promise that my next move will be less cowardly than the last.

CHAPTER 3
CARLIE

"Can you start right away? Lord knows this place could use some help," Serelle, the founder and head of Serenity House, a women's shelter, asks. Her smile is genuine.

My need for this job even more so.

"Absolutely. I'm so excited to use my experience and skills to make a difference here."

"Wonderful! There may be some marketing involved, as well, but I'm sure you can handle it." She stands. "I'll give you the grand tour. Is tomorrow good for your onboarding?"

Marketing. I haven't got the first clue on how to put together a marketing campaign for a business like this one. Do we even call it a business? "Of course."

Her phone rings, and she hesitates. "Shoot, that'll be my next interview."

"I don't understand?" I ask. She just gave me the job.

"Our business manager quit last week, and we can't afford

to let anything slip. Margins are tight this time of year and with our current contracts, etc."

"Oh, sure."

I breathe a sigh of relief as she picks up the receiver and talks softly. God, the last thing I could take would be losing another freaking job. As it is, I'm going to have to allocate twenty-five percent of my wage to Mills. Luckily, she was happy moving in with me after Carlson . . .

We've lived together before. Not long after we first met.

"Sorry about this. I'll find Nadia to show you around while I take this next appointment," Serelle says, plucking up the phone again before hitting a button.

I glance around her office from my vantage point at her door. Her shelves are packed with treasures of a life well-traveled. Her sleeveless light-green linen dress hangs off her wiry frame. Her light brown curly hair is like a cloud around her head and shoulders, lined with streaks of silver.

Kind eyes find mine, and she gives me a sweet smile as she hangs up. "Right, about tomorrow, you will have onboarding with whoever I hire today. Along with Nadia, she does all the intakes."

"What time do you need me here?"

"Oh, half eight should be good. Nadia, will you show Carlie to the executive office, please?"

A meek petite, curly haired brunette with oversized glasses appears in the hall, as if she'd anticipated this. "Yes, hello, I'm Nadia." She holds out a hand, beaming.

I shake her hand and feel like some kind of Amazonian giant standing beside her in my four-inch heels. Her weathered tweed skirt suit makes me feel overdressed. I offer her a tight smile, and she nods, walking down the hall. We pass the foyer where I first arrived and walk past the front desk. Two guys in suits sit in the plastic chairs, both looking down, both engrossed. One with his phone, the other with a tattered paperback. Neither look up as I cross the small room and follow Nadia into the office.

A long corridor dotted with plain white doors flanks us and I take in my surroundings as much as I can as she prattles on about the facilities.

Copy and supply room to the left.

Break room to the right.

Social workers and a therapists' suite take up the rest of the doors on the left, which takes us to the end of the corridor that opens up to a large open office floor space.

"Sorry, it's a little crowded." She offers up an apologetic smile as we weave through a sea of desks where staff are currently working. They look up as I walk through, nodding with tight smiles.

"Hi," says an older man, balding with suspicious light blue eyes and a crinkled shirt, crooked tie, and the messiest desk I've ever seen. His trash can is full of candy wrappers, which explains the distance between his chair and desk. Stifling a grimace, I set my eyes on the glass-walled corner office that Nadia currently stands in front of.

"This is you, and, well, the business management guy. Whoever that will be."

"Thanks." I walk inside to find a large white table that looks more like an old dining table than office furniture. Shelves run along the wall under another large window. Two non-ergonomic chairs, one grey and the other a weird orange color, sit at either end of the table. I wander to the window to find views of the city. There's one large potted faux fig, a dented trash can that looks like it's been used as the staff football, and a cart with charging docks where two bricks of laptops sit.

Good lord, no wonder the place is running on fumes. Not exactly inspiring staff morale—or any morale, to think of it.

"Thanks, Nadia. Is it okay if I bring my own supplies in? Laptop, chair, etc.?"

She looks surprised but nods. "Absolutely. You'll have to get the passwords from the tech guy so you can log in to our systems, but that shouldn't be a problem."

"Great." I give her a smile that is part excitement, part my keenness to make a difference here. Even if it's only the office decor.

"Well, since there's only the two of you for onboarding tomorrow, I guess we could do it in here." She glances around the room.

"Sounds good."

"I'll see you out, then."

We pass the bald candy guy, and he gives me a cringy thumbs up as his gaze drifts up my body. I return a tight smile and pick up my pace, ignoring the uncomfortable heat snaking down my spine. Nadia waves me off as I spill into the foyer. Instantly, cedar and spice hit me. Man smell.

Delicious.

That reminds me, it's been at least a fortnight since I swiped right. Maybe I should celebrate tonight. I could go for an orgasm or five. The second the thought forms, I remember Mills is waiting at home for me.

Guess it's my old friend Vinny. I am a thousand percent aware it's weird to name your vibrator, but hey, he's never let me down yet. And we've been together for years. No strings, no disgusting feelings, only lust and orgasms. He gives me all a girl could ever need.

I don't do love.

I stopped believing in love the day my dad walked out. Men are only good for one thing, and Vinny is hands down a better lay than most of the guys I've been with.

Much less complicated.

I walk the two flights of stairs down to the front doors of the oversized building with stunning heritage features. The first floor has been remodeled to three large spaces—two dorm-type rooms with bathroom and shower facilities and a large community room where the women and girls who end up here spend time, safe and cared for.

A stone forms in my throat as I close the heavy wooden door behind me and step into the sunshine. Summer is fading, the days cooling off, the first tinge of fall poking through in the leaves of the trees studded along the sidewalk of Franklin Ave.

I head for the subway. It will take me a solid hour to get home. But the thought of moving from the apartment I love in the suburb I know every block of seems ridiculous. Besides, who knows if this job will pan out? My heels click toward the steps as people pour up and out of the underground labyrinth. I slide to the right and squeeze my way down to the platform.

The doors to the train swoosh open, and I wait for people to disembark before stepping aboard. As soon as my ass hits the vinyl seat, I let my head rest on the window and my eyelids fall.

Here's to a new start.

The sweetest, excited, wrinkled smile greets me as I unlock the front door to my Bronx apartment. Her blue eyes light her face, hands clutched together in front of her chest. "Well? Did you get it?"

I laugh as I tug my jacket off and toss it onto the front rack, dumping my bag to the floor. "I did."

I grab her arms, and her hands close around my forearms.

"I knew you would. Imagine the difference you can make in a place like that, Carlie, sweetheart."

"Yeah, it will be something to strive toward, that's for sure."

"How do you mean?"

"It's not a glamorous outfit like Carlson's. But it will be great on my resume."

She releases me and heads for the kitchen with a wave over her shoulder. "Resume, schmesume. You're built for great things. And this is the start of something great, you mark my words, missy."

It's now that I smell the delicious aroma of Italian. Spaghetti, maybe . . . Possibly garlic bread?

I toe off my heels and pad to the kitchen to find Millie stirring something in a pot on the stove.

"How many times have I told you? You are not my maid, Mills. This is your home."

"Too many, and frankly, it's a little insulting. I like to cook, and taking care of you is one of my greatest pleasures. How dare you steal that from me." She huffs playfully, and I narrow my eyes as I close in on the stove and lean over her. She's so small. I swear she shrinks more and more each year. I plunge a finger into the hot, bubbling red sauce, stuffing it into my mouth before it burns my skin.

"Hey!" She slaps my arm.

I smile around my finger as the flavor hits.

"Good god. A girl could orgasm from this."

"Carlie Lamont, watch that sassy little mouth of yours!" The blush creeping up Millie's neck and face is adorable as she frowns at me, bewildered. It blows my mind that the generations before us lived so wild and free, unaffected by technology and social media, but bring up talk of sex, and they run and hide.

I couldn't live like that . . .

Mills turns on me, wooden spoon in hand. "You and your mouth can set the table."

I pull a face that sees a smile crack and stretch her face. But I oblige, setting two places and gathering cutlery, her favorite wine and my green juice.

"Dinner's ready," Millie calls from the sink as she tips the pasta into the colander to drain. Steam billows above her and she hisses. I'm guessing she burned herself.

"Shit, Mills. Will you let me help, for god's sake?"

She steps sideways with no argument. Not like her at all.

"You okay?" I ask softly.

She sighs. "Everything seems to be harder these days. I'm not getting any younger."

"I know, you old fossil, so take a hike and let me handle this before you end up with third-degree burns."

She rolls her eyes at me, and I suppress the need to laugh at her. Seventy-five and as fiery as she was when she was in her twenties. Where does she think I got the sass from?

"Your mom rang earlier," Mills says as she sits at the table.

"Oh." I load up two plates and carry them to the table.

Millie frowns, her eyes setting into a hard gaze that's locked onto my face.

"One day, you might want her back in your life. Take her calls, love."

That will be the day hell freezes over.

CHAPTER 4
LAWSON

I can't take my eyes off the strawberry blonde across the white desk—well, table—from me. Her brown eyes bore into my head, as if she can make my brain implode with her super vision.

And . . . she has every reason to hate me.

Sweet Jesus.

Carlie Lamont raises one elegant-as-fuck eyebrow as she sits unnaturally still, waiting for Nadia to leave the room. Nadia runs off to collect something she forgot when she arrived, in a flurry of apologies, five minutes late.

"What. The. Actual. Fuck." She stabs me with each syllable, and I brace for impact.

"Nice." I grind my molars.

"Nice? I'm sorry, are you here in an HR capacity? Or for the business management gig? Because last time I checked, you were standing in the corner, chicken shit, while I was fired from the career that took me over a decade to build."

"I'm not HR anymore," I offer.

"Well, that's great news for the working folk of New York."

"Maybe we should try for a fresh start. We have to work together."

I look around the room that feels a hell of a lot smaller than it did when I saw it yesterday. Could possibly be due to the fiery woman swallowing up all the fucking oxygen in the room.

She can hate me all she likes, but we have to work together, so we should at least try.

"A fresh start? Yeah, that's not happening." Carlie raps her nails on the desk. *The woman holds a grudge . . .*

She continues, "Why on earth did you apply for this job? Something to atone for?"

A smirk, albeit a stunning one, tugs over her mouth.

I force my gaze back to hers. "Something like that."

She scoffs. "Fuck my luck."

The mouth on her.

Jesus.

I run my hands through my hair as Nadia returns, still apologizing. She hands printouts to Carlie and me and sinks meekly into her chair with a side glance at Carlie, whose glare burns into me. It's almost as if she's scared of her. Smart woman.

Nadia's focus volleys back and forth between me and Lamont. "I'm sorry, do you two know each other?"

"No," Lamont snaps as I say, "Yes."

Fair. That's completely fair.

Carlie forces her focus from me down as she plucks the handout up from the desk with perfectly manicured pale-pink nails. Her brown eyes scan over the page.

Nadia clears her throat, and I remember the document in front of me.

Serenity House Mission Statement.

I flip to the first page and read it quickly.

It covers the founders, the goals, and the principles that guide the shelter and various community initiatives.

Everything looks great.

This is not my first time working for a non-profit, but it's the first that hits home, bringing up the early days of Grace coming to work for Ma, taking care of Mack. I flip the page.

Figures cover the paper, the payroll, operating costs, contract settlement amounts and such.

An area of business I've been missing. I guess I'm more like my old man Harry than I give myself credit for. I huff as I scan the bottom line and find it much smaller than I expected.

"Something funny, Rawlins?" Carlie pins me with her browns.

I'm as far from amused as can be when I pull my gaze from the paperwork to meet hers.

Hell, it's like having Ruby across the table from me. Luckily for me, I know how to wind up clever, fiery women.

"Not a thing, Lamont." I hold her stare until she returns her focus to the page in front of her.

"These are the most recent figures. The next annual report is due around Christmas, and that will fall into your scope of practice. We don't have the funds for an actual finance department," Nadia says with a small tentative smile.

"Oh sure. Can't wait to dig into the numbers for you." I give her a megawatt smile. I'd bet my folks' ranch that I can improve these numbers.

Turning back to the page, I catch Carlie's eye roll. Pretty sure the Mars rover picked it up.

I suppose I shouldn't be surprised . . . I find a gig that

speaks to my soul and land the job despite my lack of recent business management experience, only to find myself stuffed in a tiny office with my newest archnemesis.

This is my penance.

Well-earned. But over hell's frozen testicles am I bowing down now. From what Serelle told me, they need me here. Serenity is desperate for a turnaround before they end up another organization that couldn't make ends meet and every last woman and girl who relies on this place has nowhere else to go.

"Nadia, from a PR standpoint, which of these documents do I need to pay particular attention to?" the devil's offspring says with a forced smile.

"Oh, the last four pages are related to our community efforts and exposure."

"Wonderful," she replies with the fakest damn smile, thumbing the last few pages.

I study the fine lines and angles that make up Carlie Lamont. If she wasn't the world's biggest bitch, she'd be the whole package. What does Rubes say?

She's a ten but she's got attitude.

Now, I do chuckle to myself.

Carlie looks up from under dark lashes, and the look could melt the Arctic.

Sweet Jesus. This inner monologue of mine needs to quiet the hell down before she wipes me completely. Since we need to work together and hopefully save this place, I can't give her any reason to.

Sounds easy, in theory.

Doesn't it?

"Well, I'll let you two get acquainted and look over the reports. After lunch, we have an all-staff meeting. You can meet the rest of the team then." Nadia rises, clutching cream folders to her chest. The ones she originally came in with. "If you need anything, my line is six. Feel free to shout out for anything, I'm kinda the jack-of-all-trades around here, alongside manning—or is it womaning?—front reception?"

Is she asking us?

She seems nervous as she rushes from the room.

"Thanks, Nadia," I call out after her as she slips through the glass door.

She ducks and waves, her blue eyes lit up, before disappearing across the staffroom floor and around the corner.

"Good lord, you utter suck-up." Sharp words snag my attention.

Carlie is standing, the papers in her hand. Her crisp white work shirt, that looks more designer than it should in a place like this, is tucked into a fitted navy skirt that hugs her frame, finishing before her knees over cream heels.

I slide my hands inside my pockets. The white shirt and blue tie I'm wearing over navy slacks with black dress shoes has me feeling underdressed next to her.

"Right, if you're done staring, we should go over this page by page and makes some notes, review last fiscal year's efforts, and plan from there," Carlie says, her gaze traveling the room, looking anywhere but directly at me.

"Fine." I roll up my sleeves like I mean fucking business and drag my chair closer to hers at the other end.

"What are you doing?" she snaps, her eyes alternating between me and the chair I hauled around the table.

"I'm not shouting across the damn table."

Her face is unreadable as she turns back and rifles through her handbag, an oversized tote, and produces something like . . .

Tape?

She walks to where I stand with my hand still on my chair. Flicking a hand at me, she waits, glaring, as I push the chair back and step out of her way. She leans over, running pink fucking tape across the center of the table.

You've got to be joking.

She spins back, as if reading my mind, and points to her chair. "This is my side. That is yours. Never shall the two converge. Got it?"

That's the last damn straw.

This she-devil can kiss my sweaty nuts. From everything I learned at Carlson's, she was efficient, productive, and handled people with grace and style. I can only figure this version of her stems from what happened in that last meeting in Carlson's office.

"Whatever you say. Just . . ." I push my chair back to my end of the table and sink into it. I lean back, propping my hands behind my head and crossing my ankle over my knee, the epitome of undeterred. "Next time, put it in writing. An email will suffice. If we're going to have that kind of relationship, Lamont."

Clearly, the woman never opened the last one I sent her.

She stalks to where I sit, and I tilt my head up as she bends down, hands on those damn hips. "Not now, or at any time, will you and I have a *relationship*, Rawlins. Professional or otherwise."

I resist the urge to run my gaze over her incredible

fucking curves, planting my somewhat feigned glare on her pouty fucking lips. "Don't go makin' any promises you'll regret, darlin'." I give her my best Harry and watch with utter delight as her face twitches when the Montana accent I grew up with and the vernacular my father spouts on the daily lands.

She stands, frowning, before stepping back and squatting to run the tape over the floor, cordoning off my half of the office from hers. I sit up, leaning on the desk, realizing the door is in her half. "And how am I supposed to leave?"

She turns back from tucking the tape back in her bag. "You'll figure it out."

A soft knock catches both our attention.

Nadia.

She's trying her best not to stare at the flaming fuchsia tape over the desk and floor. "Um, Lawson, would you be able to help me with something?"

"Sure," I say, rising from my chair and crossing the stupid pink line.

Carlie folds her arms, narrowing her eyes and burning a hole in my back as I follow Nadia from the office. I leave Carlie seething as I wander toward the supply room with Nadia.

"What do you need?" I ask.

"Oh, the copier paper got stuck, and I can't manage the top half up while I remove the wedged-in paper. All the other guys are in a project meeting. Could you hold it for me?" Big eyes look up at me.

I shift on my feet, realizing we did, in fact, pass two other guys in the staff room on our way here. Nadia shuts the door, and I fold my arms over my chest, putting a few feet between us. "You sure one of the others can't help?"

"I-I can't ask Bob for help, I'm not really . . ." Her face and neck flush as her gaze sinks to the floor.

I raise a hand. "It's fine. Show me what to do."

She swallows and nods at the lid. I try to lift it, but it doesn't budge. Her hand moves along the underside, brushing against mine before she clicks a lever and the top pops open.

"It won't take long," she says softly.

I lift the lid and hoist it up. It's heavier than it looks. The watch my folks gave me moves on my wrist as I adjust my grip, forearms flexing. Nadia leans into the machine, tugging at a pile of jammed papers.

"How long have you worked here?" I ask.

A muffled "Huh?" escapes the printer cavity as she bobs up, hitting her head on the lid.

"Shoot." She rubs her head with a hand, smudging ink over her forehead.

"Geez, sorry." I push it open further. "Was asking how long you've been working here. Now, you've got something . . ." I point to her forehead.

"Oh, almost six years." She wipes at her face with her clean hand and glances at me before diving back in and removing a destroyed wad of paper. "Thanks."

I lower the lid, and it clicks shut. The machine whirs back to life as she hits the power button and I give her a nod before heading for the door.

"Lawson?"

I turn back.

"Um, thanks." Her sheepish look and ink-stained hands clutched in front of her pull a genuine smile from me.

"You're welcome."

I open the door and head back to Medusa's lair made of glass and neon-pink tape.

Time to stake out my territory.

I may only technically be able to claim half of that office, but I'm going to make it mine. And she is going to work with me to see this place thrive and drop the damn attitude while she's at it.

CHAPTER 5
CARLIE

Kill them, *him*, with kindness.

Millie's idea that she spent two hours convincing me was my best option if I wanted to keep this job and have some way to work with Mr. Montana over there.

Yep, you bet your ass I Google-stalked this small-town redneck turned Mr. All-American Business.

Keep your enemies closer and all that.

I dump a basket of muffins and a large Starbucks coffee over the pink tape boundary and into enemy territory. Rawlins doesn't bother looking up from his laptop, his big mitts flying over the keyboard.

Poor fucking keys . . .

Each swift stroke shifts the tendons across the back of his hands.

The pads of his fingers tapping with precise caresses.

Fuck a girl sideways.

I clear my throat. "Breakfast."

I sink into my chair and open my laptop. What is he doing here so stinking early, anyway?

"Already ate," he grunts, still not looking up.

Sorry, Mills, your strategy died in the water.

It's only now I realize his hair is damp. A small duffel that looks like a gym bag sits to one side of his chair by the table leg.

So, I try again.

"Get a good workout in this morning, then?" I say, lacing the words with the sweetest tone I can muster.

Urgh, it feels like acid in my throat.

"Don't work out on Tuesdays." His eyes don't leave the screen.

Okay, rude.

"Okay, I'll bite, why is your hair wet?"

Now, he looks up. "It's not wet."

"Um, yeah it is. Did you walk through a storm on your way to work after your hearty breakfast?"

His jaw clenches before he says, "Nope."

"Oh, for fuck's sake, this is me trying to play nice, Rawlins. Take it or leave it."

"I don't want your nice, Lamont. I want your professionalism. And cooperation."

I shake my head and open my inbox, muttering, "Bet that gets all the girls wet."

"Sorry, I missed that."

"Good, you were supposed to." I don't let my eyes wander up to the deep blues I can feel burning into my face.

He wants to do this the hard way? The hard way it is.

"I need the budget projection for the next quarter by the end of the day."

"Email a request."

"I'm requesting it now."

Without meeting my gaze, he sits back in his chair, loosening his tie as if that's what'll kill him. "In writing, remember?"

I hold up a finger, the universal signal for 'please wait,' and spin the office chair around to grab my tote. Inside is a large bag of my new stationery. This office is drab at best, a little more color is just what's needed.

I haul the bag from where I stuffed it after leaving the store and take my time setting up my desk. An aesthetic of hot pink, pale pink, and cream and gold, until my half of the desk looks like a working girl's paradise with gold accents.

Rawlins raises a brow over those stupid fucking blue eyes and presses his lips together.

"Get your own. If I find you stealing my stuff, I'll have your balls."

He huffs through a laugh. "Pink's not my color, Princess."

Heat floods my neck and face.

I hate that nickname. I hate everything it represents, from the ridiculous patriarchal system it stemmed from to the last person who called me that.

My dad.

Before he left with the fucking milk.

I stand and my chair rolls back, hitting the sideboard my bag sits on. "Don't call me that." I lean forward, planting my fists on either side of my laptop. "Ever."

He holds his hands up in surrender, those blue eyes a little wider as he studies my face. Like he cares. Like he can figure out the wounds and baggage that make up Carlie Lamont. Like hell he's getting a chance to find the chinks in my armor.

"End of day, Rawlins. Or the only communication you'll be receiving in your precious inbox will be from Serelle." My tone is harsh, the volume raised with my harried blood rushing through my head.

He frowns at me now.

Huh, who would have thought he would be the teacher's pet . . .

Oh yeah, that's right, I did.

I pegged him right the first time, damn suck-up.

He flicks his gaze to the side, looking outside this glass box we're in. Like Ken and Barbie in a two-for-one box.

Mortified, I find the entire staff frozen, staring through said glass walls at the two of us. We're literally in a fishbowl. A square glass enclosure made to house the shelters' most expensive acquisitions, which apparently is *not* soundproof.

"Shit," I breathe, dropping back into my seat.

That's all I need, an audience.

"You'll have it in writing before lunch, and I expect a quick turnaround, Rawlins."

"Fine." He straightens his tie and leans over the desk, stealing a muffin from the basket and sipping the coffee that's probably lukewarm by now. "How'd you know apple cinnamon's my favorite?"

He smiles his hideous megawatt grin at me before taking a bite. His Adam's apple bobs, and he swallows a mouthful of coffee to wash down the bite before tossing the muffin in the trash can by the door as he leans down, coffee in hand still.

With a click of my mouse, I flick the email to his inbox. And the *whoosh* sounds from my laptop fills the room.

"Much better, Lamont. Following orders already."

Ass!

The balls on this guy.

I catch the smuggest smile stretching his face as he pushes through the glass door and weaves through the sea of desks, chatting and saying hi to people as he goes.

Goddamn brownnoser.

How is he the people person in this office? That's always been my card, the strength that found me in PR in the first place.

My laptop pings.

Reminder: Exec Meeting – Serelle.

Hell, that's why he left. Shit.

I bite a muffin and swipe up my coffee and hightail it from the fishbowl and through the desks after Rawlins. But unlike his trip past the desks, nobody is chatting or stopping what they're doing to say hello to me.

This is his angle?

Make everyone love him, so they hate me?

Rub my shortcomings in my face?

Right, Cowboy. *Game on.*

The pink sticky note that moves with the air funneling down from the central air system sticks to the top of *his* laptop.

I scroll through the last quarter's marketing plan and PR notes. It's not much to go on, but from what I can gather, the efforts were pretty minimal. And the health of the business sadly reflects that. That's one thing Rawlins and I agree on, at least.

The telltale swoosh of a sent email sounds as I finish up a request for a meeting with Serelle to hash out some better, more effective ideas for the shelter. I mean, I could just go ahead and plan all this out—after receiving the budget, that is.

But I would rather know the lay of the land and what she'd like me to work on than get halfway through my grand plans, only to be shut down because it's not what is usually done.

The glass door opens, and Rawlins walks to his desk, phone in hand, not looking away from the screen for a second. With only five minutes to lunch, I pin him with my gaze, waiting for him to find the pink sticky note.

My written request.

Email, my ass. He has it on his computer—in detail, no doubt—it would take less than a minute to copy and paste that section of his financial report and send it on.

"Can I help you?" he says, still not looking up from his phone.

"You can start by putting your personal business aside at work."

He tosses his phone beside his laptop. "What, the coffee and muffins were from your other personality?"

My mouth gapes, and I snap it shut.

I will not lose my cool.

I will not lose my cool.

I will not lose my cool.

I point a manicured finger at the sticky note on his computer.

Running a hand through his brown hair that looks like it would feel like silk to sink my fingers into, he peels the note from his Mac.

"In writing, as requested," I say with the most saccharine tone I can rouse in his vexing presence.

Looking up, he tilts his head as if considering something. Without a word, he crumples the sticky note in his fist and tosses it into the trash, making it in from his side of the desk.

Show off.

He rolls his chair forward and opens his computer. A few seconds later, my email pings.

Rawlins, Lawson - **Request Denied**.

"The fuck? This isn't a game. I need those numbers, Rawlins."

He stands, walking to the wall behind his side of the desk where a large whiteboard hangs on the wall. He starts writing up some sort of mind map, complete with figures from the original report we studied during onboarding.

I study him for a moment. Sleeves rolled up, marker scrawling across the shiny white surface as he brain-dumps notes beside each designated bubble.

And I would have to be dead not to notice his shirt straining over his shoulders and biceps, his tight, round ass . . .

Shit.

Annoyed and needing to get my own work done, I return to the last quarter planning and reports and open a fresh blank document. I create two subheadings, 'old style' and 'Lamont style.'

I set two columns in the doc and save it to my personal drive just in case. I have a ton of contacts from working for Carlson for ten years and good relationships with vendors and events people from all over the city. Surely, since this is definitely a good cause, arranging promos and marketing events should be a breeze, right?

When I check out the shelter's socials and website, my hope deflates. The website is old, outdated, and houses almost nothing helpful for either women in need or potential donors. This will all need to be overhauled. Which means another hit to the budget. Let's hope that it is substantial enough to cover the upgrades I know it's going to require to move this place off the dire list and onto the thrive list.

I'm mid-hunt into my contacts for potential event ideas when my email pings. Hopeful, I flick over to the app. But my hope dies as quickly as it bloomed when it's Serelle, confirming a meeting.

Starting in ten minutes.

Guess I'm winging it.

It would be great to have those numbers before I head in. Maybe I can ask her for the reports, or where to find them. Deciding it's best to be early, I gather up my laptop and phone and head for the door. When I reach Serelle's office, Nadia is inside, singing the praises of none other than Rawlins.

God, this girl has it bad.

Guess that small-town charm of his works on this basic bitch.

Figures.

"Come in, Carlie. We're done here." Serelle waves me in.

Nadia gives me a tight smile as she slips past me and through the door. I sit in the chair and set my laptop and phone down.

"How's your first week?" Serelle asks.

"Good. Fine."

She smiles as if she knows something I don't. "Excellent. What can I do for you?"

The meeting goes as I expected. She shows me where to

find the reports but shuts down my better ideas in favor of more conservative ones.

Just what I was afraid of.

If her preferred tactics worked, they wouldn't be scrambling each quarter. If it's out of your comfort zone, it's most likely what you're supposed to aim for. Apparently, not everyone got that particular memo.

I make my way back to the fishbowl to find it vacant.

But as I push through the door and cross to the desk, I find a clutter of sticky notes—*my* pink sticky notes—stuck over my end of the table. Each one inscribed, in the most annoyingly neat cursive, with a category or department and the spending or budget.

The thought that sears through my mind hangs on the fact that Rawlins and his big mitts went rifling through my stuff.

The whiteboard is cleaned of his previous scribbling and diagrams. And in the center, an elegant short sentence in the same perfect cursive is handwritten on a slight angle in pink marker.

You're welcome, Princess.

My marker, that currently stands on its end amidst the sticky notes plastering my desk like a lone knight amongst a sea of fallen fuchsia foe.

Fucking Rawlins.

CHAPTER 6
LAWSON

The brown brick of Serenity House Women's Shelter towers over me as I wait by the front steps, feeling more than a little guilty about my last poor choice of words directed at the woman I have to share an enclosed space with. I should apologize.

I should eat my damn words.

The clack of heels closes in, and I look up from the message I sent Mack. I'm so far out of my depth with this fiery woman. I thought I could handle working here. With her.

Maybe I should talk to Reed instead? God knows Rubes keeps him on his toes.

Carlie's in a dress today—red—with black heels.

Fuck a man where he stands. I loosen the tie around my neck and force a platonic smile as she side-eyes me and stalks past.

Great. Just fucking great.

"Carlie, wait up."

With a sigh, she stops and spins back. "What, Rawlins?"

"Did you get somewhere with those numbers I put on your desk?"

She tilts her head, closing the space between us at the top of the stairs on the landing. She smells goddamn incredible. Like spice and vanilla, or is that something floral?

"Serelle gave me access, so I don't need your little hand-written love notes anymore."

"Love notes?" I raise both brows at her.

She made a very clear point of hating being called Princess. But by the look on her face, it didn't hit the way I assumed it would. Just when I think I have her pegged, she surprises me.

I'm an idiot.

That's most likely her MO. Say one thing, do the other.

"You know, those sticky notes you stole and then littered my desk with?" She raises her chin, and it's all I can do to not let my gaze fall to the soft, delicious-looking creaminess of her elegant neck.

The thought bursts when she says, "And who could forget the whiteboard covered in your formidable scrawl? My vibrator legit ran out of batteries last night when I replayed those words over and over in my mind."

Her red-stained lips part on a feigned desperate breath, letting her head fall back.

My last breath stalls out.

The image of this stunning, hot-headed woman arched on a bed, impaled by her vibrator, sends my blood rushing south faster than humanly possible.

Sweet Jesus.

I try to clear my throat and choke on the absence of air that should be inflating my damn lungs. I grind my molars, sliding my hands into my pockets and hoping she doesn't catch the now-stretched crotch of my slacks. "Here I was thinking you'd be face down in your pillow, crying all night at the thought of me."

She huffs a breath, raising an eyebrow. "The only way I'll be face-planting on my pillow is if I'm biting it. And nowhere in that scenario would there be you."

Well, fuck.

She throws a smile over her shoulder, so saccharine that it absolutely registers as an insult.

Christ, it's going to be a long day. I'm going to need a workout after the clock ticks over. I flick Miles a text and then drop one into our group chat, 'City Crew.'

I make it up the first flight of stairs as my phone lights up. Two messages from Miles. Four in the group chat.

"Sounds like someone needs to work on some frustration." Miles.

"I'm on shift til tomorrow. Can the boys help?"

From the boys in the group chat:

Pin her to the wall and fuck her outta ya system, bud.

Dexter.

Yeah, cos that won't land you in purgatory. You idiot, Dex.

Griffin

. . .

G riff and Dex, two twins who couldn't be more different if they tried. One the party boy and reluctant legal eagle, the other the straitlaced lawyer. Griffin is who I recommended Carlie to, but she wouldn't know, since she obviously never opened the email I sent before I quit that hellhole Carlson runs. The four of us have been inseparable since college, catching up at least once a month, more if a game is on that one of us wants to see.

The third floor is abuzz with the usual business when I walk past reception.

Nadia waves and smiles like we're best friends. Like only two people who have battled a jammed copier can be. I return the smile and wave. She's on the phone but finishes quickly and hangs up, hurrying after me. "Lawson."

I stop, my satchel swinging into my hip. "Morning."

"Yes, I just wanted to thank you for your help with the copier the other day. That thing hates me, I swear." She pushes a stray strand of hair behind her ear before wringing her hands in front of her.

"It's all good. Happy to help."

"Oh, thanks."

"Have a great day, hey." I head toward the glass corner of hell.

"Um, Lawson?" Nadia is still behind me, looking anywhere but at me.

Oh . . .

Oh.

"Let's head to the break room." I usher her to the room we barely frequent and close the door. "I think we have our wires crossed, Nadia. I'm not looking for a relationship or anything of the sort right now."

Her face flushes, and her focus remains stuck to the floor. "Okay . . ."

"Hey, it's just my life, okay? You did nothing wrong, and I would be honored to call you my friend."

Now, she looks up. "You would?"

"Absolutely."

"Oh great. I could use one of those."

I frown. What's that supposed to mean?

"Alright, well, if you're okay, I'm going to head to the office before the dragon lady starts timing my arrivals."

She laughs at my joke about Carlie.

"Carlie is the best applicant this place has had for years. Serelle was so excited she applied." She looks almost apologetic as she says it.

"I have no doubt. See you later."

"Yeah, later."

I leave the break room and walk through the desks toward the corner office. Carlie is already seated at her desk with the door open, typing away on her laptop as she glances downward at the desk and swipes up her phone. Even from here, I can hear her conversation.

"Mills, slow down. What happened?"

She rubs a hand over her forehead and through her golden waves. Nodding, she says, "It's okay, I'll get another one. Please don't stress, okay?"

Don't tell me the ice woman has a warm side . . .

She looks up to see me outside the glass door and winds up the call in a hurry.

I push through the door. "Morning." Like we didn't exchange words outside.

It took two flights of stairs to lose the boner that sprung at the image of her—

Nope. Not happening.

I sink onto my chair and slide the satchel from my shoulder. Flipping it open, I pull out my Mac, but when I go to pop it on the desk, the surface is vandalized with pink sticky notes, each one with a lipstick kiss covering the center.

"The hell?" I grunt.

"It would have been beyond rude to not return a sweet note to sender."

I pluck one of the hot-pink sticky notes up, and the instant I do, the pads of my fingers meet something slimy. I pull my hand away, turning my hand over to find . . . egg yolk?

"Jesus, woman." I stride to the trash bin as she watches, trying her best to suppress the laughter currently tugging at the corner of her mouth.

As I pull the tacky notes from the desk, she bursts out laughing.

The egg sticks, cementing some of the notes on the desk.

"You realize you have to work in this room also, right?" I growl out, thoroughly annoyed. Now the old egg smell has finally found my senses. I gag, tossing the last neon square into the trash where it damn well belongs.

"Calm your farm, Cowboy. I got us better desks. This old thing has seen its last working day."

As if on cue, a knock rattles the glass door.

"Delivery for Carlie Lamont?" the delivery guy holding a clipboard says.

"This wasn't in the budget I sent you yesterday," I say to Carlie.

"Don't blow a vessel, Rawlins, it came out of my paycheck."

That makes my mouth gape.

"Well, don't stand there like a suffocating cod. Help the man." She waves at him as she plucks up her phone and laptop and slips out the door.

"Shit, sorry." I help him wheel in the cart with two over-sized boxes. "How the hell did you get these up here?"

He chuckles. "Tricks of the trade, bud. You good with these?"

"Yeah, sure. Thanks."

"Oh, Miss Lamont has a note on the delivery slip, hold on a second." He turns the page over. "Oh yeah, she's got here that Rawlins is to assemble the desks. Guessing that's you? Fire-cracker, that one." He shakes his head, a stupid hilarious grin plastered over his face.

"Of course she did."

"Have a great day." He leaves with a wave and a chuckle, taking his flat cart with him.

I look over the boxes as the best idea I've had all week hits me.

And the joke's on Lamont.

I sit at my new large glass desk with chrome angled legs and a small black three-drawer unit that sits under the left side on wheels. It's a damn nice piece of furniture. If it wasn't sullied by the person who paid for it, it would be near perfect.

I line up my stationery and work items on the clear surface, then go back to my projections. After lunch, Nadia arrives with a small collection of black desk accessories she claims have been sitting in the supply room for years. Only the price tags on them tell me she went out and bought them on her lunch break. I'm grateful to have her as a friend and make a mental note to repay the favor. I turn the pen holder so it's square with the rest of the items and the edge of the desk.

It's then that Lamont comes in to find her pile of glass, chrome, and hardware in the spot where I would have placed her new desk. Had I been stupid enough to construct hers for her.

Not a chance.

"Enjoying your new digs, I take it," she coos. Like the shock and distain on her face as she drags her gaze from the glistening pile on the floor are completely detached from her emotions.

I check my watch. It's almost five. "You've been gone all day. Looks like you'll be here all night."

She glances at the pile of glass desk pieces before padding to the sideboard to her tote. A minute later, she's out the door, and I'm left alone in my smug glass castle all fucking alone.

The feeling of triumph that I thought would find me is nowhere to be found.

Dammit.

Griff slides onto the stool to my right at Murphy's. Dex plops onto the one on the left. "Spill it," they say in unison.

Sometimes the twin thing is freaky.

But they are some of the best people I know.

"Work's kicking my ass." I sip my whiskey.

Harry's favorite. When I first moved to New York, this bar was the place I would go when I was homesick. And after months of ordering the cheap stuff, I swapped it out for the amber that currently swirls in my glass.

"More like that pretty blonde is." Dex grins.

"Is there a minute out of any given day you're not thinking with your cock, bro?" Griffin grumbles.

I laugh at them, placing the tumbler on the coaster on the bar. Sleeves rolled up, satchel at my feet, I order another before I've finished the current one.

"No, seriously, is it Lamont?" Griff says in his serious tone.

"She's got attitude, that's for sure." I meet his gaze.

"The feisty ones are the best ones." Dexter winks at me, the idiot.

Griff puts his hand up, signaling for the waitstaff. That catches me by surprise. Straitlaced Griffin talking about women and ordering a drink.

"You coming over to the dark side, little bro?" Dex nods with a ridiculous smile.

"For the umpteenth time, *bro*, you are literally seconds older than me, it hardly counts." Griff orders and the waitress gives him a shy smile.

The brothers are two very different peas in a homely pod. Dexter is all blond-haired, blue-eyed beach boy with a grin that puts the damn sun to shame while Griffin is dark haired with dark brown eyes and a square jaw that could cut granite. Their looks and personalities couldn't be more opposite, but their ways, their speech, and their habits are very similar.

We haven't decided if we're putting that down to nature or nurture yet.

"Miles coming tonight?" Dex asks.

"Dude, read the chat. Keep up." Griff pins his brother with a look of annoyance.

"He's off today, but he'll be late," I add.

"Thanks, Laws. See, Griffin? Being a decent human isn't that fucking hard."

Griff flips his brother the bird. Very un-lawyer like. I shake my head, still laughing at these two when an extra whiskey is set in front of me.

"Long day?" a pretty brunette says.

Her black waitstaff uniform is a stark contrast to her fair skin and green eyes.

"Something like that."

"Our boy's having feisty woman problems." Dex winks at her.

Under my breath, I curse him out.

The brunette offers up a sweet smile, wiping down a glass as she checks me out. "If you need her off your mind, I'm happy to help."

It takes me a second to process that. "I'm good, thanks."

She hides her disappointment, just barely, walking away with the glass and tea towel in hand.

"Damn, Rawlins. This blonde's got you by the fucking balls," Dex says, but his attention is on the ass of the brunette now nursing her rejected ego with a scowl.

"You go. Put her out of her misery, bud. I'm going to head

home." I down the two whiskeys, letting them burn all the way down.

"You catching the game next week?" Griff asks.

"Yeah, sure. Night."

"Night," they say in unison.

Dex waves from the patch of bar he's now leaning on, talking to the waitress. As I step out into the sparkling New York City night, I've never felt so alone in my entire life.

CHAPTER 7
CARLIE

Millie hands me the chrome desk leg as I wind noodles around my plastic fork. "God, I should put tacks in his seat. Set the trash can on fire under his desk. Or glue his fucking shit to his desk."

"You know, I don't think I've ever seen you this wound up over some guy." Mills digs in the bag of hardware for a screw as I hold the leg in position, the fork still in my mouth. I pin her with my 'don't be ridiculous' look, and she shrugs.

Swallowing the mouthful, I slide the fork from my lips and drop it to my Chinese takeout box. "Uh-uh, no way. That's not what is happening here."

"Whatever you say, sweetheart."

"Millie, we can't stand each other. He got me fired."

"*Or* . . . you were unjustly fired, and he had no power to prevent it?"

She's tilting her head, her crow's feet-flanked eyes giving me that annoying 'I'm older and you know I'm right' look.

Urgh.

"No, Mills. He stood there while I was humiliated and then fired. And, to add insult to injury, they let you go, too. This is the furthest thing from what you're thinking, old lady."

"Who you calling old?" She cackles, her smile flattening the wrinkles over her face.

I love it when she does that.

When we first met, I didn't see that beautiful smile for months. She was literally homeless and trying to pay for three items at the convenience store. Three. And couldn't afford them.

A week later, she was waiting at the bus shelter outside the same store. I sat in my car, watching her as bus after bus came and went and she never boarded a single one. On further inspection, I realized she was dressed up nice, but the plastic bag by her side was stuffed with what looked like her life's possessions. Her bony, frail, liver-spotted hand never lost contact with it, not once.

I offered her a ride home and was scared she would pull a runner. As fast as that might be for someone her age. She declined, telling me she was waiting for her son to pick her up.

I wonder now how many people bought that line from the incredible little woman before me. I've also wondered how long she was displaced before someone had the guts and the heart to help. She's proud and will never tell.

When she fed me the same line the very next day with tears in her eyes, I swiped up her tattered plastic bag and took her home, my heart breaking all over my goddamn Gucci sleeve.

I got her a place in a rental not far from me. Then a job somewhere I knew she would be safe, which of course was with me. We've been inseparable ever since. Her own children, the fucking pieces of shit-eating vultures, are the reason she's left with nothing.

They have no idea what they lost.

She has a sister who lives in Florida who is none the wiser to her situation. Mills is too proud to admit defeat to her remaining family. Every year I send her there for Thanksgiving. It's her early Christmas present, but I always get her an actual gift at Christmas, too. With some excuse, like I bought it for myself and it wasn't right, too small, etc.

She buys into it, I think . . .

"Finished your dinner, sweetheart?" Mills pushes to her feet, wobbling.

I catch her wrist, steadying her on the spot before she takes the food to the trash can. I screw the last leg on and plant it onto the table, and we are ready to flip her over.

Well, I am.

Mills can supervise.

I scramble to my feet and slide my fingers under the glass top. It's heavy. I squat, thankful for the years of working out that are paying off right now, and lift it, careful to keep its weight on the front edge to prevent the glass from cracking. I groan as I lift, realizing as I rise the desk higher that the legs are going to be too heavy.

"Fuck. It's too big."

"Here, let me help."

"You are not blowing a vessel for my desk. Sit down, Mills."

"You listen here, I might be smaller, a *little* older, but I am far from useless." She shuffles toward the table as I raise a brow at that last phrase. With a *tsk*, she waves me off and grips one short edge of the glass top. "On three."

"Fine. But you have a coronary over this, and you'll never lift a damn finger again."

"Whatever, bossy girl. One, two, three."

We flip the desk, and it lands precariously on its feet. Mills steps back, holding her arms out: "Look! We did it!"

It looks . . . a little off. But it's still much better than that wreck of a dining table Lawson and I had to share. And now I can put distance between me and Mr. Brownnoser himself.

I chuckle and pad to where she stands. "We did, didn't we?" I hug her shoulders, and she reaches up and pats my cheek. I dot a kiss to the crown of her head, into the grey curls that she keeps styled. "We should go home. Past your bedtime, little lady."

A fine hand slaps the same cheek. I giggle, and she pokes her tongue out at me. The cheeky brat. Oldest damn brat in this city at seventy-five. I drag the desk back toward my sideboard on my side of the office space and decide the drawer cabinet can wait until I can rope one of the staffers into fixing it up for me.

Our fish tank is being upgraded. The desks are only the first of the changes I want to bring to my workspace. But I'll bide my time, make sure I'm staying before I sink any more into this place.

"You going to call that mother of yours back tonight?" Mills asks.

"Yeah, sure. Right after I kiss and make up with Rawlins the Brownnosed-Rat."

"Don't you forget her, sweetheart. Family is too hard to lose. Learn from my mistakes."

I groan internally.

The only family that is worth my while is the woman right

in front of me. And I hate it when she says that kind of stuff. Like she's the reason her family disintegrated to nothing. All she ever did was give until she had nothing left, literally. Stripped of her assets and down to her last penny, she ended up at the fucking bus station. So, what, her kids could live it up? If I ever—

A soft thumb finds the crease between my brows. "You're far too young and too beautiful for a frown. Wait 'til after you meet Mr. Right and fall in love. Then, you can frown and have a face like mine." Soft eyes find mine as her head tilts. "Take this old lady home, sweetheart."

"I don't believe in that kind of love, you know that." I can't help it; I wrap her in a hug. "But you know I love *you*, right?"

My eyes burn, and I suck in a random emotional breath.

The hell?

She rubs my back. "I do. The feeling is mutual, in case you have forgotten."

I huff a strangled laugh before whispering, "I haven't forgotten, Mills."

She yawns. "Time to go, then."

"See?" I hold her at arm's length. "Past your old-lady bedtime."

This earns me a slap to the arm, and I grab up my bag and hook my arm through hers. We leave the office and take the stairs steadily before spilling out into the cool night air and onto the street. Fishing out my keys, I unlock my car. I'm glad I drove today. I doubt Mills would make it home without falling asleep if we took the train.

When she's safely inside, I round the car and drop into the seat. As I start up the BMW, her eyes fall closed.

Yep, we stayed too long.

The woman's ass in front of me twerks. Bending over, she looks behind herself and right at me. I bend down, following her position and then squat, following the instructor's shouts.

My thighs burn.

Hell yes.

We raise our arms over our head, lacing our fingers as we pulse deep into the squat. I breathe through the burn, gritting my teeth. This is what I pay hundreds of dollars a month for.

Torture.

In return, I have a stellar ass, fantastic legs, and an even better waistline. I can't imagine not working out five days a week now. After years of trying every diet and exercise combo known to woman, I fell into this HIIT class, desperate to find something that worked for my body. I've never looked back.

I've never felt as strong, as indestructible, as I do now.

The shape I have after three years of working out daily as a sort of promise, a commitment to myself, is delicious. I'm not shy about flaunting it by buying the nicest clothes I can to compliment my *assets*, as Mills calls them.

I chuckle at the memory of her voicing that one during a particularly deep and meaningful conversation.

"Reverse lunge, with weight. And go . . . in five, four, three, two, one. Lunge, ladies!"

I swipe up my ten-pound weights, gripping one in each

hand, and step back into the lunge. After the pulsing squat, this feels easier and better all at the same time.

Twelve minutes to go.

Not that I'm counting.

I'm always counting. It's not that I don't enjoy the workout —I do. But mid-workout is where my willpower wanes, and I start watching the clock at the front of the class. Millie used to come along too, to watch the class, but said all the Lycra-clad women made her feel old.

She stays home these days and sleeps in. Breakfast is always waiting on the table when I make it back to the apartment.

As class finally finishes up, I tug my towel from my bag and wipe the sweat from my brow.

"Nice workout," twerking woman says, chewing gum as she closes in.

"For some," I say with a shake of my head.

"Good view?"

Um . . . Okay.

"Yeah, I prefer the mixed class, actually. Less pussy shoved in my face."

She gives me a sour look and walks off.

"Fucking hell, whatever happened to being mysterious?" I mutter.

Am I giving off desperate vibes or something? Must be time to swipe right on something with a handsome face, sizable hands, and no strings. I gather my things and head upstairs to Mills.

Sure enough, the second I crack the front door, the aroma of coffee and croissants finds me. And I find a note on the front table.

Gone to the store, then to a midweek book club, it starts early today. See you tonight, sweetheart.

I dump the bag by the door and head for the shower.

Since when does Mills do book club?

God, the short trip upstairs has done nothing for my mood. Nothing my vibrator can't fix. I strip down and turn the water on. Pulling my hair tie out, rose-gold locks tumble over my shoulders. As the sweat from the workout dries, my skin flushes with goosebumps, my nipples pebbling.

How long has it been since I took care of myself?

Heat thunders south, and I palm my breasts, letting my eyes flutter closed.

A girl could use an orgasm or three before a long, stressful day with Rawlins.

Fuck me.

My eyes fly open.

Urgh, the last man on earth I want to think about right now is Lawson Rawlins.

And just like that, my head latches onto the ridiculous idea. I groan at the thought of the insufferable man, and the second the sound reverberates on the tiles and swings back at me, my imagination transposes it to a moan.

Images of him, his ropey forearms, his deep blue eyes, and his handsome fucking face.

I'm wet.

Ridiculously so.

"Shit."

No, Carlie. Anyone but him . . .

I slam my eyes shut again, only to find more images conjured up, in all sorts of ways I wouldn't have considered.

I must be ovulating.

Even Elmo would look like my last meal during those few days.

Giving myself a little grace, I let my mind wander, and when I brush a finger over my clit, my lips part, one nipple pinched between two fingers.

My mind has Rawlins on his knees.

"Oh god."

I slide the second drawer open to find my translucent pink vibrator, Vinny.

Thank fuck.

Stepping into the shower, I sit on the bench at the far end, letting the water wash over me. As hot as it is, it feels lukewarm over my skin. I push the tip of the vibrator against my entrance.

Blue eyes and a square jaw flash through my mind, the fucking traitor.

I impale myself on Vinny and cry out as I explode around it on the first pass. Body convulsing with every soul-wrenching wave, I slap a hand to the tile, my legs spread wide.

The second it's over, all I feel is empty and alone. Bar the images of Rawlins that refuse to budge. I groan, and the noise resembles the man himself.

I need to get laid.

The sooner the better.

CHAPTER 8

LAWSON

Serelle's apologetic smile alternates between me and Satan's Little Helper to my right. Who currently smells like apples and strawberries with a hint of something heady I can't place. Her hair is twisted up, her red lipstick like a fucking stop sign.

Like I need a reminder.

Her personality is enough to repel the most desperate of men.

Okay . . . that's probably a little harsh.

"What do you mean, one of us goes?" Lamont bites out, her face stone as she pins her boss, nonetheless, with a glare.

Nope, I was right the first time. It's her, not us.

My mother would be telling me to look at the bigger picture here, give her the benefit of the doubt, and see the situation from where she's coming from. *Not today, Ma.*

"To clarify, the contract from the city that funds our executive program doesn't cover the cost of two wages after the

Christmas period. So, as of January first, the glass corner office will be one of yours. Solely."

"And just how are you going to determine who stays and who doesn't?" Lamont says, her grip around the arm of her chair tense.

I'm worried, sure. But I'm obviously better at rolling with the punches.

"Whoever makes the biggest impact stays." Serelle's gaze doesn't meet either of ours.

"So, I have around three months to make a difference?" Lamont rephrases the statement as question.

"Yes, that's correct." Serelle is game enough—or professional enough, I should say—to meet her gaze now.

"Fine. I assume there will be a three-month review, regardless?" Lamont adds.

"Yes, also correct. And Carlie," Serelle says, her face all empathy, "I know what this looks like. I am truly sorry. It was never my intention to reduce our exec team further. But funding is a citywide issue. We can only ask for our allotment each year, unless we have the man—sorry, person- or people-power to hedge a bigger project. With your background and experience, I'm sure you can understand that."

Curious just got curiouser.

Her background?

Is this a rags to riches thing?

"Not a problem, Serelle. Is that all you needed me for?" Lamont says, gathering up her phone and laptop.

"Yes, please don't let me keep you from your work. Lawson, can I have a word?"

Lamont gives me the side-eye as she rises and leaves. To sit at the wonky desk I assume she put together after we all went home. Now the joke seems a little over the top, in light of the new situation.

She leaves Serelle's office, tapping on her phone like it burns to the touch.

Serelle stands and shuts the door before pulling the chair beside me away a little and dropping into it, lacing her hands in front of her chest with a smile. "How are things going in the corner office?"

"Fine. We're working on the last quarter numbers, planning and projecting accordingly."

She offers up a tight smile before dropping her focus to her hands. "It was brought to my attention yesterday that you and Carlie have a little history." She sighs. "Today feels like one constant apology, but I want you to know that we are all here to support you. I hired you both because of your talent in your respective areas. I really hope the situation at Carlson's isn't going to make your time here uncomfortable."

Her eyes are almost pleading.

She would have to be the most empathetic boss, leader, I've ever had the pleasure of working with.

She makes Carlson look truly hell-sent.

"We get along fine. I know she blames me for losing her career at Carlson's. But I think this is a change we will thrive with."

The second the words leave my mouth, I remember that one of us isn't going to be staying.

Fuck.

"Please know, we would keep you both if we had the means to."

"I'm sure you would. And this isn't about either myself or Lamont—Carlie." Her first name on my tongue feels strange.

Too much. Too . . . familiar. "It's about the women and girls you help every day."

She gives me a scrunched-up smile and pats my hand as she rises. "Good to know. I'll let you return to your day."

"Thank you."

She rounds the desk and sits behind it as she looks up. "You're most welcome."

If there was a person to win salt of the earth, best human on earth, it would be Serelle.

And damn if I don't want to make sure I'm still working here, for her, at the end of the next three months. I wander back to the office to find Nadia waiting outside my door. Satan eyeballs her from behind her wonky glass desk, flipping a gold pen through her fingers.

I decide to put Nadia out of her misery. "Morning Nadia, what can I do for you?"

She chuckles and sweeps a stray curl of hair behind her ear and pushes her glasses up her nose. They're new.

"You get glasses? Or am I the one who's blind?"

Her body sways as she huffs a small sound and tugs her bottom lip through her teeth. "My contacts fell down a subway grate."

"What? What happened?"

She waves a hand. "Oh no, nothing like that, I was trying to pull my purse out to pay for a hotdog and they flew out, case and all, and bounced over the metal and out of sight. It's my fault really, I should be more organized. That bag of mine is so—"

The glass door opens, protesting with a whine from being hauled open too quickly. "If you are bored, Nadine, I can't find a job for you. Rawlins, I need you in here."

Nadia's eyes widen as she turns, her movements stiff and mechanical. "Sorry, I just nee—"

Lamont raises an elegant eyebrow and tilts her head, as if sizing up her damn prey.

Nadia glances to me before lowering her eyes as she softly says, "The copier is jammed again. Could you help me, Lawson?"

Lamont folds her arms, her face settling to a stonelike facade.

"Sure, come on." I take Nadia's elbow, hoping to save her from whatever is about to spray from Satan's Mistress's pouty lips.

We reach the supply and copy room, and Nadia waves at the machine. "I don't know why it hates me."

I slide my hand under the lid and catch the lever, hauling the top up as she dives in, clawing the paper from the intake. Her heels screw into the carpet, making a groaning noise, her knee-length skirt slipping up as she leans in further.

She looks set to topple if she reaches much more.

I bend over the machine, trying to help her tug the wad of paper free. She glances at me, cheeks flushing as my hand bumps into the side of hers.

"Oh." She jerks upward.

Something cracks and then she sways sideways. I pull my head out, finding the spike of her heel popping up from the carpet. Nadia clings to the machine. I try to steady her with a grip on her upper arm. My purchase on the lid slips and it slams down onto both of us.

"Dammit," I grunt. Shouldering the machine off me, I manage to push it free and remove us from the deadly jaws of the ancient copier. Nadia leans on it, breathing heavily as she fixes her hair, managing to sweep toner over her neck and cheek.

I chuckle at her. For a second, mortification crosses her face, but a laugh bubbles free as she points to my face.

"What?" I swipe at my face.

"You have black, like all over you—"

"Well, isn't this fucking cozy." The hard words snap both of our attention to the doorway of the supply room. Lamont stands, hands on hips, with a scowl that could scare a war-ready Viking.

Sweet Jesus.

Nadia plucks her glasses from the shelf by the copier and slides them up her nose.

"The machine was jammed. Hold your fire," I growl, taking a step toward her.

Both her brows rise as she looks at Nadia and spins on her heels.

Just great.

Today is one goddamn implosion after another.

"Sorry, Lawson." Nadia hands me a Kleenex.

I wipe my face and toss it into the trash can. "It's fine. I'll handle her."

I head for the door and make it one step out as a thought hits me. "Why can't you ask Bob to help?"

Nadia's face falls, her gaze hitting the floor. Her body tenses, and I'm hoping like hell the reason I'm guessing is not what she's about to say.

"He makes me super uncomfortable. After the last time . . ."

"Last time?" I prompt, my HR intuition flaring back to life.

"I can't talk about it," she says, so damn quiet it takes me a while to understand the meaning.

Shit.

"Right, let me know if you need any help. Any time, okay?"

She nods, but her arms wrap around her body, as if she's protecting herself against the very thought of needing to ask for help.

"You okay here?"

"Sure. Thanks."

I hesitate, not wanting to leave her alone. Jesus, is nowhere safe anymore? I all but stalk my way back to the corner office.

I cross the threshold to I find Lamont leaning on her desk, legs crossed, arms folded over her chest. "Done so soon?"

God above.

I grind my molars, not bothering to look at her as I sink into my chair and fling my laptop open with so much force it shunts backward on the desk.

"What, no foreplay for me?" She stalks to my desk and slams her palms on either side of my laptop, leaning down.

I close my eyes and pinch the bridge of my nose, biding my time, hoping the heat growing in my chest at her tone dissipates.

It doesn't. The instant I open my eyes, she saunters away. Those hips, that ass taunting me as she flicks her long hair over one shoulder.

Wait . . . when did she take it down?

"Never mind. In a few measly months, you and Nancy will have to part ways, and she will be my copy bitch."

I fly out of my chair so fast it topples over. Rounding the desk, I close the distance between us and fly into her space like it's the last parking spot at the fucking Super Bowl. Tightness in my chest has me tugging at my tie, tilting my head as I glare at her.

"Watch that damn mouth of yours," I growl.

Her brown eyes study my face as her lips part. When her gaze narrows, I know vitriol is about to spew from those red lips that have snagged my attention. "Rawlins, my mouth is none of your business. And unless you want to leave early with a sexual harassment charge, back the fuck up."

"What cold part of hell did you crawl out of?" I hiss.

"Hot."

I jerk my head back. "What?"

"Hell is hot, everyone knows that."

"God, you are a child."

"Takes one to know one."

Fucking hell.

"I have work to do," I say with a sigh and turn to make for my desk. It's then I see the whole of the staff room staring at us. Their expressions range from stunned to amused and everything in between.

Something creaks behind me. I spin back, fully expecting something hard flying in the general direction of my head.

What I find is worse.

Lamont is sitting side saddle on the desk, her face enraptured by faux lust. "Oh Lawson, the copier needs you. Only you. Please, you have to help me." Her hands work over her chest, up her neck as her head falls back, her eyes fluttering shut.

Something brown tweed and horrified moves to my left.

Nadia.

She-devil continues, "Ah . . . Oh, Lawso—"

"Enough!" I close the distance between us in two strides and haul her off the desk.

She slaps me. "Get your fucking hands off me!"

I dare a glance back at Nadia. The spot where she stood is now empty. Her hunched over figure hurries through the desks and down the hall.

I turn on Lamont. "What the fuck is wrong with you?"

"Me? You're the one who is fraternizing with the subordinates. Making an idiot of yourself with your Mr. Goody Two-Shoes horseshit! If anyone needs a reality check, it's you!"

The door opens. "Both of you. In my office. Now." Serelle's goodhearted smiles and gentle ways are nowhere to be found as she glares at me and then Lamont.

When neither of us responds, she snaps, "Move."

Lamont jolts to life, her face turning from stunned to mortified in a heartbeat as she walks out of the office and holds her head high, drifting through the rows of our shocked peers. All except Bob, who, of course, has a shit-eating grin plastered on his face.

I pin him with my dirtiest look as I pass his desk.

Lamont won't look at me when we sit in the chairs we were in only this morning.

Sweet Jesus, how quickly this day has turned to shit.

I rub a hand over my face and suck in a long, slow breath.

Serelle doesn't sit. Instead, she wanders to her wall of treasures, pacing a small stretch of carpet as her expression moves through a thousand shades.

I lean forward and try to salvage this. "If I could—"

Serelle shakes her head viciously, flinging a hand up.

We wait with bated breath as she paces for a few more minutes. She stops abruptly and turns to face us. Lamont gasps, holding her breath.

We took it too fa—

"It is clear to me now that your history is more like a present issue."

Lamont opens her mouth to respond, but Serelle glares at her. She shrinks back into her chair.

"The only way to sort through something like this is wade through it. Neither of you, from the intel I received, were given the opportunity to exercise your potential rights or legal options at Carlson's. I blame that toxic environment for what is happening now."

She moves to her seat and opens her laptop. Tapping on the keyboard, she cranes her neck and then taps the trackpad a few times. When she's satisfied, she turns the computer around to face us.

"This here is your—*our*—solution."

Lamont leans forward, studying the website. "It's a resort."

Her gaze flicks back to Serelle.

"Actually, it's a retreat. My friend from college runs it. Their programs are designed to target this sort of thing. She owes me a favor, so it would be pro bono." Her attention alternates between us. "I want you to pack your bags. A week should be enough time to work through the baggage between the both of you."

"With all due respect, Serelle, I can't just up and leave. I have a dependent. I can't leave her alone."

It's as if the oxygen has been sucked from the room.

I can't force my stare from her as she keeps her gaze on Serelle.

Lamont has a kid?

How did I not know that?

Surely that would have been on her file at Carlson's?

"This is nonnegotiable, Carlie. Same goes for you, Lawson.

We need you at your best; this will make sure you can achieve that. You can take your work with you, if you're worried about falling behind. The activities that are hosted every day only take around four hours. That leaves plenty of time to work and get to know each other better so we have the best versions of you both. This constant war between the two of you stops now. Honestly, it would have been easier if you were screwing . . ."

Lamont's jaw drops, her eyes tight with disbelief.

That'll be the day that ice woman here thaws long enough for a man to get close enough to—

"Now, get the hell out of my office. I'll email the details within the hour. You leave Sunday."

I rise from the chair and walk through the door, almost numb. It shuts behind me, and I hover a little as Lamont composes herself. "Carlie, I—"

"Don't fucking talk to me."

She stalks away, hips swaying, hands curling into fists.

It's going to be a long damn week.

CHAPTER 9
CARLIE

I toss clothes into my oversized luggage as Mills sits on the end of my bed, hands wrapped around her mug. The scent of her chamomile tea infuses through my room.

"I'll be fine, sweetheart. I'm not a child. I've been taking care of myself for decades."

"I know, but what if something happens and I'm not here?" I stop packing, and her hand rests over mine. The stone that swelled in my airway at the thought of leaving Mills here alone only grows.

"You like this job, right?" Mills sets her mug on my bedside and shuffles closer.

With her dressing gown on and rollers in, she looks like Sophia from *The Golden Girls*. My heart squeezes in my chest. She's my adopt-a-grandma, my best friend. My reason to fight for everything.

"Yes," I breathe.

"Good. Well, you're going. It's only a week, and I have this thing called a cell phone. I'll send you a text every day, okay?"

"Fine." I sit on the bed next to her. "What if I can't move past this? What if Rawlins and I can't figure this baggage out?"

She tilts her head. "My precious girl. You can do absolutely anything you put your mind to. I saw that the day I met you. Heavens above, you saved my life. You've already done the hardest thing a person can ever do." Silver lines her eyes. "Now, it's past this little old lady's bedtime. Night, sweetheart."

"Night, Mills," I choke out.

She forgot her mug.

I chuckle at her forgetfulness. But an hour later, it's the little things that could go wrong that have me tossing and turning.

What if she forgets to turn off the stove. What if she forgets to lock the front door or to look before crossing the street . . .

So much for sleep.

My alarm snaps me out of my restless sleep. On a fucking Sunday. I fumble for my phone. It slides from the bedside to the floor.

"Fuck," I groan.

Rolling over, I toss the blankets off and sit up on the side of the bed. My phone lights up again. A text.

From . . . Rawlins.

Urgh.

Carpool?

Not likely.

Um, I meant, can I bum a lift?

Are you serious?

This son of a bitch doesn't have a car?

Fine. But we're splitting the gas. And one syllable about my driving and you're walking.

Righto, Rubes.

Huh?

Who the hell is Rubes?

Perplexed, I shower and dress and double-check I have everything before doing a thorough run-through with Millie on safety stuff while I'm gone.

"Remember to turn off the stove at the wall, okay? Double-check the front door every night, do not rely on the automated locking system. Check it."

She swats my arm, and her brows drop into a rare frown. "Would you get out of here, already? My life is not that eventful. Book club is the most exciting thing I'll be doing while you're gone, and it's only two blocks away."

That makes me freeze, and she deflates. "Please, sweetheart, do something for you. Just this once."

I sigh and fold her in a bear hug. With my heels on, I tower over her. She slides an awkward arm upward and pats my cheek.

I'm suffocating her.

Her signal letting me know I'm squishing her. I have a habit of doing that.

"If I don't get a reply to my morning text every single morning, there will be hell to pay, Millicent DeLuca."

"Good lord, not the full name, Mom." She winks at me. The little shit.

I peck her cheek. "Love you. Enjoy your week of solace."

"You too," she says with absolute cheek.

I press the center button on the handle of my suitcase and shoulder my handbag as I turn for the door. A hand swats my ass, and I shoot Mills a glare over my shoulder. "Just as well I love you."

She cackles. "Just getting my turn in before the cowboy does."

I roll my eyes at her, and she pulls a crazy face. Scrunching my face up in a goodbye smile, I slip through the door and pad the ten steps to the elevator. In the garage, I hit the keypad on my car key, and the BMW's lights flash with a high-pitched chirp. I haul my bag into the trunk and slam it shut.

Sinking into the driver's seat, I fire her up. The low rumble of my car always sends lightning through my veins. Something my mother never understood. "Boys and men like cars, not women," she would say any time I showed interest in a car. To my credit, they were always luxury cars.

I pull out onto the street and slip between traffic, flying toward the drop pin Rawlins sent me before I walked out the door.

"Siri, take me to the latest drop pin."

"Taking you to East 73rd Street."

Lord above, slumming it, Rawlins.

When I pull up out front of a five-story attached brown-stone, I honk the horn as I pull up level with the man himself and his luggage. He stands in Levi's and a polo shirt with aviators and his usual messy brown hair parted to one side. A small piece of luggage sits at his feet.

He slides the aviators down his face and frowns.

Seriously?

I hit the trunk button and climb from the car. "If you're waiting for a limo, you'll be here a while."

He slides the glasses up onto his head and smiles. "Mornin' to you, too."

The fucking nerve on this guy. I swear, he only uses that damn drawl when he thinks it's going to piss me off.

"Whatever. Get your shit in the trunk; this doesn't have to take all day."

I sit back in the driver's seat and check my phone. Nothing from Mills yet.

Of course there isn't.

The car dips with his weight as he fills out the passenger seat, surprising me. It's been ages since I've had a guy in my car, and none have affected the suspension.

Rawlins is lean and fit . . . and looking oversized in the passenger's seat.

His aftershave fills the small space. My heart races, sending short, useless breaths to expand my lungs.

I clear my throat and secure my seat belt over my lap before flicking the turn signal and pulling from the curb and into traffic.

"Nice wheels," he says softly.

My skin is awash with goosebumps at his low tone.

Ignoring him, I tighten my grip on the wheel.

"Should take us about two hours," he says, tapping his phone.

"Yup." I let the *p* pop.

Longest two hours of my life.

"Not really one for small talk, are you, Lamont?"

"Absolutely. Just . . . not with you."

He chuckles.

"Well, we're going to have to sort it out before we both end up unemployed."

"You mean, you'll be unemployed. I have prospects."

He dares to chuckle again.

It takes every fiber in my being to not ram his side of the car into the guard rail as we merge onto the highway.

As if I would ever . . . My beautiful BMW, I would never.

But it's a fucking temptation.

With a satisfying lack of small talk, or any talk at all, we reach Hartford in under two hours. I pull into the parking lot of the retreat. The huge sign welcoming all to Cedar Beach Lodge passes overhead as we roll into the last of the free parking spots.

The place is buzzing with activity. It must be high season.

People mill about the expansive grounds. A group is in the middle of a yoga lesson to one side of the main building. A few folks lounge by a beach-type pool area that looks like it has a bungalow-inspired bar with grass hut vibes, complete with a couple of waitresses sporting coconut bikini tops.

Shaking my head, I glance at Rawlins, who is taking in our surroundings, his glasses pulled down with one hand.

I check the gauges and kill the engine.

I leave Rawlins to grab our bags as I check in. He can figure out his accommodations after he hauls the luggage in.

The girl behind the counter shoots me a nervous smile as she appears to be checking and double-checking something. "So, we have you booked for the week, with an option for ten days if needed."

I raise an eyebrow.

God no. There is no way I'm prolonging this torture.

Damn you, Serelle. Always finding a way to keep us accountable.

"Okay . . ." I study her face.

Why is she so nervous? I school back the resting bitch face that usually takes up permanent residence on my features. She taps away again before lifting the receiver on the phone. "Monty, we have an issue with the bookings."

She hums in agreement as Monty, or whoever, replies on the other end of the line. And when she hangs up with a tight smile, I know something is off.

"So, we had your last-minute booking, but your two twin rooms that were booked got snatched up earlier."

"What does that mean?"

"We only have a larger suite left."

"Okay, so I'll take that."

"No, sorry. I must not be explaining it right." She shifts on her feet.

Rawlins appears at my side with all the luggage and a smile on his smug face. "What's going on?"

"There is only one room left." The girl at the desk flickers her gaze between us like she's watching two dangerous predators and trying to figure out which one is going to rip her to shreds first.

"That's okay, we'll take it," Rawlins says.

"It's the couples suite," the girl says softly, like the words will get her eaten by the nearest predator.

"We will not." A look of horror stretches my face.

"Yes, we will. Unless you would prefer to sleep on the lawn and see the sunrise for the next seven-to-ten days." Rawlins waves a hand at the expansive outdoor area.

I drill him with a glare that heats my own face with its afterglow. I force a smile and return my focus to the girl behind the desk. "Fine."

"It really is our nicest suite. I think you'll find it most lovely." The girl tries to banish my expression of horror, now melted to a fiery annoyance, from existence.

"I'm sure it will, Jessica. Don't stress, hey." Rawlins leans on the counter, giving her a smile.

Good lord, this man is detestable.

She hands him the keys, complete with a sparkling red, and rather obnoxious, heart. She holds one up to me, the heart pink. I snatch it from her hand and stalk from the office with a sigh.

Of all the ridiculous things . . . The only two people in the state of New York who can barely stand sharing an office have to share an even more intimate space.

I'd bet my left breast Serelle set this little shenanigan up.

Double-booked, my ass.

We cross the lawn to the furthest bungalow. The oversized hut has a tropical, Bali-inspired thatched roof over its round architecture. The door is unlocked. A handle, that gives way under the lightest touch, gleams under two semi-faded hearts, one red and one pink.

Because of course it does.

I push open the door, and it swings back to reveal a studio

type room, but round. On one side, there's a kitchenette. On the other, a flat-screen, but no sofa. Who has a television and no sofa? A faux wall highlights the massive bed that is the central feature of the *Couples Suite*.

No sofa.

One bed.

Copious amounts of pillows top the bed along with rose petals and a towel rolled and twisted into the shape of a heart. A bottle of champagne and gold heart chocolates sits between them. A small tray of strawberries and what looks like a tiny bowl of chocolate fondue tucked into one side also sits on the white linen.

"Son of a bitch," I hiss, dropping my key on the small bamboo side table.

Wheels rolling over hardwood drags my gaze back to the front door. Rawlins stops, our bags in hand, and lifts his aviators up as he takes in the bungalow.

A smirk tugs at his lips, but his jaw clenches. "Now, *this* is fucking cozy."

Urgh, fuck my life.

CHAPTER 10
LAWSON

I cast my eye down the screen as I study the itinerary Serelle sent Lamont and me. Each new item is more disturbing than the last.

Couples Therapy (Daily, 10 a.m.)

Tandem Yoga (Daily, 5 a.m.)

Trust and Understanding Session (Day Two)

Meditation Hour (Daily, 2 p.m.)

Reflection and Verbalization Session (Day Three)

Role-Playing (Day Four)

Honesty Hour (Daily, 8 p.m.)

Christ.

What the hell is Serelle thinking? Lamont can barely tolerate my existence, let along all this touchy-feely shit.

I sit on the bed, pretending this is simply a bad dream that surely I will wake up from any minute now.

The noises from the very open bathroom space behind the faux wall do nothing to mute the string of curses. I assume Lamont just checked her email.

While she's in the bathroom?

Well, that's unsanitary.

I run a hand through my hair as the water turns on and then off. Lamont stalks back to the bed and shoves a hand on one hip as it cocks, and she reads the list aloud, like I haven't already read the same information.

Finally looking from her phone, her gaze falls down to me as her mouth gapes and she says, "No fucking way."

"You say that like we have a choice."

"Maybe . . . we say we went, and . . . *don't.*"

A knock rattles the door, and she turns on it like a lioness eyeing a vulture circling her cubs before stalking across the space.

Ripping the door open, she demands, "What?"

"Ah, hello, Mrs. Rawlins. My name is Man—"

She throws a hand up and he startles, faltering back a little.

"We are *not* a Mr. and Mrs. This here"—she waves a hand behind her without looking—"is my coworker Rawlins. My name is Carlie Lamont. So you will need to update your information."

"Oh, so sorry, miss. My apologies," the guy says, striking something out on his clipboard and writing a note—I assume, her name.

His megawatt smile never fades over his dark eyes, dark

hair, and dimples. His neat, pressed uniform looks like something straight out of a Scout's lineup. Only a little more casual, with his top few buttons open and wearing loafers instead of more serious enclosed footwear. "As I was saying, if I may, my name is Manuel. I am your guide for your time here. I will escort you to each activity, keep records of your progress as a couple . . ." He shifts on his feet, and Lamont crosses her arms over her chest.

He tries again. "Your professional progress?"

I rise from the bed and pad to where Lamont stands, trying to show a little support for the guy. This woman is scary as fuck when she wants to be. "Sounds great, Manuel."

I earn a filthy side-eye from Lamont, who nods to the clipboard in his hand. "So you're our warden this week. Who are you reporting to?"

"Ah, it's not really like that. More like so you can see how far you've come in your relationship after the seven-to-ten days. However long it takes."

His smile stays painted on, but his grip tightens on the clipboard.

"If you must, but this is a working relationship, Manuel. Your metrics will have to reflect that." Lamont unfolds her arms and walks away.

So much for us never having any kind of relationship. That's the most bend I've seen in this fiery woman since the day I met her.

"Lunch is at one, then meditation hour. I will pick you up from your bungalow in a few hours, okay?" Manuel smiles.

"Sure, bud. Thanks." I close the door as he leaves and turn back.

Lamont is pacing.

At least we agree on something.

"It won't be so bad, maybe we go through the motions and bide our time 'til seven days is up . . ." I offer.

"Bide our time? He's tracking our progress. Which means that if we don't make any, we stay longer."

Oh fuck, of course.

I run a hand through my hair again and she stills, her gaze stuck on the motion. A heartbeat later, she shakes her head as if snapping herself from a trance. "Well, we should discuss the sleeping arrangements."

I drop my hands by my sides. "Like, left or right?"

"More like, floor or bed," she snaps.

"You can't be serious."

She raises one elegant brow and pins me with those darkening browns.

"Whatever, I'll take the floor. You take the bed, Lamont."

Her eyes narrow over an incredulous stare. "This does not make up for Carlson's, if you're thin—"

I close the distance between us and am in her space before she can take a step away. She leans back.

"What makes you think I have any intention of admitting fault there? I gave you opportunity to fix that, and you didn't."

"What?" Her face twists with confusion.

"You could have taken that idiot for millions. But I guess opening my email was beneath you."

"What *email*?"

I study her face for a beat, looking for any hint of a lie. When I find none, I ask, "You really didn't get the email I sent you the day you were fired?"

"I lost access to all systems immediately. Hell, that snot-nosed weasel in IT was probably shutting down every bit of access I had as I was getting my ass handed to me in Carlson's office."

She never even saw it.

That takes the wind out of my sails.

Fuck.

She folds her arms as if things that come from me could only be harmful and she needs protection. "What did you send?"

"Litigation recommendations. Unfair dismissal, anything you could pin him with relating to how you were fired down to the sexism, the vernacular and insults he tossed around that day."

Her mouth gapes.

"It's not too late, you know. It still occurred. You were still disrespected and let go on grounds that wouldn't stand in court. I had Griff do some research for you, in case I'd missed anything."

"I'm sorry, who?"

"Griffin, my college buddy; he's a litigator. A damn good one."

Her mouth closes as her phone buzzes on the bed, its screen lighting up. "I have to take this . . ."

She swipes the phone up and heads for the door. As she opens it, she answers. "Hey, Mills. You okay, babe?"

The door closes behind her, and I stand in the room, wondering how I missed that Lamont is a mother. How she has a kid. And is a single parent . . .

That explains the mama bear attitude she owns. Fuck, that must be hard, especially with the hours we work.

All of a sudden, I'm jealous of the fucker that got to make a kid with her and annoyed at myself over said thought all in the same beat. With almost two hours to kill before the first activity, I open the laptop and work on this quarter's report. After a solid hour passes, the front door opens and Lamont wanders in. Her hair is a mess around her shoulders, her face flushed, like she's been exercising.

The jeans and T-shirt she's wearing are sweaty from the warm midday sun. For the first time, she forces a smile as she walks past me toward the bathroom. After collecting a few things from her bag, she disappears behind the faux wall. "Stay out there, Rawlins. I'm taking a shower."

I chuckle.

"Yes, ma'am," I call back.

A breathy huff escapes the bathroom space before water turns on.

The image of her stripping out of those jeans mere feet from where I sit winds its treacherous way through my ridiculous mind. Blood sinks south before I can wrangle my thoughts.

Fuck me.

I retrain my focus to the spreadsheet on the screen. I try three times before giving up when the shower turns off. I slam the laptop shut, shoving my head into my hands.

"Shit," a small whisper comes from behind the wall.

It's then I realize the towels are still on the bed, twisted into the heart shape.

Lamont would be needing one right about now. I rise and grab up a towel, padding for the wall. I lean on it, looking away from the bathroom. "Cold yet?"

"Just throw me a towel."

I chuckle. "Manners, Princess."

"The fuck," she mutters.

"I guess you could drip dry. You'll miss lunch, though.

Guessing all that long hair takes a while to dry. Manuel will be upset. You could blow-dry yourself." The second the sentence leaves my stupid mouth, I groan into the drywall. The words *blow* and *Lamont* shouldn't be in my mind, let alone escaping my damn mouth.

"Towel, Rawlins, before I make this uncomfortable for both of us."

She would, too.

And I'm momentarily tempted to let her come out here and take the piece of linen from my hands.

She has the spine and the confidence to pull something like that off.

Now that last phrase took me from semi-hard to concrete.

Sweet Jesus.

A hand appears around the wall, grabbing for the towel. Relenting, I shove it into her hand. My fingers brush over hers as she snags it and disappears, replaced by a breathy word. "Child."

My chuckle turns to a stifled groan as the ghost of her touch sends electricity over my skin, radiating out.

Who would have thought Satan's Little Helper could have that effect on me.

Lord above, it's going to be a long week.

anuel is right on time to collect us for lunch, which we inhale in silence before he shows us to a patch of lawn for our meditation. With his clipboard in hand, he waits as we sit on the grass, leaving at least three feet between us.

"No, no." He's waving his hands, signaling for us to shuffle closer. "It is better if I don't have to keep alternating between you both."

Lamont doesn't budge, simply lifting her sunglasses into her messy updo. Probably so she can more effectively incinerate Manuel with a single glare.

I shift closer until a measly six inches of grass is all that's left between us, earning a short-lived glower from those brown eyes. With her hair up that way, a few strands have already escaped. Her tank top has slipped off one shoulder, and the workout pants she wears make it just past her knees as she sits cross-legged with her sneaker-clad feet tucked under her.

"Better!" Manuel smiles. "Let's start. Close your eyes, please."

I shut my eyes. Instantly, every other sense is more intense. The ground beneath me, the wind that tosses my messy hair, the air that fills and stretches my lungs. I relax into nothingness.

Lamont shifts beside me with a sigh.

I guess sitting still isn't her thing.

"What next?" she asks.

"Simply breathe," Manuel says, "Feel every sensation you can. Listen to every single sound. Taste the air—"

"How on earth am I supposed to *taste* the air?" she says, annoyance lacing her tone.

I open my eyes. She's tense, rigid, and sitting upright. Her eyes are pressed shut, her face scrunched like she's in pain. I guess it takes effort to stay that sassy every minute of the day.

"You can simply concentrate on other senses, if you wish," Manuel offers.

"Fine." She relaxes slightly, her hands coming to rest on her knees, still curled into fists.

I suppress the smile that wants out at seeing her like this.

"Close your eyes, Mr. Lawson," Manuel says.

Lamont's eyes fly open and her face sours. "You need a Polaroid? Close your fucking eyes."

Now I can't help the laughter that spills from my lips. My shoulders shake with the hearty chuckle that runs away with me. This woman is always on, even when she's supposed to be powering down. It's impressive.

It must be exhausting for her.

"Stop laughing. You're supposed to be taking this seriously, remember?"

I let my laughter peter before choking out, "Sure, I remember."

Her brows lower. "Your eyes are still open."

I flatten the remnants of my smile and let my eyelids fall.

"Better," she whispers.

Those two syllables send shivers over my skin like they caressed their way over my body.

I tilt my head, trying to analyze what the hell that's about.

"Now settle your mind by counting backward from one hundred," Manuel says softly.

Hauling in a lungful that stretches my chest, I start. *One hundred, ninety-nine, ninety-eight, ninety-sev—*

"I'm sorry, how long will this take?" Lamont snaps.

I open my eyes to find her glaring at Manuel, who now grips the clipboard like a shield to his body.

Smart man.

"This session runs for an hour, Miss Carlie."

I school back the wince that automatically twists my face as he calls her by her first name.

And . . . he just got stupid.

But her face relaxes slightly. "Thank you, Manuel."

Well, fuck.

CHAPTER 11
CARLIE

Day one.

The early morning sun pokes through the bungalow window as I stretch out in the California king bed. Those West Coast folks have their shit together—this bed is bliss.

A groan sounds from somewhere on the floor. I tug the sheet up over my silk sleep camisole, only now remembering who I share a room with.

Rawlins.

I shuffle forward on the bed, sheet clutched in my hands, as I peek at the floor. He lies flat out on the hard floor, a forearm covering his eyes, the biceps bulging with its elevated position. The single blanket I tossed at him last night has slipped down, exposing his bare, toned chest and stomach.

Holy shit.

The man is built to perfection.

A raw groan slips through his lips as he stretches where he lies, and his arm falls away.

Fuck.

I scramble backward and lie, shoving my hands under my head as I roll onto my side and slam my eyes shut.

A soft chuckle turns to a strangled moan as the blanket hits the bed. "Sweet Jesus, the damn floor is as hard as it looks. Mornin', sleepyhead." Footsteps pad behind the faux wall as he adds, "You can open your eyes now, Lamont."

My eyes fling open along with my mouth.

I snap my mouth shut, remembering the pajamas I have on, the very open space we share, and the fact that this is only the first day, and night, of seven. More, if we screw this up.

I flip the covers back and rush to where my bag sits against the wall on the rack underneath the flat-screen. I dig through it until I find an oversized T-shirt and pull it on. Better.

Flinging my long hair over one shoulder, I pluck my phone up from the nightstand and send Mills proof of life.

She sends a cowboy emoji back.

I roll my eyes and click my phone off.

The one thing she and I don't agree on has always been romantic love. Call it the baggage of my trauma, whatever you want, but after the first man I ever loved decided I wasn't worth the trouble and left Mom and me to fend for ourselves, I haven't bought into the commercial concept of romantic love.

Because that's all it is—a way for companies to sell more products and services to unsuspecting big-hearted fools by attaching emotional need or the perception of it.

I'm nobody's fool. Not anymore.

"Bathroom's free." The low tone pulls me from my inner TED Talk.

Dragging my gaze from the lock screen of my phone, I meet

deep blues, an angled jaw that could rival Thor's, and messy damn dark hair.

I force my focus back to my phone. "Yep."

With only a few minutes 'til five, I opt for just brushing my teeth and washing my face before Manuel graces our doorstep.

I'll work out and shower after the morning session.

Rawlins is dressed in a T-shirt and shorts that resemble running clothes. As he shoves his AirPods into each ear and taps his phone, I realize he has the same idea as me.

Except I wouldn't be caught dead running.

Cardio never served me well, only adding to my waistline instead of reducing it. So one of my HIIT workouts will do nicely while he's out pounding the pavement. Slapping a sports watch on his wrist, he answers the door as I finish getting ready. My navy active wear is my favorite thing right now. And the fact it compliments my long strawberry-toned blonde hair and brown eyes is an added bonus.

"Good morning, my lovelies!" Manuel's exuberant greeting fills the air throughout the bungalow. I grab my phone and stalk my way to the door. I pluck the keys from the front table and hold Rawlins's in one hand, waiting for him to take it.

The key disappears from my fingers as he raises a brow. "Someone has plans."

I slip the key into the side pocket of my pants and slide my sneakers on, tying the laces.

"Well, let's get you two to yoga." Manuel turns on his heel, leading the way. I follow as Rawlins holds the door before closing it after us.

Across the resort and past the pool that's unsurprisingly vacant, we find another large grass area where people mill about. A grid of yoga mats, ready for the morning's session, cover the dewy grass.

Manuel shows us to two mats in the middle. I take the first one, and Rawlins takes the next. Manuel drops his clipboard by the next and steps onto it.

"You're doing this, too?" I ask.

"Of course. I wouldn't ask my guests to do anything I wouldn't."

I scoff and Rawlins glances at me.

"Okay, people. Shoes off my mats, please," the instructor calls. It's then I notice Manuel's bare feet.

Shit.

I squat, untying my laces. Rawlins does the same, his gaze snagging on mine as I hurry my laces free. Ignoring him, I slide my sneakers off and slip my socks into them. Music starts up, slow and rhythmic. The instructor signals for silence and then bends to one side. The group imitates her movement. I bend to the side, my body still cool and stiff from the early morning start.

We bend to the opposite side, and my limbs wake up. Slowly.

The sun rises a little more with each pose we hold, wobble through, and fall from. Not used to the stretching and balancing act of the exercise, I'm trembling by the time the hour is up.

"Alright, well done, all. I will see you tomorrow morning. Same time, same place." The instructor beams with a smile.

The crowd of early risers disperses, and I sit on the mat, tugging my sneakers back on.

"Well, that was fun," a low, breathy voice says.

I snap my attention to Rawlins. His T-shirt clings to his

toned frame from the exertion. A sheen of sweat lines his forehead.

"If you say so."

"Okay, my children, I will see you in an hour for breakfast." Manuel swipes up his clipboard with a broad smile, like this garbage rejuvenates him. Me, I'm exhausted and still recovering from trying to contort myself and hold my muscles at angles that no man's ever managed to get my body into, let alone me trying it on my own.

As if my facial expression changed, Rawlins frowns. "See you back at the house."

See you back at the house. Like it's our house. Just a normal occurrence, the two of us at home.

What the actual hell, Carlie?

Fucking yoga's bent my mind out of shape.

That has to be it . . . right?

Waving them both off, I stalk my way back to the bungalow. I need to think about something else.

Safely inside with the front door locked, I prop my phone up on a pillow with YouTube playing my favorite fitness channel's latest workout. The first burn of the squat lances through my thighs.

Much better.

After god knows how many squats, lunges, pushups, crunches, and a trillion other body weight exercises, I'm a sweaty, happy mess. I wander to the bathroom and peel off my clothes, letting the cool air caress my skin as I turn on the water. The white bathroom is a stark contrast to the wooden hut-style bedroom on the other side of this wall. The space floods with steam. It's warm and relaxing . . . delectable.

The vision of Rawlins lying on the floor bare-chested this

morning captures my mind. The toned chest, hard stomach, and bulging arms. Like he . . .

Heat sinks low in my belly.

Apparently, yoga not only loosens up your muscles, but it also destroys your sanity and rational thinking with its twisty ways. Because where the hell did that come from?

And why the hell is Vinny still in my bag and not in my damn hand?

My fingers gravitate to my now-hard nipple.

Maybe I should get it out of my system before he comes back. Leaning on the warm tile, I slide a hand over my stomach to my throbbing apex. With the first brush of my fingertip over my clit, I arch off the wall, tempted to pad back to the room to grab Vinny.

But my window of solitude this morning is closing, and I need this over and done with.

Pinching my aching nipple, I sink two fingers into my pussy.

"Oh god above," I mutter into the steam.

It's been ages since I got laid.

I should have taken care of this before I left. Now I'm stuck in this tiny bungalow with the last person I want to be thinking about while I'm grinding over my own hand.

As the telltale spiral of bliss unravels and I come hard and fast, I can't help the string of throaty sounds that slip past my lips.

My breathing settles and I wash up, rewashing my hair for good measure before shutting off the water. Stepping out onto the bathmat, I squint through the steam, doing a double take at the empty towel rack.

Urgh, the no-towel curse of the couples suite.

I swear this old hut is conspiring against us.

I pad to the bedroom to grab one from the end of the bed that was made while we were at yoga. But the bed is suspiciously empty. Save for a handwritten note.

I pick it up.

> *Carlie & Lawson,*
> *My apologies, we ran short on towels. I will send some with Manuel at lunchtime.*
> *So sorry!*
> *Elizabeth*
> *(Your friendly housekeeper);)*

For fuck's sake.

Sorry to break it to you, Elizabeth, but there is no Carlie and Lawson. I drop the note on the bed as a noise comes from just outside. Dripping wet with nothing but the pillows at my left or the entire bedspread to cover myself with, I stand frozen for a heartbeat. I scramble for something to shield against the person on the other side of the door that I'm assuming is Rawlins.

His key slides into the lock.

The image conjured by the sound shouldn't exist. It really shouldn't.

The lock clicks.

The doorknob turns.

The door cracks open.

Breaths come short and choppy as I alternate between standing my naked ground and owning this or cowering behind . . . his throw blanket. It's draped over the chair by the bags.

Could I get there and back in time and cover up before he sees the true Carlie Lamont?

A vision I'm sure will scar him for life. At the least, traumatize him to the point he might actually quit Serenity and leave me to my peace . . .

Standing butt-naked, I'm indecisive for the first time in my life.

CHAPTER 12
LAWSON

Lamont is naked and *almost* covered by my throw blanket. The door closes behind me as I stand stunned.

Recovering, I drop my key into the bowl.

"No towels," she chokes out. Her damp strands of long blonde hair hang over her chest, only barely shielded by the blanket.

I half expect her to drop the blanket in some sort of sassy statement and stalk to where she needs to go next. But tight browns pin me where I'm rooted to the spot as I fight the blood rushing south and the lancing breaths that have nothing to do with my five-mile run. I pull one earbud from my ear, slowly. Then the next. Our gaze doesn't break.

"If you don't mind." Her expression finally breaks, turning to annoyance.

"Right," I mutter, turning back to face the door.

Soft footsteps pad away, and I press a hand to the door,

letting my forehead drop to the cool wood. My entire body is on fire at the sight of her.

Serelle, what the hell were you thinking?

Right now, I'm praying Lamont used the last of the hot water, because I need a frigid fucking shower. My phone buzzes in my pocket and I push off the door and slide it out.

Ma.

How's the work retreat going?

How does *lustful dumpster fire* sound?

Fine.

Hmmm. What's wrong?

Nothing. It's exactly as I expected.

Well, almost. The stray thoughts that have been invading my head tangling Lamont and me together are a little disturbing.

Inappropriate.

Intense . . .

Do you think it will work? To improve your working relationship, that is?

I have no idea, Ma. Here's hoping.

Also, your brother wants you to confirm your numbers for the Thanksgiving dinner.

Shit, I forgot about Reed and Ruby's Thanksgiving banquet.

It's an annual thing. One of the original events they started hosting when Rubes helped Reed turn the ranch into a vacation destination slash working ranch.

Oh sure, I'll be there.

Only RSVPing for one, my love?

My gaze flickers toward the bathroom unconsciously. I shake my head, dislodging that particular thought before it takes hold.

Just one. Gotta go, Ma. Love you.

Love you too, my boy. I'm sure the two of you
will work it out.

I don't reply with anything else. What am I supposed to say? In the last few weeks, I've quit my job, landed another one with a pay cut, and pretty soon, I'm going to need to move for the first time in ten years. Serenity is too far from home, and with the pay decrease, it makes things too tight.

"Shower's all yours."

Realizing my phone's gone black, I look up to find a dressed Lamont.

"Sure, thanks."

She avoids eye contact, and I make my way to the shower. Between my run, yoga, and sleeping on the floor, my muscles could use a hot shower. The second I step into the bathroom, I'm overwhelmed by the scent that is Carlie Lamont. All floral and spice.

Goddamn, if that doesn't send my body into a frenzy.

I've shared an office with her for weeks, but this is like a concentrated shot of her.

I tilt my head, grinding my molars. "Hell."

"You say something?" A head pops around the corner.

Apparently, the risk of seeing me naked doesn't faze her.

"Nope. Out you get."

Her eyes turn to slits, but her disembodied head disappears. If only there was a door to this ridiculous bathroom.

I strip, turning on the water. Stepping into the warm stream, I roll my head on my shoulders, stretching every tight muscle as I go.

Heaven.

Well, almost.

Couples therapy. It's as stupid as it sounds.

Especially since the woman currently sitting on the floor in front of me with her legs tucked under her butt refuses to look at me.

This is going just great.

"Miss Carlie, this is a sacred space. Nothing you say here would be judged or shared. You can be honest." Manuel rests a hand on her knee, and she jerks her head back to look at him.

He gives her a reassuring nod and a smile that looks as strained as her tight expression right now. How much baggage does this fiery little woman carry around every damn day?

"Sorry, what's the question?" she says.

This time, the fire has dimmed.

"What was your first romantic relationship?" Manuel repeats the question.

"How is that relevant to a *working* relationship?" she says.

"Well, considering the resentment you seem to be harboring toward each other, I'm trying to gauge where it started and why you're attaching it to Mr. Lawson here." Manuel gives her an empathic look.

"I'm not answering that question. Pass." She folds her arms over her chest.

"Okay, that's your choice. But exploring your foundations will lead to a better outcome in the end. So think about that before your next turn, okay?" Manuel says before turning to me.

"Mr. Lawson, tell Carlie about your first romantic relationship."

"Ah, there's not really anything to tell." Lamont sneers, but I direct my response to Manuel.

"Okay, what about with your parents? Your mother, perhaps?"

"My relationship with my mother is good, always has been."

Lamont's brow flings toward her hairline.

That surprises her. It really shouldn't; she despises me.

"Good, thank you. This is part about getting to know each other on a deeper level, part giving each other the opportunity to understand where the other is coming from. Sometimes our past relationships trigger responses in our here and now. Our responses are not always conscious."

"That makes sense," I offer.

Lamont shoves a finger onto her nose before rolling her eyes.

"Miss Carlie, did you have something you needed to say?" Manuel says.

She scoffs. "Nope."

"Manuel's right, your baggage stays in this room, Lamont. Drop it and leave it."

Her eyes tighten. "You first. Or is the only thing weighing you down being your utter failure as a human being?"

And . . . we're back to square one.

I sigh. "Can I take five?"

Manuel waves a hand toward the door. I push to my feet and wander outside. The second the cool air sinks into my lungs, I close my eyes. I try really damn hard to understand why she is like this. The constant need to be on defense. To win at all costs. Why we make the smallest bit of progress, inching forward one step, only to take three back.

People wander about the facility, chatting, laughing.

This place is burning with positivity and happiness. I swear, the only spoiled apple in this resort is our relationship. Time to own this and fix it.

The way my father taught me to.

I pad inside to find Lamont holding Manuel's hand, both their eyes closed as he chants something, over and over. I study them for a beat as the scowl melts from her face. She's stunning when she's content.

Hell, who am I kidding, she's stunning when she's mad as a cut snake.

Huffing a laugh, I cross the room and sink to my seat. They both open their eyes, and Lamont squares her position to face me.

"Ready?" I ask.

"Fine." She tilts her chin up.

"Let's continue," Manuel says, looking at me.

Giving him a nod, I glance at Lamont.

"Okay, this time we are going to try physical contact. Take each other's hands, please."

Lamont clears her throat, but to my surprise, she holds out both hands. Her elegant, manicured hands. I fold mine around them, doing my best to ignore the spark that ignites with the touch. Her lips part as her gaze drops to where we're connected.

Her fingers are cold, and I squeeze them a little tighter.

"Good. A great start. Okay, this next question is harder than the last few. So, I'm going to ask it, then start the timer for one minute. You are not allowed to respond until the timer chimes. Then, looking your partner in the eye, tell them your honest answer."

I shift on my seat.

Now I'm the one who's uncomfortable.

"Mr. Lawson, tell Miss Carlie the one thing you would want her to know if this was your last sentence. The last sentence you could ever speak to her."

Sweet Jesus.

Manuel starts the timer.

Lamont wrangles the shock now slipped over her face back, and I fight to keep my expression indifferent.

I know this is a revised version of couples therapy. But even if I was sitting in front of someone I loved, this would be a hard question. With Lamont, almost impossible.

The timer goes off.

I study her face and the way she's holding herself, rigid and ready for something that's going to hurt. Like she's ready to take a hit. Only two words fill my mind.

"I'm sorry," I breathe.

Her hands jerk. She tries to pull away. As if she won't accept anything but opposition from me. We don't play nice. It's not comfortable for her.

Every small moment she's held me accountable or challenged me sweeps in. The way she is always on, always running at one hundred and twenty percent . . .

"I'm sorry. If I could have helped you in that moment, I would have. Please know that."

Her chin wobbles. Her hands rip from mine. She staggers to her feet and stalks from the room.

I turn to Manuel, and he's smiling a sad but knowing smile. "Bingo, Mr. Lawson."

"Shit," I utter.

When she doesn't return, I leave Manuel to his breakthrough. Her hair swishes as her hips sway with ferocity over the lawn toward the bungalow. I pick up the pace, lengthening my stride until I reach her. "Lamont!"

She flips me off, not slowing down.

"Carlie, stop."

A strangled noise leaves her as she picks up the pace.

Dammit.

I grab her elbow, and she teeters as she tries to shake me off. "Slow down, for god's sake."

"Get your hand off me," she grinds out.

"No."

"I swear to god. Is this your plan? Kill me with kindness until I feel something less than hatred for you? You think if we're friends, I'll give up my job so you can keep yours?"

The hell?

I tilt my head, brows plummeting. "No!"

"Let. Me. Go." Wild brown eyes flicker over my face.

I release my grip on her, and she steps out of my space. She marches into the bungalow, slamming the door behind her.

How on earth am I supposed to break through that wall she's built around herself? At this point, I think the shelter is kind of irrelevant. The more pressing issue is the heavy load this woman is hauling around. And the weight that's set to crush her if she doesn't let someone—anyone—in. And soon.

I walk to the house and open the door.

She's sitting on the side of the bed, her head in her hands.

I close the door quietly and she looks up. Her face is all hurt.

How does an apology equate to hurt?

Desperate to know what the hell is going on in that mind of hers, I brave the storm and sit on the end of the bed. "Need to talk about it?"

"God, you just can't take a hint, can you?"

I huff a laugh. "I promise it's not what you think."

"Yeah, right."

"Talk to me, Lamont."

"Not happening."

"Then talk to Manuel. Take the couples therapy sessions for yourself."

"And have it get back to Serelle that I'm a fucked-up mess? No thank you, I can handle myself."

"The way you imploded over a simple apology would suggest otherwise."

"Fuck you, Rawlins."

I turn to face her as her eyes burn into mine. "If that's what it takes."

Her lips part, but a beat later, she shakes her head. With a breathy laugh, she says, "I'm not playing that game."

I frown. "What game?"

"Where you have me fired for fucking you."

This takes me aback. "That's not—"

She stands, closing the distance until she's all but standing between my legs, looking down at me as she whispers, "I'd rather impale myself on Vinny."

Who the fuck is Vinny?

CHAPTER 13
CARLIE

Day two and Rawlins is getting handsy.

"Stop manhandling me," I snap, moving out of his space.

We stand in the middle of the lawn area by the pool. People lounge on long chairs, sipping drinks that look like cocktails. Why couldn't that be on our itinerary?

"Sure, I'll just let you fall and slam into the ground. I prefer that option, anyway," he says, giving me a deadpan look.

"This exercise is about trust," Manuel repeats his previous statement. "You fall, Mr. Lawson catches you, yes?"

"Trust is earned, Manuel, not given. I'd rather hit the ground." I straighten my tank top and shake out my body like that will rid my skin of the ridiculous tingle that's crept into every inch his hands came in contact with.

Rawlins runs a hand through his hair, flexing a bicep. "Fine, you catch me."

"I'll pass."

He blows out an annoyed breath. "We won't make any progress if you refuse to participate."

"Fine, I'll *endeavor* to catch you. Don't come bitching to me when you end up with a concussion."

He huffs and shakes his head, but Manuel positions us the perfect distance apart again, this time with Rawlins's back to me.

"Okay, I'll count you down, Mr. Lawson. Miss Carlie, be ready to take his weight."

I stare at Manuel, forgetting to ready my stance. That last phrase shouldn't hit the way it does.

Take his weight.

But after yesterday in the shower and then the failed therapy session, something about him has changed. Nothing huge, just a subtle shift in the way he speaks to me.

So, in true sassy-bitch style, I dialed up my defensiveness.

There is no way this man is hauling my walls down. He may have chipped away a few bricks, but the wall still stands.

"Five, four . . . Miss Carlie, ready?" Manuel shoots me a look that screams 'pay attention.' "Three, two, one, and fall."

I quickly spread my feet, reaching for the man in front of me, the man who has handed over his trust so easily. My palms meet his back.

Fuck, he's heavy.

I scramble to stay on my feet as his slip on the grass. We tumble to the ground in a tangle of legs and flailing arms. His head hits my chest and wind leaves my lungs.

Rawlins rights himself and turns over, pushing to all fours, looking down at me from under his messed-up hair. "Hell, you okay?"

"Ow! Shit. How are you that heavy?" I sit up on the grass, hands planted on the ground behind me.

He chuckles as he jumps to his feet and extends his hand, offering to help me up. I smack it away and scramble to my feet.

"Again. I'll be ready this time," I hiss.

"How about Mr. Lawson catches you now?" Manuel prompts.

I roll my eyes but say, "Whatever."

Standing in front of Rawlins, I force my eyes shut.

I hate this.

"I got you, Lamont," Rawlins says, his tone low and soft.

I almost believe him.

"Five, four, three, two, one, and fall."

Here goes nothing. I wrap my arms around my body, clinging to my biceps.

I tip backward, and the sickening feeling of weightlessness with no guarantee I won't hit the ground swells in my stomach. I squeeze my arms tight. I freefall for what feels like ages . . .

Warms hands slide over my arms and grip tight.

My head hits something solid. My back stops against a wall of muscle.

"Got you," Rawlins whispers, his breath hitting my neck. Shivers flood my skin, traveling up my spine. I can't tell whether it's his words or his touch, but the air in my lungs stalls out regardless.

"I—"

"Trust, see!" Manuel exclaims.

My eyes fly open, and I am acutely aware of Rawlins's steady hands still holding me to his chest. Shooting back to my feet and upright, I put space between us.

"Okay, your turn," I say to Mr. Fucking Perfect. "You fall this time, I'll catch you."

"No, we are done here." Manuel smiles at me.

"What? No, he didn't have a proper turn."

"He doesn't need to go again, Miss Carlie, he already fell. He already trusts you."

I open my mouth to object but, realizing Manuel has a point, I close it. Rawlins already took the risk on me; he already trusted me with his safety. He did his part. I feel second place again. Like this is some contest over who is the nicest.

One I'm never going to win.

After years of looking after myself, working twice as hard as everyone else to make it this far, I guess I lost the nice-girl vibe somewhere along the way. Honestly, it probably died somewhere in the ten years I worked for Carlson.

"You have free time now. Be free, my lovelies. I will see you for dinner and then honesty hour at eight sharp." Manuel waves as he heads for the communal area.

Leaving Rawlins and I standing on the grass, staring at each other.

It's fucking awkward.

"Yeah, so, sorry about crushing you." Rawlins offers a slight smile.

"Forget it. I should have paid attention."

"Is that a concession, Lamont?"

"What? No!"

He laughs, genuine and hearty, and he's . . . absolutely gorgeous.

My stomach flip-flops, and I force my attention to the lucky fuckers at the pool still sipping their cocktails. Rawlins glances to where my gaze has drifted. "Did you want to grab a drink?"

"Ah, no." I force a smile and decide it's time I got some work done. But as I turn to leave, a hand catches my wrist. I look down to where his large, warm hand holds me to the spot. "What?"

"Lawson," he says softly, studying my face.

"I know your first name, Rawlins."

"Then use it, Carlie."

My lips pop open, and heat rushes my neck and face as I suck in a breath at hearing my first name from his mouth. Somehow, I manage, "Why?"

"Consider it a nonnegotiable of this professional relationship of ours."

"We don't—"

"Yeah, you said that, but we do have a relationship. Whether you like it or not. We ought to make the most of it with the little time we have left together at Serenity."

I don't know what to say, torn between the reality of one of us leaving in a few short months and the feeling that's growing with his touch, his words. The way that having Rawlins—Lawson—in my days has become something I can count on.

"This does not mean we are friends," I add for clarification.

He runs a hand through his hair, glancing somewhere in the distance before his deep blues settle back on me. "Carlie, you and I can't be friends."

Confused, I tug my hand from his grip. What the hell is that supposed to mean?

"See you later," he says, heading for the bar area by the pool.

With nothing else left to do, I track back to the suite and get started on some work.

Four hours later, I am fighting off a tension headache and have only cleared half my inbox. I rub my eyes and yawn. It's only six, but it may as well be midnight by how fried my brain feels.

Six . . . *Shit*.

Dinner.

I grab a jacket and shove my slip-on shoes over my feet and cross the lawn to the restaurant area next to the bar and pool. Rawlins—I mean, Lawson—is still there, perched on a stool. Weaving through the tables, I wander to the bar and slide onto the stool beside him. His hand grips a tumbler with amber liquid in it.

How long has he been here?

He forces a smile as he slides his gaze sideways. "Get some work done?"

"Yes, I'm guessing you didn't? Have you been here the whole time?"

"I—"

I hold a hand up. "Never mind, none of my business."

He closes his mouth and swirls the liquid in his glass. He doesn't seem drunk . . .

"Hungry?" he asks.

"Starving, but I have a killer headache."

"Why didn't you tell me?"

"What, while I was working, and you were here . . . drinking?"

"I only switched to whiskey when the sun went down. The mocktails are interesting, though."

"Oh," I breathe.

"Pain relief first or food?"

Someone drops a glass a few feet away, and I wince.

Lawson slides from his stool and takes my hand. "Pain relief first."

I all but fall from the stool and follow as he leads me from the noisy space.

He drops my hand as we reach the grass and walk together. "You get them often?"

"When I'm stressed or forget to drink my coffee."

"But we only have coffee at breakfast."

"Yep, and it sucks."

I'm one hundred percent sure this is the cause of my headache. But I don't let on.

Back at the bungalow, he sits me on the bed and disappears into the bathroom area. The tap turns on, then shuts off. He returns with a cool, wet washcloth, folding it before draping it over my forehead. He tilts my head up with his finger under my chin, and I resist the urge to meet his gaze.

This is too intimate.

Too friendly.

"Where's your painkillers?" he asks, padding to the bag rack.

"Front pocket, on the inside."

I lie back.

It isn't until I hear the zipper on my bag that I remember Vinny is packed in the same spot.

Fuck.

If he noticed the pink vibrator, he doesn't say anything as he returns with painkillers and swipes my glass of water from the bedside table. I take the pills and drift my eyes shut, rubbing my temples, hoping it will help. The ache doesn't budge.

"Can I try something to help release the tension and ease the headache?" he asks.

"What is it?"

"My mother's technique she uses for my father. Shoulder massage with pressure points."

"Okay . . ."

He climbs onto the bed behind me and rests his hands on my shoulders. I stiffen under the large spans of warmth they bring. *Holy shit.*

"Damn, you're so tense," he mutters. Then, "Close your eyes."

"Not on your life."

He leans down to whisper by my ear, "You trust me now, right?"

I turn back, giving him an indignant filthy look.

"Let me help, please, Carlie."

"Fine, but so you know, I have mace in my bag."

"Amongst other things," he says quietly.

Heat engulfs my neck and face. I bury my face in my hands. And his chuckle dies in his throat before he clears it. His hands fall away, and I turn back. "Seriously?"

"Sorry, it's none of my business."

"No, it's not. But my headache is killing me, and your hands are so *warm* . . ."

Glancing back, I catch a small smile tugging up in one corner of his mouth. "Fine, but you get all handsy, Lamont, I'm going straight to HR."

"Well, for your sake, I'm glad that's no longer you." I wait for the words to land before busting out a rare smile for this man. "What happened to our first-name basis?"

He chuckles again before whispering, "Brat." He plants his hands on my shoulders again with a tight squeeze.

"Ah! Oh . . ."

Shifting my hair to one side with a gentle touch that sends goosebumps blooming over my body, he massages my shoulders.

Lawson's strong grip works my tight muscles over, and I can't help the small little groans that slip out as my head begins to feel a little better. My entire body is relaxed. His thumbs work their way up the back of my neck and past my hairline, and I tilt my head to one side with a heady groan.

"Fuck," he breathes.

I still, breaths burning. The harried blood in my veins is drowning out my rational thinking capabilities. I mean, he's not wrong. My body is alive under his touch. My heart hammers. These panties are ruined. And they absolutely shouldn't be.

"Sorry." His hands disappear from my neck, and the bed shifts with a jerky motion as he leaves the bedroom and pads to the bathroom. I flop back on the bed and stare at the ceiling. That's the most male attention my body has had in months.

And fuck, it felt good.

But this is *Rawlins* we're talking about.

My mortal enemy.

My competition.

My . . . *not friend.*

Urgh.

I decide to step outside to ring Mills. That way, he can take care of whatever he needs to without me around. Maybe he's not affected by me the way I am by him. Can't say I can imagine him getting off in the shower to the image of me naked. Although he almost saw that yesterday.

She picks up on the third ring.

"Hello, sweetheart? Ready to ride off into the sunset yet?" She cackles, not letting me get a word in.

"Quit it, Mills. You're not helping."

"Oh, did something happen?"

"Of course not," I rush out.

"Carlie Marie Lamont, you know how I feel about lying."

"Something's changed, Mills. He's different. I think I—he's getting to me, I swear." I pace a small stretch of grass outside the bungalow. "That's stupid, right? It's barely been two whole days."

"Time holds no bearing on such things. Sometimes it only takes one moment to change your life, for better or worse. I have lived both."

She has too.

"I mean, I guess it's a good thing we aren't at each other's throats anymore. But . . ."

"But what? Don't see yourself living on a ranch with eight babies and barefoot?"

"Would you stop with that shit? The man lives in Manhattan, and it is nothing like that. Stop daydreaming."

She cackles again.

How is this woman always so stinking happy?

"We had to do therapy yesterday." I try to change the subject slightly.

"Oh? How did it go?"

"They asked about my dad, in a roundabout way."

"Oh . . ." The one syllable comes out from her as deflated as

I feel. I've never been good at talking about my father, or the absence of him, to be more accurate.

"Well, you share what you feel comfortable sharing and leave the rest to the birds, sweetheart."

"I will. You okay by yourself?"

"I am old, not incapable. There's a difference, my girl. I'm enjoying the solitude, but I miss you fiercely."

I chuckle. "I miss you, too. I better go. Dinner's started." I glance at the communal area across the lawns. People are filing in, the tables filling up.

"Go! Enjoy yourself. You'll be back to reality before you know it."

"Bye, Mills."

"Bye, sweetie."

She hangs up, and I turn back to find Lawson leaning on the door frame. He's showered, dressed for dinner. And hell, the man is something else with his arms crossed over his chest, eyes snagged on me with a lazy smile stretching his mouth.

"It's rude to eavesdrop, Lawson."

"I wasn't. You were finishing up when I opened the door. How's the head?"

"Better. Now I'm starving."

"We better feed you, then." He winks at me.

Something that feels suspiciously like a cloud of butterflies takes flight low in my belly.

For fuck's sake.

Damn you, Mills, for putting your daydreams in my head.

CHAPTER 14
LAWSON

Carlie bolts from the chair across the small table from me and rushes from the room. What'd I say?

Manuel forces a smile and rises to go after her. Honesty hour.

More like emotional-trauma hour. If the look on her face is anything to go by.

We each have three questions. One about our families. One about our dreams. One about our greatest fear.

She almost faltered on the first one but managed a two-word answer. The second, she gave a more elaborate answer. The third . . .

Well, I'm currently sitting in this small therapy room by myself.

I guess asking if her greatest fear revolved around being not good enough hit home.

Only seven minutes in, and we've hit a wall.

I feel like the asshole, but that's the point, isn't it? To make us uncomfortable together, to become comrades in arms, so to speak. As we weave through our messy bits, we get to know each other at a deeper level, so this superficial back-and-forth defensiveness we've both tossed at each other can be replaced with something more productive.

Ten minutes pass before I leave my seat and wander into the large communal area. Manuel meets me as I reach the dining area. "Mr. Lawson, she needs a moment. We can continue together, if you like?"

"No, it's fine. Where is she?"

"Ah . . . she—"

"Never mind, I'll find her."

He turns as I head for the pool area, calling out, "Tread easy, please."

I wave a hand over my shoulder. Nothing about this is easy. I severely underestimated the impact this week would have on me. On the both of us. But the vulnerabilities it has pulled from Carlie are what surprise me the most.

I was raised with the notion that we take care of our own.

And I am well aware Lamont is not my family, but something propels me around the resort searching for her, regardless. Twenty minutes later, I find her sitting against a big old tree, knees up and head bent, her forehead pressed to her arm in the dark. Stopping mere feet from where she sits, I watch her shoulders rising and falling in a steady rhythm. The half-moon overhead illuminates the rose-gold hair around her shoulders.

"Need a punching bag?" I say softly.

A sniffle rattles her body. "Go away, Rawlins."

"Lawson, remember?"

She groans. "Go away, *Lawson*."

"I would love to. I have so many better things to do right now, but Manuel is riding my ass over this big-time."

Her head snaps up. Her brown eyes, tight with hurt, meet mine. "You're lying."

"Nope." I shove my hands in the back pockets of my Levi's.

I'm totally lying.

She pushes to her feet, wiping her face dry before closing the space between us. "Manuel's never so much as spoken a harsh word since the moment we arrived. What's your MO?"

Why is this woman always on defense?

Her trust in people, in the world around her, must be nonexistent.

"You know, life doesn't always have to be a battle, Carlie."

She jerks back, her face twisting. "Says you, the straight white male from the perfect family. The boys' club practically ensures your success, no matter where you work or how shitty you are at your job."

I tilt my head up, brows lowering. "You really think that?"

"I don't think that—I *know* that. It took me ten years to earn the corner office. Guess how long it took the guy who started with me to do the same?"

"Eight?" I hedge a guess.

"Try eighteen months."

My jaw slackens, shock flattening my features. "Fuck."

"My sentiments exactly. So excuse me for wanting to fight for myself. For being a little touchy about my fucking worth in this world."

That's it. That's all it takes to crack my heart all over my damn sleeve.

"I'm not your enemy, I promise."

Tears flood into those pretty browns all over again, the moonlight turning the moisture silver as her chin wobbles.

I fold her into a hug. She resists with a halfhearted wriggle, slapping my chest, but I don't give an inch. *"Please,* stop fighting me."

She stills before softening in my arms. I wrap her closer, dropping my chin to the crown of her head.

When she pushes away a minute later, wiping her face, I tilt my head to catch her gaze. "You want to come back and ask me ridiculous questions about myself and make me squirm?"

She huffs a strained laugh, but it peters out. "Couldn't think of a better way to cheer myself up."

I grin at her, and she snaps her head to the side.

"Come on, before Manuel sends out the search party."

She pushes her shoulders back with a long, deep inhale and walks toward the communal area. I follow behind, but my mind is stuck on everything I know about her life.

Her single-parent status, her battle to have the career she wants, watching every other person be promoted over her because they're male. The fact we are now in a very similar situation, where one of us stays and the other loses their job.

No wonder she attacks the world with wit and sass. It's most likely a learned behavior from every unjustified setback she's had that she shouldn't have.

Manuel waits patiently by the door to our small therapy room. We step inside, and the table is gone, replaced by two beanbags and a shit ton of cushions. A tray with a teapot and snacks sits in the center.

"Please, let us start again. A do-over, yes?" Manuel says to Carlie with a sad smile.

"Sure." She walks in, dropping into a beanbag.

I do the same, taking the beanbag by hers. Manuel drags a third a little closer and serves the tea before sinking into his with a crunch.

The tea is green, woody, and tart. Hot. I sip it slowly. Carlie takes a mouthful, tilting her head back as she swallows. The elegant column of her neck has my gaze fixed to it as her hair tumbles away and over her back.

Manuel clears his throat. "Right, Miss Carlie, ask Mr. Lawson his first question. It must be related to family."

Carlie nurses the mug in her hand, turning her body toward me a little. Brown eyes study my face before she says, "Explain your family dynamic to me. Everyone in it and where you fit in."

"Ah, that's not a standard question," Manuel says with a frown.

"No, it's okay," I offer, and a small smile curls up on her pretty face. "My parents own a ranch in Montana. I have three brothers. I'm the second eldest. Hudson is the oldest. Mackinlay, or Mack, is around two years younger than me. Reed is the youngest. They're all married and live on their own ranches now. We're pretty tight after everything we've been through and the way we were raised. Family is everything in a Rawlins household. My three sisters-in-law are considered my sisters. What else would you like to know?"

Carlie's face has dropped in either awe or shock.

I'm not sure if it's over the whole close-knit family thing, or the fact that I consider Gracie, Rubes, and Adds my sisters. Or if it's me being the only one not married when my brothers have figured that part of their lives out.

"Miss Carlie, since Mr. Lawson is offering, is there anything else you would like to know?"

"I—" She drops her gaze to her mug. "Why didn't you become a rancher like the rest of your family?"

"Wasn't really my thing. I mean, I grew up doing all that, but I wanted something more than chasing cows and hours spent fixing Harry's fences."

"Oh," she breathes. "And Harry is . . ."

"My father."

"Thank you, Mr. Lawson." Manuel's words seem to split the air between us, and Carlie pulls her focus from me to Manuel.

"Next question," Manuel prompts.

"Oh right, sure. Where do you see yourself in five years, career-wise?" Carlie says, her focus not shifting from her mug. As if she can't look at me when I say I will be at Serenity in five years. But after everything that's happened in my life and in the last month, the decision to work at Serenity isn't as clear-cut to me anymore.

"Honestly, I have no idea."

Her head snaps up. "Why?"

I shrug my shoulders. How am I supposed to be yet another asshole who takes yet another job from her? I've drifted around, job to job, making ends meet. No solid plan, just keeping my head above water. Getting home to Montana as much as I can.

"You are required to answer every question Miss Carlie asks," Manuel says, nodding.

"Yeah, I know." I suck in a breath. This feels like showing the lioness my flank or something equally stupid. But . . .

"I don't know what I want."

Carlie's brows lower and she sips her tea, staring at some random point on the wall.

"Last question, please." Manuel takes a sip from his own mug before jotting something on his clipboard.

"What is your greatest fear, Rawlins?"

I give her an incredulous look, and she gives me one right back. Guess even talking about other people's fears is a touchy subject for this woman if we've reverted back to last names.

"My greatest fear," I say, holding her gaze, "is not building a life I love."

The moment winds down to a beat, as if pausing somehow. Where the woman sitting beside me can see right into my weary heart, my head that can never figure out what it wants even at my age. And blood hammers through my head as heat rises and tightness twinges in my chest.

This right here is my vulnerability laid bare.

No wonder she fled the room.

This part is utter shit.

I refuse to let it bother me, holding my nerve. One of us has to bend. One of us has to bend *first*. Let it be me, since Carlie's had to fight for every inch over the last decade.

"Same," she finally breathes.

And just like that, we are on the same page.

About one thing, at least.

Manuel claps, and we both startle, looking at him. The biggest smile stretches his face as he tilts his head. "I think we had a breakthrough, my lovelies."

Carlie smiles at him, but it fades when she looks back at me. "I think I'm going to call it a night."

"Be there in a few," I say, and she returns her mug to the tray as she walks out.

The door clicks shut and Manuel beams at me. "That was *incredible.*"

"Yeah, it felt pretty good."

"I think you both offered up a piece of yourself today. It's only the first bit of progress. Onward and upward, Mr. Lawson."

"Hopefully. We both need this to work."

"I understand. Was there something else you needed to talk about?"

"Actually, I think there is . . ."

An hour later, I open the door to the bungalow to find all the lights out, bar the bedside lamp on the right. Setting my keys down gently, I toe off my shoes. I mill about, trying to find my throw blanket. Not seeing it, I move closer to the bed. Carlie is sound asleep. The blanket is pulled up over her shoulder as she sleeps on her side, her back to the middle, where the covers are folded back to reveal one side of the bed.

Turned down, ready for someone to slide in. My throw lies over the corner of that side. A note stands against the lamp. I sit on the edge of the mattress and pick up the card.

This bed is too big for one person ~ the floor too hard. Use that information as you will.

C

I glance over my shoulder. She's still fast asleep. Setting the card back on the nightstand, I release the clasp on my watch and set it beside the card gently. Tugging my shirt off, I lie in the bed.

Good god, it's so damn soft.

Fucking heaven compared to the hard-ass floor.

I breathe deep, relaxing into the mattress.

Goddamn bliss.

The second the air hits my senses, her scent takes hold. That rich floral. This close, with only inches between us, it takes everything I have to rein in the way my body responds to the mere proximity of her.

CHAPTER 15
CARLIE

I open my eyes to the muscular chest of Lawson Rawlins.

Fuck, that's right, I gave him half the bed in a rare moment of humility toward the man who reminds me of my greatest failure every day.

I take a minute to study the competition. Who is, I realize, missing a pillow. His head is on the mattress, his chin up, as if showing off his Adam's apple.

Although, after last night, it's hard to consider him just my competition. I run my gaze over the toned musculature on the other side of the bed. It's been forever since I woke up next to a man.

Okay, so it's never actually happened. My Tinder dates don't exactly stay for the cigarette, let alone the cuddle after. So I've never missed something I've never had. But watching Ra— Lawson sleep stirs up the butterflies I locked up and threw away the key on last night after our deep and meaningful conversation. I lock them down, a few hitting the metal confines of their cage. He's all angles, lips that look like I could eat him with one bite. Gorgeous brown hair I could send my fingers into . . .

My breathing picks up pace, sending heat low in my belly.

Shit.

I roll onto my back and rub my hands over my face.

A groan sees me splay my fingers apart to peek at the man.

He rolls over, reaching for something. His big mitt finds my pillow. He tugs it to himself, and my head hits the mattress. "Hey!"

His face twists as his eyes slowly open. He lifts his head, rubbing a hand over his face, his biceps flexing as he does. Deep blues finally meet my gaze, and I close my gaping mouth and grab the pillow. "Thief. That's what I get for my kindness?"

He smiles and flops back onto the mattress.

"Mornin'," he drawls in a low, raspy tone.

My stomach flips, upturning the metal cage, and the butter-flies race from their confines. I fling the covers off and pad to my luggage. Pulling out my day clothes, I head to the bath-room, not paying Lawson and his heady masculinity another glance.

After brushing my teeth, I take a quick shower and pull on my shorts and a tank that hangs off one shoulder. I put my hair up and apply some light makeup.

Day four.

Role-playing. This should be interesting.

I can't wait to see what crazy shit Manuel has for us today. As much as I hate to admit it, I'm kind of enjoying this week. I predicted it would be hell, being trapped in these confines with Lawson.

But it's . . . not?

I don't hate it the way I predicted I would.

"You done?" he says from near the faux wall, still out of sight.

"Yeah, sorry."

He steps into the bathroom, still bare-chested. His Levi's are crumpled. I guess he slept in them. That must have been uncomfortable.

He moves to the sink and brushes his teeth as I finish up my hair.

How very domesticated of us.

Spitting, he washes his face and runs a wet hand through his hair.

God, I want to do that.

"You good?" he says, and I realize I'm staring.

I clear my throat. "Yep. See you at breakfast."

"Sure. Be there in a bit."

I walk from the bathroom to the door, grabbing my key as I leave. At the dining area, I grab a table for two and order breakfast. My food arrives as Lawson drops into the seat across from mine. "You forgot your phone," he says, sliding my phone over the table.

I take it, and the screen lights up with a missed call from Millie.

"Shoot, I should call her back."

"Go ahead."

"One, I wasn't asking for your permission. Two, if you don't mind . . ." I wave him away.

With a small smile, he rises and finds a seat at the bar before ordering from the menu. I dial Mills, and she picks up on the second ring.

"Hey, sweetheart, how you doing?"

"Hey, Mills. You good? I missed your call."

"Oh, I was wondering what day you're back. I couldn't remember."

"Hopefully home Sunday night. You sure you're okay?"

"Yes, love. Just lonely, I guess."

That squeezes my chest. It's the first time Mills has been alone since the day I took her home from the bus shelter. I kind of forgot she would be alone, too. Sometimes, my blinders really are a disadvantage.

"You want me to call you tonight?" I ask.

"Yeah, that would be nice. Oh, also, I have something to tell you. But have a great day, hey."

"Tell me now."

"No, it can wait. Bye, sweet."

I hang up and finish my food. Laughter spills out from the bar. Lawson is talking with the bartender. Her face is lit up with amusement and wonder as he holds his hands out, gesticulating like a toddler as he recalls some story. Manuel sits beside him. I didn't see him come in. They chatter back and forth about things before Lawson slides from the stool and appears in front of me.

"You're quite the entertainer, Rawlins. I never knew that."

"Nah, just like seeing people smile, is all."

That tracks. He's always Mr. Sunshine in the office.

"Well, we should go to our first session." I stand and swipe up my phone, sliding it into my back pocket.

He crooks his arm and nods to it with a smile.

"Yeah, I'm good."

He narrows his eyes playfully. "Damn, worked for Reedsy."

"Who?"

"My youngest brother," he says with a chuckle.

"The cowboy thing isn't going to work on me."

"Noted."

I walk away, heading for the communal building to check the list and see which room we are in. When I find our names, I roll my eyes. *Mr. & Mrs. Rawlins.*

The fuck, Manuel.

Lawson leans over my shoulder and huffs a laugh. "The man is relentless."

"We'll see about that." I stalk to our designated room.

Inside, I find said resort guide with a ridiculous smile plastered over his face. The clipboard is adorned with pink and blue paper.

Oh, goody.

"Good morning, Miss Carlie," he quips.

"Don't you Miss Carlie me, buddy. What's with the list out there?"

"I have no idea what you're talking about?" He frowns, but the side of his mouth tips up.

I swear to god.

"Mr. and Mrs. Rawlins?" I rest a hand on my popped hip.

"Well, that's who you are today, for this session."

I open my mouth to tell him the fuck off, but Lawson rests a hand on my shoulder. "You're going to have to explain that one for us."

I glance at Lawson's calm face.

"Today we role-play, yes?" Manuel turns the clipboard so we can see the colored paper slips trapped under the clip.

"Okay . . ."

"We are going to role-play partner responses and problem

solving. Given, this is usually part of the couples therapy. But Serelle wanted us to keep to the original programming as much as possible."

"For fuck's sake," I mutter.

"Alright. We can do this. It's just pretend, right?" Lawson says.

I hold him with a glare before relenting. "Fine. You want me as your old lady, Rawlins? You got it."

I snatch the pink slip that Manuel holds out to me. Lawson takes a blue one.

How very retro.

"Okay, so on each slip is a problem that you must bring up with your spouse—well, partner, I guess. We run through one until there is a resolution, and then it's the other person's turn. Does that make sense?" Manuel's gaze alternates between us both. I nod and Lawson does the same.

"Alright, ladies first." Manuel beams at me.

Eat dirt, Manuel.

I read the slip. Money problems. Easy. I turn to face Lawson and read the words on the paper. "I want to talk about the mortgage."

He studies my face briefly and says, "Sure. What about it?"

I glance down at the paper. It says we've missed the last three payments.

Who does that?

"We've missed the last three payments," I report.

"Oh shit. Okay, well, how are we going to find the money for them?"

"Why are you asking me?"

Manuel leans forward, a finger held up. "Remember to use the language you would like to receive."

I draw in a lungful and set my shoulders back. "How will *we* find the money?"

"Do you have any savings?" he asks.

I press a hand to my hip. "Do you?" The tone comes out harsher than I intend.

Lawson rubs a hand behind his neck as he looks down at me, his gaze slipping to my mouth. "Yeah, sure. We can use mine."

"Mr. Lawson, the problem must be solved by both of you."

"Half can be covered by my savings?" Lawson says.

"You don't sound so sure about that," I say softly, closing the gap between us.

"I'm sure." His hands hang by his sides. "What about you, you sure?"

"That I want to pay half of a bill?"

"Yeah, that," he breathes.

"Absolutely." The word is no more than a huffy breath.

"Yes! A successful outcome." Manuel's excitement propels us apart like Moses parting the Red Sea.

I drop my gaze to the floor.

Shit.

How the hell did we get so close?

"Next up, you are going to be your respective parent and role-play how they would solve something. Mr. Lawson, who do you choose, your mother or your father?"

"My father."

"What is his name?" Manuel asks.

"Harry." Lawson's gaze hasn't left me, but I can't bring myself to look at him.

"Miss Carlie, who do you cho—"

"My mom."

"Oh, okay, great. Here are your slips." Manuel hands us new colored pieces of paper.

I look at mine, studying it like it's some ancient treasure map that takes years to decipher. Looking anywhere other than the man whose deep blues swing back to me every other heartbeat.

"Mr. Lawson, you may start." Manuel nods.

Lawson moves closer. His feet parting a little, he dips his head. "Darlin', I have some bad news."

I look up into those deep blues tightened with sadness.

"What is it?" I whisper.

His jaw feathers as he takes my shoulders in his arms. "Ma's gone."

Ma? His mother? My mother? By the way he's looking at me, I'm guessing it was mine. His Adam's apple bobs, his chest plummets.

"Okay? Whe—I mean how?"

Immediately, my mind flicks to Mills.

"Heart attack, last night."

I glance down at the notes on my card.

"But she was only fifty."

"I know, seems a goddamn waste of a good woman."

"Oh," I rasp. This feels so real. Not a pretend scenario in the slightest. The emotion in his face is very real.

"Stop." I try to pull my shoulders from his grip.

He reaffirms it. "There's something else."

I stiffen in his hold. "What?"

"I'm—" He glances to Manuel who nods, slowly. "I'm leavin'."

I freeze, deer in headlights stuff. Every muscle rigid. What, did these people dig through our pasts to find the most triggering thing they could find to throw it in our faces? And why the hell am I doing this with Rawlins?

I rip my arms from his hold and stalk from the room.

The door opens behind me as I march down the hallway, fighting back the tears.

"Carlie! Wait."

Fuck you, Lawson. Fuck you.

Large strides close in behind me, and he grabs my arm. "Hey, stop."

I turn on him, finger shoved into his chest. "You enjoy that? Dragging up the most horrible part of my life and tossing it in my face?"

He steps back, his face widening with surprise then falling with empathy. People have stopped what they're doing in the large communal space. Guests playing chess, those playing cards, and the few others sitting in the reading area all look up. At us.

"No, it's not like that."

"Really? Then tell me why you would recreate something so personal, so *hurtful*?"

He holds both hands up in surrender.

"Did you know my father left with the milk when I was a little girl? I was eight years old, Rawlins. But I'm guessing you already knew that. Did you do some digging before we came here? Or did Serelle let that one slip?"

Shock settles over him, and I swear I hear his molars grinding from here.

"No—I . . ." He hangs his hands and tilts his head as he takes a step forward. "Of course not. Not everyone in this world is out to fuck you over."

"Yeah, right." I huff a raw sound as he opens his mouth to

say something. "You know what, forget it. How could you and your perfect existence ever understand?"

Before the first tear falls, I make it to the big tree on the other side of the resort in under three minutes.

My ass meets the ground as the first sob tumbles out.

CHAPTER 16
LAWSON

Carlie's missed lunch and now dinner. She was a no-show for our therapy session, and it's about time for honesty hour as I wait for her outside the communal building.

Manuel walks in, clipboard in hand. I get a glimpse of strawberry blonde traveling behind him, and I release a breath. The last eight hours shouldn't have felt as long as they did.

"Mr. Lawson, Miss Carlie, shall we begin?"

"Fine," Carlie says as I nod.

We walk in silence to our allocated room. The beanbags are still there from last night.

I try to catch Carlie's attention before we go in, but she ignores me, even after our gazes snag when Manuel steps inside. I drop onto a beanbag as Carlie pours the tea.

She hands me a cup without looking.

I take it, letting my fingers brush hers.

She sucks in a breath before pouring another mug for herself.

"Alright. Tonight is freedom-of-speech night. This is where you can say whatever you need to, to get anything you want off your chest. Mr. Lawson, you first."

"Ah, I want to apologize for earlier."

Carlie rolls her eyes, still not looking at me.

"Good. Miss Carlie, your turn. What would you like to tell Mr. Lawson?"

She sips her tea, not offering anything up.

"Alright, Mr. Lawson, is there anything else?"

"I want you to know I didn't know about your dad. Nor would I ever use that information to hurt you. I wasn't raised like that."

The drawl earns me a lopsided, albeit sad, smile from Carlie.

I lean over and whisper, "Still offering up my punching bag services if you need them."

Now she looks at me, her eyes narrowed and dark. "Careful what you wish for."

I chuckle at her, and her smile grows.

Much better.

I would let this little woman pound on me her hardest if it meant getting that hurt out and replacing it with a smile like the one she just gave me.

"Miss Carlie. How about now? Anything you want to say to Mr. Lawson?"

She replaces the mug to the tray and tucks her legs underneath her.

"I think you should figure out what you want to do in life. I think not knowing is slowing you down. You're smart, and people love you. You could do or be anything you want."

That's the nearest thing to a compliment this woman has

ever given me. All I can do is stare at her. She drags her gaze from mine and looks at Manuel.

"Thanks," I utter, swallowing against the stone now swelling in my throat.

Look at that. She stopped hating me.

Wonder if the devil needs a cardigan . . .

After another thirty minutes of mundane small talk and no more breakthroughs, we call it a night. Carlie and I walk back to the suite in silence. We go through our respective bedtime routines, and when I slide into bed, there is a wall of pillows running down the center of the king bed.

"Just as well. You tend to be handsy, Lamont."

She screws up her face, rubbing hand cream into her hands, wrists, and up her arms. The tiny silky pajamas she's wearing barely cover her chest. A sliver of her stomach is exposed. The tiny shorts only just cover her ass, leaving her long legs, currently bent as she leans over to moisturize them, to go on forever.

In my T-shirt and boxers, I feel overdressed. She turns her head, still bending over, and her hair falls around her face. While she runs the cream up and down her left leg, I have to send my mind anywhere but fucking here.

Harry's fencing.

Mack on deployment.

Reed and Ruby's accident.

My first apartment and the rodent problem we had . . .

Rotting dead rats . . .

I breathe through the heat lancing my core and sending my cock impossibly hard as she flicks her hair over her shoulder, a squall of floral and spice wafting at me.

Clearing my throat, I lie down and roll over, facing the wall on my side. "Night."

I turn out my lamp.

She moves on the bed, then her light goes out. "Night, Lawson."

We lie there in silence, listening to each other's breathing, before Carlie says, "Can we keep whatever happens here between us? I don't need the entire office knowing I was a blubbering mess over my absent father." The last few words are weak.

That takes the wind out of my sails.

"Of course. Your secrets are safe with me, superwoman."

She huffs a small laugh. "Thank you."

"I meant what I said earlier, Carlie. Not everyone is out to screw you over. I'm certainly not."

"We'll see."

I resist the urge to roll over and shake the paranoia out of her. Fearing everything and everyone is no way to live.

No way at all.

Trust exercise—take five.

Carlie steps onto the platform, harness and rope attached to her body. A helmet on her head, she clings to the side rails with a white-knuckle grip.

"I've got you, let go," I call to her from the other side of the rope bridge. I hold the other end of her harness, the belay rope to catch her if she falls. Literally.

She shakes her head furiously.

"Mr. Lawson will keep you safe, you can step out."

"What if he gets distracted?" she says.

"I won't." I reaffirm my grip on the rope.

Honestly, even if we fall from here, it's only around six feet. Not a big deal. But by the look of terror on Carlie's face, we may as well be six miles up.

She takes one shaky step onto the tightrope line.

"Good, now another one," I coax.

For someone so fearless in her work life, I'm surprised to find she has a fear of heights. At least, that's what I think it is. She takes another step and then another. "Good girl, come on."

She looks up at me at that. Something in her brown eyes I haven't seen before swells.

She straightens a little, gaining more confidence as she goes. Stepping within arm's length, she flies into my arms as I reach for her. The air huffs from my lungs as she wraps herself around my body, burying her face in my chest. "God, that was terrifying."

I rub a hand over her hair. "You did good."

She looks up to me before moving around me onto the platform. I double-check my harness, and Manuel instructs Carlie on how to belay my security rope. She nods, moving closer to the edge of the platform as I step out.

"Slowly, Mr. Lawson," Manuel calls up.

I slowly make my way across the tightrope. It's too easy. I glance back to see Carlie watching with bated breath, the line hanging between her fingers.

Her phone rings, startling her.

The line drops through her fingers.

"No, don't let go!" I yell as my footing slips.

I scramble to reclaim my footing, arms flailing.

A second later, my back hits the ground. The air rushes from my lungs and I gasp like a fish out of water. Flat on my back, I lie there, stunned. I slam my eyes shut to stave off the burn that's eating its way through my empty chest.

"Oh fuck!" Harried steps clunk down the wooden ladder, and I open my eyes as a blur of blonde swings over my face. Fine fingers palm my jaw. "Lawson! Oh my god. Manuel, get some help."

I choke on my first painful inhale.

Something soft rubs my face. Floral and spice shroud my senses.

"Say you're alright, please?" she begs.

Hands wander over my chest. She presses her ear to my chest. I stifle a chuckle, but a groan escapes in its place. Her head lifts, and I find her face twisted with worry. Eyes shuttering closed, she sags with relief as I say, "Still alive."

I cough through the next few breaths, and she insists I sit up. I brush the grass and dirt from the back of my hair. A quick hand clears the debris from my back, and I still at her touch.

"Sorry, you had grass . . ."

"Thanks," I offer.

"Can you stand?"

"Sure. I'm fine."

To prove my point, I rise to my feet and brush off the rest of the dirt and grass. Carlie worries her bottom lip between her teeth, a gesture I've never seen on her before, and it affects me in ways it really shouldn't.

"Is your head okay?" she asks.

"Yup, I'm fine, Princess."

Her face goes from concerned to stone in less than a heartbeat.

Shit, wrong thing to say.

"Yep, back to your old self." She stalks off, and I'm left standing under the tightrope as Manuel appears at my side. "Your baby mama is a fiery woman, Mr. Lawson. Your hands will always be full, hey. You're one lucky man, brother." He slaps me on the shoulder and walks off to the communal area.

My *what*?

Just what the hell is on that clipboard he carries around?

Needing a way to lose the frustration building up after the past few days, I decide on a run. Not the smartest decision in the middle of the hot day, but if I go back to the bungalow now, I'm likely to say something I'll regret. So my feet hit the gravel track skirting the lake by the resort.

T-shirt saturated and out of breath, I turn back for the bungalow. My mind is a little clearer, and I'm in desperate need of a shower. I walk inside to find Carlie's back as she types away on her laptop, earbuds in her ears. She doesn't notice me walk in, so I head for the bathroom.

Once I'm free of sweaty clothes, I step into the shower. The hot water is incredible over my aching muscles. I wash my body and hair before stepping out and wrapping a towel around my waist. I can hear Carlie's music blasting through her earbuds from here. How loud is her music?

I grab my deodorant and apply it as she dances into the bathroom, twirling to whatever song is blaring in her ears. She doesn't see me until she swings back . . . In her underwear.

She stumbles to a halt with a gasp. "What the fuck?"

Not attempting to cover up, she glares at me as she pulls one earbud free.

"You dance around almost naked most days, or today a special occasion?" I give her a smile.

She plucks the other earbud from her ear and places them both on the vanity. Hands dropping to her hips, her eyes narrow under lowered brows.

I can't take my eyes from her stunning curves, the red lacy underwear that accentuates her shape. Ample breasts, pushed up in the lacy bra, bounce, as she steps into my space.

All sass, this woman.

"For your information, there is nothing special about this situation or today."

She runs a finger from my clavicle to my belly button. My cock is rock hard instantly, blood thunders through my body, every inch of my body alive with her proximity.

She tilts her head. "And it will be a cold day in hell when those mitts touch this body. Freezing. Arctic. Fro—"

I catch her face in my hands, and my mouth is barely an inch from hers as I say, "What if I like the cold, Princess?"

She rears back, her palm connecting with my cheek a second later.

CHAPTER 17
CARLIE

I shouldn't have done that. My palm burns, and I should *not* have done that. Lawson stares at me, unmoving, as I wait for his anger.

None comes.

Instead, he turns his head so his other, non-reddened cheek faces me.

"Need another go?"

I open my mouth to—apologize?

To take my hurt out on him? To . . .

He turns again and faces me. "I take it that name is what your dad used to call you."

How the *fuck*?

It's all I can do to nod. I guess I shouldn't be surprised; he's Mr. People Person, after all.

"I'm sorry he did that to your family, Carlie. Truly, I am. I can't imag—"

I press a finger over his lips and shake my head. His gaze drops to my mouth.

He's standing in only a towel with water droplets scattered over his toned chest, shoulders, and arms. A girl could climb this man like a tree and never come back down.

Except I won't.

I can't.

He's my peer. My competition. My rival.

He may have started as my enemy, but I guess somewhere along the way I've downgraded him to just the guy who is trying to steal my place at Serenity. Not the oxygen from my lungs.

Is it my place?

Should it be his?

Urgh, this is why I don't have friends. Don't do people, period. Mills being the only exception, of course.

Lawson crosses his arms as goosebumps cover his skin.

"Sorry, I'll let you get dressed." I wander from the bathroom and slip my own day clothes on. After the tripwire of whatever it was called this morning, I needed a change of clothes. Who would have thought dancing around the bungalow to your favorite Ariana Grande song would be so distracting you'd end up in your underwear in front of . . .

Lawson Rawlins.

I swallow. Hard.

Fuck. There's not a professional boundary we haven't crossed now. He's almost seen me naked. Seen me in my underwear. Watched me sleep, no doubt. Witnessed my fears and been present while I bared my soul. I don't know anyone else on this earth who has ever had that privilege.

Not even Mills.

Was this what Serelle was trying to do here?

Break down our walls?

I guess in a few days, I can ask her.

The city bustles around me as I slip out of the train station and march for the Serenity building. Outside is a gathering of women and children, the doors to the building still locked.

As they should be this early. The sun has barely made it up over the horizon.

Luckily for three mothers with pale, drawn faces and worry etched over their features that I'm guessing would look beautiful in any other situation, I have a key.

"Morning, ladies." I give them my best smile.

One hugs her daughter into her side. The others barely pay me any heed as they look anywhere but at the corporate woman letting them into the sanctuary. Unlocking the enormous double doors, I push one open and stand to the side. I have no idea what happens now, only that they all look like they could use a hot cup of tea and a shoulder to cry on.

The mother and daughter, their clothes soiled and a small backpack on the mother's shoulder, enter first. It's only as they walk inside that I see the discoloration on the woman's cheek.

Oh my god.

The others wander inside, moving through the foyer where I usually take a left and ascend to the upstairs offices, some heading for the bunks and some for the small sitting area littered with vibrant cushions. Nobody speaks. I take in their clothes, their hair, their sallow and brave faces as they settle in. Have they been here all night?

Just the way Mills would have been.

Scared.

Alone.

Vulnerable.

Fucking unacceptable.

I cling to the door with one hand, fighting back the emotion unraveling with every second I stand here watching them. Remembering why I came in early—to get a head start on the work I missed during the last week at the resort—I push from the door. I'm ready to pad upstairs when something tugs on my pants.

Startled, I look down to find a small girl. Big eyes peer up at me. She has messy blonde hair splayed over a jacket and a dirty yellow dress underneath, finished with gum boots. "Please, miss. Can you help my mommy?"

I squat, bringing my gaze eye level with hers. "What's wrong honey, where's your mommy?"

"She's over there, but she's too sick to come inside." She turns back, looking out onto the sidewalk.

"Show me?"

She takes my hand, and my fingers wrap around hers.

We walk down the stairs and around the building. A woman sits on the ground, her back leaning up against the brick. She shivers, her dark hair covering half of her face. I close the distance and look her over. "Are you okay?"

When she lifts her head up, her battered face steals my breath.

Fuck. I press a hand to my mouth.

She needs to be in the hospital, not the shelter. But at least the shelter would be safer than the street.

"Can you stand, if I help?" I ask.

Her chin wobbles, and I squat down. "We can go inside and get some help from there."

She shakes her head. "No, he'll take her."

"He's not allowed inside. I'll contact the police and the medics, but you have to stand for me, okay?"

After a beat, she nods. Her shaking hands land in mine, and I help her to her feet.

Once inside, I make sure the woman and her little girl are settled and call the services. The next call I make is to Serelle. She should be here. Someone should be here twenty-four seven. Not just during the day. It's not enough.

I can only imagine how this would have played out if it were mid-winter.

When the police arrive and the medics have the woman in their care, I retreat to the foyer and lean on the wall, observing, just taking in the real-time daily Serenity workings. The difference we are making.

My gaze snags on the little girl of the woman the police are currently talking to. She plays at her mother's feet. A sad smile tugs on my lips as burning flushes behind my eyes.

"Hey." A low rumble sees me turn back.

A tear dislodges, spilling down my cheek. The deep blues I spent a week in forced proximity with tighten with worry. A crisp white shirt with rolled-up sleeves and a dark blue tie over navy pants, he's all Office Rawlins today. Mr. Business.

"You okay?" he says, thumbing my cheek dry.

No.

Maybe?

I turn back to glance at the little girl. How many more exist in this city?

How many more women have nowhere to go?

How many stay because of that factor?

How many never leave, until it's too late . . .

Nausea floods my chest, burning.

"Excuse me." I bolt upstairs, spilling into the women's bathroom. My eight-dollar coffee and brioche return in a grizzly fashion, splattering all over the toilet bowl.

Breathing in a long, deep lungful, I splash my face with water before fixing my makeup.

The second the door to the bathroom gives way under my hand, I find Lawson. He leans on the wall by the restroom.

"You don't have to keep tabs on me, Rawlins."

"You're here early." His eyes are full of worry, nothing else.

"I wanted to catch up. What's your excuse?"

"Same."

"I guess having a week away wasn't great for business."

"I have full faith we can catch up and then some."

"That makes one of us."

He chuckles and falls into step as I walk past, heading for the fish tank.

"You opened the doors early?" he asks as we walk in and dump our belongings.

"The shelter needs to be open at all times . . . I couldn't leave her out there, she—"

A stone explodes in my throat. I screw up my face, desperate to stem back the emotion that is trying its hardest to claw its way back up from the pit of my stomach.

Lawson stills, his hand frozen on his laptop where he slid it onto his glass desk.

My chin wobbles.

Fucking traitor.

What the hell is wrong with me?

One week away with this man, and I go from impenetrable to inconsolable.

I clear my throat and turn back to my bag.

Baggage.

We spent a week unpacking ours, and this is the outcome. The soft version of me. The weak, blubbering mess that is Carlie Marie Lamont.

Fuck it.

When I turn back, Lawson is standing mere inches from me. "Need a hug?"

I scoff at him, but the sound breaks, disintegrating into a muffled sob.

Fucking great.

He's wrapped himself around me before the next breath fills my lungs. A large, warm hand runs over my hair, and I suck back a wobbly breath.

"We can do something about it, Carlie. We have that privilege. But we're going to have to work together."

I compose myself and push from his hold.

Part of me doesn't want to leave. It's been a long, long time since I have felt at home this close to a man. So long, it's merely a vague memory. And I think it's all the weeks we spent hating each other, being in each other's business. After all, attention is still attention, regardless of whether it's negative or not. Looking at him like I hate him is still looking at him.

The way we were before Manuel and his clipboard feels like an old skin we've shed. We've changed.

I've changed.

Who knew seven whole days could do that to a person.

I dry my face for the second time in an hour and set my shoulders back. "Right, in that case, we should dig deep. Get on the same page and make plans to make this place thrive, no matter which one of us stays."

A sad smile blooms over his face. "Sure, Miss Carlie, let's do that."

I chuckle at his use of Manuel's name for me.

His smile stretches to a grin.

Said it before, and I'll say it again. The man is gorgeous. Not that those words will pass my lips in any audible fashion.

Ever.

We get to work. Running the numbers. Brainstorming marketing, planning, and sponsorships. I order in lunch, and we don't leave the fish tank for anything. It's after four by the time Serelle comes to find us. We're sprawled out on the floor. Lawson sits on one side of our spread-out papers and projections. I'm on the other side, leaning against the glass wall under the whiteboard, surrounded by the budgets and marketing materials from previous years.

A soft knock is followed by the door opening as Serelle enters. "How's it going?"

"We're taking another pass at the historical data to make a better, more advanced plan moving forward," I say.

Lawson rises to his feet, tugging his tie off and lowering a hand to help me up. I take it and stand beside him.

Serelle crosses her arms, raising a brow and doing her best to flatten a smile. "I see camp worked wonders."

"Yeah, we're best buds now, hey, Lamont?" Lawson messes up my hair with a hand. His fingertips work over my scalp.

Good lord . . .

He doesn't make space between us, and his sandalwood and spice shrouds me. My body responds to the proximity instantly. I blow out a settling breath before I slap him away. "Get off me, Rawlins."

Serelle chuckles. "Well, almost, then. It's good to see you two getting along. I knew you'd be friends. You both have such strong reasons to be here. I had a feeling about you guys. Keep up the good work. I'll need those updated reports and quarter one's projections around Thanksgiving."

"We'll have it ready." Lawson closes the door behind her, and when he turns back, he stretches. "You know what? I could use some fresh air."

"Need to go walkies, do we?"

"Abso-fuckin-lutely."

I huff a small laugh at the longest drawl-infused yes I've ever heard.

"You want to come?"

I still.

Yes.

No. I mean . . .

I clear my throat. "I'm good. I'm going to tidy up and call it a day. It's been a long day."

"Sure. I'll see you tomorrow, hey?"

"Yup. Tomorrow."

He grabs his wallet and walks from the office as I slump into my chair. It's been a long day. My body is weary. Achy, actually.

I clear my throat again, and pain lances down it.

Oh great.

Just when we finally make it onto the same page. I finally have a real, concrete purpose for what we're trying to achieve here . . .

And a tiny army no one can see readies its ranks to take me down.

Fucking hell.

CHAPTER 18
LAWSON

Lamont is late. It's raining cats and dogs outside, and she's not here.

Actually, at ten a.m., I think that's considered a no-show. I wander to reception to ask Nadia if Carlie's contacted the office. The receptionist is nowhere to be found. I walk twenty feet and knock on Serelle's door.

"Come in."

"Oh hey, Carlie isn't here."

"Yes, she called in sick this morning. She sounded awful. Kept repeating herself in the hoarsest voice, poor girl."

Dammit.

"Right, thanks."

Serelle holds a hand up. "Are you okay?"

I tap the wall with my knuckles. "Yep, good. Thanks."

She narrows her eyes at me. "If you need the day off for any reason, I'm okay with that. Laptops were built to be mobile." She winks before waving for me to close her door.

I nod and shut the door.

Settling back into the office, I run through the numbers, double-checking the balances against last quarter, this quarter, and the projections. After I come to the same conclusion four times, I decide there is somewhere else I'd rather be. I stare at the empty desk across the room.

I fling Carlie a text asking how she is.

It sends but doesn't get read.

Should I go check on her?

No, I can't.

I shouldn't.

Could I?

I can't show up at Carlie's place. That's certified stalker shit. Isn't it?

Then I think of her home alone, having to parent a kid while she's ill. Stressing over work and being sick. Dammit, I wasn't raised to ignore my gut. Right now, it says I should be taking care of her.

Maybe I could just check in?

Take some food.

To lighten the load.

That's reasonable. That's what a friend would do.

I pack up my laptop and reports and grab my bag and jacket. Shoving my phone into my pocket, I head for the front desk again, hoping Nadia is there this time.

"Hi Lawson, how was the retreat?" Nadia beams at me.

"Good, it was good. Do you have Lamont's address? I have to drop around to check on her."

"Oh, we don't usually give out . . . You know what, let me ask Serelle."

"Sure."

She phones the boss quickly and returns the receiver with a smile. She writes down an address and hands me the sticky note. "Serelle said take soup."

"Thanks, will do."

I make it downstairs and check in on the women and children Carlie let in yesterday morning. The mother with the little girl she was worried about is still here. Her daughter plays happily as she chats with one of our social workers. The update will cheer Lamont up, I'm sure.

Running through the rain, I make a quick stop at the convenience store for chicken soup and noodles. I grab two just in case Carlie's daughter needs something to eat, too. I toss in a couple of chocolate frogs for good measure and grab an Uber to her address.

The building is much newer than my apartment building and I'm buzzed in by a doorman. Shaking off the rain, I take the elevator to the fourth floor. I cross the corridor to apartment 406 and knock. If she's sick, her kid might not let me in, stranger danger and all. Adds would never let Hattie answer the door at my place.

No movement sounds from inside, and I'm about to knock again when the door opens. An old lady with curled grey hair and blue eyes looks up at me. Her tiny frame is swathed in light-blue pants and a matching button-down top. She smiles at me then tilts her head.

I lean back, double-checking the apartment number.

"I'm sorry, I must have been given the wrong address." I run a hand through my hair.

She assesses me carefully with tight blue eyes. "Lawson?"

"Ah . . . Yes?"

Who is this?

Carlie's grandma is in town? She never said anything. But then again, that's no surprise.

"Why don't you come in," she says, nodding to the bag in my hand.

"Sure. Is Carlie okay?"

"Oh, that poor girl is as sick as a dog."

I follow the old lady through the apartment. It's amazing. Much newer than mine. The kitchen is bigger than my bedroom. The white tiled floor gives way to floor-to-ceiling windows and views of the city. The living room is white and cream, with a large flat-screen to one side by a hallway that leads to what I assume are the bedrooms.

"Let me go and see if she wants visitors." The old lady toddles down the hallway leaving me in the kitchen. I go ahead and put the soup and treats in the refrigerator. I drop my jacket and bag on the dining table, sliding my hands into my pockets. Carlie's place is incredible.

"She said you can go in. Second door on the right. I'll fix her some of your soup, our girl hasn't eaten since she got home yesterday." The old woman putters to the kitchen cupboards as I wander down the hall and knock on the door softly.

"Carlie?"

"Come." The word is so soft, and far too low.

I open the door. She lies on her side, facing away from me. The blanket is pulled up to her shaking shoulders.

Shit.

I walk around to the other side and sit on the edge of the bed. "You've got a fever."

"Thanks for the update." Her browns narrow at me. She coughs, and the whole bed shakes.

Dammit. I lean over, resting the back of my hand on her forehead. She's on fire.

"You had Tylenol?"

"We ran out, and I don't want Mills going out by herself in this weather."

"Mills?"

"You just met her, Lawson. Keep up."

"Millie is your grandma?"

So, no daughter.

"Not my grandma. My Millie," she rasps.

"Okay . . ."

"Another day." She coughs, and her face pales in front of me. With a groan, she rolls over. "Help me up, will you?"

I scoot around the bed and take her hand. It's freezing. She trembles as I help her out. An oversized T-shirt hangs off her frame, barely covering her ass. "Where are we going?"

"Toilet, I've been needing to go for ages, but Mills isn't really the muscle around here."

I chuckle. Guess that makes me the muscle today.

I walk her to the en suite, her legs shaking the entire way. She turns back, grabbing the door as we reach the bathroom. "I can take it from here, Rawlins."

The door shuts in my face, and I make my way to the kitchen. Millie is ladling soup into a bowl on a tray. "Here, I got it." I take the hot container from her hands.

I practically tower over her. She's so small and frail.

Now I understand why Carlie was worried about leaving her alone for a week.

"Thank you, young man. This old woman isn't as capable as she used to be."

I return to Carlie's room and sit the tray on her bedside table.

"Lawson?" My name is almost a whisper.

Walking to the door, I lean my head on it. "Yeah?"

"I—I'm . . ."

Retching echoes and slips out under the door.

Sweet Jesus.

Knocking, I say, "Coming in. Okay?"

"Okay." The word is more a sob than a syllable. I find Carlie collapsed on the floor, her cheek resting on the toilet seat.

Fuck.

I hit the tiles with my knees and rub her back. "Hey, we need to get you some medicine."

"Urgh, I know."

"Are you going to be sick again?"

Her eyes close. "I don't think so."

I grab a hand towel and wet the corner and wring it out. Dabbing her mouth, I toss it into the sink before standing and sweeping her up off the floor. She moans. The movement must hurt her aching body. I lay her back in bed and prop her up on the pillows. "Stay right here. I'll be back in twenty."

A soft whimper tumbles from her lips as her head lolls onto the pillow and her eyes close.

Back in the kitchen I find Millie cleaning up the kitchen. "How is she?"

"I'm going out to grab some supplies, you need anything?"

"I'm fine. You go, she needs more than I can manage."

"Be right back, okay?"

Grabbing my wallet, I slip outside and down the elevator. In the foyer, I tap my phone, hunting for the nearest pharmacy. Two blocks. Too easy.

Eight minutes later, I have a bag of Tylenol, ibuprofen, and electrolyte drinks in hand as I spill from the elevator and stride for apartment 406. Millie opens the door for me before I have a chance to knock. It's then I notice the camera mounted to the left of the door. Lamont takes her security seriously, I see.

Smart girl.

"I had to take her a bucket." Millie wrings her hands.

"Okay, you have something to eat and have a break. I'll take care of Carlie."

She gives me a sad smile and pats my jaw like we're family. I tug off my tie and roll my sleeves up as I toe off my shoes and head into Carlie's room. The bucket is empty when I reach the bed, and Carlie is still shaking with fever.

"Time for your medicine."

"Yes sir," she croaks.

I sit her up and hand her the pills, twisting the lid from one of the electrolyte drinks. She takes them and rests back on the pillows. "Thank you."

"I'll check your temperature in twenty minutes." I set the drink on her bedside by the soup.

I turn to leave, and fine fingers wrap around my wrist. "Stay?"

"You want me to stay and cuddle, Princess?"

Instead of reaming me out over the nickname, she huffs a strained laugh and closes her eyes. I stand for a beat, wondering when that changed. When her eyes open and I haven't moved, I nod to the bed. "Permission to come aboard?"

"Granted, but keep your hands to yourself."

"Yes ma'am."

The sweetest lopsided smile breaks on her face.

I climb onto the other side of her bed, sitting at the top and leaning on the headboard. "So, tell me about Mills, your not-grandma."

She rolls her head on the pillows, studying my face before she says, "We met at the convenience store once. I didn't know it at first, but she had no family here and nowhere to go."

"Now she lives here with you?"

A pretty smile blooms as she says, "She does."

"Never would have taken you for a softie, Miss Carlie."

"Huh, who you calling soft? You're the one taking care of your archnemesis."

I hold her gaze for a moment before muttering, "Not anymore."

"You think you've been upgraded to the friend zone, do you?" Delight consumes her weary eyes.

"Oh, absolutely, otherwise you'll be getting my bill in the mail tomorrow for all this pampering."

She chuckles, but it deteriorates into a cough.

"I'm so tired," she rasps. "So cold."

Rolling over, she presses into my side, hunting for warmth. I slide my arm around her and lean my head back on the headboard. It's been a long few weeks. I could just close my eyes . . .

". . . Touch me, please."

I blink against the darkness, remembering where I am. Carlie is still up against my side. My arm is numb from her lying on it for hours.

"More," she whimpers.

Fever dreams?

I check her temperature with the back of my hand. The devil's lair has nothing on the heat of her forehead. Shit, how long were we asleep?

I try to retract my arm, and she mumbles, rolling over, burying her face into my chest. Blonde waves fall over my arm and shoulder.

Even in the darkened room, the elegant features that make up Carlie Lamont take me aback. Maybe more so.

I run a hand over her hair and brush my hands over her neck. She's too hot.

"Carlie, wake up."

"Mmmmm, no."

"We need to get some more medicine down, you're burning up again."

Her head rises, so slowly she looks out of it. Hell, she probably is, going by the mutterings that woke me up. "Lawson?"

"Yeah, right here."

"I love your drawl."

I chuckle.

She jerks, blinking. "Did I say that out loud?"

Running a hand over her forehead, I double-check her temperature. "Come on, you need some painkillers."

"Did you know Millie has a boyfriend . . . his name is Henry." She's gazing nowhere in particular as she continues in a whispering tone, "Met him at book club."

"Did she? Good for her."

She tilts her head back. "You think so?"

"I do. Everyone deserves love."

"You are such a sap." Her eyes are half closed again.

I lift her from my body and sit her up. She sways on her

seat. I pop the pills from the pack, and she opens her mouth. I drop them onto her tongue and press the drink into her hands. She swallows the pills, and I lie her back on her pillow.

"I'll be back in a minute," I say, leaving the bed. I pad into the kitchen, where the lights are all still on. Millie sits in an old armchair, watching television. She looks up at me. "Oh, how is she?"

"The fever's pretty bad, but I gave her some more painkillers. You needing anything?"

I come to stand by her chair, and she takes my hand in both of hers. "No, sweet boy, I'm fine."

It's been a long time since anyone called me that.

"You holler if that changes, okay?"

"Alright, Cowboy." A cheeky grin pops on her face as she goes back to her show.

Cowboy? What on earth has Carlie been telling her?

I grab a glass of water from the tap and stretch, checking my phone.

Missed call from Ma.

A text from Miles.

> Where are you bud? Missed you at Murphy's tonight.

> Sorry, man, taking care of a sick friend. Catch you up next week, hey?

I send the text and turn the screen off.

I'll get to them tomorrow. I look around for a clock before remembering my phone is in my hand. Man, I'm exhausted, too.

9:15 p.m. stares back at me.

I use the main bathroom and head back to Carlie. She's awake when I come in, and her gaze doesn't leave me as I cross the room to her bedside. She holds up a hand. "Why are you so nice to me?"

I sit on the bed by her side, and her hand reaches for my face. Her fingers brush over my jaw. Sweet Christ, how the contact sends my body into an unregulated frenzy.

Tenderness from this woman will be the end of me.

"Why do you say that?" I ask.

"I thought you hated me . . ."

"I've never hated you, Carlie."

Her eyes narrow. "You sure?"

I chuckle. "Yep."

"No."

"No?"

"Not yep."

Realizing what she's asking for, I brush a stray strand of hair behind her ear and say, "Yes ma'am."

Her lips part, her gaze drops to my mouth. "If I wasn't sick and ridiculously disgusting, I would—"

Her eyes close. Her chest plummets, and I'm pretty sure it has nothing to do with the illness.

"Get some rest. You text me if you need me, okay?"

"No, don't leave," she whines.

"I don't think I should stay, not this time."

Her face slackens, as if the penny's dropped and she picked up on the 'next time.' I cup her cheeks and press a kiss to the crown of her head. A promise to return.

A promise, period.

"Night, Princess."

"Goodnight, Cowboy."

I smile at her, hesitating by the door before I slip out into the hall and pulling the door almost shut. I give Millie my number before seeing myself out.

Making it home, finally, I find Miles outside my apartment. And the shit-eating grin on his face tells me all I need to know.

He's onto me.

There's no keeping secrets from Miles Hammond.

CHAPTER 19
LAWSON

"Spill, bud." Miles cracks a beer and flops onto my sofa.

"Nothing to spill, how about you?"

He tilts his head with an incredulous look. "Are you paying house calls to all your coworkers or just one fiery blonde?"

I toss a packet of nuts at his head and grab a bottle of water. I'm too tired for anything else tonight.

Miles turns on the game and we settle into the old sofa that barely holds us both. I really should buy another one. As it is, I'm going to have to move. If I stay on at Serenity, that is. It takes me far too long to commute to work every day.

"So, you been fraternizing with the enemy, Rawlins?"

That didn't take long.

I can't help my smile as I take a pull of water. "Nope, no fraternizing."

"Yeah, right, you spent how many nights in a bungalow together?"

"Seven."

"Seven nights and not a thing happened?"

"Sorry to disappoint, bud."

He shakes his head, but his face isn't filled with amusement as I expected, it's etched in concern. "When was your last relationship of any kind?"

"You oughta talk, four years is insane. And you're a firefighter, shouldn't women be falling at your feet?"

He rolls his eyes at me. "Pretty sure the hours I keep scare off any potential contenders for serious relationships. That and the fact that every shift may be my last."

He loves to play that fucking card, real funny.

Because it's absolutely not.

"What about another firefighter, then?"

"Yeah . . . my unit is my family, be like kissing my sister."

I chuckle and he drops the subject, returning his gaze to the game. My phone rings and I remember Ma's missed call. I push up from the sofa and swipe up the phone.

Gracie.

"What you doing up so late, little mama?" I answer.

"Mack is snoring beside me. Said I had to tell you the good news before I went to bed."

"Oh yeah, what good news?"

"You're staying with us for Thanksgiving, Laws."

"Damn straight, little woman."

She huffs a laugh. "Oh shoot, don't make me laugh, now I gotta pee."

"TMI, Gracie."

"Never."

"You good?"

She sighs and I imagine her running her fingers through my

little brother's hair the way she always does when they're in close proximity. "Yeah, I'm good. How's your new job going?"

"Pretty great actually, but there's been a slight hitch."

"Oh?"

"Yeah, turns out one of us goes at the end of the three-month probation period. Budget constraints or something."

"Oh, that sucks. Well, I hope they choose you. You deserve this, Laws."

"Maybe."

Carlie's worked years to get where she is, being passed over for promotions time after time. I'm not sure I'm the one who deserves to stay on.

"What do you mean, maybe? Of course you do, you do an amazing job. With everything you do."

I chuckle. "Thanks for the vote of confidence. Love you, Gracie."

"Love you, too, Laws. Night."

I tap the phone and hang up.

"How's she doing?" Miles asks. He's been a Gracie fan since the day I came home and told him about her showing up in my brother's—my family's—life.

"She's good."

But it's Rubes he would steal away from my brother given half the chance. Lucky he's good at putting out fires, because that girl burns him down every time she's in town. Which brings us to Addy. She took to Miles like a duck to water with Miles's dad being a chef like Adds's mom. They swap childhood war stories that have the entire group in stitches whenever we get together. They both had to be the foodie experiment guinea pigs, which always ended in some hilarious tale.

"How is it that you Rawlins boys pull the most amazing

goddamn women? Save some for the rest of us, will you?" Miles gives me a pointed look.

"Milo, that's like a grand total of three. Pretty sure there's a few left."

He holds up four fingers, mouthing the number. I toss a cushion at his head, and he harrumphs. "Could have fooled me."

How this man is still single is beyond me. A handsome, buff, kind-hearted firefighter. Go figure.

I tap out a message to Ma, even though I know she won't check her phone 'til tomorrow morning.

"Man, is it cool if I pass out on your sofa? I'm done."

"Yeah, of course. Up for a run in the morning?"

"Sure, bud."

I pad to my bedroom, unbuttoning my shirt and shrugging it from my shoulders. I should text Millie and see how Carlie is doing. But it's late, and I don't want to disturb her. I know Carlie will have her phone on silent. I opt for texting her instead.

How you doin', Princess?

The message sends.
The dots appear.
Shit, I hope I didn't wake her up.

Still breathing, Rawlins.

I smile.

Good to know.

The dots oscillate and then disappear.

They pop up again and then vanish, so I send one of my own.

Night.

Night.

I shower and pull on my boxers. When I lie in my bed, I can't shift her soft words out of my head. "If I wasn't sick . . ."

That's all it takes for my brain to run with it, sending every last drop of blood south. I roll on to my side, ignoring the damn raging hard-on a few words from her lips has given me. Thinking of anything else, I shove a pillow over my face, like it will help.

An hour later, I'm still wrangling with thoughts I shouldn't have. Carlie in only a towel in the bungalow. Her between the sheets in those silky pajamas that barely covered her gorgeous ass. The swell of her chest as she slept mere inches from me.

Sweet Jesus.

My cock throbs from studying the curves and elegant angles of her.

I roll over into the mattress, but the pressure does nothing for the ache in my cock.

"Fuck."

I'm never going to fall asleep with a goddamn hard-on.

I tug my cock free, fisting it.

It's her pouty lips and elegant hands I want around my cock right now, not my hand. Christ, the woman is laid up in bed, sick as hell, and here I am fucking my hand to the slightest thought of her.

I'm going straight to hell.

The sound of her soft whimper, her tiny moans when I carried her to her bed, her body pressed to mine . . .

I come all over my stomach.

Now I have something to atone for, Princess.

My feet hit the pavement. Heavier footfalls pound beside me, harsh breathing the only sound exchanged between Miles and me. We hit the five-mile mark a little way back, and neither of us is showing any sign of slowing down. With only a week until Thanksgiving, my head has been full of numbers for the last few weeks.

Carlie made a full recovery and is back to giving me attitude like nothing else. I swear, now that she knows me better, she's taking this thing between us to DEF CON 1. We spend an ungodly number of hours in the office. Arriving early and leaving late, trying to prep and plan for the first quarter like we've been tasked with saving humanity.

Perhaps we have?

The performance outcomes of quarter one decides who stays and who moves on. Besides the fact I am desperate to make a difference, the idea of not working with Carlie annoys me more than the idea of leaving. We've got under each other's skin, but in a good way now. It feels like something that's a rare find in this life. Hell, maybe we really are friends.

That grinds my gears like nothing else, and I stumble to a

halt on the pavement, pressing a hand into my side, walking a tight circle.

Miles turns back before slowing to a walk and meeting me at the edge of the sidewalk. "What's going on? Talk to me, Rawlins. Or I'm calling Ruby."

I try for a laugh, but it comes out strangled.

"Ah, shit. I knew this would happen."

"You knew what would happen?" I look up into the brown eyes that are filled with empathy and a streak of amusement.

"You and the feisty blonde."

"She has a name, Milo."

I rarely call him that, because he hates it. But the guys referring to Carlie as the 'feisty blonde' almost makes my skin crawl.

Like she's some stuck-up bitch with no depth.

She's far from shallow.

She's impossible and incredible.

She's stunning and sassy.

She's gor—

Oh fuck.

My face must have registered the realization, because Miles slaps my shoulder. "You're a goner, bud."

"Fuck off, Hammond."

"Hey, I never said it's a bad thing." He grins at me.

I bend over, gripping my knees. The deep breaths flooding my lungs still burn. And he's right. The line between love and hate is a fine one, and I just obliterated it out of existence.

"Come on, let's grab a coffee. My treat, you poor sap."

I shake my head at him.

"It's all downhill from here, you know." The joy on his face contradicts his words. Asshole.

"Your turn's coming, Milo."

He snaps an arm around me, pulling me into a headlock. I uppercut him, and we fall apart laughing.

Coffee. Coffee would be good.

The closest Starbucks is luckily not too busy this early in the morning, and we grab coffee and bagels. Miles heads off, making me promise to text if anything develops between Carlie and me, and I make my way home to shower and get ready for the day.

An hour later, I'm running out the door, already five minutes late.

When I reach the office, I do the rounds, saying good morning to everyone but Bob. Him, his candy trash can, and sideways deviant looks can go die in a hole.

Carlie sits at her desk, working at her laptop when I open the door to the fish tank.

She looks up and smiles as I pad to my desk. "Coming in late already, tardy Cowboy?"

"Three minutes is hardly late, Princess."

She stills and frowns. "On time is late by default."

"Oh yeah, and I guess you're going to report me to HR?"

"You know that guy is useless," she says and returns her focus to her screen.

"Hopeless, more like it," I mutter and sit at my desk.

I'm one hundred percent sure she's referring to me. Old wounds take ages to heal. And my being here must remind her every day of the worst day of her career. Hell, I only now just stopped thinking about it.

Nope, still think about it.

She was right when she said I was here to atone for something. I absolutely am. But her losing her job is only one of the wrongs I need to right in this world. I run through the semi-finalized plan for the next quarter and attend to my emails.

A discrepancy has been noted on the sponsorships and city funding—by Bob, of all people. Tempted to disregard his comment, I flip through the pages and come to the same conclusion.

Dammit.

I'll need to double-check those numbers, maybe confirm with the respective departments that the figures are still correct.

I dial the city and speak to the community liaison first. She confirms the city's budget as Serelle said. One confirmed, one to go.

Three large sponsors are responsible for half of the funds needed to run Serenity. Their generous donations of millions of dollars keep these doors open for the limited hours they are, during daylight hours.

I wonder what it would take to keep them open twenty-four seven?

I dial the first number and speak with a receptionist, who promises to put my request in writing to the finance department, who will get back to me by end of day.

Not ideal.

I dial the next company. I have my confirmation in under five minutes.

Great.

The last set of digits goes straight to an automated voice. "The number you have called is no longer connected."

I check the number I dialed.

It's correct.

I try again and get the same response. I google the company

only to get a 404-error page. Well, *that's* not good. Running a finger over my screen, I search for their sponsorship percentage.

Eighty percent.

Our biggest sponsor.

Christ.

CHAPTER 20
CARLIE

Lawson is running his hands through his hair, muttering to himself. I would say it's the pressure of the upcoming holiday in a few days, but we've had more important issues in the last month, and nothing's had him this worked up.

His constant hushed monologue is doing my head in. I push from my chair and stalk to his desk. "Tell me what's going on."

I fold my arms over my chest and lean on his desk beside his chair as deep blues lined with worry flick up to me.

"We have a problem. A fucking big one."

"What?" I push off the desk and turn so I can see his screen. He points out the name of one of the major sponsors for Serenity.

The Align Group.

"Yes, what about them?"

"They went bankrupt."

"No. When?"

"Two months back. I rang to confirm the donations for next

year, and the line was disconnected. So I googled them. It took some digging, but Griff asked around, and they're up for tax fraud. And they were our main sponsor. Like without them, we all go home next quarter."

Shock steals my last breath on its way out, and I grip the side of his desk, leaning closer to the laptop as if that will make things clearer. "How did this happen, and why didn't they communicate this to us? We need to talk to Serelle and let her know. Like now."

"No, wait."

"Lawson." My tone is low and reprimanding.

"Wait, just give me ten minutes. If I've learned anything from years in business, it's that once you put a narrative out there, it takes on a life of its own. If we can sort this out before the Christmas period, nobody needs to get fired, the shelter stays open, and what if . . ."

I pace at the side of his desk, mulling over his idea. "What if we can gain more than just the sponsorship we lost, and have enough to cover the shelter to operate twenty-four hours?"

Lawson leans back in his chair as I continue, "If this doesn't work out and we can't replace the sponsor we lost and Serelle realizes we lied to her, we'll both lose our jobs. Who knows who will be in this fish tank after us. Will they even care about those women and children?"

"It's a risk, I know. But I think it's one that's worth it." He runs a hand through his already mussed hair. And I want to close the distance between us and sink my fingers into it. Then my mouth over his.

"Let's do it." My own words startle me.

"You sure?" he asks.

"Yep, business is always a risk. Without risk, there's no

growth. And we need growth more than anything else. Maybe we could set an event to pull in better sponsors?"

He smiles up at me. "You think you can plan and pull off a sponsorship gala?"

The overwhelming realization of what we have schemed hits me. I'm one woman in the city that never sleeps, needing to plan a gala—preferably before January first, with less than four weeks to pull it off.

Fuck.

"I—"

Lawson stands and closes the distance. "Tell me what you need me to do."

"Give me a second," I whisper, rubbing my hands over my face and turning away to pace again. "It should be a Christmas gala. You know, hit people when they're filled with the festive —a.k.a. giving—spirit."

I spin back, throwing my hands in the air. "Yes! That's it!"

It's then I see the entire staff floor enraptured as they stare at the fish tank. We must have been more intense than I realized. I force a tight smile and wave to Bob, the loser who has a smirk plastered on his damn face.

Urgh. That man is insufferable.

"Stop pacing," Lawson says, rising from his chair. "You're scaring the children."

"Huh, you oughta talk with your manic monologue earlier."

"Carlie, we'll get this sorted. We can ask for outside help if we have to."

"No thank you, my reputation has taken a big enough hit after Carlson."

"I thought of that, and I have a solution for you."

I stop and meet him in the middle of the office. He folds his arms over his chest, those roped forearms of his flexing with the movement.

"Spill it," I say.

"So, Thanksgiving is in two days. I need to go back to Montan—"

"You can't leave now!"

"Hold your horses, Princess."

I narrow my eyes at him. That name has taken on an entirely different meaning now that he knows my story, has taken care of me, and still calls me it with his tone that feels like . . .

"You're coming home with me. We're going to go to Montana and spend the long holiday weekend planning, making calls, and using the best resource we have."

"And what's that?" I ask, raising a brow.

"Who."

"Pardon?"

Annoyance lances through my veins. How can he be taking this any way but serious right now?

"You mean who, not what."

"Okay, fine, tell me who is our greatest resource when planning a gala."

The grin stretching his mouth sends warmth to my chest. "Ruby Rawlins, that's who."

"Your sister-in-law? Doesn't she live in Montana?"

He blinks, and stares at me as if waiting for the penny to drop.

"Sister. And yes, she does live in Montana, but she was an event planner from the east side before she married Reed. Did a heap of big galas and stuff."

"Hold on, you mean Ruby *Robbins*?"

My jaw drops to the floor.

Surprise contorts my face. I'd seen the woman in action at a few events my clients were invited to. If anyone could pull off a gala at Christmas, with only four weeks' notice, it would be Ruby Robbins.

"You know Rubes?" he asks.

"I—"

"That's great, this will be even easier than I thought."

"I don't exactly know her. I've just admired her work, for years. But then she . . . vanished."

"Moved to Montana, actually."

"Oh," I breathe, stunned.

"She's going to love you, Princess."

"Okay . . ." I can barely respond, my mouth gaping.

I don't know what else to say. For the first time in, I have no idea how long, I'm at a loss for words and excited out of my skin for something close to my heart. A trailblazing woman who takes no shit. In my area of interest, no less.

"So I'm coming to Montana with you, then?"

"Millie is most welcome, too. Reed and Ruby host a Thanksgiving dinner every year on their guest ranch."

"N—no, she goes to her sister's place. It would just be us."

"Sure. We all good, then?"

"I don't know, I can't think straight . . . Why didn't you tell me about Ruby?"

"I didn't know you were a fan." He shrugs. "Come on, Princess, let me ride off with you into the sunset. Just this once. It's for a good cause."

Now I find my composure and roll my eyes at him. "Does that line really work, Lawson?"

He chuckles, and the biggest smile stretches his face. "I wouldn't know, never used it before."

"Mills, make sure to pack your extra charger for your phone. And your medication bag," I call out from my bedroom, busily throwing anything I could need for a Thanksgiving dinner and ranch life into my luggage.

God, never thought that sentence would run through this head. Ever.

"Got them, Mom."

I smile at her comeback. Cheeky little lady.

When we're both ready for the airport, I order an Uber. We stand in the foyer of our building as we wait.

"You won't do anything I wouldn't do, will you, sweetheart?" Mills looks up at me, patting my cheek.

"Absolutely not. Besides, is there anything you wouldn't do?"

"Touché." Her eyebrows lift. "I mean it. You look after yourself, and if his family is no good, you come home, okay?"

"It's only a couple of nights, Mills. Not a month. Besides, I doubt they'll be around much. We have a ton of work to get done. It's a work weekend."

"Sure, honey. Sure."

The smile on her face doesn't slip. Not for the whole Uber ride to the airport nor when we check in and drop our luggage off. I'm about to text Lawson when he appears by my side.

"Ready to get lost in the middle of nowhere?" he whispers into my ear.

Millie's eyes light up, and I give her a harrowing glare before the smile I'm tamping back slips.

The PA calls for the Florida flight passengers, gold class, and I walk Mills to her gate. "I'll pick you up in a week, okay?"

"I'll be here, sweetheart."

I fold her into a hug. I always hate our one week a year apart. I know it's silly, but it feels like I met this wonderful woman too late. And the time we have left is finite. So much so that any time apart makes me nervous.

"You better be, Mills."

She pats my cheek again and pulls the handle up on her small carry-on. With a wave to us both, she makes her way to the small line at Gate 5.

"Bye," I whisper.

The gate agent takes her ticket, and she passes the roped off area. Before disappearing, Mills turns back, and her cheeky smile is back on her face as she lifts a hand to her forehead. Is she tipping a nonexistent hat?

Good lord, she's so corny. But a chuckle leaves my lips, and her eyes light up as she looks to my left and smiles.

Right at Lawson.

I stare at the dwindling line of strangers at Gate 5, and jerk with a start when the PA announces our flight.

Great Falls, Montana, here we come.

"Ready for this, Princess?"

I turn back to find Lawson shouldering a backpack. His usual casual dress is ready for the Montana weather, with his trench coat over his arm. Hell, I hope I packed enough warm clothes.

"Ready, but we are going to have to come up with a new nickname. I'm not going to your family for the holiday with you calling me Princess."

"Sure, what do you want me to call you?" He takes my bag, and we walk for our gate. After I show the hostess both our tickets— Lawson's hands are full—we make our way onto the plane and to our seats.

I take the window seat as Lawson puts our carry-ons overhead. He drops into the seat beside me, and we're shoulder to shoulder. We haven't been this close since I was sick. I fasten my seat belt and watch as he struggles with his. The buckle's bent?

"Here, let me take a look." I flick it over and slide the metal back in place. Leaning over, I click it into the latch and pull the lap strap tight.

"Thanks," he rumbles, his breath sinking into my hair.

"You're welcome," I say, releasing the belt.

His hand catches mine. "I mean it. Thanks for coming with me. I can't imagine trying to fix this Serenity disaster on my own."

"Of course. And I'm pretty sure the problem belongs to both of us."

If I didn't know better, I'd say he's nervous about something.

"Are you okay?" I ask.

"Not much of a flier." He forces a smile.

Who would have thought? I plant my earbuds in my ears and turn on my favorite women-in-business podcast.

We take off, and by the time we reach altitude, Lawson is white-knuckling the armrest. I pull one earbud out and study the tight features of his face. Every angle is accentuated. He looks terrified.

"Hey Cowboy, you need a hug?"

He snaps his gaze to me. "Maybe."

I pry his fingers from the armrest between us and lace my fingers with his. "You're okay."

But he shakes his head.

His dark hair falls onto his face before he brushes it back and quickly reaffirms his grip on the seat with his other hand.

"Lawson, look at me."

He turns his head too slowly, like a ventriloquist's doll would.

I palm his jaw. "Breathe."

"I know to breathe, it doesn't make it any easier. There's a reason I only go home a few times a year."

"You need something to distract you, then?"

"That would be good."

I take my belt off, shuffling closer.

"No, put that back on!" His eyes widen.

"I will, after."

"After what?"

I pull my hand from his and cup his face with both hands. "This."

I cover his mouth with my own. Lips exploring over his, I nip his bottom lip and pull back a little. The fear holding him before has melted to something more intense. Need.

His hands leave the seat, trailing up my neck and into my hair as his mouth crashes over mine.

A heartbeat later, a voice from behind tells us to get a room. I chuckle, breaking away, and find Lawson breathing heavy and deep.

At least those breaths will be useful. I think . . .

He studies my face before settling back into his seat. Every few minutes, he glances at me. I slide my earbuds back into my ears and lean back and close my eyes.

Well, that boundary is shot to shit.

We can still be friends, right?

Seven hours and one more languid kiss after a bunch of semi-scary turbulence later, we land in Great Falls, Montana. Lawson is quiet. And I don't push. We got through the flight. All's well that ends well. He grabs our carry-ons, and we disembark.

A few minutes later, we're strolling through the terminal the size of my local post office to find our luggage.

"I got it," Lawson says as our bags travel around the conveyor belt at a turtle's pace.

I hear the squealing before I see the source. A blonde who I recognize and a brunette who I don't rush toward us.

CHAPTER 21
LAWSON

The biggest smiles light up Rubes's and Gracie's faces as I'm ambushed with exuberant hugs. Gracie's ever-growing belly prods my side and Rubes all but strangles me as I drop the bags and hug them so damn tight.

"I missed you two."

Gracie leans back, her hands sinking into her back. "You should come home more often, then."

Yeah, right. Who's going to distract me on every flight when I'm traveling solo?

"You packed for an entire family, Laws?" Rubes asks as she scans the two luggage bags and two carry-ons. Her pretty browns narrow, and it's then she notices the woman to my right. "Oh, hey. I'm Ruby. You must be Carlie. Lawson didn't tell us you were coming."

"Hi," Carlie says, her face lit by ecstatic wonder. She is fangirling big-time over Rubes. It's kind of funny. She holds out a hand, but Ruby waves it away before pulling her into a hug.

"It's lovely to finally meet you. Lawson hasn't shut up about you since he started the new job."

"You're choking her, Rubes," I say with a chuckle, and she releases her.

"Sorry, it's just that Laws never brings anyone home." Ruby tilts her head, alternating her gaze between us.

"We're so excited to have you here." Gracie holds out her hand and Carlie shakes it. "The hugs are a bit awkward. Maybe next time?"

"Mackie-boy let you out of his sight? Or did Rubes steal you?" I ask, knowing how protective my little brother is of his wife. Always has been.

"The last one. But I text him so he doesn't freak out." She smiles, resting a hand over her belly. Gracie being ten years younger than Mack and them meeting the way they did after everything they both went through, Mack has every right to be protective of his wife.

She's in good hands with Rubes.

"Let's go home, Laws. Reed will be dying to meet your plus-one the second he reads his texts. I can't wait to see the look on their faces when we get back."

"Should I be worried?" Carlie whispers as she leans into my side.

"Nah, you'll be fine. Just don't piss Harry off."

"Oh, does that happen often?"

I chuckle. "Only if you're Rubes."

We follow the girls to Reed's big black truck, and Rubes helps stash the bags in the back before we head for home. "You and Carlie have a cabin by the stream. We are booked up, so you have to share." Her and Gracie share a conspiratorial glance.

Gracie clears her throat. "Sorry, with your plus-one, you're better off with your own space, Laws."

Nice work, girls.

It's not like Carlie and I haven't shared a space before. We do it every day at work. And the retreat was a success, in close quarters. But the kiss on the plane lingers on my mouth. The feel of her elegant hands around my jawline. Her breath mixing with mine and the soft sound she made as we parted.

I didn't imagine the chemistry there.

I couldn't have. I've never felt anything like it before.

Carlie doesn't look at me, sitting in the back seat with me as Gracie rides shotgun and Rubes drives. Carlie is watching Ruby as if she can't believe she's in the same space as the great Ruby Robbins. I'm saving that particular story to tell Rubes later.

I've never been prouder of my sister than the moment I realized how big of a deal she was on the New York event planning scene. Okay, maybe the day she put Harry in his place was that day, but . . . The way Carlie speaks about her, I have no doubt Rubes accomplished all that and more.

"How long does it take to get to the ranch?" Carlie asks.

"An hour and a half," Rubes replies.

Carlie's smile wraps around her face as she leans over and says softly, "Thank you for bringing me."

I turn my head, my lips to her ear. "As if I would have left you behind on Thanksgiving, Lamont."

A small huffy breath puffs against my cheek when I pull away, and she's frowning.

I slip my phone from my pocket and send her a text.

What's with the long face?

Long face?

Why are you frowning, Carlie?

You called me Lamont.

You don't like Princess, so . . .

I need a new nickname, Cowboy.

Guess we'll have to figure that out this weekend, too.

Guess so.

I can't get those plane kisses out of my head, so I hedge my bets and tap out another message.

My family can be a bit much sometimes. So, if you're in need of distracting this weekend, I owe you one. Well, two actually.

I'll hold you to that 😁

Yes ma'am.

She glances at me sideways.

Keep that up, and I'll have to collect before we even make it to the ranch.

I huff a chuckle, and Gracie turns back to meet my gaze. "You good?"

"Yeah."

She smiles at me and takes a quick glance at Carlie, who's tapping on her phone.

My phone vibrates and I look down at the screen.

> If the road gets too rough, I might have to collect.

Sweet Jesus.

Come on, Rubes, do a guy a solid and hit a pothole.

> That all it takes?

> Maybe . . .

The truck does in fact hit a pothole, and Rubes swears under her breath. My sister is more and more like my brother every damn day. She worries over his big black shiny truck just the same.

Carlie's hand slides underneath mine. I close my fingers around hers.

I text back.

> You're serious?

> I don't like not being the one in control when it comes to cars.

Figures.

She runs every aspect of her life like clockwork. I always thought that was driven by ambition. Maybe it's fear of failing, instead?

"You two good back there, or do I need to pull this truck over?" Rubes says.

"Hey, that's my line." Gracie laughs, her hand rubbing her belly. "Got to practice beforehand, you know."

She's going to be a great mama.

"No, we're good," Carlie says, retracting her hand. The loss of her touch is immediate, and I hate it.

I'm way past the friend zone. And after the flight, those moments of distraction . . .

Miles was right, I'm a goner. I've gone and fallen for the one woman I can't have. I shouldn't want. We're competing for the same position.

She doesn't date.

We can't afford any distractions from the disaster threatening to end Serenity for good, leaving women and children vulnerable.

And the last, but still very real, aspect of this scenario— eight short weeks ago, this woman hated me.

We loathed each other.

What happens if it doesn't work out? Does hate rear its ugly head again, only to leave me broken?

The white cabins with their red trim on R & R Ranch are spectacular. This time of year, as fall turns the landscape around them a pretty orange hue, even more so. I carry our bags up the few steps and onto the small porch.

Carlie follows, our carry-ons in her hands.

I push through the door and set the luggage down as I take

in the space. The guest cabin is separated by a wall. The living and dining area is open. The only door to the bedroom sits to the left of the dividing wall. One of Gracie's landscape oil paintings of the mountains outside hangs on the wall.

The sofa, flat-screen, and fireplace fill the right, and the small ranch style kitchenette fills the left.

Carlie wanders through the door to the bedroom, looking around. I follow, hands in my pockets as she takes in the quaint space Rubes created for guests.

"Ruby and Reed built this place into the guest ranch. My brothers and father built the cabins and renovated the largest barn, which you'll see tomorrow night. Rubes has an eye for decorating."

"That she does," Carlie says, running a hand over the blankets before she backs up to the side of the bed, her calves hitting the mattress. She flops down starfish-style and waves her arms up and down the covers. "This place is incredible, Lawson."

"It is. You tired?"

She yawns as the words leave my mouth. I could curl up on this bed and recreate our hours tangled together when she was sick. Less the sick part, that is.

"I'm wiped. What do we do for dinner?" she asks.

"Rubes texted. She's going to drop a welcome basket off later. Fruit and snacks and the like."

"Oh, that will be perfect. Maybe I'll just nap until tomorrow." She sits up and pats the bed beside her. "Come here."

It feels like the tension between us has changed. Everything is more familiar. More heightened.

I pad to where she is but don't sit. Instead, I look down,

trying to find the words I've been wanting to say for hours. Since the plane landed.

"What?" she says, a rare shy smile gracing her face.

"I—" I study her face. I can't ruin the working relationship we have. But every day I spend with this woman is more intense, more tortuous than the last. Deciding words won't cut it, I palm her face. Her lips part as her brown eyes tighten. "How about instead of Princess, I just call you mine?"

Her little gasp has her head jerk back from my hands.

Fuck.

Too much.

Too soon.

You idiot.

I resist the urge to step away. Carlie stands, her hands hanging by her side. "I want to try something," she whispers.

I stand still, waiting as I swallow against the rock in my throat.

"You're not needing a distraction, right?" she asks.

"Well, that depends . . ."

The blood racing south says I absolutely do. Anything to take my mind off the stunning woman in front of me.

"I mean, you're good. This is not just a coping mechanism?"

Fuck.

She means . . .

"I'm good," I rasp.

Her hands cup my face before dragging my mouth close. Her lips brush over mine. "You sure?"

I nod before pressing my forehead to hers. I couldn't fight this moment off if I tried. How many weeks have I imagined touching her, kissing her, takin—

"Stop thinking, Lawson."

"Yes ma'am."

"Fuck, when you talk like that . . ."

My mouth tips in a crooked smile. "How'd you mean, darlin'?"

"God above." A hand sliding behind my neck, she pulls my mouth down to hers.

I can't control what happens next. Cupping her face, I pull her up off the bed and spin her round. We're all heat, dancing around each other, and she meets me where I'm at. Fine fingers glide up my neck and into my hair.

One hand presses over my heart as she herds me backward to the edge of the bed. Dropping onto the mattress, I slide my hands down her neck, losing contact for a second before I grip her hips, and she crawls onto my lap.

Rocking forward, she moans a little. The sound is goddamn intoxicating.

Just as needy for this as I am, she devours my mouth, her hands weaving their way through my hair.

I'm rock fucking hard underneath her.

Sweet Christ, this woman is my version of heaven.

She is heaven, period.

I may as well have died and left this earth for all I care. I take everything she offers up, my hands wandering up her ribs, and she breaks away.

"We should . . ."

Her lips are parted, her breaths now short choppy bursts, color flushing her features. She's stunning, freshly kissed and out of breath. I can only imagine how incredible she looks freshly fucked.

I press my forehead to her chest with a groan.

She chuckles, running a hand through my hair. "Thank god for turbulence."

"Fucking hell," I breathe. I can't do anything more, only exist, trying to catch my breath around her.

"Laws—"

The front door rattles under a hard knock.

Timing, Reed, timing.

"Hello?" my youngest brother calls, back from being out on his tractor, no doubt. Rubes probably texted him to come home since I arrived with Carlie and had made a point of not telling my family ahead of time. Easier that way.

Ma would make it a big deal and all. I want Carlie's weekend to be great and productive. None of those things can happen with my meddling family. They mean well, but—

"Is that Reed?" Carlie's face lights up.

"Yep. Come on, we should get this over with."

"I heard that, Laws." Reed's voice is muted through the door.

Carlie chuckles, tossing her head back. I dot a kiss to her sternum and her laughter fades, brown eyes settling back on my face as all amusement disappears, replaced by a sliver of the need it was just captivated by. She runs a thumb over my bottom lip before closing her eyes briefly and rising from my lap.

Shifting myself in my jeans, I head for the door and swing it open. "Reedsy, how's things, bud?"

He opens the screen door and walks in. I tug him into a one-armed hug, and he smacks the side of my head. "You know Rubes needs a heads-up if you're bringing a pretty girl."

Carlie walks up, stopping by my side. "Hi."

"Howdy." Reed beams, folding her into a hug before I have

a chance to tell him not to. As he releases her, he glances at me, fixing his hat. "Well, aren't you the prettiest surprise we've had around here in a long while."

Carlie huffs a laugh and smiles. "Thank you, glad to be of service."

"Oh, I like this one, Laws."

I roll my eyes at him. This one, like there have been others.

"Alright, I'll let you go back to . . . whatever. The boss wants me home for supper. You're welcome to join us." Reed tips his hat before stepping outside.

"The boss?" Carlie asks, glancing at my brother.

He gives her his best grin. "Rubes."

Her eyes light up as she pulls her bottom lip through her teeth. "Oh, dinner with Ruby Robbins . . . Can we?"

"I'm going to need that request in writing," I tease.

She raises an eyebrow but pads to her handbag, rifling through it and mumbling a phrase under her breath before returning with a pink sticky note and placing it on my forehead.

Reed cackles where he stands as I peel it off and hold it out to read.

Scrawled over the square pink paper is *Please, Cowboy, I'll owe you one.*

I shift my gaze back to catch hers as desperation twists her face. She's absolutely gone over meeting Rubes. It's damn adorable.

I know the feeling of being gone all too well as warmth floods my chest with her plea.

CHAPTER 22
CARLIE

I sit on a white Adirondack chair next to *the* Ruby Robbins. Well, Ruby Rawlins now, but still. I'm fangirling so stinking hard, I'm terrified I'm going to make an absolute fool of myself.

"So, you need a gala four weeks from now?" Ruby asks me.

It's all I can do to nod.

Lawson works fast.

I grip the wine glass she handed me twenty minutes ago when we came outside and left the men to wash up. Merlot. It's floral and rich. Lovely.

"Do you have any idea of the type of guests you need for the sponsorships? Do you have a curated event list already, or access to one?"

"I—no, I mean, I'm not sure. Serelle seems to play most things close to the vest. But I have contacts from Carlson's I can use."

"Great, I have a list, but not everyone on it will be a good fit. We should make a new list. A venue will be the hard part, catering even harder this near to the date."

"I was afraid of that." I swirl the crimson liquid in my fine-stemmed wine glass and take a sip.

Ruby gazes into the fire, as if choosing her words carefully. "Laws is just—"

"I know. He's the kindest man I've ever met." I hope everything I say isn't coming out weird or like I'm trying too hard. I'm not used to the feeling of not being the most successful woman in the room. As self-centered and shallow as it sounds. But I've been running on defense for so long, this is . . . nerve-wracking. I lower my gaze to the wine, turning the stem in my hands.

"Hey," Ruby says softly. "This place, this family. Safe space. The safest. Nothing you do or say will change anyone's mind about anything. Blanket statement. That should really be a Rawlins Hallmark card." She scrunches her face at me with a kind smile.

"Thank you," I breathe, seeing the tangle of emotion lining her eyes. The great Ruby Robbins, who I've admired for years, is letting me in. I have only ever known her on a professional level. And like one does when you barely know someone, I assumed her life was brilliant. Perfect.

"Of course." She studies my face, her brows dropping the slightest bit. "I never knew what family meant until I came out here. Reed gave me that. These people will change your life."

"From what Lawson tells me . . . you did the same for his brother."

She huffs a laugh. "Let's just say we both found what we were looking for."

"That's incredible."

I sigh, tilting my head back to take in the big, beautiful Montana sky riddled with shimmering stars strung across the dark inky blanket.

"Yeah, it is."

I glance at her, and she's beaming up toward the man who has appeared behind her, his hands gripping her shoulders, as he leans down and presses a kiss to the crown of her head.

Lawson sinks into the seat by mine. "Get some things sorted?"

"Working out the new guest list options." In the firelight, I can't take my gaze from his face as he stares into the flames. "You catch up a little?"

Lawson pulls his focus from the fire. "Yep."

"Well, we have a big day tomorrow," Reed says, pulling his wife up and into his chest. "Night, y'all."

"Night Reedsy, night Rubes." Lawson smiles up at them.

A heartbeat later, we sit in front of the fire, just the two of us. I down the last of the wine, letting it warm my body as it goes down.

"It's so beautiful out here," I say softly.

"Sure is." Lawson's gaze is on the whiskey tumbler in his hand.

"Don't you miss it?"

He chuckles, but it fades. "All the time, but it's not who I am. At least, not anymore."

I can understand that. We work hard, sometimes for years, for the lives we want. I know it better than most. And when you finally get to a place where you feel like you can take a breather, it's worth every hard patch you lived through. There's something to be said for making a life you love.

I've never seen a barn in real life, but this one exceeds every expectation I could have had. The wide double doors are adorned with so, so many fairy lights. The long, wide driveway is filling up with pickup trucks at an alarming rate as I lounge on the small porch, rocking in the hanging chair. This place truly is like something out of a movie.

The door to our cabin creaks open and Lawson appears, our coats in his hand. "Ready for the full Rawlins experience, Princess?"

I stand and close the distance between us.

He cleans up nice. Really nice.

Clean-shaven, his hair a little messier than how he wears it at the office, a pale blue button-down shirt rolled up at the sleeves over dark Levi's, and . . . are those cowboy boots?

"You look edible," I whisper, running my fingers over his jaw.

His deep blues darken as he slides a rough hand behind my neck, tugging me into his chest. "I could fucking devour you right here."

"I don't think the guests came for dinner and a show, Cowboy."

"Too bad."

"Isn't it," I say pushing a little way away from him. His hand slides from my neck, and he bends his head down. "Party time, snoodlebug."

"What the hell kind of name is that?" I scoff.

"Pookie bear? Snookums . . . or maybe you're a sweet cheeks." The shit-eating grin now splitting his face is contagious.

"I will have you know"—I sway down the few steps on my stilettos, looking over my shoulder—"I am none of those things, Lawson Rawlins."

His huffy laugh turns strained as I turn at the bottom of the stairs, looking up at him where he now stands on the top step. I blow him a kiss and his jaw feathers. A beat passes and he descends the stairs holding up my coat for me to slide into.

"Are you forgetting something?" I ask.

"Don't think so. Dressed, shaved, warned the gorgeous girl by my side about my family . . . Nope, I've remembered it all."

"Close your eyes." I lean down to the bag Ruby dropped off earlier that I hid under the stairs.

"No?"

"Lawson whatever-your-middle-name-is Rawlins. Don't you deny me a thing."

A breath chugs from his chest and his eyes fall closed.

I pull out the black hat and slide it on his head. And . . .

Oh. My. God.

Holy shit.

There is no way in hell I'm getting my ovaries back in their cage now. "Open your eyes, Cowboy."

The small smile that blooms over his face is priceless. It steals what's left of my resolve when it comes to this man. I thought he was hot in a tie and a rolled-up work shirt with those ropey forearms and that gorgeous hair. Now—

A finger slides under my jaw, lifting it shut.

"I—"

He leans in, cupping my face with his palm. "Thank you."

Really, the hat was for me.

"What for?" I breathe.

"Reminding me who I am."

My mouth is agape again. This weekend has been one incredible surprise after another, and we've barely started. We have two more nights here. Two more days of this place that feels like another world.

"We should head in there before the girls come out and drag us in." Lawson adjusts the hat on his head.

"We should."

He crooks an arm, and this time I take it. Like it's my god-given place on earth.

We cross the gravel drive, somewhat precariously thanks to my heels, and arrive at the doorway. Inside is simply magical. Long cream sails are draped across the ceiling with more fairy lights. Long tables adorned with white tablecloths, cream plates, and silver cutlery with candles and flowers dotted through the center of each. Acoustic country music weaves its way through the big open space where people mingle, chat, laugh.

I'm jostled when Reed rushes over, sliding an arm around my middle and sweeping me out of Lawson's space as three women descend on him with more glee than I ever thought possible. "Watch out, or you'll end up collateral damage," Reed says with a chuckle.

"Laws!" the three women scream in delight at once, arms reaching as they close in.

Ruby I know.

Grace I recognize.

And the third must be Addy.

He's smothered in hugs and kisses on the cheek as he tries

his best to hug all three tight. I only just make out the choked words that leave his lips. "I missed you guys so damn much."

If ever there was testament to the shape of a man's heart, this would be it. Three women who absolutely adore him.

The black hat topples to the ground, and Reed releases me so I can pick it up.

"Nice touch," he says, winking. His own hat on his head gets a subtle tip as he adds, "Make sure you save me a dance, Miss Carlie."

Miss Carlie.

He reminds me of Manuel, happiness personified, so I guess it fits.

"Rubes, Gracie, you remember Carlie." Lawson extracts himself and folds me into his chest.

Ruby rolls her eyes at him with a laugh. Grace says a soft hi and hugs me lightly, kind of sideways.

"Adds, this is Carlie. We work together." He waves at the pretty brunette with big brown eyes and curly brown hair. "Carlie, this is Addy, Huddo's wife."

"Hi, it's amazing to meet you all," I say.

"Where is that big brother of mine?" Lawson says.

"Tending the bar tonight with Mack." Addy nods to a long rustic bar where two cowboys in hats are busy serving drinks. "They lost the toss this year."

Lawson laces his hand with my own and we wander through the long tables toward the bar. I feel a little out of place in a cocktail dress and heels. But when I take a closer look at Ruby's outfit, something right off 5th Ave, I feel much better.

One white hat bobs and weaves behind the bar as the man wearing it serves drinks and makes change. The other, in a black hat, smiles at me and wipes down the counter before tossing the tea towel down and rounding the bar. "You must be Carlie. The Reed grapevine travels at lightning speed round here. I'm Mack." He pulls me in for a hug then fist-bumps his brother.

"Busy as ever, Mackie-boy," Lawson says with a grin.

Mack points a finger as he returns to his post, his face turning to stone. "You're cut off already." His face splits with a grin as the man I assume is Hudson flicks him on the jaw and comes out from behind the counter, sliding his white hat off with one hand and one-arm hugging Lawson. "Hey bud. So good to see you."

Lawson pats him on the back, hesitating before he lets go.

Emotion burns behind my eyes. God, he must miss his brothers. His family. And I haven't even met his parents yet.

"Hey, I'm Hudson. You must be the firecracker who's keeping Laws on his toes, hey?"

Heat flushes my neck and face. The hell? Since when do I blush at the mention of Lawson?

"Yep, that's me," I force out before leaning into Lawson's side.

Mack hollers for backup, and Hudson glances over his shoulder.

"Y'all have a good night, you hear?" Hudson says with a smile before tapping Lawson's hat with a finger and wandering back to his station and taking an order.

"Overwhelmed yet?" Lawson asks, bending his head down.

"No." I'm being honest. I love seeing him in his element. Seeing this side of Lawson Rawlins. It's endearing.

"Oh my lord! Will you look at that!" A woman's voice cuts through the air, and we spin back. A blonde woman in her sixties stands by an old cowboy, who looks . . . suspiciously like an older version of Hudson.

"Ma," Lawson calls, closing the distance as she folds her son into a hug. Even from here, I can tell it's one of those warm hugs that only a mother can give. That unconditional love makes.

A second later, the old cowboy has his hat in his hand, and Laws moves in for another one-arm hug. This lot are ridiculous. When the hugs are out of the way, his father moves across the floor to where I stand. "Howdy, darlin'. Welcome to the family tradition."

"Hi, I'm Carlie." I hold a hand out for him to shake, and he chuckles. A heartbeat later, I'm wrapped in strong arms, looking over his shoulder to Lawson, whose face is utterly amused.

By the look on mine?

"Harry Rawlins, you let that sweet girl go before you suffocate her." His mother's smile stretches her face.

Harry releases me with a nod and smile.

"Hun, you look just stunning." Lawson's mother casts her eye over my dress.

"Thank you, Mrs. Rawlins."

"It's just Louisa." She pats my cheek like Mills does, and I tamp back the emotion that rises with the gesture.

"Lawson, it's so good to see you, my boy. You make sure she's taken care of." Louisa cups her son's cheek before following her husband, who is making the rounds chatting to guests.

"Yes ma'am," Lawson replies a little too late, his gaze stuck on his parents.

I move to his side and lace my fingers with his. "I think I'm in love."

He drops his head, his mouth brushing over my ear. "That was quick."

I turn my head to the side so my lips brush his jaw. "With your family, Cowboy."

He nudges my shoulder with his.

I fight the urge to climb this man like a tree right here and now.

A glass clinks against a well-timed fork, and Lawson ushers me to the head table where his family now sits. Reed stands, a glass in his hand and Ruby by his side, her hand in his as he waits for quiet.

"Thank y'all for coming out tonight. This Thanksgiving gig has kind of become a tradition, and it is our honor to have you all at our table. Here's to the people we love. Family." He looks around our table. "Friends." He casts his gaze over the tables and finally says, "And those of you who have chosen to spend your holiday with us. Happy holidays, happy Thanksgiving. Let's eat!"

Ruby pushes up on her tiptoes and dots a kiss to his cheek. They sit as a silver cart rolls out from the door near the bar where I assume the kitchen is. It reaches the table, and Reed carves the first slice of turkey as waitstaff file from the same door, dropping plates in front of each guest. The chatter quiets as everyone eats.

Dessert arrives twenty minutes after the main meal is done, as if on some silent cue. I can't believe I am living a Ruby Robbins event. It's perfection. Between the decorations, the food, the ambiance, and the mood, it's utterly ethereal.

After dessert, the mood swings and upbeat country songs

vibrate through the barn. Lawson's family are the first people on the dance floor. I scoff a laugh as Harry sweeps the floor with them all. The old man has the moves. He takes Louisa for a turn, and then Ruby.

When he appears at the table, his hand extended to me, I shake my head.

"Come on, darlin'. It's not a party unless you're dancin'."

"Go on, Princess. We can dance later." Lawson whispers in my ear.

I narrow my eyes at him as I stand and place my hand in his father's. The smile that spreads on Lawson's face is worth any amount of songs. Even country ones.

Twirled without warning, I huff a laugh, righting my foot-work before Harry slides his arm around my waist. I'm swung around the dance floor as happiness radiates from me with every quick, exuberant breath.

It's heady and foreign.

Something I can't control . . .

I love it and hate it all at once.

CHAPTER 23
LAWSON

Carlie swings around on Reed's arm, the soft twang of country music floating around us. And I sit, rooted to my seat and whiskey tumbler in hand, as tension builds in my chest. Growing with every song she dances without me.

Reed leans in to say something. The music drowns out his words as I watch his lips move before cracking into a grin. Carlie tosses her head back with a laugh that would smash through the stars, seeing them fizzle and plummet to the ground.

The telltale heat of jealousy winds its way through my veins.

I throw back the last mouthful, and it burns.

Like it goddamn should.

Jealous of my little brother. Loser territory, if it ever existed, and I'm the fucking king.

The song dies out, and something slower starts up. From

across the table, I see Ruby wink at her husband as she sips her merlot.

I have no idea what's gotten into me when I stand and stalk to the other side of the table by Ruby's side.

She looks up, taking another sip. "Laws?"

"We're dancin'."

"Oh, I would love to, but my feet are killing me." The smile on her face paired with the mock-innocent look tells me she's full of shit. "Send my husband back to me when you're ready, hey."

These two totally set me up.

Dammit.

I lean over and swipe my hat from the table and push it onto my head before I close in on Reed and the woman who oughta be in my arms right now. Not his.

"Cuttin' in, bud." I wave a hand between them.

Reed reaffirms his hold on Carlie. "Yeah, we're not done, *bud*."

Carlie tries and fails to tamp down a grin as Reed whisks her away from me.

Like fuck, little bro.

As he makes the mistake of spinning her around with one hand, I step in and slide my arm around her waist, pulling her to me.

I'm a damn Neanderthal. It's not my best moment, I'm aware. But the heat washing its way through every inch of my body at watching her happy in some other man's arms is suffocating me.

Even if it is my brother's.

I pull her closer, dropping my face into her hair as we take up the rhythm of the song. Her hands move, one sliding across the back of my neck, the other pressing into my chest over my heart.

The first useful lungful floods in.

"Lawson?" she whispers.

"Yeah?"

"Thank you for bringing me with you."

"My pleasure, Princess."

We sway our way through the song that will always be my favorite from this single second on. I lift my head and meet her gaze. Silver lines it.

"You okay?" I rasp.

She scrunches up her face and nods. "I'm great."

Rubes drifts past, closing in on Reed on the other side of the dance floor. So much for sore feet. Somebody bumps into my shoulder, and I turn to find Mack and Gracie, my brother wrapped around his wife from behind as they shimmy across the dance floor. Gracie's belly leads the way as Mack dips his head to her ear, and she smiles and rolls her head back, planting a kiss on his cheek.

Hudson sits at the head of the table, Addy on his lap, her arms around his neck as they watch their daughter, Hattie, wander around, collecting flowers from everyone's table.

Fuck, the love and adoration are everywhere. This family of mine is pure heart and soul.

"Now I understand." Carlie's hand slips from my chest to my jaw as she holds my gaze.

"What do you understand?" I ask.

"Why you're such a nice guy." Her attention wanders around the room, landing on my brothers and their wives, finally resting on my parents who sit at the table, Ma tucked into Harry's side. The old man's eyes are closed, whiskey in hand, as he sways his head to the song. "You're so lucky, Lawson."

"Yeah, I am," I rasp.

Christ, what I wouldn't give to have what the rest of my family has found.

Carlie yawns, her hand pressing over her mouth.

"Bedtime," I whisper into her ear.

"No, Grace isn't leaving. So I'm staying. Even Hattie's still up. I don't want to be the one to not keep up."

I chuckle. "It's not a competition, Carlie."

"I know, but it would be rude to leave so soon."

As if on cue, Reed and Rubes waltz their way over. "Bedtime, Laws." Reed wriggles his eyebrows at me like an absolute idiot.

"Thank you so much for bringing our favorite brother home to us, Carlie." Ruby leans in for a hug, and I release the woman in my arms so she can hug my sister.

"You're welcome," Carlie says, the words wobbling a little. She's still a little starstruck by Rubes. Completely understandable—the woman is the eighth wonder of the world. All three of my sisters are, if I'm honest.

"Night," I say, wrapping Carlie back into my chest.

She laces a hand with mine for a beat before turning in my arms. "We should say our goodbyes, then."

I lean down, pressing my forehead against hers. "Yes ma'am."

With quick goodbyes and a questionable promise to visit Ma before we leave, we grab our coats and make our way back to the cabin. Carlie walks beside me.

"Geez, how did it get so cold in such a short period of time?" she asks, looking up at the star-studded sky.

Clear skies, cold days.

No one ever said Montana was the Bahamas. I open the door and hold it as she walks inside. I close the screen and pull the wooden door shut tight. The fireplace is crackling away as we step inside. No doubt Rubes would have made sure firelight was warming our cabin, and all the guests' cabins, while we were all having fun at the dinner.

Flopping on the sofa, she slides off her heels. "The fire is bliss."

I tug my coat off and hang it on the hook on the back of the door. "So, you're sleeping there. Must be my turn to take the bed."

Her mouth pops open on a gasp.

The grin splitting my face is ridiculous. "It's only fair, after the bungalow."

Removing her coat, she stands and closes the distance between us. "If I remember correctly, I gave you half of a king bed."

Easiest catch of my life.

Hook, line, and sinker.

I resist the urge to claim her beautiful face with my palms and devour those pouty fucking lips as every drop of blood sinks south and the air in my lungs turns to ash.

I tilt my head and clear my throat, like that'll damn well save me. "Yes, you did. But we're having a pillow wall, can't have you getting all handsy on me in your sleep."

I walk toward the bed to set up the pillow wall. To see just how far she'll let me take this before she stops me. I tug the hat from my head and toss it onto the chair in the corner of the room. I toe my boots off and remove my belt before grabbing the pillows and set them in a line down the center of the bed.

Turning back, I find her right where I left her. A look of desperation sits over the rise and plummet of her too-quick breaths . . . as her chest heaves. Her hands hang by her sides.

I know exactly what has her held to the spot. Because it's been paralyzing me for weeks. It's been responsible for every stupid emotion I've had to fight off, for the strings that tug at my heart gripped in her elegant hand.

Slowly, I pad to where she stands. Brown eyes lift to find my own.

"Lawso—" Her voice breaks.

I take her face in my hands. Without a word, I sweep her up and into my arms. "Bedtime, baby."

A little huff tumbles through her parted lips, but her gaze doesn't leave mine.

We reach the bed as she says, "Put me down, *please?*"

Her voice is unsure, like I crossed some line that kissing her apparently never did.

I set her on her feet, and she takes a step back. "I can't. I'm sorry."

I shake my head. "Don't be," I breathe.

"I—you . . ." She turns her back to me. "Can you unzip me?" Her words are so soft, like she's afraid to ask after she thought I wanted something more.

Damn every last man who's hurt this woman. The world can go fuck itself for the damage it's done.

I unzip her and turn her back to me with my hands on her shoulders. "I can sleep on the sofa if you—"

Her finger presses over my lips. "No, the pillow wall will suffice."

I smile underneath her touch.

"Besides, I'm used to having you beside me now."

I pull her closer and plant a kiss on her forehead. "If you snore, Princess, you're on the sofa."

She huffs through a strained giggle before her lips brush against my jaw.

And fuck.

I'm rock hard. The desperation for her is a catalyst low in my core, sending its blistering response into every fiber of my being. The need for this woman will surely kill me, but if she needs slow, we go slow. If she needs anything, it's hers.

"I'm going to shower . . ." she whispers, breaking eye contact.

I swallow past the rock in my throat.

Tortured is a man so close to what he wants most in this life, only to be held back by some invisible wall the men before him erected.

What I wouldn't do to take down that wall for her. Piece by piece with my bare hands, if I have to. If she would let me.

The shower turns on, and I amble to the living room and drop onto the sofa. Running my hands through my hair, I blow out a low breath and hang my head.

Fuck, I'm so gone it hurts.

My heart had to go and pick the only girl I've ever met whose heart is locked away. The rusted chains around it are secured with a triple padlock of sassiness, the keys long lost to a deep sea of independence. The shield she uses to keep me from finding my way in, her ambition and work addiction.

But it just so happens I was raised by two of the most loving, capable people who would go to any length to give a person what they need. To take care of their own. In true Rawlins style, I won't quit on Carlie. Not until she has everything she's ever wanted and maybe a few things she never knew she needed.

The small sigh that sounds from the bedroom sees me push off the sofa and pad to the bed. I turn back to the coat rack and grab out my boxers from my bag. Making quick work of my own shower, I slide into my side of the pillow-wall-separated bed. Once I'm settled in, hands behind my head and eyes closed, the pillow in the center at my shoulder slips.

I open my eyes to find browns studying my face.

Her hands are tucked under the pillow her head rests on as she lies on her side. Her lips purse and roll as she sucks in a breath.

"Yeah, Princess?"

Her hand slides out from under the pillow and traces the angle of my jaw. "Night, Laws."

Laws.

Not Rawlins, or even Lawson.

Just Laws.

I roll over, studying her face. Her hand reaffirms on my jaw. Her eyes light before she breaks eye contact and her hands drops from my face, sliding back to her side. I grab it before it can disappear and press her palm to my lips. "Night, baby."

Emotion rolls through those pretty features, and I close my eyes before the sight of her beside me, her hand still clutched in my own, can take me down.

CHAPTER 24
CARLIE

The cabin living room floor is littered with documents. Plans. Guests lists. And venue options and details. Ruby sits on the floor, her laptop to one side as her fingers fly over the keyboard.

"I can get the Met, maybe . . . Anna owes me a favor." She chews on the end of her pen.

"The Met?" I ask, my mouth gaping.

"It's on the 'maybe' list, don't get your hopes up."

"Holy shit," I breathe.

I knew she was good, but this is—

"How's it going out there?" Laws calls from the bedroom, where he's elbows deep in financial backup plans, should this all crash and burn.

Despite the excitement of working alongside Ruby, my mind keeps wandering back to that kiss yesterday after we arrived. To the moment Lawson carried me to the bedroom like I was the most precious thing he'd ever held.

And . . . that right there is why I don't do relationships.

I can't afford any distractions. With the stakes so high for both Serenity and my career, now is not the time to let my guard down. I don't actually know when that would be a good idea, if I'm honest.

That thought alone scares me.

"Okay, we have our first round of invites nailed down, anyone who doesn't respond within twenty-four hours goes on the backup list, and we send out round two. This way we are guaranteed to have a waitlist instead of waiting for guests to take their time and decide. We want to create the illusion of scarcity. When an opportunity is fleeting, the right people bite. We want the elite who have appearances to uphold. A lesson I learned from Anna a long time ago." Ruby slides two lists across the hardwood floor to me.

"That's brilliant."

"That's how you get a sold-out event with highfliers, babe."

"Can you big-sister adopt me, pretty please?" I ask, pleading hands clasped in front of my chest and all.

She chuckles and places her laptop on her legs, which are now crossed as she sits by my side. "Working together regularly would be nice. I'd like that. I've missed the high life a little, if I'm honest. And I would love to take Reed to some things, if he ever had a week off."

"You guys are busy out here."

"So much."

"You always have guests? Year-round, I mean?"

"We do, for weddings, parties, and other events. We're always running, but there isn't anywhere else I'd be. My heart lives here, you know?"

"I think I'm starting to understand that."

She smiles at me. "Good."

"Do you think we'll make the numbers we need for guests and sponsorship?"

"Let me make a few calls, then we'll have a better idea."

"Of course," I say softly, gathering up the paperwork and heading to the bedroom to give Ruby some space.

I drop on my side of the bed, placing the papers on the bedside, and lie on my stomach. "I think you and I are going to have to stay friends just so I have a direct line to Ruby."

Lawson looks at me where I lie, my head by the papers he's working on, his laptop to one side. He turns a pen through his fingers as his deep blues slide toward me. "Friends? Nah, we can't be friends."

His voice is low. The insane timbre to it rumbles like a warning.

I sit up, pulling my hair around my neck so it drapes over my chest, my brows dropping. "We can't?"

"Nope." He turns back to his screen, tapping something out.

I'm confused. I thought, at the very least, if we had to work together and no longer hated each other, we would be . . .

Oh.

Ohhhhh.

You idiot, Carlie.

Yep, we definitely crossed a line.

Fuck.

Footsteps close in on the bedroom. "Carlie?"

I meet Ruby at the door. "What did she say?"

I bite down on my bottom lip, holding my breath.

"She said . . . the booking for the twenty-fourth's payment defaulted. And it would be her pleasure to help a cause as incredible as Serenity. We have the Met."

I throw my arms around Ruby. I hug her way too tight and can't help the way my inner child jumps around like an absolute fool. I don't care, I'm so excited. So impressed. So in awe of the woman in my arms.

Oh yeah . . .

I release Ruby, and she grins at me. "Send out the first wave of invites tonight. We'll talk tomorrow. Oh," she says, leaning around me, "Laws, Reed and I are heading to Great Falls for a few hours. Can you guys hang out at the house in case any guests need anything?"

"Sure, not a problem. See you for supper?"

"Absolutely." She collects her laptop and her notes before exiting the cabin, leaving me in her wake, one infused with gratitude, completely humbled and a whole lot inspired.

I turn back to find Lawson grinning at me. "You good, Princess? Not going to faint from excitement?"

I pull a face and poke my tongue like an utter child. But, hell, this weekend has been incredible. I haven't felt this excited, this free, since . . . I have no idea when.

"Come over here and pull that face," Laws rumbles.

I want to.

I really do, but the line we crossed is starting to blur. If it gets any fuzzier, I won't be able to find it when I need to retreat back across.

I don't know how to get past the walls I built around me. I lost the key to this prison a long time ago. I'm used to operating on autopilot of just sex, no emotions. Just meeting a physical need, no strings.

This is the first time I've ever wondered what would happen if I wanted more.

I do. I want more.

With Lawson, I want—

A hand tugs me toward the bed. Disconnecting from my inner monologue and looking down, I find Lawson sitting on the edge of the bed, me standing between his legs.

"Overthinking this is a really bad idea," he rasps.

"You should probably stop that, then."

His hands splay over my ribs, his thumbs rubbing the soft flesh of my belly over my T-shirt.

His warm hands send a ridiculous heat through my body, homing in on my core.

"I don't do relationships, Lawson," I whisper.

He glances at his hands, his gaze studying the path his thumbs take for a beat before looking back up. "Why?"

Because I'm broken.

Because the first and only man I loved didn't feel I was enough to stick around. And the wound he left has ruined every attempt I've ever made to have love in my life.

Hence, I no longer believe it exists.

"I don—I no longer believe in it," I say, unable to look at him.

"It?"

"Love, I don't believe in it. I believe there is companionship and there is lust. But love, that's . . ."

He stands and cups my face. "Baby, you are literally surrounded by it in this place."

He means his family, right?

I open my mouth to respond. His thumb drags over my lips, and he shakes his head. "Challenge accepted."

"What?" I breathe.

"I accept the challenge, to show you love does exist and how much you deserve it."

"Lawson," I plead, shaking my head.

No.

The stakes are too high.

We work together.

Only one of us can stay. Best case, we go our separate ways; worst case . . .

"We're literally fighting to save Serenity, we can't afford the distraction. Not now." I study his gaze for some hint of amusement. Like this could all be a huge prank he wants to play on me. Payback for our early days at Serenity and that one time I imitated him and Nadia. Well, only Nadia. But still, a low point in my life, and in my career.

The lowest.

"Love isn't a liability, Carlie. It's an asset. If my family shows you anything, it's that." He tucks a stray strand of hair behind my ear and dots a kiss on my cheek before leaving out the front door.

He might have a point.

Maybe he has a point?

No.

There's no point to this. He can't convince me something intangible exists. He just can't.

As much as the little girl inside me wants him to be right and me to be wrong, I know he's not. Somewhere along the line he'll realize either I can't be loved, or I was right, and love's simply something we create in our heads as we chase an illusion of happiness. Then, we're both going to be left shattered.

It will always end that way.

Always.

The clatter and clink of Ruby and Lawson washing up is almost drowned out by their laughter. The Montana night air is crisp, and I grab the blanket draped over the arm of the swinging porch chair and wrap it around my shoulders.

"Thought I'd find you out here," Reed says, sitting on the chair beside me. He leans back and pushes off the porch with his feet, sending us swinging.

With a stifled squeal, I grip the chain beside my head.

He leans back on the swing, laying an arm along the back as he stares out into the vast wilderness around us. "Ready to go home?"

Home.

The concept feels odd since I've been out here.

"I think so."

He turns to me and leans forward. "Thanks for spending the holiday with us, hey."

Why is this family so goddamn friendly? What is with the niceties every other hour? They make my life feel empty and shallow. Making a big deal out of the simplest things. This is what Lawson grew up with? The constant interference and people being in his business . . . It's no wonder he fled to the city.

Urgh.

Going straight to hell for those thoughts.

"If you ever need a break from the hustle, a cabin is yours, just flick a text through."

"Smooth. This how you get all your business, cornering people on porch swings?"

Reed leans back, searching my face as he frowns.

I'm a bitch, I know. But honestly, this salt-of-the-earth shit is getting old.

"You're family. Not business, darlin'."

I scoff. "Okay."

"You want to tell me what's eating you?" he says softly, concern etched all over his features.

How the hell . . . ? I flick my hair around my neck and refuse to meet his gaze. "I have no idea what you're talking about."

I snap my focus to the starry night sky over the inky blue mountain and whispering grass fields.

"It's okay to let people in, Carlie. You're not the first strong woman to be loved or taken care of. Just ask Rubes."

He stands and messes up my hair with a hand before giving me a two-fingered salute. What the hell's that about?

"Yeah, right," I breathe as he disappears through the door back into the house.

I spend the rest of the night talking to Ruby, ignoring the Rawlins men as much as possible. We came here to spend the weekend sorting out this colossal work disaster, so I focus on that. Not the gorgeous man who brought me here. Or his eyes that see right through my fucking soul like they have the right to. Or the way a little part of the wall I built crumbles away with every interaction we have.

No, I'm not letting the distraction ruin my career, my life. Steal everything I've worked for over the last ten years.

No fucking way.

CHAPTER 25

LAWSON

My apartment is too quiet. And far too lonely after spending the weekend and then some with my family and Carlie.

I drop my bag inside the door and flick the light on. Four days went as fast as four hours, and after one non-eventful flight home, I made sure Carlie got home okay before catching an Uber home.

With a plan and a backup plan, including the gala, I'm hopeful we can pull Serenity out of the red and have the place thriving, if not improving exponentially.

Despite that, things feel off with me and Carlie. I have no idea what she and Reed were talking about on the porch our last night in Montana, but whatever it was, she's been distracted since. Closed off, even. The gut-sinking feeling that I've ruined everything twists, turning my stomach contents of airport food and a cold coffee to lead.

"Dammit." Fingers threading through my hair, I slump onto the sofa. "How could I be so fucking stupid?"

I pull my phone from my back pocket and tap out a message.

Carlie, thanks for the weekend.

Nope, scratch that. I delete it and start again.

Carlie, if this weekend was uncomfor—

Urgh.

I delete that, too, and toss the phone onto the sofa. I flop backward and stretch out on the cushions. The day's done and dusted at around nine in the evening, and I couldn't be bothered to text the guys. With a groan, I close my eyes, resting my forearm over my face.

Let's hope we can pull off the rest of this quarter and the next before one of us ends up leaving.

My phone buzzes, the screen lighting up.

Carlie.

I fly up off the sofa embarrassingly fast, fumbling the phone. I slide the bar across and answer.

"Hi."

"Hi, yourself. I got home and realized I have the wrong bag."

I snap my gaze to the bag by the door. Not my bag. Her rose-gold luggage sits against the wall by my front door.

"Damn, you need it now, or . . ."

"Well, yeah."

"Oh, so." I rub a hand behind my neck, my words suddenly drying up. "You want me to bring it over?"

"If it's not too much trouble. Besides, I don't think my Gucci will look any good on you tomorrow at the office."

"You never know."

"Laws, I need my things. Please?"

"Okay, I'll be there in a bit."

"Thank you."

The line disconnects. I stare at the bag by the door. How did I mix that up with my silver one? I guess I wasn't really paying attention to the luggage, only to the woman traveling with me.

Not one to look a gift horse in the mouth, I swipe up my wallet and keys and grab the bag, leaving the apartment before my pride can take a hit. The woman needs her things.

It takes forty minutes to get to Carlie's, and when I get there the foyer is quiet. It's almost ten. Shit. I head to the elevator and hit the button for the fourth floor. When the rising cubicle slows with a ding, I step out of the sliding door and head for her apartment. I raise a fist to knock but hesitate.

I've never been so self-conscious trying to do the right thing before in my life. After the last night, things seem different—and not in a good way. Needing to know either way, I raise my hand and knock.

The door opens a moment later, revealing a bed-ready Carlie. Her hair is up in a messy bun and her face washed, free of makeup. Navy satin pajamas, a button-down top and long pants, cling to her curves. She's stunning.

"Thanks," she breathes, taking the handle from my hand.

"Sure." I slide my useless hands in my pockets. "Well, it's late and I should get home. Do you have my bag?"

"Oh yeah, come in."

I step inside, and she closes the door. "Sorry, I'll go grab it. I opened it before I even realized it wasn't mine." She walks through the apartment to her bedroom. I lean on the doorframe and wait as she slides the bag from the bed and rolls it toward me.

"Promise I didn't look at your stuff." The cheekiest smile blooms over her gorgeous damn face.

"My Spider-Man undies are safe from prying eyes, then?"

Her laughter echoes through the apartment, and it's then I realize I didn't see Millie.

"Where's Millie?"

Her laughter fades. "She doesn't get back for another three days."

"Right."

"Just me here for the next few nights, which only happens about once a year." She studies my face. It takes all I have to not push off the doorjamb and take her face in my hands, crash my mouth over hers, and devour her where she damn well stands.

"Laws?"

I clear my throat. "Yeah, sorry, I'll go."

She gives me a shy smile.

Since when is this woman shy around me?

I frown, taking my bag from her and making my way toward her front door. Reaching it, I turn back. She's hanging back in the space between the entrance and the kitchen, her bottom lip worried through her teeth.

If I didn't know better, I'd say she's just as confused about this as I am.

A moment passes as we stare at each other, the tension so thick you could mold it with your bare hands. She gazes at my face before settling on my mouth.

I should leave. "I—"

"Law—"

"Sorry, I should," I rasp, nodding sideways to the door.

"Sure, see you tomorrow." Her face falls as if that's the last thing she wants.

Deciding not to push her, I turn back for the door. I have the handle depressed and the door open an inch when she crowds me from behind, her hand slamming onto the door at my shoulder.

"No." The word is barely more than a whisper as the door clicks shut. I drop my head to it as her warmth disappears from behind me.

"What are we doing, Princess?" I grumble into the hard surface.

"Honestly? I have no idea. I've never been so back and forth about anything in my entire life."

The tone she uses, almost accusing, has me spinning back. She stands, hands by her sides and chest heaving, mere inches from me.

I close the last of the distance between us. "Tell me what you want."

"I—"

"Don't overthink it or attach some misguided notion that my motives are anything but straight down the line. I'm not built that way, and you know it."

She huffs a breath, her face turning desperate, like she's been denying herself something for so long the restraint is painful.

"You know what? I'm deciding for the both of us."

I cup her face. When she doesn't move from my hold, I crash my mouth to hers, running my tongue along the seam of her lips. She opens, and I claim her. Palms snap to my chest, pushing, and I break away, searching her face as it registers every mood on the scale of human emotions.

Finally, it settles on a combination of surprise and need.

"Tell me to leave, and I will." I give her one more chance to send me away.

Brown eyes burn into mine as she doesn't breathe a word.

"Fuck, Carlie, baby. You've been driving me insane since our first day at Serenity."

A small smile tips up her lips, but she swallows. She's never been so quiet, ever. I tilt my head, tracking a thumb over her bottom lip. "Talk to me, Princess."

Her eyes close, and she leans into my touch. "I can't." Her words are threadbare.

"Look at me," I grind out.

Her eyes remain closed as she places her palms on my chest. They slide up my neck, and her gaze finally meets mine as I collar an arm around her waist, tugging her into my hold. "Let me in, baby. It's been long enough."

A breathy sob slips from her lips as her fine fingers move over my jaw, and she pulls me down to her. "Don't you dare break my heart, Lawson Rawlins."

"Not going to happen."

"You can't promise that." Her gaze searches my face.

"I can promise you I will break my own heart before I let yours take a hit."

"Can I have that in writing?" She smiles, and it's meek and wobbly.

Fuck. Her Achilles heel, offered up to me on a silver damn platter.

"Will be on your desk in the morning, baby."

Pushing up on her tiptoes, she brushes her lips over mine. I stand, letting her explore as her hands wander, breaths turning choppy. Fingertips run over the angles of my face, lips nipping my own, as I grip her waist with my hands, holding her close.

My cock stretches against the confines of my Levi's, and I drop my head, kissing my way up her neck. She's soft, delicious. Like I knew she would be. I run a hand over her belly, and her breath hitches.

"Laws, please."

Hands sliding under her ass, I pull her up and onto my hips. Her legs wrap around my waist, her mouth devouring my own. I turn back and slam her into the door. Hands tugging through my hair, she gasps. "Fuck, too many clothes . . ."

I suckle my way down her neck to her collarbone. Her back arches off the door, offering up her hard peaks that are straining against the silky fabric of her pajama top. God, how much I want to drag those into my damn mouth.

Thrusting my hips against her, I pin her to the door. Making sure she is secure and won't fall, I work on her buttons, slow like. Taking my time, I flick one open, then another.

Brown eyes burn into me as if pleading with me to hurry the hell up.

I slow my pace a little to see the reaction I get.

She doesn't disappoint, pouting before trying to rip her pajama top from her body.

"Slow down. We're savoring this."

Her eyes widen. "We are?"

"Absolutely," I rasp. The last button pops free, and I drop my mouth to her breast, sucking the nipple. She bucks against the door with a wild little whimper.

She's fucking perfect.

"Oh fuck, Lawson."

I roll the hard peak with my tongue, earning a fist that clamps down in my hair. I bite down and suck the burn that would follow away with one long draw, letting her nipple pop from my lips. Her shoulders are set back onto the door, her head tilted to one side as she writhes against it.

"Baby, look at you." I brush my fingers over the side of her temple, and she turns to face me. My fingers brush over her lips. "More?"

"More."

I peel her from the door, walking through the apartment with her wrapped around my waist. Her hands wander my face, her kisses dotting over my jaw and down my neck. I lose my footing as I groan into her neck before we reach her bedroom.

"You sure?" I rasp.

"Yes, Cowboy. I'm sure."

I set her down on her feet, and she steps back, putting distance between us as she slides the pajama top from her shoulders and it hits the floor. My rock-hard cock turns impossibly harder, throbbing as each breath burns through my lungs. My body vibrates with each heartbeat, blood thundering through my body, concentrating south.

"Now the rest, Princess."

"Who knew you'd be bossy in the bedroom?" Her words are full of sass, as is the curl of her lips as she slips a finger behind the waistband of her pajama pants on each hip.

They join her top and she stands in only black lace panties, stealing the last of my breath at the sight of her.

CHAPTER 26

CARLIE

Who knew standing naked in front of this one man would have me nervous? I don't get nervous with men.

It's never been serious enough to bother.

Until now.

Now, the way Lawson makes me feel is unsettling, like something wild and free with a life of its own. My body trembles as I stand, chest heaving. The wisps of air gracing my lungs despite their desperate rise and fall sears.

I'm out of control. I have no say in the way my body responds to his.

I love it. I hate it.

I *need* him. Every inch of me burns, the only way to douse it being his touch. I'm not sure when this happened, but somehow, he snuck past the wall I so meticulously built to keep people out.

Possibly, it had something to do with the shape of his big heart.

"You tell me to stop, and we will." His knuckles graze my jaw, his blue eyes searching mine. "But hell, Princess." His voice is pure gravel.

I don't want him to stop, even if he—we—could.

I close the distance between us and slide my fingers over his jawline and into his hair as I breathe, "No stopping. No second-guessing. No holding back."

"Don't need to tell a man twice," he growls.

He fucking *growls* at me.

Rough hands grip my ass, and I'm back up on his hips a second later. Hungry open-mouthed kisses travel up my neck, and I roll my head back as my eyes flutter shut with the ecstasy.

Oh god.

He doesn't move toward my bed but the en suite, and I drop my gaze back to him. "Where are we going?"

"After an entire day traveling, shower first."

I huff a laugh. "'Course."

I mean, I showered. But he's still in his day clothes. The thrill of getting to strip Lawson drives me wild. I tug at the hem of his polo impatiently.

He chuckles as we step into the bathroom, and he sets me down on the vanity.

Not where I want to be.

He takes a step back and flips the water on in the shower. I slide off the marble surface and close in on him as he turns back. When I tug on his shirt this time, he raises his arms, and I toss it up and off before letting it fall to the tiles.

Urgh, he's fucking perfect. Toned, just as I remember. All angled muscles and a light dusting of chest hair. The five-o'clock shadow on his jawline adds to the heat radiating from his darkened eyes.

The resort seems like ages ago, or maybe it's the immense change in how I feel about this man making me feel like the journey was long.

I let my fingers wander over the planes of his chest, up and over his shoulders and down his arms, hesitating as my fingers reach his. Lacing them through mine, he closes in on me, pushing my back to the glass door of the shower. "Fuck me, seeing you this way is even better than that sassy little mouth of yours."

His mouth devours mine. I open, desperate, wanting him everywhere.

Wanting him, period.

I send my fingers down his hard stomach, hunting for the fly on those Levi's. Too impatient to wait for him to break from the kiss, I flick it open, shoving his jeans and boxers past his hips. Without losing contact, his tongue swirling against mine, he kicks the jeans to the side.

Heat and wetness flood my center as he grinds his hard length into my apex. I send my hands through his hair, tugging on it to coax him away from my mouth.

Blue eyes the darkened shade of a deep ocean undertow burn into mine.

"Shower, remember . . ." I choke out.

He nods, pressing his forehead against mine as he briefly cups my face. "Shower."

It's when he steps back, taking my hand, that I see the full, raw, bare man in front of me. And holy fucking hell.

If I wasn't on fire before, I am now.

Strong, muscular legs, a flat, hard six pack supporting his toned chest, bulging biceps, and ropey forearms.

God, I'm drooling, I just know it.

Fuck.

Perfection has nothing on Lawson Rawlins.

"You're staring, Princess." He tugs my hand, and we're in the shower a heartbeat later. Instead of washing the long day of travel away, he pulls me into the water stream, hand sliding into my hair as he tugs my head back, closing his mouth over mine. Water rains down over his back and shoulders as he protects me from the hot spray.

Steam curls around the small en suite space, obscuring the visibility. Clouding my head as it goes. Or maybe that's the man gripping me tight, eating me the fuck alive.

I—

I need . . .

I can't breathe.

Fingers curling into his shoulders, I whimper. He breaks away, his gaze studying my face. "Tell me."

Tell you I want to ride your perfect face?

My hands tremble.

Tell you I want to be impaled by the only man to turn my hardened shell into a brittle, useless facade . . .

I try to haul in a useful parcel of air and fail.

Tell you—

"Stop. We're not overthinking this, alright?" His hands grip my face, tilting my gaze up to his.

"I feel like I'm unraveling," I whisper, the last syllable breaking.

He tilts his head, his jaw feathering. "With me, you're supposed to."

His words are earnest, the tone so raw and low, my face crumples. He folds me into his arms, and I sink my face into his neck.

God, this must be what safe feels like.

His hand tangles in my hair as he holds tight. Just holds me.

My unwavering disbelief in love starts to crack. Like the first sign of an earthquake through a cement wall, the crack races up the wall and the broken chip pops from the very top.

I'm done for.

Thoroughly screwed if this goes south.

Lawson releases me, his thumb brushing over my cheek. "I want to see your face fall apart, but not like this. There're better ways to crack this beautiful mouth open."

He dips his head to my neck, suckling, and my breath hitches. He plants hot kisses over my shoulders before his lips close over my hardened nipple. Automatically, my hands slide into his hair, wandering around like they fucking live there. Puttering lazily, as if this moment could last forever.

His lips release my sensitive nipple with a pop.

"Fuck, how long I've wanted to do that, Princess."

"Stop talking about it and do it."

His hand slaps my ass. "Bossy little thing, aren't you."

"Only when it's something I really want."

I'm manhandled against the tiled wall as he sinks to his knees.

"Laws—"

"Not yet, you don't get to say my name yet."

"What?" I breathe.

He looks up, hair wet, on his knees, water droplets littering his skin, and smiles. "Give me a minute or two."

His large hands spread my thighs like he's going to . . .

"Shit, you don't have to."

He glances up with a raised eyebrow. "This, you're worried about? Trust me, baby, if I don't get my mouth on this gorgeous pussy I'm going to fucking implode."

He ducks his head, widening my legs before his finger traces over my entrance.

"Can't have tha—"

One hot, languid sweep of his tongue through my center and I'm buckling against the wall. "Fu—Oh, god."

My hands slap to the tile by my sides. I try desperately to hold myself up as he licks and suckles my clit. Heat pools rapidly in my core.

He bites down, and I jerk against the wall. "The hell?"

A brief grin plays over his lips before he suckles away the sting, and I melt against the tile. "A—again, please. Lawson."

"You like that, baby?"

I nod, the desperate movement harried.

"We can do better."

He dives back in, flicking my sensitive nub with his tongue. Two fingers push into my aching center, and I whimper, eyes shuttering closed as my head lolls to the side.

An orgasm builds, weaving its delicious heat through my core, starting to radiate.

The sting registers as he bites down again. This time, he pumps his fingers slowly as he suckles away the discomfort.

And I explode around him.

One hand grips down on my hip, holding my pussy to his face, and I rock through the blissful waves. Lawson coaxes every incredible wave higher, pumping his fingers, sucking down hard, not letting the contact break. My mouth agape, I can't take my eyes off him as he wrings out the last waves tumbling through my center.

Going limp against the tile, I try to find words to say who knows what. What do you say to the man whose face gave you the orgasm of your life?

Pretty sure those words don't exist . . .

The buzz starts to melt into my bones as my breath returns to normal, and all I want is to see the way he breaks under the same scrutiny.

"Up." I tug on his hair, sliding a hand over his jaw as he stands. "Wall."

He shakes his head. "Shower first, Princess. Then I'm all yours."

"Fine. But just so you're aware . . . this goes both ways."

"It always has, Carlie."

We're not just talking about the pleasure we can give each other, I don't think.

Needing a moment to process that one line, I kiss his cheek and push through the shower door to grab my towel. I dry off and find him a towel before padding to the bed. Checking my phone for any messages or missed calls from Mills—there are zero—I lie on the bed, wrapped in my towel.

The ceiling stares down at me as I scan its pale surface, hunting for the meaning in the last few weeks. How everything I believe is currently being challenged by the very naked, very gorgeous man in my shower.

The water shuts off, and I breathe in a lungful. My body still buzzes with his touch. With the thought of touching him. Seeing his handsome damn face wrecked. I sit up as he pads toward the bed, a towel wrapped around his hips.

He runs a hand through his damp hair, biceps flexing, eyes

pinning me to the bed where I sit. But when he closes the distance, I do something I swore I would never.

I drop from the edge of the bed to my knees.

I look up.

I'm on my knees. For a man.

The part that pulls relentlessly at my heartstrings is why I want to do this. I'm desperate to make him feel good. To make him fall apart for me.

Determined, I slide a finger behind the towel and lift my gaze to his.

"On your knees for me, Princess?"

"Don't let it go to your head, Cowboy."

He smiles, a crooked stunning thing kicking up on one side of his face.

"Open your mouth, baby."

I tug the towel down, and it crumples onto the floor.

"Yes sir."

CHAPTER 27
LAWSON

Carlie takes my cock in her hand and swirls her tongue around the tip, taking the pearl of pre-cum that leaks with the motion. I groan, hands fisting at my sides. "Fuck, baby."

"You like that, Laws?" Big brown eyes look up at me, and it's almost my undoing. Almost.

"Fuck, you have no idea," I grind out.

I swear her eyes darken with that one phrase, and she takes me further into her mouth.

Sweet fucking Christ.

It takes all I have to stay rooted to the spot, to not slam into her pretty mouth as her pink lips slide down my cock. She sucks her way back up, and I groan. I tangle my hands into her hair to hold myself still. With every long, savoring pull of her mouth, it takes more and more to not fuck that pretty mouth, rough, the way I'm desperate to.

"Princess, unless you want it all, you better stop."

"Uh huh," she mumbles around my rigid shaft, her thumb tracking across the sensitive skin beneath my balls. Heat licks up my spine on the next stroke of her perfect damn tongue over the tip.

Yes . . . ? No?

No, don't come?

No, she doesn't care?

"Carlie," I growl, my grip in her hair tightening.

She shakes her head.

Fuck, woman.

She slips a hand down to her pussy, her thumb brushing over her clit on a whimper, and I lose it.

Palming her face, I slam into her mouth. Her eyes water, her whimpers turning into moans. Her fingers wrap around my wrist as she takes me deeper and deeper. Her flawless breasts bounce with every thrust I make into her mouth.

She cries around my cock as she comes, riding her fingers as I release ropey shots onto the back of her tongue.

"Ah, fu-uck, Princess."

She swallows, taking every drop I give her. Her trembling fingers leave her pussy as she stands. When we're eye level, she slides her fingers into my mouth. I groan, sucking them clean. She tastes incredible. Without breaking our gaze, she thumbs the smear of cum over her mouth back in between her lips.

"Now you can go, Cowboy."

Fuck, that's the last thing I want to do.

I haul her into my chest, wrapping her in a tight hug. Her body trembles against mine.

We stand in each other's warmth as our breathing settles. And it's not until goosebumps flood her skin that I let her go. "Need me to tuck you in?"

"Not this time." She huffs a laugh, pushing up on her tiptoes and brushing her lips over my own. Fine fingers claim my jawline as she whispers, "I expect that written request first thing in the morning."

I close my eyes.

"What?" she breathes.

"Nothing." I smile around the word.

"It's not nothing, Lawson." Her voice sounds . . . worried.

Of course it does. This is out of her comfort zone.

I open my eyes to find her chewing her bottom lip before she says, "Just tell me. It was bad, wasn't it?"

I shake my head. "Nope. We're not doing that. I know exactly what I'm getting with you. After this weekend, I hope you do, too."

She opens her mouth to respond, but I lift her jaw up with a finger, closing those pretty lips before dotting a kiss to them. "I'll see you in the morning, Princess," I whisper.

I dress and see myself out.

Hoping like damn hell I didn't just ruin everything.

I get to work an hour early, and the office is quiet. The few women waiting outside were grateful for the early entry, and after making everyone tea and putting out snacks, I head upstairs. Sleeves rolled up and tie already crooked, I get to work on finalizing the new plan before we meet with Serelle.

There's just one catch—I don't think we can tell her about the loss of our major sponsor. Not yet.

I think we should wait until the gala. And then, if we can't replace them, we'll let her know.

It's a risk.

But if Serelle figures we'll never recoup the loss, people will lose jobs. Those women downstairs will have nowhere to go.

Is it really a lie if it's simply withholding information?

I'm in the middle of contemplating my own character flaws when floral and vanilla shrouds me from behind.

"Morning," Carlie whispers into my ear as she leans over, lips brushing my ear. A to-go coffee cup plonks on my desk.

I spin around on my chair, looking up into her gorgeous brown eyes. This morning they look a little different. More . . . mischievous? Happier?

The smile stretching my face sends one blooming over hers. "Ready for this morning's meeting, Princess?"

She sighs. "I really think we should tell Serelle about the sponsor. Withholding that part makes my skin crawl."

I take a sip of the coffee. It's good. It's hot.

Swallowing, I study her face. "No, not yet."

"What? Why not?" Her brows lower as she sips her own coffee.

"Well, if we replace the gap at the gala, it's a nonissue."

"But if we don't?"

"There's a risk that we all lose Serenity."

"Lawson, that's not—"

"I know. I know you're going to say it's misleading and it's lying, but really, it's just better management. This is what she pays us to do. Manage things. And risk is part of management."

"I suppose."

"We are the ones who keep this place funded and growing; that's our job. And we will do it."

"Fine. But I want it on record I was up for telling her about all of it. And what do you plan on telling her about the Christmas gala, then?"

"Well, we promote it that the gala is to extend opening hours and operations."

"It is that, too, I guess."

Worry is etched all over her face, she wrings her hands as her eyes tighten, but she nods. "Let's do it. Between you and me and our secret weapon, pretty sure it will be impossible to fail."

"Our secret weapon?" I raise my eyebrows.

"Ruby Robbins." She gives me a little head tilt lined with sass before padding to her desk and dropping her bag down. "Right, Rawlins. Get back to work."

I chuckle at her and spin my chair back to my workstation. "Yes ma'am." And as automatic as breathing, I give her a two-finger salute. The prettiest damn smile a man's ever seen blooms on her face as she holds my gaze for the moment before it slips, and she opens her laptop.

The gravity of the action lands a heartbeat after my fingers leave my forehead.

Yup . . . this man is done for.

The men in our family have a little tradition of saluting their captain. My father salutes Ma. Hudson, Addy. Reed, Rubes. And Mack—the ex-soldier he is, putting us all to shame —he salutes the hell out of his Gracie. Because a man without his captain is a ship lost at sea.

He may be sturdy in his own right, but she is his direction. His unwavering anchor.

I can't pull my focus from the woman across the room as

this sinks in. It steals the last thought I have, replacing it with a fresh, overwhelming intensity.

One I have no idea if she reciprocates or even could.

The stone that grows in my throat makes me choke on my coffee.

Carlie looks up. "You okay, Cowboy?"

"Yeah, Princess."

She smiles, none the wiser to the hurricane of emotion in my head and heart, and goes back to her work without missing a beat.

Yep, totally fucked.

"Someone pour me a drink," I groan, forehead hitting the wooden bar as Griff slaps my back. Dexter whistles for the waitstaff, waving them down as Miles walks in. The city crew is all here.

I was already three drinks in by the time the boys got off and made their way here from the high-rise they work in for their old man. I guess being partners in one of New York's most-prestigious law firms has its perks—Griff offers to take the tab, apparently since I'm in no state to make financial decisions.

"Fuck man, what the hell?" Miles chuckles as he slides onto a stool by Griff.

"Our boy's fucked, Milo." Dex plasters a shit-eating grin over his stupid face. "She's gone and sunk her damn talons into his soft country-boy heart. Poor bastard never stood a chance."

"I'm right here, Dexter. Right fucking here," I grind out.

He pats my cheek like a little old lady on the subway would. I slap his hand away.

"Like you're one to talk. You're always chasing some skirt." Griff scowls at his twin.

"I like to keep it casual and play the field, brother. Unlike you, you robot. When's the last time you were within three feet of a woman?"

I lean forward and try to catch the waitress's attention again. "Hello?" I wave a hand, almost toppling from the stool.

Griff's grip closes around my biceps. "Woah, bro. This ain't no rodeo."

Every time we drink, they let rip with the country boy jabs. Hate to break it to them, but this man hasn't been on a horse for over ten years. Honestly, compared to my brothers, I'm no country boy. Just a joke straight outta small-town Montana.

I don't fit in here any better than I fit in back home.

Figures, since I literally work in a homeless shelter.

Fuck, this is depressing.

I sway on the stool, and strong arms prop me up. I turn back to find Miles. His kind eyes are lined with worry and a dash of amusement. *Fuck off, buddy.*

"Come on, my man. Time for bed."

"No, I need to get this off my chest." I struggle to stay on the stool. But being manhandled by three guys makes my fight fruitless. A heartbeat later, we're standing on the sidewalk, waiting for an Uber. Miles is strong-arming me so I stay standing on one side, Dex has the other in his rough grip. Griff waves at the Uber driver as the car slows, and we climb in.

Sounds like a bad joke . . . Two lawyers, a fireman, and a businessman climb into a cab. I chuckle, and Miles shakes his head at me. "Bud, the hell. You're going to be hurting in the morning."

I turn my head, slow like, since every effort takes so much. Only to meet his deep browns, and all I can think of is Carlie and the way she's going to rip my heart to pieces. I groan. "Already am, Milo. I already am."

CHAPTER 28
CARLIE

Mills wanders through her favorite shit-and-glitter shop, as she calls it. The cheap shop is what it is. Where you find all sorts of mindless items to waste your change on.

She got home last night, not wasting a second to connect with Henry, as they sat on the phone for hours planning their first date like a couple of teenagers. Now she's nervous and in need of distraction, so here we are.

Me, on the other hand? After an entire day without Rawlins, who called in sick, I was up for anything besides sitting around, overthinking. So, shit-and-glitter retail therapy it is.

"Oh, this is pretty." She holds up a pink glass heart that fits in my palm, almost. It's a little too big to fit comfortably. "You should get this for your desk. It matches your aesthetic, or whatever you young people call style these days."

She drops the glass heart into my hand, and all I can do is stare at it. The replica of my own heart is uncanny. Shiny and unused, really. Hard but fragile at the same time.

I can just imagine it would smash to smithereens.

The sliver of doubt that crept in with Lawson's absence raises its ugly head.

"Put it back, Mills. I have enough crap."

Her face falls. I don't miss the way she slips the heart into her shopping basket as she walks away from me. I won't be surprised when I find it later in my room somewhere. Her heart is always in the right place, unlike mine.

"You almost done, my sweet?" I ask, following her, lost in my own turbulent thoughts.

"Nearly. I want to grab some more bathroom supplies."

She disappears around the end of the aisle as I slow to peruse the candle section. I could use some more tea lights. One can never have too many candles.

My phone pings in my bag. I slide it out and swipe the message open.

Ruby.

Joy floods my veins like it does every time she texts or emails. I will never get over being in her circle . . . Am I in her circle?

Lawson surely is.

I shake my head and focus on the message.

All set for the 24th at the Met. How's the guest list RSVPs coming and the catering?

Guest list is stellar. We are almost at capacity between both our lists and your invite method. Caterers are a go. We should pull this off

Wonderful! Reed and I will be in town the day
before. Also, I hope you don't mind but we
RSVP'd for the whole family, since it's always
months between Lawson visits.

Of course! That's amazing. I'll keep that
between us. It'll be a lovely surprise for him.

Great, I'll let you know when we land on the
23rd.

Thank you 🖤

She hearts my message, and I click my phone off with a content smile over my face. If twenty-year-old me could see this conversation, she would be squealing, jumping out of her skin.

My phone buzzes again as I go to return it back to my bag. I turn it back over and find one more text from Ruby.

Tapping the screen, I read the words and my breath stalls out.

We are just so thrilled Lawson has you in his
life 🤍

We.

His entire family.

This close-knit family stuff builds a pressure behind my ribs that I've never felt before. A soft, fine hand closes around my wrist. "Ready when you are, sweetheart."

I snap my gaze from where it's still stuck on my phone to Mills. She tilts her head before I drop the phone into my bag. I wouldn't know how to respond to that text, even if I wanted to.

"Let's go home." I take the basket from Millie's arm and pay for her items, which earns me a frown and a breathy chastising at the counter where a young girl bags the items.

Out on the sidewalk, we wander to the next tiny family-owned business. A fresh produce shop. Millie disappears inside, claiming to need vegetables. I hover by the boxes of fresh fruit angled for display as an old man in a navy apron bags up citrus fruits for a lady to my right.

Millie reappears with three bags of vegetables, standing in front of the grocer and slipping him cash before I can pay.

The triumphant expression on her face makes me chuckle. Feisty little old woman. "Done, now we can go home." She sets her shoulders back, walking for our building. It's three blocks, and I settle in beside her without a word. I'm too lost in my thoughts to shoot the breeze.

Just when I think I understand this thing between Lawson and I, something tosses a wrench into the works.

"You're far too quiet, young lady. Spill it." Mills loops her arm through my own as we cross the street.

"I think I—"

Her eyes snap up to mine when the tone of my voice registers.

"I'm not sure I'm cut out for a relationship, Mills."

She slaps my arm with her free hand. "Fiddlesticks. Strong women have successful relationships every day."

I chuckle at her, but it's breathy and weak.

I don't feel strong. I feel pulled in every direction, unable to choose one.

I don't believe in love. At least not the fairy-tale type. There is no such thing as meeting one person who fixes everything. That's useless bullshit. But . . .

And it's a big but.

Lawson has debunked so many other things I've held onto to keep my heart safe for so long. He's not trying to get promoted over me. He takes care of me before he worries about himself. He's selfless that way. Lawson Rawlins is all heart, and fuck if he doesn't rile me up in a way I never thought possible.

I wouldn't swipe right on this man. He's not a good time, he's . . . a lifetime kind of thing.

That right there scares the hell out of me.

I asked him not to break my heart, and the man promised to break his before he let mine take a hit. What kind of guy does that?

A magnificent one, that's who.

On our floor, I slide the key into the door and let us in.

"Ugh, Mills." I close the door behind me and lean against it, letting my head fall back, hitting the wood with a thump.

She turns back, startled. "Montana was that good, hey?"

"No—"

She folds her arms and pins me with her 'don't you dare lie to me, little miss' expression.

On a sigh, I breathe, "What if I can't give him what he deserves? Hell, I barely believe in the concept of love."

She closes the space between us, her expression softening as she rests a hand on my shoulder, looking at me. "If love is anything, my girl, it's a risk. But when you find the right man? It's a non-brainer."

I huff a strangled laugh. "It's 'no-brainer', Mills."

"Yeah, that one. That's what love is when you find it. It will be the easiest decision you ever make."

"It doesn't fix my baggage."

She shrugs. "Who says it needs fixing? Geez, leave it behind and replace it with better possessions."

I frown at her before raising an eyebrow. "What?"

"I'm saying, replace your luggage or whatever you call it with things you place more value on. Like family, the one you create. Not the one you left behind. Honey, you already did it once before. Hence, I'm here."

She turns away, heading for the kitchen. "Listen to me." She waves her hands in the air with a manic laugh. "I'm freaking Dr. Phil."

Our little lady watches far too much daytime television now that she's not working.

Good, it's about time she was a lady of leisure.

It's my pleasure to take care of her. I always will.

Hours later, I slide into bed, exhausted from the nonstop reel of what-ifs and scenarios playing through my head. Laying my head down on the pillow, I jolt as something hard digs into the side of my face.

"What on earth?" I utter, sending my hand under the pillow.

Cool, hard angles meet my fingertips.

I pull out the pink glass heart. Setting it on my bedside, I lie down, head on my pillow and hands under my head. Now, staring into the endless pink nothing of the heart, I let myself wonder for the first time what it would be like to be someone's priority. Someone's everything.

I ignore the pulse of dread in my gut as my body fights this new willingness to let go and hand my heart over to a man. That's how I drift into the deep sea of new dreams, with thoughts of Lawson beside me. His warmth. His love. My fight. My determination. One big, beautiful life.

Our life.

As the first tear soaks into the pillow, I force my eyes closed, reprimanding myself for my wishful thinking.

The photocopier, the stinking relic that it is, just ate my motherfucking menu mockup.

The hell?

With a frustrated groan, I head for the one man I know can fix it. My cowboy. Copy wrangler from the hills. I chuckle as I swing into the fish tank with a, "Hey, give me hand?"

Lawson looks up from his screen, his handsome face breaking into a smile. The kind that lights up his eyes and my stupid heart.

Settle the fuck down, heart.

And I see you, ovaries, and you can just sit the hell down.

He follows me to the copier room, hands in his pants pockets, sleeves rolled up as always, tie crooked from him fussing with it the way he does when he's thinking.

He turns back to shut and lock the door, and I realize how much I know about this man. It sends a jolt of joy tangled with fear down my spine. "The copier ate my mockup. I need it back."

He chuckles and crowds me against the machine. At least in here, no one can see us, unlike our glass office that feels like we're reality TV stars and the whole entire staff floor is waiting for a fight or for us to fuck and get it over and done with.

"First, this." His hands take my face as his mouth descends over mine.

I open, unable to put up any sort of a fight when it comes to Lawson. He sweeps in, plundering my mouth, setting my body on fire. My legs widen automatically as he moves between them. My hands wander through his hair. He nips my bottom lip, and I tug on his hair, now messy from my fingers crawling through it.

God, I love him this way.

Fuck.

Fuck. Fuck. Fuck.

No, no, that—this—is not happening. I push him away.

His brows fall. "You okay?"

"No. No, I'm not."

I swallow and choke on the movement. I shove my face into my hands. Each breath starts out shorter than the last as I lean on the copier. It groans, a plastic whining sound, protesting my weight, and the floor hits my ass. Dots flood the peripherals of my vision.

"Dammit, Carlie." Lawson is by my side a heartbeat later.

I can't breathe.

"Laws—"

I claw at my chest.

"Breathe, baby. Come on."

A strangled whimper leaves my throat at his soft tone. As if every action he takes and every word he says reinforces the overwhelming epiphany that just took me down.

My hands cramp, my face stiffens. What the hell is happening to me?

Thumbs rub over my cheekbones as he demonstrates deep

breaths. I hold the blue eyes in front of me with my gaze, like they are my last lifeline.

"You're panicking. You have to focus on your breath. In, one, two, three, four. Out, one, two, three, four."

I haul in a breath and hold it before letting it go.

The tingling in my hands starts to fade.

"Good girl. Tell me three things you can see."

"I—" He tilts his head, giving me a reprimanding look. *Fucking bossy damn cowboy.* "Paper. Disposable cups. Stapler."

"Two things you can feel."

My hands gravitate to his chest. "Heartbeat. Warmth."

"Good, now, tell me one thing I don't know."

Pretty sure that's not part of the grounding technique. "Nice try, Laws."

"Humor me."

"Why?"

"Because nobody gets that look without something significant affecting them. Tell me, Princess," he rasps.

I can't deny him. Not when his desperate face is tangled with so much worry.

I run my fingertips over his jawline, ghosting them over his bottom lip. "I want you more than anything before," I mutter.

His Adam's apple bobs, and he closes his eyes. "Just promise me one thing."

The words are so raw, my breath hitches. "Anything."

"Take your time, make sure you're certain. 'Cos there's no coming back from this for me."

He dots a kiss to my forehead before rising, flipping the copier lid open, and manhandling the machine. The menu mockup presses into my hand before he leaves, closing the door and shutting me in.

Sitting on the floor with ink staining my fingers, my heart pounds against my ribs, protesting its way free. Like if it could leave and follow behind him, it would.

And I don't know what the hell to do with that.

Not a damn clue.

CHAPTER 29
LAWSON

After a long day and a long-ass run to try to process everything flying around in my head, I slide the key into my apartment door and let it loose. It's dark inside. The lamp I always leave on in the corner by the sofa is off. I pull my phone from my pocket and tap the flashlight feature. The small bright light floods the living room.

Everything seems to be in its place. I sweep a hand over the wall. It's then I notice something on the floor, fluttering in the draft from the open door. I hunt for the light switch again, only to find it taped over.

"What the hell?" I utter. I shine the beam at the taped-up switch. Next to the switch, a pink sticky note is attached to the wall.

Leave me off is scribbled over the note.

I move the light to the floor and scan the closest sticky note.

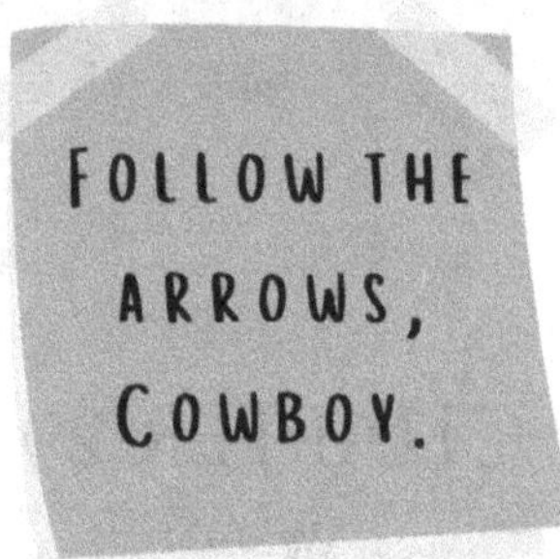

The smile that stretches my face would look ridiculous if anyone could see it. Luckily for me, the goofy smile that rose with Carlie's nickname for me is safe from being seen in the dark. I turn back and kick the door closed.

Following the arrows, I track over four more sticky notes before I find one on the wall by my bedroom.

I look down to find an oversized silver candle with three wicks sitting on the small side table by the door. My side table by the sofa. She must have moved it. Tossing my backpack onto said sofa, I light the candle as instructed. Sulfur infuses the air as all three wicks burn to life.

Replacing the matches, I find another sticky note.

> TAKE ME WITH YOU, FLIP ME OVER WHEN YOU STEP INSIDE THE BEDROOM.

I step inside the darkened bedroom, and when I flip over the small square pink note, it reads . . .

> PRESS THE BIG BUTTON, COWBOY.

With a chuckle, I hunt around the doorframe for a button. Finding a round button just below eye level, I press my palm into it.

Fairy lights flicker to life, illuminating my bedroom.

And . . . the stunning blonde draped over my bed.

How the?

"Hi," she breathes. Her lips curve into a smile as she lies on my bed, propped up on the pillows on the side of the bed I never use. Like she knows where she belongs.

Her hair is pulled around one side of her neck, cascading

down her shoulder. In only black lingerie, she is the most addictive illusion. I can't take my eyes off her.

Instantly, blood sinks, sending my cock to aching hard in seconds. Harried breaths whip from my chest.

"Hey, Princess. What's all this?" I rasp.

"Aren't you going to ask me how I broke and entered your apartment?"

"Nah, you can take anything you want."

"I plan to," she says softly.

Now she leans forward, her finger beckoning me closer. As I close the distance between where I stand and the foot of the bed, she crawls toward me.

Fucking crawls.

Her long legs are bare. Her brown eyes hold me where I stand as she reaches the end of the bed and rises onto her knees. My hands ache to hold her, but I let them hang by my sides as she explores my face with the pads of her fingers. A fine worship, inch by inch.

"I love the way you feel. The angles that make up your jaw, your cheekbones. All of it," she whispers. Her hands move over my chest, and she straightens, amusement flooding her face. "Nice shirt."

Ah, fuck.

"Is this so you remember where you come from?" She giggles.

I glance down at the Montana shirt Ma sent me. Her not-so-subtle way of reminding me to come home whenever I can. "Something like that."

But I don't belong in Montana—*here* is where I'm needed. Here is where I want to build a life.

I swallow past the stone growing in my airway.

She scared me the other day in the copier room. The way she freaked out over being close . . . the way it smashed my heart up watching her falling apart.

It's not that I can't handle her emotions or her attitude. That's not it at all. Seeing her hurting was one of the hardest moments I've lived through. It may as well have been my lungs suffocating.

Leaving her sitting on the floor was the hardest thing I've had to do in a long while. But if I've learned anything from managing the anxiety that plagues my family, space and time help. As does a safe place to fall. And I want to be that for Carlie more than anything.

Only, she has to let me in first.

Really let me in.

"Carlie," I rasp.

Her fingers fall from my face.

"Lawson?" My name is torn between a plea and a whisper.

"Talk to me. Tell me what you want." I can barely get the words out, terrified she'll tell me something I don't want to hear.

"What do you mean?" Her thumb sweeps over my lips, my jaw, as the pads of her fingers track through my hair.

"This thing between us, serious or not serious?"

Studying my face for a beat, she sucks in a breath. "Serious."

Thank fuck.

I groan as she slides her palm over my chest, letting it hover over my heart.

"I can't promise I know how to do this right. But you would be the first man to ever make me want to try." Her head tilts to one side as her face breaks.

Sweet Jesus, baby.

I cup her face and smash my mouth to hers.

She claws at my shirt, and I raise my arms for her to remove it. Breaking apart briefly, it flies across the room, landing somewhere by the bathroom door.

"God, Laws, you're addicting."

I chuckle. "You oughta talk, baby, in those fucking panties."

Her hands make quick work of my boxers and running shorts. I really do need a shower. After almost ten miles of pounding the pavement for a little solace, I'm all dried sweat and stink.

"I need to shower first."

"No," she whines.

"Yes, trust me. You'll appreciate the clean Lawson much more than the smelly one."

"Maybe," she says, but sits back on her heels. "You have five minutes, Cowboy."

I fly into the bathroom like a man on a mission and am out in under four minutes. Fastest shower in history. Every minute I'm away from her is too long.

I don't bother with a towel when I hop out, opting for speed over dryness. I'm dripping wet when I make it back to the bed.

Carlie climbs me like a damn squirrel up a tree, and I hold her on my hips, devouring her neck.

"Oh my god, you're still wet," she says with a giggle.

I shake my head like a dog, sending droplets over her, the bed, and the floor. A squeal flies from her mouth as she holds up two hands in front of her face, laughing. Her head tips back.

The sound of her happiness lights a fuse in my veins.

My chest warms to the sound of it.

My body vibrates with need for this little woman.

"God, where have you been all my damn life, baby," I growl, dropping my lips to the soft spot below her ear. Her laughter peters out, turning to a moan as she settles on my hips, her hands running into my hair.

"Waiting here, for you. It took you long enough."

I huff a breathy laugh, but she takes my face in her hands. "You make me feel things I never thought I would have the privilege to feel. Things I . . ." She glances at the ceiling as a strangled sound leaves her lips. "I didn't believe this kind of pull between two people existed before. Before you."

"You didn't believe in what?"

"I don't . . . I didn't believe in love. It's so manufactured, it hardly feels real, let alone attainable."

"That's damn sad, baby." I run my hand over her cheek and cup her jaw. "Lucky I came along then, hey."

"Maybe."

"Maybe?"

I toss her on the bed, and she giggles. I crawl over her, planting my hands on either side of her head, caging her in with my knees. Errant drops of water fall onto her gorgeous skin.

"You need me to show you what it looks like?"

"What *what* looks like, Laws?"

"Love, baby."

She studies my face, hesitating. "Just a peek."

I kiss her, hard. Hungry.

She breaks, letting me in.

I claim every part she lets me, and when she's left breathless—as am I—I track my kisses down her neck, over her collarbones.

"This underwear is stunning, you're stunning, but it's coming off," I rasp.

She arches her back, and I release the clasp. A heartbeat later, the bra hits the wall somewhere and drops to the floor. I brush my lips over one hard peak and then the other. My girl arches off the bed with a little whimper and a mewl when I clamp down around the delicious peak.

I have her writhing underneath me as I splay one hand over her ribs, holding my weight with the other. Her skin is so soft, the taste of her is intoxicating. I kiss and suckle my way over her belly. Hands dig into my hair as I descend lower and lower down her body, inch by fucking agonizing inch. My rock-hard cock presses into the mattress, only reminding me I'm nowhere near where I want to be.

But this is me showing her love.

Taking my damn time.

Because my gut tells me this moment is an important one, and over hell's frozen balls am I screwing this up for her. For us.

"Laws, please," she gasps.

I nip and kiss low on her belly, readjusting my knees to be inside her thighs. "Patience."

She moans, and I swear she utters something that sounds like, "I don't have any when it comes to your hands on me."

Shuffling backward, I widen her thighs with my hands and track my finger up one creamy thigh, then the other, careful not to touch the sensitive places she is desperate for me to find. I get a protest in the shape of a huff when I take my sweet fucking time, tracking my thumb around her pretty little clit without touching it.

"Lawson *goddamn* Rawlins, I swear."

I huff a laugh, but who am I kidding, I'm as strung out as she is. I sweep my tongue through her center with one long, languid stroke, and her back flies off the bed, hands turning to fists in my hair.

"Oh fuck," she whimpers.

"Slow down, my girl. We're taking our time."

With a moan, she plants a kiss into my hair and lies back down. I send my tongue through her soaked pussy again, and fuck if my balls don't tighten with her taste. I could survive the rest of my life just eating this gorgeous woman out. I'd never go hungry again.

With a suckle of her clit, I have her writhing on the bed, hands sliding down the covers, hunting for my hair again. Where they fucking belong. I swirl my tongue around her sensitive nub before pushing two fingers inside.

She gasps, hips bucking. "Fu-uck . . . Laws."

I curl my fingers, biting down on her clit.

I'm rewarded with wave after wave as she tightens around my fingers, her body quaking with every single one. The pretty little whimpers tumbling from her parted lips are the best fucking sound I've ever heard. She rides my face and hand until her orgasm ebbs.

I look up, my mouth still on her sweet pussy when she rises off the bed, looking down at me. Fine fingers curl around my jaw, tugging me up toward her as she breathes, "More."

CHAPTER 30
CARLIE

I want Lawson's weight. I want his touch, his kisses. I want all of him.

God, it's been how long—maybe never?—since a man has drowned me this way. I'm all out of air. I was the second he stepped through his bedroom door in the candlelight.

I want to . . .

I scramble over the bed to where he now stands after giving me a mind-blowing orgasm with his mouth, chest heaving, taking me in. And I climb this man like the damn tree he is.

I want him to feel this intense, ridiculously overwhelming feeling I have for him. I pepper his face in kisses, tracking them down his neck. His throat works as his hands slide underneath me.

"Prin—" he chokes.

"Shhh. My turn."

My turn to shower him in every mushy feeling I have for him. In every tug of my heart that I swear you could see on my face from space. Fingers in his hair, I claim his mouth with mine. Hunting for permission, I tighten my grip, and he opens.

He's hard underneath me. My soaked pussy grinds against his hard stomach as I devour him.

My hands tremble as they lower down his neck and back up under his jaw. He catches my gaze, and we can only stare, desperate breaths puffing from our lips, mingling in the small space between us.

"Ca—"

I press a finger over his lips.

His face falls, and he swallows.

"Still my turn, Laws."

I release my legs, sliding down until my feet hit the floor. But I don't stop, sinking to my knees.

"Fuck, baby. The sight of you on your damn knees. Is there anything more incredible . . ."

"There is, actually." I slide him into my mouth, not breaking eye contact.

"Christ, *woman*."

He shakes where he stands, every inch of his muscular body vibrating as I take him into my mouth as far as I can, wrapping my fingers around the base of him. With one intense stroke, I pull up with a pop, leaving him stranded.

"Good girl." His face curls in a half snarl as his lips part, hands folding around my face. "More."

Without hesitation, I sink him into my mouth. Swirling my tongue, I tease his engorged tip.

Fuck. His grip on my face turns punishing.

I graze my teeth over the tip before taking him deep again. This time, he moves. Hitting the back of my throat. I fight back the tears that swell with his need. I love that I can give him this. That he can take what he needs with me.

It's incredible.

I clamp down around him, sucking my way back up. Reaching his tip, I sweep my tongue over the small opening, taking the salty offering he gives me.

He groans, low and raw.

A heartbeat later, rough hands haul me to my feet. A hungry, wet, open-mouthed kiss covers my mouth. His hands tug me back onto his hips as he moves forward, hitting the bed before he drops me onto it. I huff out a sound that's a tangle of surprise and absolute need. Lawson cages me in for a kiss before he stands and slides his hands behind my knees.

His thumb circles my clit before he sends two fingers through my soaked entrance. "This right here is mine, Princess. Don't you ever forget it."

I shake my head.

No forgetting here, Cowboy.

I ache for him. My clit throbs with an agonizing jolt with every heartbeat.

"Please, Laws."

He hauls me to the edge of the bed, raising my hips upward to his. "Keep begging, baby. Go on, see what it gets you."

Beg. The fucker wants me to damn beg.

. . . I absolutely will.

"Come on, Cowboy, give me every sweet fucking inch of you."

"Sweet?" He raises an eyebrow.

"You heard what I said," I say with a smirk. Winding this man up is one of my favorite pastimes.

He tilts his head as his jaw flexes. His arms tense as he lines the tip of his cock with my entrance.

"Please, Laws . . . Every. Single. Inch."

His grip tightens as his stare burns into me. As if he's trying to decide who this is going to destroy more, him or me.

I slide a hand up my ribs, cupping my breast before rolling the nipple between my fingers. My eyes flutter shut as my back leaves the bed.

"Fuck me," he growls.

The second my eyes open again, he slams into me with a force that sends me backward on the bed. I gasp, grappling with the stretch needed to take all of him.

Oh fuck.

FUCK.

"Law—" I cry out, but the word disintegrates as he pulls out and slams into me again.

His hand wraps around my calf, lifting my leg over his shoulder as he thunders into me. His face breaks a little further with every demanding thrust.

Warmth winds through my core, and the tantalizing sparks of release taunt me, building with each move Lawson makes. I send a hand to my aching clit.

Deep blues burn into me as he smacks my hand away. "Nope. Not yet, Princess."

I huff an indignant sound, removing my leg from his shoulder. His only reply is a smirk as his movements slow before he settles over me, fists digging into the mattress on either side of my head. "You poutin' on me, Princess?"

"Give me what I want."

"Don't be so goddamn impatient. You'll get what you need more times than you can count. You just have to trust me."

I open my mouth to respond, but something deep in my chest snaps. I swallow around the emotion it brings and simply nod.

This is it . . . the moment I give in to a man.

Surprisingly, I don't hate it.

His cock must have fucked with my logic and reason.

Because, *shit*.

His knuckles brush over my jaw, and he takes my mouth with his. I arch up, wanting what he's giving up. For me.

Deep, methodical thrusts snag my attention, turning me into a writhing mess underneath him once again. I adore him inside me. We fit. We better than fit.

We're . . . heaven.

"Laws, I can't—"

I can't stop the blinding orgasm that's tugging me off the edge and into oblivion.

"Good girl. Milk my fucking cock. Get used to it, because you'll be doing it again and again before we're done."

His mouth sinks over my nipple. He sucks, nips, and suckles until the waves of ecstasy leave me ragged. I lie limp, hands over my head, and he stills for a beat, kissing my neck and nipping my jaw.

"Keep count for me, Princess."

"Count?"

"That was number one."

Oh shit.

I huff a chuckle, and he slides a hand under my shoulders. "We're moving."

I'm on his hips again as he walks from the bedroom to the kitchen. My ass hits the counter, and he spreads my thighs with his palms, slowly. His gaze snags on where we're joined.

His body is alive with exertion, a light sheen of sweat making him look like some kind of god.

"Laws . . ."

I don't know what I want to say. Only that I need to say it. Without the luxury of words, I trace a hand over his cheek and down his jaw.

He pulls out, slowly, letting the tip rim my entrance, and it steals my breath.

"God, fuck, Carlie. How the hell are you this damn perfect?"

I can't breathe. I can't manage to catch any amount of useful air in my lungs. Lawson's warm hand cups the back of my neck, and our foreheads are pressed together.

"Breathe, Princess. Fuck, you're so tight. Relax for me."

"Too big," I breathe but manage a nod.

Sex has never affected me like this before. It was simply another basic human need on Maslow's pyramid to be taken care of. There's never been a connection. Only a physical thing where we both got off.

This . . .

This is taking a wrecking ball to my heart.

Making every word, every touch, every kiss . . . Obliterating.

I'm free-falling.

And it's terrifying.

"Lawson, please."

"Tell me what you need."

"Stop." I press a palm to his chest, and his eyes flood with worry. "No—don't. Urgh. Please, I just—"

"Hey." He cups my face. "Anytime you want out, say so."

"I want to . . ."

My hands shake as he pries their white-knuckle grip from the counter's edge. "We can stop."

"No. No, I don't want to stop. I—it's . . ."

"Overwhelming?"

"Yeah, that."

"I know, baby. Fuck, I know."

His jaw feathers. I take my hands from his warm hold and wrap them around his jaw. This is affecting him as much as it is me.

I search his gaze and find a mix of need and vulnerability.

Oh.

I huff a sound that's halfway to relief.

Trust.

That's what he asked for.

So that's what I'm going to try to give him. Along with everything else he needs. I drag his mouth down to mine, letting my lips brush his as I say, "I've never done this before, but I really want to with you, Cowboy."

He chuckles, dotting a brief kiss to my lips. "Me too, Princess."

"Now that we settled that . . . I'm collecting on those orgasms, Lawson Rawlins."

"Yes, ma'am."

His hand travels into my hair, wrapping it around his fist. He tugs my head back, and a heartbeat passes before he slams into me with a darkened gaze.

I'm clawing at his shoulders, unable to stop myself. Hell, it's as if he's unraveling me from the inside. It's addictive. It's bliss.

My breasts bounce with every thundering thrust.

Earning me the agonized expression now growing on his face. God I could come just watching this man annihilate my body with his.

As if on cue, he sweeps a thumb over my clit. "Come for me, baby. Now."

I shatter on the next exhale, moans tumbling from my lips.

"God, fuck. You have no idea what you do to me when you come around my damn cock, Carlie."

I couldn't respond even if I wanted to.

Drowning in his words and in the full length of him as he seats himself deep, I can only stare at him as he scoops my pliant body from the counter and heads back to the bedroom.

"Where are we going?" The question is redundant. Completely. Because what do I care? But if I don't say something, do something, I'm likely to fall apart.

I am *not* going to be that girl. The one who cries during the best sex of her fucking life.

"We're not done yet, baby."

He sits on the bed, up by the headboard, and leans onto it, his arms falling by his sides. "Save a horse, darlin'."

It takes a hot minute for me to gauge his meaning. When I do, I can't help but decide to take a little of the control back. I rise on my knees, letting his cock fall away. Our groans tangle as we both cope with the loss. I spin around and plant my knees on either side of his hips. Pulling my hair over my shoulder, I look back.

Slowly, ever so slowly, I lower onto his hard length. Holding his gaze, I wait until I'm fully seated before whispering, "This what you want, Laws?"

"Fuck yes. You gotta move."

He's desperate for me to move, judging by the way his hands knead my ass, willing me to rise.

And I do.

Excruciatingly slowly.

His head falls back onto the headboard, and a smile fueled by pure satisfaction blooms over my face.

"Sweet Jesus, woman, looking at you like this. Was worth every insult you ever threw my way."

I chuckle and hover with his tip only just lodged in my entrance. "This has you all fucked up, does it?"

"Hell yes," he growls.

I cant my ass a little and fall until the full length of him is sunk deep inside. My breasts bounce and the sensation drives me insane. Fuck, I love this for us. This is the most turned on I've ever been. I fondle my breasts and rise again. "Eyes on me, Cowboy."

He snaps his deep blues open and takes in my figure swallowing his cock, my hands on my breasts, before his gaze locks with mine. "Bounce, baby."

"You want me to bounce, you're going to have to give me your hands, everywhere."

With a wry smile, he pushes off the headboard and closes the space between us, my back flush against his chest. He cups my breasts. "Show me that bounce, Princess. Bounce on my fucking cock until you come all over it." He nips my ear, teeth grazing down my neck, and I whimper.

His swollen length twitches inside me.

My reminder to get moving.

I roll my hips, and the pressure is delicious.

On a whimper, I lay my head back on his shoulder. I need a moment to savor Lawson inside me. Just a—

Sting spreads over my right ass cheek.

I jolt, crying out, rising a little before falling again.

"That's it. Need another one?"

"Lawson . . ." His name is a plea that disintegrates on a cry.

Fuck. I'm not going to last another few seconds this way, let alone however long it takes to get him off watching me bounce on his cock.

With a squeeze and a tweak of one of my aching nipples, he breathes, "Now, Princess."

I rise and fall, my hands gravitating behind me and into his hair.

Lawson vibrates beneath me. His grip shifts to my waist briefly before a hand fists my hair. With a subtle tug, my head tilts back, forcing me to arch my back. The new angle he's created between us is too much. I rise and fall, faster and faster, chasing the pleasure I've never had before. Not like this.

I'm bouncing. Desperately hunting my release. Up and down his every inch.

"Fuck, Carlie. Fuck."

I whimper. Unable to form a single word.

Breasts bouncing, head pulled back, I explode around him with a strangled cry.

"Oh fuck. Laws—god above," I mewl as my soul comes apart at the seams. My heart twists in my chest as he roars behind me, one hand slamming my hip down, the other pulling me back further as he utters, lips brushing my ear, "This is what you do to me, Princess. Only you."

Thrusting up into me with erratic movements, he sends his hot release inside me.

With a groan, he releases my hair, pulling me into his chest. His arms are wrapped around me a heartbeat later. He mumbles something into my hair I can't catch over the noise of my own pounding heart. But warmth floods my chest, and I turn and plant a kiss to his sweaty brow.

Something hard and cold chips from my heart.

The warmth he gives up for me finds the opening and claims it. Making my heart swell. Cracking the hardened veneer surrounding it. Setting it to shatter.

One more act of adoration would send it plummeting.

"Seeing you fall apart is the most incredible thing I've ever witnessed," Lawson breathes. "Fuck, you're beautiful, baby."

I'm pretty sure this man can read my mind . . . Because damn, that last blow was everything.

Fuck, if this is love, I'll take it.

CHAPTER 31
LAWSON

Strawberry blonde occludes my vision when I wake up Saturday morning. Warmth pressed against my body. My cock is now rock fucking hard for the woman in my arms. I plant a kiss into her hair, careful to be gentle and not wake her. After our first time—which will be stored in my memories for a lifetime—we had another and another. As if making up for lost time.

We both stopped counting after the third round.

But my girl has a healthy flush on her pretty damn cheeks, and the fact I put it there may just be one of my proudest moments.

"Mhmmmm." She rolls over in my arms.

I toss the blanket over our heads as she blinks awake, her perfect body pressing against mine. God, what I wouldn't do to devour those perfect fucking tits right now.

"Morning, Princess."

"Mornin', Cowboy," she drawls.

I chuckle and roll her onto her back. She looks up at me.

Her big brown eyes are an abyss of emotion. From surprise, to need, to adoration.

"Breakfast time, my girl." I cage her in, nudging her chin up with my nose as I kiss her neck.

"Great, I'm starving."

"Me too."

I travel down her soft-as-fuck skin, dotting kisses as I go.

"God, Laws, you're insatiable."

I chuckle against her skin, which makes her writhe with a giggle. Her hands shoot down, gripping my shoulders. The sheet covers us both, and in our makeshift tent, she peers down at me. "God, I want to. So badly. But I have to get my errands done before Mills gets home. Rain check?"

I drop my head to her belly with a groan.

"We'll have heaps of time later, I promise." Her hands run through my hair.

"Just one taste?" I beg.

My cock is aching to be wrapped in this sweet pussy. But if I can give her one moment to keep her satisfied throughout the day, I will.

"Fine," she breathes. "Only a taste, I've got to get ho—"

I sweep my tongue through her center.

She spreads her legs like her soaked pussy is my goddamn smorgasbord. And it fucking is.

I suckle her clit, then lick her entrance before concentrating over her sweet, sensitive nub. I pop my head up, licking my lips. "All good now."

"Oh . . . no." Grabby hands shove my shoulders down, hips bucking up in a pleading motion.

The smile that cracks my face is ridiculous.

It's just too easy, Princess. And I fully intend on giving her an orgasm before she leaves my apartment to start her day.

"More, baby?" I rasp.

Her whimper as she fondles her breasts is all I need. I dive in, sending my tongue deep into her pretty little cunt, pinching her clit with my fingers while the other hand pushes two digits deep inside her.

With a few strokes into her tight pussy, I have her writhing on the bed.

So . . . I take it all away and push up onto my elbows.

"What? No!" She snaps up off the bed, leaning on her elbows.

"Something wrong?" I raise an eyebrow.

I'm an asshole, I know. But I love seeing her needy as fuck for me. This strong, incredible woman who folds for me. It's damn addicting.

"You want it, you sit on my face," I say with a growl.

"No, I can—" She frowns, chest heaving. "Please, just give me more, Laws."

I shake my head and crawl up the bed. Caging her in, I sweep an arm under her and flip us over.

"Now, on my face."

She searches my expression for a beat before moving up the bed on her knees.

"Hands on the headboard, Princess."

"O—kay."

I knead her ass with my hands. She moans but doesn't lower her soaked pussy.

"Are you sure?" she whispers.

"Down. Now."

She doesn't move, and I slap her ass. Hard.

"Oh fuck," she breathes.

I grip her hips and plant her pussy over my mouth.

Which earns me a whimpered, "Oh fu-uck. Laws . . ."

I would tell her she's a good girl, but my mouth is full. In the best fucking way possible.

I suckle, lick, and fuck her tight cunt with my tongue. Slowly, she starts to rock her hips, her hands sliding over the headboard.

I lap at her entrance, and her chest caves.

I bite down on her clit, and she cries out.

I suckle the sting away, and she screams my name.

I rim her entrance with a finger, and when I feel the first flutter of her pussy, I slide two fingers inside, curling them forward.

The sweet sounds that tumble from her parted lips as she comes all over my damn face will keep me hard for weeks. I'll never be able to top this moment. Her first time on my face. Big brown doe eyes looking down, holding my gaze, as she falls apart above me.

Fucking priceless.

Fucking priceless, Princess.

Dex and Griff run ahead as we make our way around Central Park. The only reason those two run is so they can drink on the weekends. Never having wanted for a thing save the silver spoon in their mouths they grew up on, the boys are down-to-earth, considering their massive wealth.

When we first met in college, Miles, me, and the brothers, I was always waiting for the penny to drop. For them to realize that, unlike the three of them, I'm not from money. At least not from their caliber of coin.

"Catch up, Rawlins." Dexter glances over his shoulder.

"Why are you so slow this morning?" Griff spins, running backward before tilting his head in an exaggerated thinking pose.

"Oh yeah, that's right. Our boy got laid," Dex yells back.

Fuck me.

"Leave him alone, you dipshits." Miles's voice booms from behind, his footfalls pounding the track as he closes in. I slow a little, looking back to find him winding through the other runners.

"Where'd you come from, bud?" I ask as he catches up.

We hit an equal stride, and he grins at me.

"Not you, too," I rasp.

"Never. I, unlike those ingrates, am happy for you. 'Bout fucking time."

The smile breaking over my lips as I pant to keep up his stride would put the Joker to shame.

Miles slaps me on the shoulder. "Saw you lot fly past. Starting without me these days, are we?"

"Nah, bud. Never." But my grin doesn't slip.

"Fucker," he huffs and leaves me in the dust.

Ass.

I pick up the pace and catch them all before overtaking them as we reach the starting point. I pace a few laps before heading for the food cart and grabbing a water.

"What took you so long?" I quip when Griff files in by the truck, holding his side like his once-a-week run isn't railing him with a stitch right now. Dexter flails to a stop by his brother. "Remind me why we do this every fucking weekend?"

Miles strides over, cool as a goddamn cucumber with his ridiculous firefighter fitness. "Got to keep you in line somehow, Dex."

"Would you please go and stand over there," Dex says, waving him away. "How are any of us supposed to get laid with your man candy ass hanging around?"

Miles chuckles and messes up Dex's hair with his oversized hand, flexing forearm, and bulging biceps. Hell, Dex has a point, bu—

"You're out, too, Rawlins. You two both stand somewhere else while we wait for the rest of the running babes to come in." Dex is still waving us off, his brother rolling his eyes as he checks his phone. "Come on, track tramps. Lycra ladies. Jogging jezebels."

It's all a joke, we know that. The guy doesn't have a serious bone in his body. I'm guessing he really needs to ge—

Miles pins him with a look we can all read, one that means Dex has gone too far. "Disrespect. Yeah, that'll get you laid every time. Cut it out, Dexter."

Dex holds his hands up in a 'don't shoot' gesture. A sheepish look crosses his face before he schools it back to his usual goofy expression. Sometimes I wonder what woman would take him on. He's kind of a lot.

"Sorry, Dad." Dexter wanders off to the drink truck and grabs a Gatorade.

"Come on, Laws, let's leave these two. Give me a hand holding down the sofa?"

"Sure thing."

I wave to Griff, who barely glances up from his phone, his face twisted by concern. He manages to nod, and we hike it five blocks to Miles's apartment. As a member of FDNY Engine 53, his new apartment is closer to work. And a touch larger than mine. We take the stairs to the third floor. He unlocks the door, letting us in.

"Want a drink?" His head disappears into the refrigerator.

"Nah, I'm good. Thanks." I wander around the apartment.

"So, spill it." He thumps my shoulder with his enormous mitt before flopping on the sofa. I swear the thing groans.

"What's to tell, bud?"

"You and devil woman?"

"Her name's Carlie, Miles."

He huffs a laugh and smiles. "That's all I need to know." He sips his drink and points the remote at the television. A ball game flicks onto the screen.

"Oh, our station received an invitation to a Christmas gala for Serenity. Nice work. Our crew is off that night, we'll all be there. Your family coming?"

My mouth gapes.

Carlie.

Carlie and Rubes.

But most likely Carlie, since—

"Hold up. Are you only going to hit on Rubes?"

"So, she *will* be there."

"Don't, bud."

"Would never. But the second she's done with that little brother of yours . . ."

"Ain't going to happen. Now who needs to get laid?"

"I talk a good game, but I'm no home-wrecker, Laws. I'm happy for her. I am."

You would think those two grew up together, the way he talks about her. But he's known her as long as I have, less a few months, I suppose. Her first visit back here after she and Reed became a thing, they met.

They hit it off instantly. Been friends ever since.

Miles is a good friend to have, so I won't begrudge Rubes that.

I sip my water, and he chuckles, returning to the game.

Shithead.

Sunday comes and goes, and Monday is here before I am ready to acknowledge its existence. The only perk of a workday is spending hours with Carlie. She's been busy with Mills coming home, and I didn't want to take away from their time together.

She loves that little old lady like her own grandma.

In truth, she's growing on me. A bundle of baked goods and some Miami trinkets arrived at my door Sunday night. And when Carlie texted me a few minutes after the delivery, I couldn't stop smiling.

Millie feels like family.

Carlie feels like—

"Mornin', Cowboy." She wanders in, her bag hanging off one arm. Her coat is over the other, her heels wet from the first snowfall. I'm guessing she didn't drive today.

"Morning, Princess."

She glances at the open door to our office and turns back to shut it. Now I wish we weren't walled in with glass. Because the way her black skirt suit hugs her curves, the sway of her damn hips . . .

I'm closing the distance between us before the blood supply can resurface to my brain. Halting just before I end up backing her into the wall and covering her body with mine, I divert, leaning over and gripping the edge of her desk as she sinks into her office chair.

"You okay?" she asks.

Fuck, she smells incredible.

"Yeah," I choke. Who am I kidding . . . I'm sporting a raging hard-on at work, and the entire staff floor is now bearing witness to my lack of self-control.

"Lawson, sit. I'll email you."

I open my mouth to protest, but instead, I peel myself away from the only fucking thing I've ever wanted this damn bad and force my ass into my chair. I open the laptop, adjusting my crotch as I do.

"Open your Gmail, Laws," she says softly.

"What?" I snap my eyes up to where she's tapping on her laptop.

"Not your work account, okay?"

Okay . . .

I bring up my Gmail account. She rises from her chair and walks to my desk with a pink sticky note. If I was hard before, now I'm concrete.

Her email address is on the note.

thecowboysprincess@gmail.com

I tap out a hello and send it off.

I huff a strained chuckle with the little air left in my lungs. If this is what fucking this woman and then leaving her for two days feels like, then . . .

My email pings.

Heat slips down my spine as I read her email.

Hello Cowboy,
I missed you. Fuck, I missed you like four or five times in the shower last night. Then one more this morning before I even made it out of bed.
Your Princess.

Fuck me.

"Yes, please," she whispers.

Hell, I said that out loud?

I tap out a reply.

Hey Princess,
This is going to be damn hard, working across from you for hours and not touching you. Not tasting you, baby. Longest workday ever, hands down.
Your Cowboy.

Hmmm,
Well, you get break times, don't you? I've never had sex on a copier before . . .
Princess.

Christ.

I tap out a reply, my keystrokes so uncontrolled my desk shakes.

Princess,
You will be the death of me. But yes, copier sex would be a first for me also. Just curious . . . Where else?
Cowboy.
P.S.
I hope your panties are soaked because you have me rock fucking hard, woman.

She huffs a little giggle, and it goes straight to my damn balls.

Sweet Jesus.

Brown eyes burn into mine from over her laptop. And then she drags her bottom lip through her teeth as if she's considering something.

Hands gripping the arms of my office chair, I stifle a groan.

She must pick up on my tension, because her lips part, and she moans a sweet little noise. She shrugs her jacket off, leaving the pale silk blouse molded over her perfect fucking tits.

I push the laptop away as my forehead hits the desk.

Jesus fucking Christ, woman.

CHAPTER 32
CARLIE

I shut and lock the door the second Lawson crosses the supply room threshold. He's crowded me by the door before I have a chance to catch my breath.

I'm starving for this man.

He hauls me up the door and it rattles.

"Fuck," he grinds out.

Warm hands manhandle me, carrying me on his hips across the room. My ass hits the copier, and I am all hands in his hair, legs wrapped around his waist. My heel falls from my foot as he devours my mouth and litters kisses down the column of my throat.

God, a girl could get used to this . . .

But the chances of getting busted in this small office are high. Somehow, the thought drives me wild. "Laws, give it to me, please."

He chuckles, his lips vibrating against my neck. "So fucking needy, Princess."

"Our window will close if we take too long."

He groans, flicking the buckle of his belt before spreading my thighs. Notching at my entrance, he holds my gaze with his. I take his face in my hands, and my lips part as he gives me every inch.

My head falls back. He flicks a button on my blouse, pushing my blouse aside before his lips capture my nipple.

"Oh god, Laws."

He slams into me, every blissful stroke sending me higher.

The door rattles under a knock.

"Hello, is someone in there?" Nadia calls, her words slightly muted by the door.

"Oh shit!" I whisper.

Lawson's forehead presses to mine, the cheekiest smile tugging one corner of his delicious mouth up. "Fuck, Princess. This ain't going to last long."

Right now, that's probably a good thing.

He thumbs my clit as he rasps, "Come for me, baby."

I explode around him, and he groans through his release, his hands gripping my hips with force.

I pant through my next words. "She'll be back with a key."

"Yeah, probably."

He doesn't let me go. Despite the fact we are most likely seconds away from being busted, I don't want him to, either.

"Carlie," he breathes.

"I know, Cowboy," I whisper, but guide him backward with my hands on his chest. Sliding from the copier, I fix my skirt. He readjusts his pants and belt and runs a hand through his hair.

The door opens and I spin on my heel, grabbing the first item I can reach.

Toilet paper.

Fantastic.

Laws chuckles at me before taking a few random stationary items from the shelf as the door pops open. Nadia's face turns stunned, then melts to disappointment as she sets her shoulders back. "Sorry, are you done? I need the copier."

"Yeah." Lawson clears his throat. "Just needed these." He holds up the folders, and are those highlighters? Whiteboard markers, maybe . . .

Why do I care?

"Okay," Nadia says, eyeing the toilet roll in my stupid hand.

I force a smile and walk from the copy room like the carpet is on fire. Lawson is hot on my heels when we run right into Serelle.

"Carlie. Lawson. My office, now."

Turning back and marching for her office, she beckons us with a finger over her shoulder.

"Shit," I whisper, shooting Laws a worried look laced with annoyance.

"I'm sure it'll be fine." His hand brushes mine.

I put space between us.

Fuck. God, I'm so stupid. I've broke every fucking rule I've ever had. I can't lose this job. I can't do that to Mills again.

We file into Serelle's office and sink into the chairs in front of her desk.

She leans back in her chair and steeples her hands with a frown.

Fuck.

Fuck. Fuck. *Fuck.*

"When were you going to tell me the scope of this gala you're planning?" Her gaze alternates between Lawson and me.

"I mean, that's incredible, but what happens when the funding doesn't meet the expenses?"

I have to do my best to tamp down the hysterical laugh that wants out. She's worried about the size of the gala.

"The Met has donated the space. The catering has been funded, and the remaining service providers were within budget." I hold her gaze.

"Oh, wow. I didn't realize you had connections to the Met. Color me impressed." Serelle's hands slap the desk with enthusiasm.

My body sags with relief, but I try not to let it show.

Lawson glances at me with a smile. "Actually, it was a team effort. My sister worked in events before she decided to stay in Montana. She's been helping plan."

"Oh, well, that's wonderful. Let's hope we can raise the funds to keep you both on board for the next year." She slaps her armchair and leans into the desk. "Funding has always been an issue. I'm glad you found a creative solution for this. But I'm not surprised. I hired you both with this potential in mind, and you've proven me right. I won't keep you from your work." She nods, dismissing us.

I rise and walk from her office.

She's proud of us.

And we're lying to her.

In multiple ways.

Withholding the real financial situation of Serenity House. Plus the fact that Lawson and I are . . .

What exactly are we?

As I make it back to the fish tank, I'm in a trance of disbelief when I drop into my chair. I face-plant into my hands and groan.

We are so fucked.

If this doesn't work out, we are royally fucked.

I will be a princess standing in ruins. Who knows if my cowboy will still be by my side if this all goes sideways.

I try—and fail—to hold my composure as *the* Anna freaking Winston waits for me at the entrance to the Met. Life goals officially accomplished. I can die happy now.

Last night's snowfall litters the ground, and I hug my coat closer with one hand as the wind decides to pick up.

Mills tugs at my arm, which hers is looped through. I was so starstruck, I forgot I invited her to come along this morning. Someone has to keep me grounded. Besides, she put up a convincing argument.

Apparently, she's old, and to deny her the chance to meet a woman like Anna Winston would be the cruelest of sins.

"She's so elegant, look at her." Millie nods, excitement lighting her sweet face as she wobbles her way up the steps. I hold her steady, calculating each stride I take to keep her safe.

We ascend the steps to the museum, and Anna's face breaks into a smile. "Carlie, lovely to meet you." She extends one fine, manicured hand, and I shake it. My mouth moves, but I can't form a coherent word to save myself.

"Hello," she says to Millie. "I'm Anna. Come on in. Let's make a start on curating a space for your gala, shall we?"

Millie's mouth actually gapes, and now I feel less stupid for not uttering a word in the presence of one of my lifelong idols.

"Say something," Mills hisses at me.

Like what? Shit, I missed my window. We walk behind Anna as she leads us into a large open foyer. The biggest Christmas tree I've ever seen stands on the central platform, strangled by lights and decorations. An oversized star illuminates its top.

Still following Anna, albeit a little slower as I look around in awe, we pass under archways lined with festive garlands and through double doors into a grandiose room.

I've been to the Met before but never during the holiday season.

It's stunning. It's breathtaking.

Millie and I cross the threshold into the event space. Inside is spectacular, with a high ceiling, large floor space, and steps flanking the entire far end of the room with a stage.

"Oh wow, this will be perfect," I say, and Anna turns back.

"I thought so, too." She offers me a smile, making me relax. Millie slides her arm from mine and wanders around the grand space, touching the walls and the trim, gazing through the large, tall windows as she eyes every detail. Kid in a candy shop.

"Are you sure this will be available for the twenty-fourth? I wouldn't want to put you out, being such short notice and all," I say, the waver in my voice too audible for my liking.

"Of course. I booked it for Serenity the minute I spoke to Ruby about your event. I admire what you're doing for the city. For the *women* of New York."

Holy shit.

Now I can die happy.

"Thank you," I breathe. But it's not only me, it's the entire team. Lawson and Serelle play just as big of a role in Serenity's success as I do. "Really, it's a team effort. We are trying to make the House thrive, not simply survive."

Her face falls, tugged down by the most elegant frown I've ever seen. "Is the House in trouble?"

Ah, the moment of truth. The split-second decision I have to make whether to lie to the most amazing woman I've ever met, or to spill the beans. An entire can of messy, hideous legumes that could have Lawson and me fired should they get back to Serelle before we've solved this problem.

"A figure of speech, I guess. I think we can do more to help the women of this city. As we should."

A tight smile stretches her lips. "Well, in that case, may I suggest some activities for the night to help with your fundraising goal?"

"Absolutely, that would be incredible."

We chat back and forth about possible options for the night's entertainment from prizes to donation options and more. Her knowledge on big events like what we are trying to pull off is impeccable. No wonder she and Ruby get along like a house on fire.

"Have you known Ruby long?" Anna asks.

"No, she's actually my coworker's sister-in-law."

"Ah, another cowboy, hey?" Her smile is almost cheeky. Apparently I'm not the only one who finds the whole cowboy vibe attractive.

"What time can we be here on the 24th to finalize preparations?" I ask, changing the subject.

"As soon as we open at nine."

"Wonderful."

"Is there anything else you need to know?" she says, handing me her card. I stare at it and its gilded front lying in my hand. Millie appears by my side, slipping the card between her fingers as she looks it over.

Do not lose that, Mills.

"I think we've covered everything. Thank you. And thanks again for fitting Serenity in."

"Oh, my pleasure. Say hello to Ruby for me, will you?"

"Of course."

"Now, I have a board meeting, but feel free to look around and make your own plans. Best of luck for your event, Carlie."

My hands are shaking by the time she leaves us alone in the event hall.

"Holy motherfucking shit," I utter.

Mills cracks up. "You did great, sweetheart. I loved watching you in your element. You really are good with this stuff."

I roll my eyes at her, and she pats my cheek like the little old lady she is. I clutch her hand briefly before taking a final turn around the magnificent space that will be ours for an entire day and evening. I walk the steps up to the stage, imagining the fundraising layout. The tables lined up. A space for dancing just below as the evening draws on. The musicians will be to the left of the stage. The donations table, inconspicuous and small, will be by the door to catch folks on their way out.

And of course, a Christmas tree to encourage gifted donations for the women and girls. That should be in the center . . .

I sigh and smile as I cast one last longing gaze over the space.

No wonder Ruby loves doing this. The hope and potential have my body abuzz with something I haven't felt for years.

Excited to bring happiness to people.

Excitement, period.

CHAPTER 33

LAWSON

After hours spent fixing the last of the decorations and settings for the gala—with Ruby's help, of course—my bones are weary. Who knew building out a space for a prestigious event would be so damn intense. The boys all came to give us a hand. Miles for the muscle. Dex and Griff got put on centerpiece duty, not daring to argue with Rubes.

Damn, it was amusing. Bossy little sister had all three of them sorted out.

Reed worked his tail off, scaling things to hang lights, despite the Met staff insisting he was an occupational hazard. That got a chuckle out of him.

Ruby and I sent Carlie home early to get ready and spend some much-earned time with Millie before tonight. She's been killing herself over this gala. And since the whole 'lying until we can fix this problem' thing was my stupid idea, I feel responsible for her current exhaustion.

Plus, Rubes wanted to add some extra touches to the enormous space as a surprise, and I can't wait to see the look on

Carlie's face when she experiences the full Ruby Robbins experience.

I straighten my bow tie, brushing imaginary lint from my tux. I'm nervous.

As I fucking should be—I could have sunk everything by withholding Serenity House's real situation. And I fully intend on taking the blame if this implodes on us. It's the right thing to do.

Besides, I made a promise to Carlie to protect her heart, and this is definitely included. Her work, her career, is her life. She's done well for herself and kept a roof over Millie's head. God, how many people can claim that level of humility?

I double-check my hair in the mirror and don some after-shave. It burns my skin after the second shave of the day. I highly doubt five-o'clock shadow is Met-Gala appropriate. Or maybe it is . . .

My phone lights up.

Are you on your way? Don't be late picking us up, okay, Cowboy?

I chuckle and tap out a reply.

Wouldn't dream of it, Princess.

My little control freak. Who am I kidding, I love it. I grew up under the guidance of a strong, capable woman. My brothers each married one. It's familiar to us.

And Carlie just fits.

Inexplicably so.

My phone lights up again.

Ma.

She's been jumping out of her skin since she received the invite. Which is hilarious, since it came from Rubes.

But I know she is dying to spend time with Carlie and be part of our lives for even a moment. My mother is the essence of unconditional love.

I send a message back.

The message pops with a heart.

I swipe up my wallet and keys and head downstairs. The Uber I ordered waits out front. Not exactly a knight in shining armor. I don't even have my own vehicle, for fuck's sake. Carlie offered to take her car, but that defeats the purpose of me picking her up.

I settle into the back seat and relay my instructions to the driver. He nods, and we're heading for Carlie's a heartbeat later.

"Close your eyes, Princess."

My entire family and the rest of the work crew are already inside. Me, I pretended to leave my wallet in the Uber, getting Reed to escort Millie and Henry inside so I could be the one to take Carlie in. Her hand slips inside mine, and I check her eyes are in fact closed before leading her toward the steps of the Met.

I take her in.

Her body is wrapped in a slinky black dress that highlights her delicious figure, dipped low to show off her cleavage that'll have me scowling at every fucker who so much as glances her way. Massive soft waves of hair tumble over her right shoulder, pinned to one side. Strappy silver heels poke through her split hem with every step, as does one long elegant leg. A fluffy dark coat keeps her warm.

Dammit, I should have kept my attention straight ahead, because now I feel the need to adjust myself in my suit pants.

And the way she smells.

Sweet Jesus, it's going to be a long damn night.

"Steps, Princess. First step now."

She steps, a little awkward as her grip around my biceps tightens. "Is this really necessary? I was literally part of the prep crew."

"You were, but I want this night to be everything it can be. Humor me?"

"Fine. But if I face-plant on the concrete outside the Met in front of the most incredible event I've ever been a part of, I will never forgive you."

I chuckle. "Deal."

She hums a disapproving sound, and I lean in. "I've got you, baby."

We ascend the steps, and I halt her before the doors as they check our names off the list.

"Thanks," I say to the tall guy in the suit with an earpiece and wire before turning to Carlie. "Eyes closed, remember?"

"At this rate, we'll be late."

"Not late, making an entrance."

"Good lord, what does that even mean?"

We walk toward the event hall where two more men in suits hold the door handles. They open the doors simultaneously as we approach and wave us in with polite smiles.

"Open your eyes."

We cross the threshold to the gala as she flicks her eyes open.

"Holy shit . . ."

Above us, a glittering blanket of fairy lights imitates the night sky. Round tables with white tablecloths fill the floor, surrounded by golden gilded chairs with white sashes. In the center, a giant Christmas tree, almost putting the foyer's tree to shame, stands lit up like . . . well, Christmas.

Traditional Christmas songs play softly over the speakers, the croon of a Dean Martin holiday album tangling with chatter, clinking champagne glasses, and laughter. Waitstaff wind through the crowd with appetizers and fresh drinks, all dressed in black and white.

Women in evening gowns and men in tuxedos populate any free space between the tables, some already sitting at their designated seats. The string quartet is seated on the stage, waiting for their cue.

"Lawson," she gasps.

Her eyes swell with tears, and she scrunches her face, trying to stem their fall.

"Merry Christmas, Princess."

"Oh, yeah. Merry Christmas." Her eyes study my face as her lips curl into the prettiest smile.

"Come on, let's find some people."

We find Reed and Ruby first, and Carlie all but flies into Ruby's arms.

"Hey, you like our extra little touches?" Reed says, beaming like it was his idea.

"Yes, I do, very much." Carlie smiles at him.

Ruby slaps his shoulder. "He says our, but it was all Lawson's idea."

She turns to me, her mouth agape. "What did you do?"

"Just added a few details. Nothing much." I grin at her, and she narrows her eyes.

Smart woman.

Mum's the word on the new activities on the agenda for tonight. Who am I to spoil the biggest PR event of her career?

"Ladies and gentlemen, if you would kindly take your seats, the entrée will be served momentarily," the emcee—one of New York's bravest—says. Miles meets my gaze. He's one hell of a showman when he wants to be something other than a broody motherfucker trying to keep us in line. Tonight is about raising money for Serenity, a cause he is one hundred percent behind.

"Oh! Miles." Carlie leans in as we wander the room to find our table. "You didn't tell me Miles was the emcee; I thought it would be someone at the office. I like this much better."

I'm hoping the guests here tonight do, too, and dig deep for our charming firefighter as he hosts the night. Millie sits with my parents as we file in and find our seats. Mack and Grace arrive next, Gracie as radiant as ever and almost due to give birth. I'm surprised that brother of mine let her venture this far from home. Hudson, Addy, and Hattie take their seats next as Reed and Ruby fill the last two at our table.

The gang's all here.

My family.

Our family.

And it feels fucking right.

Ma is deep in conversation with Millie as the food comes around. I saw my parents at their hotel earlier when Reed and Rubes finished the prep and went back. I spent over an hour catching up on things back home, but all anyone wanted to talk about was Carlie.

In true Rawlins fashion, my brothers saluted like idiots every time someone said her name.

Only to earn eye rolls from me and knowing looks from Gracie.

From our table, I spot the work crew at a table headed by Serelle and who I assume is her husband. The rest of the tables are packed with New York's most wealthy, chatting away like this is an everyday thing for them. Hell, it probably is.

"Uncle Lawson?" Hattie tugs at my sleeve.

"Hey, sweetie, what's up?"

She leans closer, her little face screwed up as she darts her gaze around the table. "Why is there so many forks?"

The scrunched-up expression on her face makes me chuckle, and I tamp it back before saying, "One's for eating, the rest are for slingshots."

"Ooooh, okay. Thanks."

"Laws, you did not just tell her that," Addy says, shaking her head, but the smile that claims her face is priceless. Hudson leans back, his arm wrapped around the back of Addy's chair, his gaze full of adoration as he watches his small daughter pick up each fork and inspect it.

As the food rolls out and the band starts up, the story of Serenity House and the impact it has had on the folks of New

York tumbles from Miles's mouth. He has the entire room enraptured by the time he comes to the part that's had my stomach in knots for weeks. Asking for donations to keep the House up and running. To add to our impact, service, and facilities.

Carlie grabs my thigh under the table. Her grip is so tight, I resist the urge to flinch. Instead, I slide my hand under hers and lace our fingers together, leaning into her. "Breathe, Princess. We did everything we could. People will put their money where their mouth is, you'll see."

I sound more confident than I feel.

As Miles announces donations will be accepted at the table by the door and online, I feel Carlie's pulse kick up where her wrist is pressed to mine.

"One last matter of housekeeping before the entertainment for the night. Donations close at midnight. So make your mark now, ladies and gentlemen. Leave your legacy and go big."

He sets the microphone on the small table behind him and exits the stage. Chatter floods in as men and women get out their phones around the room. On the back of each person's name card is a prompt to donate above a QR code. People start scanning and tapping as the chatter rises.

"This is what we came here for," Pa says, pulling out his phone and sliding on his reading glasses. My brothers all do the same.

"I need some air." Carlie squeezes my hand, rising from her seat and winding her way through the tables before she disappears through the double doors.

"I think that's your cue, Laws." Grace rests a hand on my arm, nodding at the doors.

I dot a kiss to her forehead and make my way after Carlie.

Outside the doors, I find her pacing, her hands wringing in front of her as she stalks a small strip of marbled floor, heels clacking as she worries her bottom lip through her teeth.

She spins back, striding toward me, and I step into her path, gripping her shoulders. "Hey, tell me."

She shakes her head, shaking my hold free.

"Carlie," I plead. "We're going to make it."

She snaps her gaze to mine. "You don't know that, Lawson."

"No, I don't. But you have to have a little faith."

"Faith? If we hadn't—" She scans the foyer quickly, lowering her voice to a whisper as she says, "If we hadn't lied, we wouldn't be in this position."

"But we wouldn't have had a chance to make things better, either."

"It's a million dollars, Lawson. *One million.*" She huffs a furious sound before waving her hands through the air. "I will not lose this job. I will not."

I know it's a big gap to fill—

Hang on, what's that supposed to mean?

Is she going to blame everything on me and offer me up as the sacrificial lamb to Serelle so she can keep her job?

"Carlie, don't do this!"

She marches for the door. I follow behind, catching up as she makes it inside. The second we do, the noise is deafening. Women at every table are waving their hands, phones, and purses.

What the actual hell?

I flick my gaze to my family's table. Addy's laughing, holding her hands over Hattie's ears. Gracie is cheering as

Mack stares at her, arms crossed over his chest. Ma has spun around on her chair, but Ruby is . . .

On the goddamn stage.

"Okay, ladies, this one is really special. And I know you're going to love him as much as we do. Next up in our auction is none other than the man who takes care of business for Serenity House, Lawson Rawlins! Come on up, Lawson. Ladies, hold those bid cards high."

CHAPTER 34
LAWSON

"What the hell is going on?" I growl.

Carlie looks as shocked as I am. "I have no idea. Anna said we could use other initiatives if the donation goal wasn't met, but we only started taking donations. I don't understand."

"There he is! Come on up, Laws." Ruby waves at me, and the entire room turns to stare at Carlie and me standing by the door.

Fucking hell, Rubes.

I set my jaw and start for the stage.

Fine fingers clasp my wrist, and I turn back. Her big brown eyes are tight when she says, "I'm sorry."

I have no way to respond to that.

I stride for the stage, and Rubes pats the upholstered seat where I'm guessing the last guy sat as he was auctioned off to the highest bidder. I take the steps two at a time, and that gets a reaction from the audience. Apparently, the wealthy women of New York like a fit guy.

Just my luck.

Ruby gives me a shit-eating grin as I sit on the chair, tugging at my bow tie.

She leans over, holding the microphone behind her. "Untie it and lose a button or two. You'll raise more money, Laws."

I give her the foulest look I've ever mustered as she messes up my hair with her free hand.

Yep, Rubes is a dead woman.

Begrudgingly, I do as she asks.

"Alright, ladies. Don't let this one get away."

I watch as Carlie drifts to our table and sits in her seat, dumbstruck. I see Adds snickering. I shake my head at her.

Huddo gives me a thumbs up, and Mack shakes his head while Reed imitates feinting like a southern belle in need of goddamn vapors. This is why my family should have stayed in damn Montana.

"Shall we start the bidding at five thousand?" Rubes coos.

The hell?

A paddle shoots into the air. Some older lady in a shimmery pea-green outfit.

Christ.

"Can I get six thousand?" Rubes slinks behind my chair, shoving my hair forward and into my face. I shake her off but leave the hair messed up and half in my face. At this point, who really cares? My dignity died as soon as I crossed the threshold minutes ago.

I count a total of ten paddles as they fly into the air.

Well, fuck.

"Oh ladies, play a little hard to get, hey?" Rubes laughs and leans down, whispering, "Sell it, Laws. Come on, I know you can."

With a grunt, I resist the urge to flip her off. But seeing as Serenity's entire existence hangs on raising enough money, I do as she says. I tug at the bow tie and slide it from my neck, letting it drop to the floor. Next, I shoulder off the jacket and roll up my sleeves.

I glance at Carlie. Her face is unreadable, and not in a good way.

"Ten thousand!" a platinum blonde in a navy dress yells from a front table.

Trying my best to keep a straight face, I let my gaze burn into Carlie's before I lean back, manspreading.

"Twenty thousand," another screams, jumping up and rattling her whole table.

Rubes closes in by my side. "Did you want to say something to the ladies, Lawson?"

I swing my focus back to our table. Carlie's hand is over her mouth as she leans into the table. I take the microphone from Ruby's hand and hold it to my lips as I growl out, in my best Montana accent, "Yes ma'am."

Ruby's eyebrows meet her hairline as she smiles, moving the microphone closer to her and says, "And what would you like to say?"

Serenity is riding on this money. This fundraiser is the difference between us surviving or sinking. Without this money, all one million dollars of it, the women of this city will lose a lifesaving resource.

"Save a horse, ladies." I let the words rumble from my chest.

The crowd goes wild, figures flying from lipsticked mouths faster than the shells of an automatic weapon.

Ruby simply walks to the edge of the stage and holds up a hand.

The room goes quiet as she raises the microphone to her lips. "Can I get one hundred thousand dollars?"

Three women send their paddles into the air.

Holy fucking shit. *Christ, Rubes.*

Through the ruckus, I swing my gaze back to our table.

Carlie's seat is empty.

Double fucking shit.

Dammit.

"Can I get one hundred and twenty thousand?" Ruby calls.

Two paddles fly up.

The third lady is whispering to who I assume is her partner as he shakes his head. What the hell was that dynamic going to be?

"One hundred and forty," Ruby calls.

Both paddles fly up again.

These women have more money than sense. God above.

"One hundred and fifty."

Two paddles are raised again. This time, they stare each other down. If it wasn't my virtue on the line, it would be hilarious.

Why the hell did I have to say 'save a horse'? World's biggest idiot right here, sitting on this fucking chair.

"One hundred and fifty-five thousand."

Only one paddle shoots into the air, the crowd so silent, you could hear a slingshot fork hit the pristine carpet.

"One hundred and fifty-five thousand dollars. Going once." Ruby looks around the room, like there might be someone else to enter at the eleventh hour.

"Going twice . . ."

The room is still.

"Going a third time, ladies. Your very last chance." Ruby moves to my side.

"So—"

"Two hundred thousand," a voice yells from the back.

I can't make out where or who she is with the stage lighting in my eyes. The last lady in the auction sits, shaking her head as she sets her paddle down.

The crowd's gasps around the room drown out any rational thought.

A woman walks through the crowd with an air of elegance that has us all stunned as Ruby smiles at her.

What the—

"Lawson, meet Anna Winston. Board member of the Met, editor-in-chief of *Elegance* magazine, and one my oldest friends in the event space." Rubes leans over, signaling for me to tidy up.

Anna steps onto the stage, and I stand, clearing my throat.

She looks me over. "A reasonable price to pay I suppose, for young love."

I swallow, a little taken aback . . . and a whole lot confused.

Rubes beams at me as she ushers both of us off stage. The next guy to be auctioned off is Miles. As he walks on stage in his firefighter gear, the room is chaos.

A soft hand guides me through a side door, and we emerge in a hallway that's littered with doors to what I assume are smaller rooms.

"Thank you for what you're doing for the women of New York, Lawson. It's my pleasure to help you achieve it. But I'm afraid I was not bidding for myself." She opens a door on the left and leaves it ajar as she tilts her head so elegantly. "Have a wonderful night; you both deserve it."

I can only stare at her as she leaves and reenters the gala.

I run a hand through my hair, hoping against all hope the person she bought me on behalf of isn't going to hold me to the 'save a horse' comment.

Guess there's only one way to find out . . .

The smaller room is set up for conferences and such. A polished large oval table fills the space, ten plush leather chairs surrounding it. A small sideboard sits at the back of the room. In the half dark, I find Carlie sitting at the head of the table.

Her legs crossed, she starts rapping her fingernails on the polished surface.

I close the door and flick the light on.

Instantly, the hurt that's scrawled over her face is a kick to the chest.

"Fuck, I'm sorry—"

She holds up a single digit and rises from the chair.

"Is this how you planned on securing Serenity's future?" She narrows her eyes, her lips a thin line. She flicks her hair behind her and sets her shoulders back. "Figures."

The actual hell, woman?

"You know me better than that," I snarl, unable to tame the annoyance lacing my veins.

How could she think I would . . .

"Do whatever you want, Rawlins. We're done here."

How fast did she flip her switch on me?

Sweet Jesus.

Fortunately, I wasn't raised to give up on a good thing. When she stalks past, I catch her arm.

Her eyes meet mine and the fire from only a second ago fades before me. "Don't," she chokes.

"Don't what, love you?"

Her face breaks.

"No, Carlie. You don't get to bail at the first sign of trouble. No fucking way."

Her chin wobbles as silver lines the dark eyes that roped in my heart on the first day I met her.

"Look, I understand you have to fight for everything. But I'm not one of those things. There's no fight here. I come willingly. Always will."

A sob slips from her, and she moves a little closer, her hand resting on my wrist.

I track my knuckle over her cheek, and her eyes flutter closed.

"I made you a promise, Princess. And fuck, I intend on keeping it."

"What happens when we don't make the quota tonight? Serelle will still let one of us go . . . If I stay, you'll resent me. If I go, I'll resent you. There's no winning here, Lawson."

"We haven't even crossed that bridge yet. Why are you doing this?"

She pulls away and hugs herself. "Because! There is no way we're making a million."

"Hell, someone probably already put a cool million on Milo. If Rubes is smart, and we both know she is, she'll auction Griff and Dex off as a set, that'll surely get us over the line. You'll see."

"No, I won't. I can't risk Millie's security or my career."

"I would never ask you to. Will you please at least wait until the donations are tallied? Give me that much, please."

She looks everywhere around the room, avoiding my gaze as I close in on her. She backs into the wall, and I cage her in. "I will find a way. I won't let you down, Captain."

She tilts her head, her face twisting.

She knows about the captain thing?

Ruby.

Fuck me.

Her fingers tremble as they ghost over my jaw. Searching my face, she opens her mouth to say something but rolls her lips before worrying that bottom lip through her teeth.

"Please, baby. You could break my heart, but I would really rather you didn't," I breathe.

"Fucking Anna," she utters, her chest heaving under choppy breaths.

"I like Anna. She gave me this little moment."

"Fuck it." She palms my face, drawing my mouth down to hers.

I crowd her against the wall. Devouring her mouth, I splay my hands over her ribs. The thin material of her silky dress offers no barrier as her warm skin burns into my palms.

I drift my thumb over a pert nipple straining against the material. She whimpers, sagging a little, and I put my leg between hers, holding her up. I run a hand up her thigh that's hosting an almost indecent slit in her long, shimmery dress.

A little moan slips from her lips when I find her panties.

Soaked.

"Fuck, Princess." I sweep two fingers through her wet center. Dropping my head, I tug her dress down to find her braless. Sweet fucking Christ. I close my mouth over a pert nipple as she rocks on my leg, chasing friction.

"Laws," she rasps. "Table."

I scoop her up and stride three paces to the oval table, putting her down on it. As I lean back to adjust my position, she slams a hand into my chest.

"Fuck you, Lawson Rawlins, for making me fall in fucking love with you." She seethes through rapid breaths. "Before your stupid handsome face and kind big-ass heart, I was completely fine on my own. Now . . . look at me."

"I am, baby, and you look edible."

"I am not edible. I'm ropable."

"You can hate me while I fuck you, I promise."

"I—"

"Or we can stop."

"Don't you fucking dare."

I chuckle, and she huffs an annoyed breath.

Christ, I love her this way.

"You want to hate fuck, baby?"

"I do hate you, for fucking with my emotions. My heart. What is wrong with you, why are you so nice?" She's in my face.

I grip her throat, and her eyes light with surprise that fades to a heated desire on a level I've not yet seen from her.

"Making you come while the people in the room next door prove me right is going to be worth every sassy word that leaves those pouty damn lips."

Taking a step back, I release my aching, rock-hard cock, and she moves. Standing with her back to me, she leans over the table a little and slides the silky dress up and over her ass. Her long legs ending in high heels, her perfect ass canted up to me, she scowls over her shoulder. "Fuck me like you hate me. Oh, that's right; you did before."

"I never hated you, but I can still make you scream, Princess."

I don't give her any warning or go easy.

I slam into her, and the whole fucking table moves with a groan. I slap a hand over her mouth as a stunned cry flies through her lips.

She bites down on my hand, and I thunder into her.

Her legs tremble and my own release threatens to take us both down as I slide a hand beneath her, swirling my fingertips over her clit.

She unravels, bucking against the table.

I can't help the roar that leaves my throat as I shoot hot ropes into her.

If this is makeup sex, I'll take it.

Hell, I might even be the one to pick the fight next time.

CHAPTER 35
CARLIE

With the last eligible bachelor auctioned off, we get to my portion of tonight's entertainment. I hate public speaking. Love public relations and building connections, but speaking in front of a crowd of this caliber . . . that's another torture entirely.

"Hello everyone." I hold the microphone too close, and it squeals before I can put distance between me and it.

The room is silent.

Great, why is it my job to deliver the serious portion of the night? How are you supposed to follow the hottest auction in New York with these sobering facts and stories? Determined, I set my shoulders back, remembering the impact we have had on women and children. On someone's mother, someone's daughter. Aunt. Niece.

"Now is the part where I have you squirming in your seats for an entirely different reason." I clear my throat. As if feeling the vibe plummet, others do, too.

I point the clicker toward the backdrop behind me that's been set up for our presentation tonight. Serenity House's logo and mission statement flash onto the screen.

"Every year, more and more women are in need of shelter. It takes on average twenty-one days to apply to a non-emergency shelter and be placed. However, three women are killed by domestic violence every single day in the United States . . ." My speech covers the statistics highlighting the need for more beds, more services, and extended hours. And I finish with a tear-jerking story of a woman named Alysandra. ". . . as fingers dig into my windpipe, I realized I had to leave. My home, my sanctuary was tainted, I wasn't safe. I hadn't been for a long, long time. I had been praying for things to just get better. For him to do better. It was after he lost his fourth job in three months, that the—" I swallow back the emotion and suck in an inadequate breath. "The bruises came. The hurtful words and punishing physical altercations. And I remember thinking, my mother's heart would be shattered if she saw us like this. With nowhere to go, I stayed. For another month. It wasn't until I started finding unexplained bruises on my six-year-old daughter that I finally found the strength to leave. I had failed her, and in the worst way possible. But I would not fail her again. We left in the middle of the night, and by the time I fought my way free of the house and his rage, we ended up in the alleyway by the Serenity building. That was the first day in years I'd been able to finally take a breath."

I pause and scan the room. Hankies and tissues are shoved in women's faces at every damn table.

I swallow and force a smile before ending my pitch. "Alysandra and so many others like her and her daughter are why Serenity needs your help. Currently, we are at capacity. But through the kindness of others, we hope to extend our operating hours and house capacity, along with adding fundamental services to get women back on their feet and regain their independence, including reentry into the workforce and counseling. So, I ask, humbly of you, to donate. Thank you."

I turn off the microphone and rest it on the small table by the chair. I leave the last slide with the smiling faces of some of our past guests at Serenity, hoping their stories will influence the people in this room to donate as much as they can.

Lawson meets me at the bottom of the stairs, his jaw clenched, his cheeks shimmering with tears that have streaked down his face. I cup his jaw, and he grasps my hand. "You killed it, Princess. Look at all those shattered hearts."

He turns back to the people at the tables, now busy quietly discussing. Devastation wrapped around a few. Couples pulling checkbooks and phones out as they flip over their name cards to scan the QR codes to donate again.

"God, I hope it's enough," I breathe, and Lawson pulls me into his side.

"Me too, baby. Me too."

The night recovers as the music rises and folks migrate to the dance floor. Before I have a chance to object, Harry is asking for the first dance, and I can't say no.

He spins me around as Lawson looks on, sitting with his family.

"You've done one hell of a job here, darlin'. You should be proud," Harry says as we travel across the dance floor.

"It was a team effort," I say with a small smile. I study his features, looking for pieces of Lawson in them. With every beat of the song that passes, I find familiar angles and those deep blues that have held me captive for weeks. Mostly, it's the kindness and unwavering support that I now know Lawson inherited from his father.

Lawson has no idea how lucky he is.

"Somethin' weighing on your mind, Carlie?"

He swings me around, and we turn back the other way, my dress twisting over my legs with a slow swish. I can't look at him, and his grip on my hand squeezes briefly. "A problem shared is a problem halved." Harry nods with an encouraging look.

"So much rides on these donations. Without them . . ."

"You'll find another way."

I look up into his eyes, so similar to the ones I adore. "I don't know if I can."

"Luckily for you, darlin', it's a *we*, not an I."

I huff a laugh.

He's right. Of course he is.

"That son of mine isn't going to let you down, and neither are we. If this is important to you, it's important to us."

"That's so generous of you," I say, trying not to let the emotion swelling on my face show.

"You do for family." He spins me out and catches me on the return. "I have a feeling that includes you."

My mouth pops open as a smile grows on his face. The song ends, and he leads me back to the table, returning me to my seat. Louisa rises, saying, "Must be my turn, my love."

"Yes, ma'am," Harry says, nothing but deep love running through his gaze.

The two words register, sending warmth through my chest. A warm hand slides over my own. I turn it over, lacing my fingers with his, my focus still stuck on Harry and Louisa as they cross to the dance floor for the slower song, and he wraps her in his hold automatically.

Hashtag marriage goals.

Millie grins at me from across the table. I know that cheeky damn look. What have she and Louisa been scheming up?

Warmth leans into my shoulder as Lawson's hand tracks a path over my palm. "Care to dance, Princess?"

The smile that blooms on my face is second nature.

Was Harry right?

Am I in way over my head?

"Tell me," he prompts.

I rise from my seat, not letting go of his hand. He follows before striding up to the dance floor and pulling me to his chest. I slide my hand behind his neck, one palm over his heart. And that moment when jealousy got the better of me while he was being auctioned earlier resurfaces, just a little, with his proximity.

This right here is the reason I don't believe in love. Relationships are messy and end badly over half the time. Even so, the thought of some other woman—

The thought of not having Lawson in my life . . .

He cups the back of my head. "Breathe, Carlie. You did good, and I'm so fucking proud of you, baby. It will all work out."

The stone that's nudging its way up my windpipe explodes.

Fuck.

I grip him tighter.

Well, if the folks at work didn't know what lies between Lawson and me before, they do now.

Feet burning in my too-high heels, I slide into an Uber after the last guest has gone home and I've put Mills and Henry in separate Ubers to get home. Lawson slides in beside me, loosening his bow tie the instant the door closes. We pull away from the curb and drive through the city.

We roll through the holiday-themed 5th Ave, the colorful lights reflecting over the windows and rolling over our faces. I turn to find Lawson's gaze on me.

"Come with me somewhere tomorrow," he rasps.

"Where?"

"You'll see."

I smile at him, and a yawn slips out. "Sure, not too early?"

"Not too early." His face is soft, eyes full of something I don't recall ever seeing before, and I can't place it in this moment.

I frown, and he kisses my hand before hauling me across the seat and into his side. "But, first, we are going to sleep for hours, tucked up together. Tangled in the damn sheets like we're never going to leave."

"Hmmm. Sounds perfect."

He huffs a soft, raw chuckle. His breath tickles my neck, and I roll my head to one side. He plants kisses on my neck, and before we have a chance to remember we're not alone, the car pulls over to the curb.

"Home sweet home," the driver says.

I look out at the small three-story building that houses Lawson's apartment. "Thank you."

Lawson slips from the back seat, appearing at my door as it opens. I climb out, and he takes my hand. Bed cannot come soon enough. I carry my heels in one hand, my coat wrapped around me as the snow falls steadily, settling on our hair and clothes.

The perfect end to a perfect night.

My feet are burning from the cold sidewalk now, and I tiptoe as quickly as I can toward the front door. A heartbeat later, strong arms sweep me off my feet, and I am wrapped in a warm embrace against Lawson's chest as he strides for the door.

"A girl could get used to this," I whisper.

"That's the plan."

My amused smile slips a little before I school it back into place.

Surely, I can do this. For Lawson. For what we have . . . How many chances do you get in one lifetime for this kind of *love?*

The word.

One syllable.

A whole shit ton of weight dragging it to places in my heart that shouldn't exist. We push through the door, and Lawson walks the three flights of stairs, refusing my requests to let me walk to save his efforts.

"Not a chance," he growls.

We reach his apartment, and he nods to the door. "Key's in my inside pocket."

I slide a hand into his jacket, the warmth sending a buzz

through my fingertips. Probably from going from being so cold to his heat . . .

I slip my fingers inside the pocket and produce his keys. He steps forward, and I insert the key in the lock and turn it. With a click, the door unlocks and opens. I retract the key as he kicks the door open. I chuckle. *That's my cowboy.*

After spending time with his family, I know now just how grounded, how rugged and real they are. But the one thing that outshines all that is their devotion to each other. It's fucking humbling.

It's a reminder of what I grew up without.

I yawn again, and Lawson kicks the door shut. "Bedtime, baby."

"Hmmm. I could sleep for a week."

"I'd let you. If I had the choice, we wouldn't leave my bed for weeks."

"You'd stay with me through the messy bits, wouldn't you, Laws?"

"Yes ma'am."

My heart actually melts in its boned cage, the liquid remnants seeping through. Yes, for this man, I want to try to do this thing that's taken on a life of its own.

I couldn't not, even if I wanted to.

Because I am irrevocably and entirely in love with Lawson Rawlins.

Fuck.

He presses a kiss to my forehead and whispers, "I love you, Carlie."

Four words.

Just four . . . and they send me into a panic.

What if I screw this up?

I search his gaze, the way he looks at me like I'm the most precious thing he's ever known. He's literally handing over his heart.

To me . . .

What if—oh god—

Double fuck.

CHAPTER 36
LAWSON

The park's dappled sunlight hovers as the trees overhead sway with the midday breeze. Carlie is lying beside me, her head on my arm, the both of us tucked under a fleecy throw and lying on the picnic blanket. Her eyes are closed as the folk of New York enjoy Central Park's relaxed Sunday hours.

A lazy Sunday in Central Park.

A well-earned one. Our food gone, we doze in the sun.

My family is taking in the sights, with Ruby and Addy as their guides. I'm sure Ma's in her element following Hattie around. She's such a devoted grandmother. Almost as devoted as she is to being a mother.

Clouds skim overhead, dotting the crisp blue sky. The snow from last night is scattered in clumps around the park, layered over weighed-down tree branches, on the tops of benches, and melting to small puddles over the paved areas, sending folks stepping sideways as they avoid them.

The park is busy, filled with people enjoying the last day of solace before going back to the grindstone.

Carlie hums, rolling over beside me as her eyes open. "Why'd you let me fall asleep." She smiles, her fingers tracing the angle of my jaw.

Right now, if I could capture this moment and tuck it away, I would. This right here would be enough to carry me through my darkest moments. I'm not naive enough to think a love like this comes easily. Strong women are a force of nature.

One that's worth every hard day.

My mother has taught me that.

Then Adds.

Then Rubes . . .

And finally Grace.

I dot a kiss to Carlie's forehead. Hopefully, I will have the privilege to live my life alongside the best one yet. The woman currently tucked into my side under the fleecy blanket we brought for our picnic slash outdoor nap. "You were tired, Princess."

"I'm not tired anymore . . ."

Her brown eyes darken.

"Baby, we'll have to take this picnic indoors if you keep looking at me like that."

She chuckles, rising a little to peck my lips.

Now she's gone and done it. I roll over, pinning her down. "You grab the blanket, I'll get the food basket, we can be home in ten."

"That's too long," she groans.

I chuckle into her hair. "I can have us there in eight," I growl, nipping her bottom lip.

"Get a room!" some guy yells, flying past on his scooter.

Fucking New York.

"Grab the blanket, baby. We're outta here."

I scoop Carlie up, and she manages to grab the basket with one hand and the blanket with the other. As I take off at a run with her in my arms, her head falls back as a hearty laugh tumbles through the prettiest damn parted lips. The basket thumps against my side and I manage to dodge the blanket trailing between my legs as I run with a waddle.

Reaching the edge of the park, I set her to her feet, the basket falling to the ground. She steps over the blanket to cup my jaw in her palms. "How do you manage to make my life so much better with even the littlest of things?"

I sink my mouth over hers briefly, barely leaving her panting lips from mine. "It's supposed to be easy, that's what makes it the real thing."

Hell, loving this woman is as easy as breathing. I take off in my waddled run again, and she cracks up.

"Are you sure? Because you have been anything but easy, Lawson Rawlins," she teases.

I nip her ear, slowing a little. She moans ever so softly, propelling me faster again. When we make it to my building, I'm well and truly out of breath. But I don't want to put her down.

Ever, if I can help it.

I push through the front door and take the steps two at a time, letting the burn sear its way through my legs. I drop my gaze to hers, and her face is tightened with something between shock and . . . awe.

Goddammit, how one parent can screw up his daughter so bad that something as simple as a man caring for her has her in disbelief. Hope he rots in his own karma in whatever life he chose over her.

"Don't look at me like that, Princess. I might never let you go."

Figuratively and literally.

"Y—you mean it?"

"I don't break promises, Carlie. And I sure as hell won't be breaking anything else where you're concerned."

Her chin wobbles a little, and she scrunches her nose up. A beat passes as she schools her face to something less emotional and says, "And to think . . . I used to hate you."

Her fingers brush over my jaw, her thumb ghosting over my bottom lip. That's all it takes to have the blood plummeting south, and I set her to her feet and have the door unlocked and opened in a heartbeat.

"I take it that particular phase has passed?" I wink at her.

"Somewhat . . ." She smiles, her bottom lip tugged between her teeth as her browns darken.

"Sassy little woman, I have the cure for that attitude of yours."

"You do?"

"Abso-fuckin-lutely."

"My mouth just runs on its own accord around you. I need it, Cowboy."

I chuckle, tugging her closer. Taking her face in my hands, I smash my mouth to hers, and she crushes her body against mine. Fuck, she's the softest thing, and I can't get enough of her.

She tugs at my shirt, and I pull it from my back, tossing it away. Her coat goes next. The warmest damn coat I'm sure has ever been made joins my shirt. In under a minute, we stand naked and out of breath. Impatiently, I grab her ass, kneading it before hoisting her to my waist. She's hungry, pressing open-mouthed kisses over my jaw and neck.

"Fuck, you drive me goddamn crazy, Princess."

The cheekiest smile blooms on her face. She likes that she makes me this way. *Two can play that game, Carlie Lamont.*

I stride to the nearest wall, and her back meets it with a thud. A little gasp escapes as I bend my head, closing my lips around her delicious hard peak. Her hands are feral in my hair, pushing and pulling in desperation as I suckle the nipple and lose it with a pop.

"Oh, fuck, Laws." The sweetest little moan slips when I palm her other breast, nipping the tight bud. She's out of breath, rocking her hips into me, hunting for friction in a movement she can barely manage, pressed against the wall.

I don't move.

I don't give in to her sweet-as-fuck little plea for me to touch her.

Instead, I brush my knuckles over the skin below her belly button.

She whines in protest. "I hate you."

I chuckle.

"Payback, Princess," I rasp.

Who am I fucking kidding? This is torture for me as much as it is for her. This sassy little woman is mine, and I will push her damn buttons and pull the most intense pleasure I can from this writhing, perfect body as I can. I want her to implode with the way I make her feel.

I want her as desperate for me as I am for her.

Something neither of us can walk away from . . .

"Laws, please. Fuck me before I die an early death."

"This won't kill you, baby."

"You sure? I'm on fire. You know if I die, you're responsible for Mills."

That takes me aback, and I cup her face, studying her expression. Without overthinking, I let the first response be the one I go with. I nod.

Her face breaks.

I kiss her trembling mouth and whisper, "I will always be there when either of you needs me. And for the moments you just *want* me around."

"I—yo—oh, god."

I rub my thumb over her cheek, catching a stray tear. "Don't cry, Princess. It's my privilege to love you."

"God, how the hell are you so fucking perfect?"

I laugh now, an amused sound that travels around the room. "Far from that, I'm just your first mate."

"You realize I know what that means for your family, right?" Her eyes study mine as she cycles through heaving breaths.

"Yeah, I do."

She huffs a laugh. "That's what this is, isn't it?"

It's a tangle of a statement and a question, like the words couldn't decide. She can't decide.

"Yes ma'am."

Now she sobs, her face twisting with every ragged tumble of incoherent words she's trying desperately to tell me.

I swipe the tears from her face as they fall.

"I—We—urgh . . . I know I already told you I love you, but I just figured out, like ten seconds ago, how much. Do y—are you, I mean, is it this deep for you?"

I study her gaze as I tuck a rogue strand of hair behind her ear. Her brows lower further with every heartbeat that passes while I try to put into words how obliterating this feeling I have for her is.

I grind my jaw as my throat thickens. "There is no place you could wander to that I wouldn't follow. This sass of yours has got me addicted. This incredible mind, your big damn heart . . . all of it. Mine, until the day you decide otherwise."

Emotion hits her features, and her hand flies up to her mouth, stifling a gasp. She lets out a sniffle before raising an eyebrow playfully. "Possessive looks good on you, Laws."

I moan and drop my face into the crook of her neck. "You drive me to places I've never been before, Carlie. I have about as much say over my heart now as the sands have over the tide."

"Then stop making me wait." She cups my jaw with fine hands, tilting my head up and my gaze to hers. "Fuck me, Cowboy. Just the way I like it, please."

I open my mouth to tell her 'yes ma'am,' but a finger presses over my lips. She wriggles from my hips and sinks to her knees. A second later, her mouth closes around the tip of my cock, and I slam my palms to the wall.

Brown eyes look up at me from under long gorgeous lashes. Perfect pouty lips that give me a run for my money every damn day are wrapped around my rock-hard shaft. It only takes three strokes to turn me to full Neanderthal mode. I haul her up, hands gripping under her arms, and onto my hips as I stride for the bedroom.

"No, the sofa," Carlie rasps.

"You going to save a horse on the sofa, Princess?"

"It's the right thing to do, those poor horses and all."

I sink onto the sofa as she plants her knees on either side of my hips. A heartbeat later, I'm lined up to her soaked entrance, and her hard peaks brush over my chest as she rolls her head back, arching her back. Fucking little temptress knows exactly what she's damn doing.

I've never been a man to complain about getting what he wants, so I take one ample breast in each hand, sweeping my thumb over both nipples at the same time.

"I just want to sink onto you . . ." she breathes.

"Hell, baby, I want that, too. But we're going slow. We make these moments last. You don't rush the best parts. And darlin', you are the best part."

"Fuck, I could orgasm from your damn words, Laws."

I chuckle before flicking each nipple, one after the other.

Carlie hums, rolling her hips, and the head of my cock slips inside her.

Fu-uck me.

I let my hands drift to her waist, holding her where she is. I want to feel her wet heat wrapped around my tip for the rest of my damn life. "Christ, woman, way to send a man to heaven in one tiny fucking move."

Her mouth is a little O as she wriggles ever so slightly.

My grip tightens on her. Hell, I thought our first time was incredible. We've barely started, and this is already blowing that memory out of the water.

"Laws, I need to move . . . *Please.*"

The beg on my sassy woman is damn addictive.

"I'll give you an inch for every time you beg."

Her brows lower, mouth gaping. "And how are you going to stop me from taking it all?"

I rise, quick and nimble from training and running, and flip her onto her back on the sofa.

"That's cheating," she utters, but her hand slides down her

belly toward her sensitive spot that is no doubt driving her crazy.

So I pull out and step back.

"Lawson!"

I lean down, sliding my hand under her knees and pull her toward the end of the sofa. Before she has time to object, I flip her over. Pulling her hips up, I don't stop until her perfect ass is canted up to me. Her slick pussy glistens with need.

All of a sudden, I'm fucking starving.

CHAPTER 37
CARLIE

A rough tongue catches me off guard as it sweeps through my center. I was prepared to be impaled . . . This, this is pure bliss, and I can't control what it does to me as Lawson devours my pussy like a man starved.

He tugs on my clit with his teeth, and my back curves, sending my breasts into the seat and pulling a mewl from my lips. My legs tremble, hands gripping the cushion supporting my chest and head. My ass is so high in the air I should be mortified. But for Lawson, I'm just desperate.

I'm dying for every tiny touch he gives me.

He plays my body like he's its conductor.

"Fuck, a man could get used to this view, this taste. Spread those pretty thighs a little more for me."

I wedge my knees into the edges of the sofa, but my left knee slips.

"Hmm. Technical difficulties. And I want you spread for me, Carlie."

He grips my hips, turning me ninety degrees. My chest now

rests on the back of the sofa, and he nudges my legs so wide, I have to curve my back once again to support myself on the back of the sofa, ass canted toward him as he drops to his knees.

Like the fucking king he is.

That makes me his queen.

I stifle a chuckle at my lame-ass thought.

A hand slaps my left ass cheek, and I jerk, glancing back.

"Focus, Princess."

"I am."

He raises a single brow.

"On you being on your knees for me," I whisper.

"You like that? Me worshipping you?"

"Fuck yes."

"Good." The word is almost a growl.

Without another word, he grips my inner thighs just shy of my entrance and runs his tongue over my soaked center, suckling my clit.

All thoughts of kings and queens fizzle out as I moan, tempted to bite down on the sofa.

"Hell, you're drenched, baby."

"Less talking, more fucking, Cowboy."

"Bossy little woman," he says, shoving two fingers inside me without warning.

"Ah, fuck. God yes," I whimper, wriggling my hips, needing more.

Needing Lawson to fill me up.

Every last inch of him inside me is what I'm salivating for.

He pumps his fingers in and out. "Look at you, Princess. Dripping wet, soaking my damn hand."

"I don't want your hand. It's not enough," I rasp.

He retracts his hand and rocks back on his heels.

"Don't you dare stop," I say on a groan.

His breaths are now choppy, and I see the way he's restraining himself. So, I rise a little and tilt my ass at his eye level. "Please, Laws. Please, I'm burning up for you. So desperate."

He raises an eyebrow. "I'm listening."

"Come on, let me have it, one delicious inch after the other." I grab my breast, squeezing it before rolling the nipple between my fingers. "Oh, fuck, Cowboy."

Rising, I sweep my hair over one shoulder and turn a little so he's looking at my profile. I slide a hand down my belly and sweep a finger over my aching clit.

He fists his cock, his eyes closing as his head falls back. "Sweet Jesus, Carlie."

I sink two digits into my aching core, and instantly my breathing hitches, my heart slamming into my rib cage.

"Look at me, Lawson." My tone is harsher than I mean it to be, but it gets the desired result.

His eyes on me, unwavering.

"Should I just fuck my fingers until I come?"

"Let me see you do that." He shuffles closer, his hand still working his cock.

I swirl my fingertips over my clit and can't help the whimper that tumbles through my parted lips.

He reaches for me, aiming for my breast. I swat him away.

"Mine. You watch."

"Fuck, now you're making me earn it? This is your version of slow?"

"It is. And if I orgasm, you watch. You don't touch. Got it?"

"Got it," he rasps. His words are gravel.

He's right where I want him.

I'm going to make sure my cowboy feels every second of this. Gets every blissful experience I can give him. The overwhelming desire to make him feel good has me dragging this out.

How fucking selfless of me.

I slip two fingers back into my soaked pussy.

The things a girl has to do to treat her man right . . .

I tamp down a smirk, and he tilts his head. "Fuck, Carlie. What the hell is going on in that head of yours?"

"Just you and your big cock, Cowboy. Promise."

He huffs a laugh, pumping his cock harder. "Please, let me touch you."

"Nope."

I roll my nipple through two fingers, letting my eyes flutter shut, just to drive my point home.

Urgh, those last four words just made everything ten times worse.

Drive my—

Rough hands spin me toward the back of the sofa. My thighs are nudged wide, really wide, as Lawson winds my hair around one hand and tugs my hair backward.

"Sorry, Princess, that's not going to work for me. I can't not touch you."

He thrusts upward, and I'm filled completely in the space of a heartbeat.

"Ah, fuck! Laws!"

I grip the sofa with one hand, lacing my fingers through his at my hip. He turns my head to the side, capturing my mouth. A beat later, he breaks the kiss, saying, "Good girl, keep screaming my name."

He thunders into me as his hand leaves my hip. I cant my ass to get a better angle, and he fills me even deeper. Oh god, that's—I'm going to—

Fuck.

His free hand collars my throat as my back presses into his chest and his lips brush the shell of my ear. "Every fucking day for as long as you'll have me, this is exactly where you will come, wrapped around my cock. This is my job, got it?"

"Got it," I rasp.

"Good, good girl. Now milk my fucking cock. Then do it again and again until I fill you up, Princess."

I don't respond—not verbally, anyhow. Instead, I raise one hand, reducing it to two fingers and press them to my forehead in a salute.

His jaw feathers and he thrust into me so deep, so hard, the blissful heat of release swells and explodes, sending me over the edge, wave after delicious wave.

Before I have time to recover from the orgasm of a lifetime, he's hauled me onto his hips, and we're on the floor, on the rug by the coffee table under the flat-screen.

"Hands and knees," he barks.

I take my time lowering to the floor and arching my back before offering up my aching pussy, still wanting—no, needing —more.

"By the time I'm finished with you, we will have fucked on every surface in this tiny-ass apartment." Lawson takes my hips, slamming into me before I can formulate a response.

After I catch my breath from his delectable assault, I glance over my shoulder. "Promises, promises, Cowboy."

"You need it in writing, Captain?"

His face goes through every emotion as he waits for me to respond.

"I trust you. Have your way with me anywhere you want."

"Careful what you wish for," he grinds out.

I roll my eyes at him, and he flips me over, the air rushing from my lungs as my back hits the floor. Hips hauled upward, my legs wrap around his waist automatically as he sinks into me with a heady groan. "Every time I think it can't get better, it fucking does."

I can't respond.

Each punishing stroke is deep, ratcheting up this blissful sensation in my core, sending an ache through my clit. I reach for it, desperate to ease the throbbing need.

Lawson growls—he fucking *growls* at me—as he swats my hand away, gripping my ass with one hand and flicking my sensitive nub with his other.

"Oh, fuck!" I jerk with each harsh flick he sends over my little bean.

It's painful and delicious all at the same time. He slows his pace, alternating between long, languid strokes and harsh flicks. It sends me higher and higher with each movement.

"God, look at you, fucking writhing around my cock, Princess."

He flicks my clit then leans over. "Show me those pretty pouty lips panting."

He flicks it twice and slams into me before pulling out so, so slowly.

I grip the rug beneath me. Arching off the floor, I tremble.

Lawson rubs his fingertip over my clit. "This sweet little thing is driving you crazy?"

He flicks it again.

I moan and meet his gaze. "*You* are driving me crazy."

He offers a smirk back, and . . .

Flicks again.

"Oh fuck, Laws. Please. *Please* . . ."

"You going to come on my cock again, Carlie?"

"Please, yes."

He flicks again.

This time, he sinks into me slowly, all the while pinching my clit.

"I hate you," I hiss, rocking my hips, waiting for the burn to subside. Wanting the bliss back.

And he gives it to me.

Fuck, how he gives it to me.

Lawson slams into me, one hand reaffirming on my hip, the other sliding over my lower belly before his thumb takes up a rhythm over my clit that pushes me higher with every tantalizing sweep of the pad of his finger.

From harsh to soft.

On the next deep, rough thrust, I explode around him. Bucking off the floor, a steady train of whimpers flies from my lips. His name, or parts of it, syllable stacked upon incoherent syllable, spewing from my mouth.

"Good girl. Fucking strangle my cock. Go on."

He keeps up the pace, but his strokes turn sloppy, his grip tightening.

"Your turn, Cowboy. Fill me the fuck up."

His lip curves on a half snarl as he does exactly that. With a low, raw growl, he sends ropes of heat deep inside me.

I go limp on the rug, closing my eyes as a shadow and warmth close in and hover above me. I open my eyes to find myself caged in by Lawson. His hands, on the floor on either side of my head, hold him up. He leans down, still inside me, and kisses my lips, my cheeks, my temples, and finally my forehead.

I slide my hands into his hair, forcing his gaze to meet my own as I say, "Mine."

Before he has a chance to respond, my phone vibrates in my bag where it hangs on the back of his front door, the sound noticeable now that our breathing has settled against the silence.

Lawson rises, leaving me to the rug in my boneless state.

"Oh fuck," he utters as he hands me my phone.

Twelve missed calls from Mills.

No.

No, no, no, no . . .

Oh my fucking god.

I'm tucked into Lawson's side as the Uber travels from his apartment to mine. God above, could they go any fucking slower?

"Can you go faster, *please*?" I hiss.

Lawson's hand wraps around mine. The way his touch, his words seem to crack away at the hardened veneer around my heart. Right now, I wish that veneer was still flawless, because the thought of Mills needing me for hours and me not hearing her calls has the picnic food rising all on its own.

Twelve missed calls over four hours.

When I finally got through to her, she was breathless.

She's been lying on the floor for four fucking hours, while we—while I—

"Oh god, I'm so fucking selfish." I shove my hands into my hair before dragging them down my face where I leave it buried.

God knows what damage she's done to herself.

Hell, she could be bleeding internally, and nobody would know . . .

Lawson's phone rings.

"Yup, she's at Carlie's, I'll shoot you the address. Meet us there, bud."

He hangs up, not bothering with goodbyes.

"Miles is on shift; he took the call. He's meeting us there."

I sag against his side as the first tear spills over and rolls down my burning cheek.

If anything happens to Mills, I will never forgive myself.

CHAPTER 38
LAWSON

Carlie flies out of the Uber as it breaks away from traffic and slows for the curb.

Fuck.

I follow, thanking the driver briefly before a swift exit. The ambulance is already here. Lights flashing still, it idles by the curb, one paramedic still prepping or whatnot in the back with the doors open.

I rush inside, finding Carlie pacing by the elevator. I slam a hand over the up button repeatedly.

"That won't make it go faster," she says weakly, biting down on her thumb.

The second it dings, she flies past me, grabbing my hand and yanking me in with her. One small gesture that speaks volumes. This woman's hell-bent on taking on the world on her own. Now, anxious and upset, she wants me by her side.

I fold her into my chest as the doors close. "Breathe, Carlie. She will be okay, we will make sure of it."

"Don't say that." She pushes from my hold, brown eyes tight with emotion.

"Let's just assess what trouble Mills has gotten herself into when we get up there, hey?"

As if on cue, the elevator dings, and the doors swoosh open.

We're at her front door a heartbeat later, but it's open with Miles waiting in his firefighter uniform.

"Hey Carlie, she's in the bathroom, and she's been asking for you."

"Hey bud," I say as Carlie flies through the apartment toward the bathroom. "How's it look, Milo?"

"Not great, but she seems like a fighter. As far as we can assess on scene, she's fractured her ilium."

"Little words, Miles."

"She's broken her hip on those marble tiles." His face is all sorts of concern wrapped in empathy.

"Fuck." I rub my hands over my face with a groan.

Poor Millie.

The fact she's been lying here for hours . . .

"Has the delay of getting help made it worse?" I ask.

"It's difficult to say. The hospital docs can tell you more after they give her a full assessment."

"I should find Carlie," I utter.

He claps a hand on my shoulder. "She was in a fair amount of pain when we got here, but from the second the meds kicked in, she hasn't stopped talking. She likes you, bud." He gives me a wry smile.

"Thanks for coming." The words are weak, and they don't quite fit. But what else can I say?

I head for the main bathroom that Millie uses as her own.

More EMS staff stand at the bathroom door by a gurney, and I can hear Carlie talking softly to Millie before I see them.

Carlie kneels on the tiles, clutching Millie's hand. Her face is wrecked but still dry. Millie is watching the paramedics as they go about securing her onto the backboard. She has a C-collar on already and an IV in the hand.

"We're going to have to roll you over, Millie, to place the board underneath you," a young paramedic says. "Suck on the whistle, sweetheart, this might hurt a bit."

Millie's shaking hand raises to her mouth as she places the long green whistle between her lips. They allow her a handful of deep breaths on the whistle before Carlie moves, and they turn Millie onto her side.

She cries out in pain.

Carlie's face breaks.

I round the room and pull her into my side, dotting a kiss to her hair. Her fingers grip the opening of my shirt as she turns into my side but doesn't break her gaze from Millie.

She trembles against me, and I hug her tighter, feeling helpless to do anything else.

With the board in place, Millie is lowered back down onto her back. She groans as her eyes flutter shut.

"Oh god," Carlie whispers.

"Keep using your whistle, Millie," the female paramedic says, now at her head. "We're going to take you downstairs to the ambulance and then to the hospital. That okay with you, hun?"

Millie nods, her eyes still closed as she sucks on the whistle.

"Can I go with her?" Carlie says, and I release her as they lift Millie from the floor, still on the backboard, and carry her into the hallway where they rest her on the gurney.

"Of course, you're her granddaughter?" the young guy asks.

"Yes." Carlie's response is without hesitation.

"Your hubby can follow, but he'll need to park in the visitor parking lot."

Carlie glances at me, and I give her a small smile and a nod. "Be right behind you, okay?"

I don't bother correcting them; if I have my way, this woman will be a Rawlins. When the time is right for both of us.

Carlie holds Millie's hand as they roll her out of the apartment and into the elevator.

Miles files in beside me. "Tough gig, poor little lady."

"Yeah," I rasp.

"You good, bud?"

I swallow past the stone in my throat. Me? No way am I worried about me, but Carlie and Millie, fuck, I'm shook up for them both.

"I gotta go, Miles. Text you later. And thanks for being here."

"Anytime, Laws. You look after those girls of yours."

He turns back and helps pack away the gear as I double-check for my wallet and keys. I lock up after the last paramedic leaves and order an Uber. Right now, I'm wishing I had a damn car.

A message pings my phone.

Bring the car, cowboy 🩶

On my way.

I file inside and grab the keys to Carlie's car. By the time I get down to the parking lot under her building, she's sent me three texts with explicit instructions on not wrecking her baby.

> I can drive, Princess. Take care of your Mills.
> Be there in ten.

The hospital's smell, clinical lighting, and constant busy noise brings back a flood of memories from my brother's time in the hospital after we almost lost him. Every tour we knew it was a gamble, that he may or may not return home to us. Those few days after he was hurt in action and not knowing anything but the scarcest details were a literal nightmare.

Striding through the corridor, I take in everything I can, hunting for the curtain number Carlie gave me.

4

When I reach the curtain I'm after, a small, elderly man waits, his hands in his pockets, his gaze staring at nothing in particular as he stands guard. Almost stoic.

Henry.

The tension on his face is one I recognize immediately.

"Henry." I stop a few feet away.

"Lawson, hello." His voice is low but steady.

"How's she doing?"

"Carlie's in there with her. They're waiting to send her to X-ray."

"Good. You need me to grab you a chair? It might be a long wait."

"I'm old, not useless, son." He glances up to me now.

I nod, offering what I hope is a reassuring smile.

His jaw feathers. "Sorry, this has me all kinds of stressed out. It's been a long time since I've had to worry about someone apart from myself."

"No, it's okay. I know what it's like."

He holds my gaze for a moment before sighing.

I can tell by the worried look on his face that this is eating him. "Hey, you want me to grab you a coffee, tea, anything?" I offer.

"Ah—no . . . maybe a tea?" He shifts on his feet, as if unsure about anything right now.

"On it. Be right back."

I head for the nurses' station to ask where the cafeteria is. Armed with instructions, I head that way through the corridors and into the maze of the hospital. Five minutes later, I have found the small but bustling space. Once I have a tray with steaming lidded beverages, I make my way back.

Rounding the ER nurses' station, I find Carlie talking with Henry and who I assume is the doctor. She glances my way, and I can tell the news is not good. Her face is pinched, her hands wringing in front of her as I file in beside her.

"How about we go to the family room and discuss our options." The doctor offers me a small smile.

"Sure," Carlie breathes.

I hand her the coffee and Henry his tea. He nods his thank you, and we follow the doctor.

"You needing anything else?" I lean down and say to Carlie as we reach the family room, where the doctor holds the door open for us. Three green upholstered chairs that look like they've seen better days are lined up against the wall by the door.

"No, I'm good. I'll see you in a bit."

She walks inside, indicating for me to stay outside. Henry ambles in after her, throwing me an empathetic look. I'm not included.

I get it, Millie is her family.

But I thought . . .

I was, too?

We're big on including everyone in everything we do in our family, so it stings a little that she's shutting me out of this. Ultimately, it's her choice.

Maybe the degree of separation is better. I can be of more help if I'm not too close . . .

Despite the self-reassurance, something churns in my gut. Because this feels a lot like those walls of hers are going back up.

She's hurting. Instead of leaning on me, letting me in to help take care of her and Millie, I'm on the outside.

Possibly, I'm reading too much into this.

Or not.

Nope. This is not about me. This is about Millie and Carlie . . . and Henry?

Confused and hoping this isn't the start of the end, I sink into one of the chairs outside the family room. Like they knew not everyone who walks these halls is privileged to be included. Not everyone fits.

That is a kick to the chest.

I force the worry from my head, trying my best to think of anything but being without her. Not being the person she wants around no matter what. I set my coffee on the floor at my feet and run my hands through my hair.

Christ.

The seat vibrates. No, my phone is vibrating in my back pocket.

I pull it out to find Serelle calling.

How did she find out about Millie? Did Carlie already fill her in?

I slide to answer. "Hi, Serelle."

"Lawson. Thanks for picking up on a Sunday."

Her voice sounds off.

"No worries, what's happening?"

"I don't really know how to say this, so I'm going to say it plainly. I couldn't be more disappointed. Honestly, this is not how I imagined hiring you and Carlie would end. I will see the both of you in my office first thing tomorrow morning. You better have one hell of an explanation for this."

Without another word, the line goes dead.

Christ all-fucking-mighty.

CHAPTER 39
CARLIE

"**I**'m not leaving her, Lawson. You go and sort it out. I'm not leaving."

His blue gaze studies mine before he nods. "I'll take care of it."

I have Millie's fine, frail hand wrapped in both of mine. She's only been out of surgery a couple hours, and it's six a.m. on Monday morning. The steady beep of the machines feeding her drip whir with a reassuring rhythm.

Apparently, our plan to fund Serenity with a gala and fly under the radar with our dirty little sponsor secret didn't hold out.

Someone in the wealthy circles in attendance probably spilled. Hell, they wouldn't even have known they were doing it.

Nobody knew the stakes for Serenity apart from Lawson and me.

I would go to bat for the House, I really would, but my priority lies in this hospital bed beside me.

This time, the cowboy will have to ride alone. I have full confidence he can salvage this. He's a brilliant business manager and even better people person.

I keep repeating the thought over and over as Lawson dots a kiss to my forehead and walks from the room, off to face the firing squad alone.

I would feel bad, but my heart has already been ripped from my chest yesterday and now all I feel is . . . numb.

Scared and numb, if that's at all possible.

I can't take anything else. I can't carry another load. For I would surely waver.

Not an option.

God, my thoughts are ridiculous. Probably the fact I'm running on twenty minutes of sleep. I sent Henry home around midnight, but I'm sure he'll be back as soon as he's allowed by the hospital staff.

Mills murmurs, her fingers flexing between mine. I turn on the hard hospital chair and pat her arm. "You're okay, Mills. Just take it easy."

She licks her lips, scrunching up her face as she squints and forces her eyes open. "Urgh, this place tastes like old socks."

"I think that's what happens when you sleep with your mouth open for six hours straight, my sweet."

Her gaze settles on me, and she frowns. "You had those clothes on yesterday. You haven't been here all night, I hope."

"Where else would I be, Mills?"

"Lordy, sweetheart." She tries to move and winces. "Not like I was going anywhere."

That's all it takes. The thought of her going someplace I can't follow. Tears swell and fall instantly.

She swallows, squeezing my hand now in her upturned palm. "I wouldn't leave you like that, I promise."

Ugly sobs chug from my lips, despite the firm line I'm desperately trying to hold them in. I put it down to next to no sleep. My emotions are all over the place.

"Chin up, girlie. No tears for this old lady, you hear?"

"I was so scared. You . . ."

She tugs on my hand, and I stand and lean down to hug her. Her hand, the IV still lodged into it, rubs my back. Hell, I should be comforting her, not the other way around.

"Too many hours alone with your thoughts, sweetheart. That'll do it every time."

"I know," I mumble, and she pats me like I'm the one who needs healing.

As I break away from her hold, she gives me a sad smile and tilts her head. "I love you more than life itself, Carlie Lamont, but I know this is more than just me laid up here. Spill it, girlie."

"No, it's not."

Her brows fall. She gives me her 'now or I'll keep asking' look.

"I can't do it, Mills. I love him—god, so much. But I can't do it."

She studies my face for a moment, her eyes tightening as they line with silver. How long has she wanted this for me? Too long.

Hell, she took to Lawson like he was a son. He'd be the first she's not interfered with, like this is the real deal and we're not playing pretend anymore. Not like the casual flings and the few guys I brought home before I decided it wasn't worth the risk.

"Which part in particular can't you do? The bit where

someone cares about you? The bit where someone has your back, all the time, no matter what? Or is it the bit where you hand over your heart, having to trust one last person?"

When I fall apart at her last words, we both know the answer.

The glass heart Mills bought me that day pops into my mind. Knowingly or not, she gave me the exact replica of how I see my own stupid heart. Hardened and fragile, all at the same time.

Only now, Lawson's grip rests around it.

His hold. Whether that's to keep it safe or wring the life out of it before he leaves, I guess, is the part I'm too terrified to face and find out.

I don't believe in grand gestures.

Hell, not so long ago, I didn't believe in love.

Chemistry and physical pleasure, yes.

Love, no.

My belief system is changing right before my eyes. As if the evidence of how wrong I have been simply keeps unfolding before me with this man.

I'm in awe.

I'm in disbelief.

I'm wholly out of my comfort zone.

"I know how hard it's been for you to let people in. But honey, sometimes the heart recognizes what the head cannot understand. That boy isn't built for your head, we all know you have that part mastered, he's built for your *heart*."

"God, Mills," I say before sinking back into the chair and burying my face in her blankets.

"Besides, Henry and I are getting pretty serious. We're going to need our own space, eventually."

I chuckle through a sobbing breath. She smiles at me with tears in her eyes.

Look at us two.

Pair of mushy crybabies over two men who have turned our little existence on its head.

Half our luck.

With Mills comfortable and the day only just begun, I down a double-shot cappuccino and stride into the office. I'm hoping to catch Lawson before he's called in to see Serelle.

But when I reach the fish tank, it's empty.

Not just empty. It's vacated.

What the actual hell?

His belongings, usually arranged so neatly on his desk, are gone. Bob wanders in with a box of what I assume are his office supplies. The smirk on his face when he claims Lawson's desk makes my cappuccino reappear in my throat.

"What the fuck are you doing?" I snap, tossing my bag on my desk.

"Leveling up." He puffs out his chest, running a hand through his greasy, almost nonexistent hair, the smirk not wavering in the slightest.

"Like hell."

I storm from the fish tank. Where the fuck is Lawson, and why in Lucifer's lair is Bob at his desk? I march through the staff area, making a beeline for Serelle's office. Her door is closed as I round the corridor, and two guys sit in her office as she turns her laptop around, showing them something.

I pull the door open, not caring in the least as it hits the wall with a bang.

"I beg your pardon," Serelle hisses.

"Where is he?" I growl.

"I assume you mean Lawson?"

I tilt my head, snapping my hands to my hips.

She sighs and the two stunned guys murmur as they rise from their seats and file outside. I close the door and lean on the desk. "What the hell is Bob doing in our office?"

"He's your new assistant. I can only keep one exec, and apparently it was you."

I raise an eyebrow. "You're going to have to fill me in."

"Like you and Lawson did when we lost our most significant sponsor?"

I lean on the desk, palms flat. "We made the *executive* decision to correct that before it became a concern. You know, what you hired us to do."

Serelle clears her throat and stands. She gravitates toward the shelves lined with personal items and photographs. "When I started Serenity, things were hard. Like really hard. I was young, female, and the cause was . . . well, let's say not the most popular. Nobody wants to soil their reputations with getting involved in the uglier side of humanity. Not back then they didn't, at least. It was a daily struggle to keep this place afloat and open as much as possible."

"But you made it. You're still here."

"Yes." She turns to look at me. "We are. However, recklessness never served anyone well, and what you both did was reckless. So much so, now we no longer have the budget for the

House. I should have let you both go. But Lawson wouldn't hear of it."

"You fired him!"

"He quit."

My mouth gapes.

What? No.

"W—why?" I stammer.

"I guess he's protecting his own," she breathes, picking up a photo of her and a man. The man's arm is slung around her shoulders. Their smiles are pure happiness.

"I don't understand."

"He quit so you could keep your job. He was protecting you, Carlie."

"I thought there was no budget for either of us."

She huffs a laugh. "That cowboy of yours is very resourceful. He promised to have the gap in funding filled within the hour. And he did. The Robbinses, as in Richard Robbins and his wife, have pledged the rest of our funding. Something about a good tax write-off. Honestly, I'm not concerned about their motivations, only the fact our doors will stay open."

"Ruby," I utter, falling into the chair.

"If Bob isn't a suitable assistant, I'm happy to swap him out with Nadia."

Her words catch me off guard.

"Sorry, what?"

"Bob. He's not the best at productivity. If you would prefer Nadia, I can make that happen."

"Actually, I don't think Bob has a place here at all."

Her brows knit before she says, "What do you mean?"

"I think you should talk to Nadia and the other female staff.

He has an unofficial rap sheet around here—of the sexual harassment kind."

"Oh my god." She sinks into her chair. "How long has this been going on?"

"You'd have to ask Nadia. Lawson found out first, but since he's not here to be her buffer anymore . . ."

"Anything else that's been happening right under my nose I need to know about?"

I want to tell her there was one workplace romance that developed in the last few months.

I want to tell her we should probably invest in a new copier for many reasons, and not just the one where—

"If you're hesitating about mentioning you and Lawson, I'll save you the angst, we *all* knew."

Her serious expression flips to amusement as my own falls with surprise, heat filling my neck and face. "Oh."

She laughs. "Carlie Lamont, PR extraordinaire, spitfire and hurricane all rolled into one. You know that's why I hired you, right?"

"No?"

"You reminded me of myself when I was your age. And without that fire, this place would have died a quick death a long time ago."

It's all I can do to smile as every sentiment she lays between us hits.

Like purpose.

Like home.

"When I brought you two on, I had a little dream of retirement. Leaving the two of you at the helm. Me, sipping margaritas in the Bahamas. But now . . ."

"Now he's gone."

"He is." Her expression is sad but empathetic.

"I—"

She holds up a hand. "Time will work it out. I trust your choices. I have from the start, but this place needs growth. And we needed Lawson to do that."

"We both did."

I don't know why I said that, but it has me rising from the chair and through her door.

"Carlie?" she calls after me.

I turn back to find the older woman smiling, her hands laced under her chin, elbows propped on her desk. "Don't ever lose your fire."

"Yes ma'am."

I find Nadia at her desk in the foyer, but Serelle calls her in a second later.

Serelle's words take their toll. My eyes swell and blur, and I spin back, heading for the fish tank. I open the glass door and clear my throat. "Out!"

Bob leans back in Lawson's chair. The fucking balls on this douchebag.

"Now," I growl.

A crackle through the air turns to a whine, and we all freeze as the oldest PA system in existence fights to come to life around the office. "Bob, effective immediately, you're fired." Serelle's deadpan tone echoes around the large room. Every set of eyes homes in on the fat, balding man in Lawson's chair.

"What the fuck did you tell her, you bitch?" He's out of his chair and in my space a heartbeat later.

"Me? Nothing. Your ass has been officially handed to you by all the women in this office you preyed on. You did this to yourself."

He raises a hand, balling it to a fist, as spittle flies and I dodge sideways.

I catch his wrist and kick the side of his knee, not taking my gaze from him as he crumples to the ground in a lumpy, bald, disgusting heap. "Get out, and do not come back."

"You'll be hearing from my lawyer," he chokes as he pushes to all fours and then rises on wobbly feet.

"Excellent, a direct line to relay every sexual harassment and assault case to. You're a gem, Bob, really."

Cursing me out under his breath, he swipes up his box of shit and leaves.

Good fucking riddance.

I follow him out for good measure and slam the office front doors behind him.

A small chuckle slips out from behind me, and I spin back.

"I can almost taste those margaritas." Serelle shakes her head and wanders back to her office.

CHAPTER 40
LAWSON

It's been thirteen days since I quit Serenity House, and not only have I not heard back from any of my twelve job applications thus far, I also haven't heard a word from Carlie. I scroll through each application, double-checking their status.

No change.

Not one application has moved forward.

To add insult to injury, the letter confirming my lease on my apartment is expiring in four weeks, requiring me to re-sign, sits on the coffee table, mocking me with its crispness and neat type.

Fuck my life.

I'm officially at rock bottom. At the ripe old age of thirty-eight. I think I may be having my midlife crisis a smidge early. How fucking sad is that . . . And the thing tearing me apart is the radio silence. Not hearing from Carlie. Not seeing her. After working together and then being with each other every hour of every day, this smarts like nothing else.

I send Gracie a text.

She's on bed rest for the next week as we await with bated breath for the arrival of the babies.

> Hey Laws. How's the job hunt going?

>> Not great. How's them babies? Ready to meet the world yet?

> I wish they would. Mack says hi.

>> Hey bud.

> So, nothing on the job front, hey?

The text sounds more like Mack than Grace.

>> Nada.

> We always have a spare horse or two if you wanna come home . . .

>> Ha ha. Harry would pitch a fit. Besides, all the good ranches are taken.

> No seriously, you do incredible work there, it's your calling, Laws.

And we're back to Gracie.

>> Thanks, Gracie. Hopefully I can find something that will keep me being useful. I really need a wage again. My lease is almost up.

The dots appear and then vanish. They pop up again.

I want to ask . . .

> Nothing from Carlie.

Oh Laws. I'm sorry.

> Yeah, me too.

Why the hell are you giving up so easily, bud?

Mack.

What, are they playing pass-the-phone? Luckily, I know them both well enough to recognize who sends what.

> I'm not giving up, Mackie-boy, simply respecting the woman's space, is all.

Um, okay . . .

> What's that supposed to mean?

Grace said you should go after her.

I did not.

> Carlie is decisive, independent and has her plate full with Millie. The last thing she needs is me bothering her.

Sweet Jesus, bud. It's not bothering when you're helping out. You do for family and that girl is family

Careful Mackinlay, you're starting to sound like Harry.

The man has foresight we all wish we had. Besides, I'd hedge a bet she's waiting on you to make a move. She seems about as stubborn as Harry.

I laugh out loud at that one.
Mack has a point.

Gotta go, see you next week. Send me pictures, Gracie. You know, when they're all cleaned up and cute.

Of course. Love you, Laws.

Love you too, Gracie.

The dots appear and then disappear.

Love you bro. Go get your captain already.

I chuckle at his affection. Our family has always been in each other's pockets, but after Mack's injuries on tour, we kind of all took it up a notch. Nothing like almost losing a brother to get your priorities right.

I shut the laptop and change into Levi's and a polo shirt. Grabbing my keys, I swipe my wallet off the entry table and order an Uber.

Here goes nothing.

I did not think this through.

Pacing outside Carlie's apartment, I can hear the television on inside Carlie's apartment, the sound punctured by the occasional chatter.

Saturday. She should be home, right?

My heart has permanently lodged itself in my throat.

Sweet Jesus.

What if she tells me to take a hike? What if she doesn't want to see me . . .

Fuck, I shouldn't have come.

"Fuck," I groan, running a hand through my hair. Footsteps pad toward the door. I glance to the small camera by the doorframe that has a direct line to her phone.

Dammit, I forgot about that.

No escaping now.

I should have brought supplies or something.

I briefly close my eyes as the door locks click open on the inside. Letting my arms hang by my sides, I try to find the words I want to say to her.

Something like *I want to help*.

I want to make sure they're both okay.

I'm desperate to make sure Carlie is taken care of when she kills herself to care for Millie and put in forty hours a week—minimum—at work.

The door opens.

I haul in a useless breath, my jaw feathering as I wait for the door to reveal the strawberry blonde, her elegant face, those brown eyes that see right through me.

Instead, Henry steps out. "Lawson, are we expecting you?"

"Ah, no sir."

I rub a hand behind my neck. Hell, should have called first.

Remembering why he would be here, I ask, "How's Mills?"

"Bossy." He smiles around the word. "But improving every day, thank god."

We stare at each other for a heartbeat before he opens the door wider. "Did you want to say hello?"

"I—"

"Carlie's at work, but Millie would love to see you." He practically beams at me.

I huff a strangled sound, but relief doesn't find me.

"Sure," I breathe and follow him inside as he closes the door.

"She's set up in the living room. Easy to get to the bathroom and kitchen that way."

I find Millie reclined in her chair. When she sees me, she sits up. A little sound that registers like pain slips through her lips. I sit on the arm of the chair by hers, and she clasps my hand in both of hers. "We have missed this handsome face." A hand rises and pats my jaw.

Henry grunts as he lowers onto the three-seater, as if reminding Millie he's here.

"Jealousy is not your best color, Henry." Millie frowns at him but winks as she returns her gaze to me. "Our girl is at work. Hard at work without you, I might add."

"Good, she belongs at Serenity, Mills."

Her frown returns. "And so do you."

I shake my head.

"You think she's better off without you?" The words are soft. "Because I can tell you now, she is absolutely not."

"It's her choice, Mills. Not mine."

"Poppycock. That girl needs a shove in the love department. Lord knows she loves you. She's afraid, is all. No one's bothered to stick around for her before." She studies my face for a beat. "But you, you're different. You stuck with her even when you couldn't stand each other. You're loyal to a fault, my boy."

I don't know what to say to that. Henry is nodding like every word Millie speaks is truth.

"She's at work, and I think she would love some help." Millie waves me off.

"Go get your girl, Lawson!" Henry pipes up, pumping a fist into the air.

Not wasting another second, I mutter a thank you and see myself out.

Pulling up the Uber app one more time, rethinking the whole no-car thing, I order another ride.

Here goes nothing.

Again . . .

CHAPTER 41

CARLIE

The fish tank floor is littered with printouts. Budgets. Marketing. PR plans. Company org charts. And so on. Despite having a business degree similar to Lawson's, spending a decade in PR means I'm out of practice when it comes to business management.

Technically, I'm qualified.

Practically . . . not so much.

What was Serelle thinking, letting him quit?

I sigh, shifting the laptop off my sweater-clad lap as I lean over and hunt for the forecasts and projections for the House for the next quarter. I need to redo the current budgets and projects to accommodate the influx of donors after the Robbinses sponsored us, and their friends and associates followed suit.

Now we are set to thrive, not just survive.

It's exciting and terrifying. God, I cannot screw this up. Every choice I make feels like the wrong one. I close my eyes with a sigh. "Where are you, Lawson?" I groan, slapping papers over my face.

A knock rattles the glass door.

I let the papers fall away from my face.

The man himself stands there. "Right here, Princess."

I drop the papers to the floor, mouth agape.

If I hadn't gotten a solid seven hours of sleep last night, I'd say I drifted off on the piles of paperwork and this is simply a dream. He takes a step into the fish tank. I scramble to my feet, but I really can't figure out what to say first.

To apologize for ghosting him while I'm sorting out my abandonment issues.

To cuss him out for quitting a job he loved for me.

For being so stupidly selfless.

It's been almost two sleepless weeks of being back and forth on whether I can do this and trust myself not to ruin everything every time something gets hard, like I did when Millie was in the hospital.

That was unforgivable.

Mills was so cranky at me.

"Carlie . . ."

I suck in a wobbly breath, running my bottom lip through my teeth. I want to respond. Now I know what I'd go with. Just sorry. Plain and simple. He deserves more, but I—

"Need a hand, Princess?"

His gaze casts over the paper-strewn floor. Always so selfless.

"No," I manage. "I don't need a hand, Lawson. I need—"

I scrunch my face up as the emotion commandeers my ability to speak, running all the logical thoughts I had from my mind.

He closes the distance between us. "Tell me."

His knuckles brush over my cheek, and my eyes fall shut at his warmth. His touch.

Oh god, I missed him so fucking much.

"I ain't askin', darlin'."

I huff a breathy laugh and open my eyes at the phrase his father uses. It suits him. It's evidence of the man he is. The family he comes from. The devotion he has to his family. To the people he loves.

"What if I can't?" I whisper.

"Then I'll wait until you figure it out."

"What if it takes months?"

My chest caves when a small smile pops up on one corner of his mouth. "Even if it takes us years."

"Us?"

"Yes ma'am."

I huff out a sob, my palm landing over his heart. His big damn heart . . .

"In that case, I have something for you." I break away and pad to my desk, rummaging through the drawers before I find what I'm looking for.

I return to Lawson. He's where I left him, as I left him. As if proving the point on his patience.

I swallow and hold the hard glass object in my hands.

Before I can get a word out, his hands fold over mine.

"I know I can trust you, Cowboy." My words are soft but steady. "It's going to take me a little time to get used to being one-half of somethin—"

His forehead drops to my own. "Something this incredible."

"Yeah, that. But . . . I'm scared."

"If it's your heart you're worried about, baby, don't be. I keep my promises."

"I know, I'm not. It's yours I can't trust myself with. But I'm willing to try for real, if you are."

He breaks away a little and opens my hands, the pink glass heart sitting in my palms. "So, this is my heart?"

I nod, but that's not quite right, either. "It's ours."

And right now, it sits in my hands, now cradled inside his.

"It's perfect, Princess."

"My part is the fragility of it, but the shine, also. That I can give you."

"And mine to protect," he rasps as his hands curl, his thumb brushing over the smooth, hard surface. "My part, the permanent, unmoving. The way it will not yield. Always standing true for yours."

Tears burn behind my eyes.

His hand falls away and he cups my jaw, tilting my head up. "Now tell me, Carlie. What do you want?"

A smile grows over my face. "I'd rather show you than tell you, Cowboy."

I push up on my tiptoes and brush my lips over his. "I want this." I kiss his jaw. "And this."

Dotting kisses down his neck and over his Adam's apple, I breathe, "And definitely this . . ."

It bobs as he chuckles. Leaning to one side, he places the heart on the desk.

"My turn."

"It is?" I raise a brow.

"Abso-fuckin-lutely, Princess."

He hauls me to his hips and walks from the fish tank.

"Where are we going?"

"The best make-out spot in this place."

We round the supply room to the copier, and I laugh so hearty my head falls back.

"I could fucking eat you, baby," he growls. "Look at you, happy and—Christ—damn edible in these sweatpants."

"This does it for you? Not my expensive designer skirts and heels?"

"That works, too. Maybe it's not the clothes at all." The ridiculous grin on his face has a smile growing on my own. But it falters as his head dips and his mouth finds my peaks through the lopsided T-shirt I have on.

My hair is up in a bun, and I slip a finger into the band, releasing it. Strawberry blonde waves tumble over my shoulder, and he groans. The sound vibrates around my nipple and all of a sudden, I'm at a loss for air.

"Goddamn, Carlie."

My ass meets the copier, and I spread my legs, making space for him to get as close as possible. My hands in his hair, I can't breathe when he slips my T-shirt from my body, his fingers releasing the clasp on my bra, his lips falling back to my aching nipple . . .

"Oh god."

"Baby, he ain't here. Just your cowboy."

A strangled, desperate chuckle slips through my parted lips.

My cowboy.

Mine.

A fire is lit, well and truly, low in my core. Now the last thing I want is to be wearing clothes. For him to be wearing clothes. I wriggle on the machine, and the plastic creaks.

"Patience, Princess."

"No."

"No?" His head pops up. "Sassy little woman, aren't you."

"It's one of my best qualities."

He chuckles. "I know."

I slide forward, and he catches me in his arms, letting me down onto his hips. "Take me home, Cowboy."

"Mills might—"

"Your home, Laws."

The second the door to Lawson's apartment closes, he has me pinned to it. I open for him. He takes everything, devouring my mouth, hands scaling my ribs, a thumb brushing the underside of my breast.

Damn, I can't wait a moment longer.

Two weeks without this man is too long.

Far too long.

"Wait, I want to do something first." He breaks away, cupping my face with his hands.

"What is it?" I breathe.

He opens my bag, pulling out the glass heart. He takes my hand and walks into his bedroom. We stand in front of his dresser as he makes room in the center and places it there. "Safe as houses."

I huddle into his side, lacing my fingers with his. "Safe as houses." I tilt my gaze up. Adoration fills his deep blue eyes as he plants a kiss into my hair.

I push him backward, and he grins as the back of his legs hit the bed. After a well-placed shove to his chest, he sits on the end of the big bed and spreads his legs, not giving me a second before he pulls me into his space, trapping me there.

"Now, where were we?" I whisper, cupping his jaw with both hands. His blue eyes have darkened, his breathing picking up the pace as I send my hands through his hair. Deft fingers toss my T-shirt away once again. My bra disappears quicker than before, and my breath hitches as warm lips close around my peak, and we pick up where we left off.

"Fuck, Laws."

He rumbles something I can't make out, releasing the nipple with a delicious pop.

"Don't stop, please . . ."

Teeth clamp down around my other peak and heat tumbles down my spine before growing in my core. I lose my tangled fingers from his hair and make quick work of my jeans, needing them gone. In only panties, I reclaim his jawline in both hands, sinking my mouth over his.

A tight grip finds my hips as his palm travels up my rib cage, cupping a breast. The other hand tracks the pads of his fingers over the cleft of my hip and inside my thigh, running along the edge of my panties, now soaked.

His finger slips past the elastic barrier, and I moan. A sound he swallows down, taking it in as his own breath.

"Never going to happen," he rasps as he breaks away.

The overwhelming need for Lawson sends my body trembling. I wave him backward. "Back, on the bed. All the way."

Ignoring my instructions, he stands and is naked a moment later. He slides his hands down my ribs and over my ass before pulling me up onto his hips. "There so many spots we can do this that don't include the bed."

"Fine," I breathe.

We're in the kitchen a heartbeat later, the small counter hitting my ass. I'm clawing at him as he dots hot, wet kisses down my neck, over my collarbones, and nips the flesh of one breast. I plant my hands behind me, leaning back, and he spreads my thighs, dropping his head between them.

"Fuck, baby, damn soaked."

I grip his hair with a fist holding his mouth where I want it. With the first sweep of his hot tongue through my center, I buck off the counter, falling back.

The few items he had on the counter in a small tray are knocked to the floor with a smash. A breathy chuckle against my pussy, and I'm writhing on the countertop, grip firm in his dark hair.

"Ride my face, Princess. Fucking ride it. Then I'm going to fuck this tight little pussy until you're screaming my name."

I whimper as he suckles down hard on my clit.

Promises, promises.

CHAPTER 42
LAWSON

Carlie laid bare on my kitchen counter is the way I want to end every fucking day. Every long, hard day should be rewarded this way. For the both of us. Grabby hands pull on my wrists. Her brown eyes darken as her fingers pluck a nipple.

Fuck me.

"You hungry?" I ask, and her head pops up, brows drawn, tone obviously not lending to her current mood, and it catches her off guard. I smile, playing with her.

"No." She slides a hand down her belly, slipping a finger into her soaked center, and I almost ditch what I had in mind. Almost.

I open the refrigerator and lean down, turning my back to her. "I'm starvin'."

A little huff sounds from behind me.

My smile widens.

I grab the can of whipped cream and the strawberry jam.

Perfect.

I turn back, letting the refrigerator door fall closed, and she's sitting at the end of the counter, hands gripping the edge. Her expression is a tangle of confusion and annoyance that falls away to surprise when her gaze dips to the items in my hands.

"I'm fucking starving, baby. Lie down."

"You wouldn't . . ." she breathes, her gaze alternating from the cream and jam to my face.

"I absolutely would. Now. Lie down." The words are more of a growl as every last bit of blood sinks south at the sight of her bare on my kitchen counter.

She huffs a breathy "Fuck" and does as she's told.

I like this Carlie.

For a little while, anyway. I couldn't go without her smart mouth keeping me on my toes for too long. Her eyes don't leave my face, her breaths cycling deep and quick as I shake the can and flip the lid off with my thumb. It hits the floor, rolling away as I step up to the counter.

"Close your eyes, Princess."

With a quick warning glance, she lets her eyes flutter shut.

I survey her soft skin, the delicious angles of her curves, her breasts, the dip of her stomach, the frame of her hips that gives way to the place I want to dive into and never return. Shaking the can once more for good measure, I squirt a perfect circle around one nipple. The instant the cold cream hits her skin, she hisses, hands curling around the long edges of the counter.

"Laws . . ." she breathes.

"Keep 'em closed," I rasp.

A tentative smile curves over her lips, her grip turning white on the counter when I pepper more cream on her breast.

I run a line of the glossy white topping down her center, stopping just before the sweet nub I'm sure is driving her crazy right now.

I round the counter so I'm at the end, spread her thighs, and strategically place more cream up each thigh, stopping short of her entrance.

"Lawson Rawlins, don't you dare." She swallows hard.

I squirt the cream over her clit, letting it fall and cover her pussy.

"The hell . . . you didn't," she whines.

I chuckle at her. I've never seen her so wound up. So desperate. It's magnificent. I reach for the jam and twist the lid off before dropping dollops over her skin, little ruby pearls of jam.

Now I really am fucking starving, looking at her spread for me, splayed over the counter.

She's damn delicious.

I pad to her head and bend over, kissing her mouth. "Hold on to the counter, Princess."

Not giving her a chance to respond, I lick the cream from one breast.

Her back leaves the counter on a whimper.

I clean the cream from her sweet, fleshy breast and suckle the nipple, then move to the other.

Her hands are white-knuckled around the edge of the counter when I'm done, and I slowly make my way down her belly, feasting my way south on a smorgasbord of strawberries and cream.

Fuck, this might be my favorite memory of this fiery little woman yet.

Running my tongue over the last of the whipped topping on her belly, I move to her clit. One hard suck and she's crying out my name, her body trembling on the hard surface.

"Hold still, I'm hungry." I grip her thighs with a rough hold, shoving them wider as I devour the sweet goodness from her throbbing nub, sweeping my tongue over her entrance. The combination of strawberries and cream and Carlie is heady. Overwhelming.

My cock throbs, agonizingly so.

The telltale heat spikes low in my spine and my balls tighten, and I have to take a breath. Fuck, there is no way I'm losing my load to the counter instead of inside my favorite fucking human. I clamp a hand over my cock.

As the urge subsides, I dive back in, but now she's sitting up. Brown eyes burn into mine as her chest rises and falls in rapid succession. "Why'd you stop?"

I groan. "You're—"

"You still look hungry to me." Her hands are in my hair, fingers tangling as she sends me back in to finish what I started.

I would chuckle at her, but I'm too desperate now. I may have started this little picnic to tease her, but hell, now I'm the one strung out for this.

I send my tongue through her center, and her legs fall away wider as she leans over, cradling my head against her chest. I tilt my head up and suckle a nipple into my mouth. Her back arches, hips rocking forward.

Fuck.

"Fingers, please," she utters.

I slide two fingers inside her, nibbling on one hard peak as she moans my name between strings of curses. Her hands cup my jaw as she looks down at me before she shoves my face back to her pussy. "You're still hungry, baby. Eat."

"You have no idea," I growl.

I lean to the side of the counter and drag a stool to the end. Planting myself on it, I slide my hands under her knees and pull her to the edge until her pussy is in my face, my mouth lined up with my feast. "No coming until I tell you, you hear?"

She scoffs a laugh and rolls her eyes at me.

I shake my head at her with a smile before diving in. I run a slow, strong stroke of my tongue through her, curling it as I lap up the cream. Swallowing, I lick my lips.

Fuck, a man could die like this. From the pure torturous bliss of it.

I lick and devour the last of the cream, thumbing the trail still on the inside of her thighs into my mouth intermittently, dragging this out for as long as possible.

The more time I take, the more wound up she becomes, until my girl is writhing on the hard countertop. I'm an ass, I know, because I have been purposely avoiding the one place she is desperate for me.

So I'm not surprised when her hand releases the edge of the counter, and two fine fingers ghost over her clit.

I take her hand, lacing my fingers with hers as I drop my mouth to the sweet little nub. It quivers in my mouth on the first suckle.

"Oh fuck, Laws."

She's so close.

I lift my head, running a finger through her entrance. "Not yet, baby."

"No, please . . ." she cries.

"So fucking desperate to come, Carlie."

Her back leaves the counter, brown eyes boring down on me, her face twisted with agonized annoyance. "I—"

"You want more, you can either beg for it or tell me just how *mine* this pussy is."

Her brows fall.

I can practically see the cogs turning as she goes back and forth on which one she'll relent to. Either is fine by me. But I want her to know she's mine and that I'm not going anywhere.

I stand and cup her face in my hands. "Beg or confess."

Her browns line with silver, and still no answer spills through her lips. "Confess," she whispers.

"I'm all ears." I drop my forehead to hers.

"I love you, Lawson Rawlins. I'm yours." She huffs a breathy laugh. "My pussy is yours. And . . ."

"And?" I lean back, searching her face.

"Please, Cowboy. Please fuck me. I need you. I want every part of you. Every amazing fucking inch of you."

"Both, I'm impressed."

She leans closer and nips my bottom lip. It stings a little before copper slips into my mouth.

"Oh, you've done it now, Princess."

"I have?" Her eyes widen as they flicker over my face.

"Oh yeah." I slide her from the counter and onto my hips. "Now I'm going to make you wait so long."

"No, Laws." Her hands palm my jaw. "No, please."

I love her begging. Not because it makes her submissive, but because the way she needs me makes me feel whole. Like no matter what, I'll be able to take care of her. Of us. No matter what comes our way.

I wander to the bedroom with her resting on my hips.

"The bed? How vanilla, Cowboy." She narrows her eyes at me.

Ignoring her sassy little barb, I sit on the bed and manhandle her until her back is to me. She looks over her shoulder with a lazy smile. "Wanna watch me bounce, Cowboy?"

"Fuck yes."

She lines herself up with my aching cock. And fuck, I can't wait another damn second. I grip her hips, slamming her downward as I thrust up.

"Oh god, Laws." Her head falls back, strawberry blonde waves swaying down her back.

This is it. The sight of her, her bare curves, her hair over her back, small shoulders dipping to a slim waist that ends with her perfect round ass now bobbing up and down on my cock.

My grip on her hips tightens as I groan.

She rises slower this time, looking over her shoulder.

"Good, Cowboy?"

"Fuck, baby. Jus—" I still her with my hands.

Fuck.

"Don't you dare, Lawson Rawlins. I plan on fucking you on every single surface in this tiny-ass apartment."

I huff out a strangled laugh and she lowers, so damn slow my head spins. Each breath burns its way through my chest. "Move, we need to move, then."

She rises, losing me from her delicious heat. I groan, reaching for her.

How the tables have turned.

Fuck, I'm pathetic for this woman.

And she damn well knows it.

She walks backward, beckoning me with a crooked finger. "Come, Cowboy."

I leave the bed, my cock aching at the loss of her.

"Follow me, Lawson . . ."

Any-fucking-where, Princess.

Any-fucking-where.

CHAPTER 43
CARLIE

The ache in my chest at the sight of this man strung out and desperate for me is a new high I'll never tire of.

I wander backward into the bathroom. Spinning back, I pad to the vanity, catching my reflection as my skin meets the cool surface. Lawson crowds me from behind, his hard length digging into my ass as he folds me in his arms and meets my gaze in the mirror. "God, I fucking love you," he growls dipping his mouth to my neck.

"Show me just how much," I whisper.

My legs are nudged apart by his knees.

His hold releases, and one hand wraps my long hair around a tight fist, the other wraps around my throat, tilting my head back.

He lines his cock with my soaked entrance.

"You want me to show you how much I love you, Princess?"

"Yes."

My head is tugged back a little further.

"Every inch I give you is a million little ways of how I love you." He slips inside me, rimming my entrance, stretching me with his tip.

My mouth waters.

I know he was just inside me, but fuck, this is different. I feel coveted. Wanted. His.

I cant my ass, wanting more.

I get another inch.

"Two million ways . . ." he rasps, his voice gravel.

My mouth falls open on a soundless gasp. His teeth find the soft flesh under my ear.

Another inch.

"More," I whine.

"Greedy little woman, aren't you. So much for that sassy little mouth. Give you a couple of inches, and you fall apart for it."

"Fuck you."

His low, heady chuckle rumbles through both of us.

But I get another inch.

Hell. I want it all. Now.

"Laws, please."

I'm clawing at his neck, my arms cradling his head as he groans into my ear.

Another inch . . .

"Oh god," I cry, my pussy clamping down with the first edgy feeling of an orgasm. He withdraws, and the words tumble from my lips, "I fucking hate you."

He growls at me. The gravel tone sends my body into a frenzy. I buck my hips, wanting everything he can give me.

"You can take it all this way, baby?" His hand tightens around my throat as I nod.

"Good." He slams all the way in. "Million to infinity. Don't you ever forget it, Princess."

"Infinity . . ." The word is a broken plea. A reminder of how deep this thing between us goes. How indestructible his promise to me is. I turn my head, hunting for his mouth. It drops to mine, his kiss searing.

I clamp down around him, my fingers frantically flicking over my clit.

"Not yet," he rasps. His hand releases my throat for a second as he laces my fingers with his before reapplying our tandem grip around my airway again.

Every thundering thrust has my body shaking. I open my mouth to—

His thumb hooks in the corner of my mouth. I suck it in, and he bites down on the soft flesh where my shoulder meets my neck.

He thrusts deeper.

Oh god. Heat whips through my core, sparks uncoiling as I whimper a string of incoherent profanities.

"Fucking *wait*," he growls.

"I—I can't."

"Christ, baby." He grips my hips, slamming up into me as his movements turn sloppy and erratic. I unfold around him, the bliss starting in my core and spreading through every damn limb as wave after wave crashes through me and I come, dragging Lawson's release along behind mine.

He growls, spilling warmth inside me as his grip on my throat wavers and his face sinks into the crook of my shoulder.

"Sweet Jesus, Carlie, the ways I love you are too many and not enough all at once."

I roll my head back, letting it rest on his shoulder. "Lucky we have forever to work through every single one, Cowboy."

"Yeah, lucky."

Mills looks amazing in her new outfit, which we spent far too many hours to find. She looks full of life once again. Back to her normal, brilliant self. After months of recovery, she's sprung back like no one else.

Her main motivator? Well, he's currently waiting in the foyer downstairs with my own.

We have a double date.

The boys, as we have affectionately titled them, have been planning this dinner for two weeks. Apparently. I double-check my own outfit and reapply my lipstick before sliding into my heels.

"You look . . . stunning, sweetheart." Mills pats my cheek as I turn back to her.

Long dangling silver earrings, almost touching my shoulders, tinkle as I move. My favorite spring dress sways around the tops of my knees.

Millie's eyes swell with what I'm guessing are happy tears. I really hope they are.

"Mills," I breathe.

"Look at you, all grown up." Her head tilts.

I roll my eyes at her. "Very funny, little lady."

She scrunches up her nose. "I'm so proud of you. You know that, right?"

I suck in a breath and hold it, hesitating before I say, "What's this all about, Mills?"

She takes my hands in hers. "My life would have turned out so much different if it wasn't for you."

"No—"

"Let me finish," she scolds, and I release a huffy laugh, tears now welling in my own damn eyes.

"This in here." She presses a palm over my heart. "You guard it well, and now I know why. It took a little while, but we all figured it out. You hid it well because it's so stinking big. The things you will do, the people you have helped . . . will help. Honey, some angels walk this earth with us, and I'm certain you are one of them."

"Mills," I breathe, a sob slipping out after the syllable.

"Now, no more tears. Two handsome men are waiting on us and I have no plans on disappointing either of them."

Either of them?

Oh, Mills. I chuckle and sweep my fingers under my eyes to dry my cheeks. This little lady changed my life. She thinks I'm her angel, but she has no idea how much I think the same of her. I would have lived a meager, lifeless, and loveless existence without her.

I truly believe that.

Ten minutes later, the elevator doors ping and we stride from the small space, her arm looped through mine. In unison, Lawson and Henry turn, whatever conversation they're having stalling as their gazes lock onto us and their faces go slack.

Mills squeezes my upper arm where she grips lightly and whispers, "I have a good feeling about tonight."

"Don't do anything I wouldn't do," I whisper into her ear.

She laughs, the hearty sound sending her head tipping

back, her face stretching with the happy motion. We close in on our boys, and Mills extricates herself from my proffered arm, favoring the one Henry crooks for her. "Thank you, my love."

He beams down at her.

"Geez, Henry, trying to show me up?" Laws chuckles, offering me his arm.

I slide my own through his, pressing into his side as he plants a kiss to my temple.

Henry glances at me before smiling at Millie. "Doubt that will happen tonight, young man."

What is with all the cryptic bullshit?

"Do we need to order an Uber before they give away our reservation?" I ask Laws.

"Our ride's already here."

"Oh. Well, let's go."

"Let's." Millie walks for the doors, Henry keeping up— almost.

I chuckle a laugh at her. Someone's hungry.

The double doors glide open, and we spill out onto the sidewalk, right in front of a new grey Chevrolet Colorado sitting by the curb. Lawson opens the front passenger door. "You ride up front with me . . ." He waves a hand, gesturing for me to climb in.

"Laws?" I glance between the luxurious interior and his handsome damn face.

"I'm your driver tonight."

Millie's hand presses over her mouth. The little shit is trying not to laugh, I swear.

"This is *yours*?"

"Yes ma'am."

"Lawson," I say, stunned, searching his face. The pickup is impressive. It's so Lawson.

"Perk of the new job. You're looking at the newest executive HR recruiter for Goldman Sachs."

"That's incredible!" I throw my arms around his neck. "Congratulations, Laws. You deserve it."

I break away, and he ushers me into the car. With a slap to my ass, he closes the door with a wink and then helps Henry with Millie.

I twist in my seat. "Did you know about this?"

She shrugs in her seat in the spacious back row.

She damn well knew, alright.

I'm happy for Laws—I am—but something doesn't sit right with his new job. Lawson's the good guy, he's the one people go to when they need an ally. He's the one who fights for the right thing, always.

He's a people person.

The man himself slides into the driver's seat as Henry closes his own door. Laws fires up the pickup and slides it into gear. It rumbles, and he sits there for a moment, hands on the wheel, seemingly lost in some sort of trance.

"Young man, I am not getting any younger back here." Millie's words have the four of us cracking up. Laws flicks the turn signal and pulls away from the curb. And fifteen minutes roll by, along with the city lights of the only home I've ever known. Finally finding a parking spot, Lawson swings the big pickup into the space like he's been doing it his whole life.

I guess he has.

Maybe it's true . . . you can take the boy out of the country, but you can't take the country out of the boy. Or is it the man out of the mountains?

The little Italian restaurant is lit up. The red and white tables inside are almost full. It's busy.

My door opens, and Laws extends a hand. "Come on, Princess. I'm starving."

The memory of our countertop picnic floods back into my mind, but I manage to climb out of the truck and help Mills down.

Once inside, the maître d' checks our booking before taking us to our table for four. Settling in, I sit beside Lawson as Henry sits in front of me across the table.

"Nope this will not do," Millie mutters. She pats Henry on the shoulder. "Carlie, honey, take my seat. I want to see this handsome face while I slurp up spaghetti."

"Seriously, Mills?" I rise and take the spot by Henry. Now I'm facing Laws, and he shoots me a happy smile. These two are adorable. Millie sinks into the seat by Lawson, and Henry reaches across the table, taking both her hands as she sighs and says, "That's better."

"Evening, can I take your order? Perhaps start with some drinks?" a waiter in a black-and-white uniform says, his hand poised over his tablet.

"Give us a minute, will you, honey?" Millie pats his arm like he's her long-lost nephew.

He gives her a forced smile and wanders to another table.

"Actually, I'm not very hungry," Millie proclaims. "I'll have the entrée, maybe a small glass of wine."

She's picking up the menu, studying like it's the most inter-esting thing in the world. We order and enjoy the world's silkiest pasta with the most amazing sauce, and then dessert arrives, the richest chocolate lava cake that's ever been created.

I swear it on my father's grave. Whenever that blessed event should occur.

Millie's looking around, like she's looking for someone or something.

What is up with her tonight?

Henry yawns. "I could turn in early, actually. Long day and all." The acrid scent of sulfur drifts through the large room.

"What? No, Henry." I rest a hand on his arm. "Are you feeling okay?"

He tugs at his collar.

"Oh no. You need some water?" I pour the table water into a glass and shove it between his hands. I look for waitstaff, but they all seem to be busy moving around the room to each table, handing out something small before darting to the next.

"Maybe it's this table. Bad feng shui or something." He rises, and Millie does the same. I glance back at them, confused.

What is going on here? I stand and help Millie as she shuffles closer to Henry, now heading away from our table.

"Another table sounds good, Henry. I'm not in the mood for company now."

"Mills, what are you up to?"

Henry guides her to a spot a few tables down. "Whatever you need, my love."

It's then I find the waitstaff lined up along the wall, their hands clasped in front of them and smiles on their faces. The house lights dim, and the many lit candles now burn brighter.

I turn, looking around the room. The other patrons have fallen silent as I notice the dozens of candles dotted around the restaurant and on every table. Some patrons are still lighting their table candles frantically.

"Mills, what's going on?"

She smiles at me, happiness radiating through her gaze as she laces her fingers together in front of her chest.

The restaurant is a buzz of flickering candles, my now laden breaths, and the odd throat clearing. Henry swirls a finger in a stirring motion, telling me to turn around.

I—

My body moves of its own accord. I find nothing at first, then deep blues beaming up at me from . . .

Lawson is kneeling on the floor, on one knee.

Oh fuck.

"Hey, Princess."

"Hey, Cowboy," I choke.

"Tell me."

"Tell you what?"

He smiles up at me, but I can see his chest heaving with every breath, his grip tight on the small velvet box in his hand. He runs a hand through his hair, messing it up a little. The sight takes my breath away.

"Tell me what would make you the happiest in the whole world, and I'll make it happen."

"I—" Emotion closes over my throat, but after a heartbeat, I whisper, "You."

"Well." He chuckles. "That's really good to hear, especially since I thought you might want this." He cracks the box open.

A princess-cut solitaire on white gold sparkles in the candlelight.

Tears spill now, burning their way down my cheeks.

I drop to my knees, taking his hands in mine.

He chuckles again. "You're supposed to stand for this part, baby."

I shake my head. "Nope."

He dots a kiss to my forehead and slides the ring onto my finger.

"Lawson," I manage. "You forgot—"

"Marry me, Carlie Marie Lamont."

"That sounds like a statement, not a question, Lawson Rawlins."

"Yes ma'am."

I sob a huffy chuckle.

"Sassy Cowboy."

He tilts his head, raising his eyebrows, as if needing to hear the answer he already knows is coming.

"Yes, of course. Always."

"Christ, woman. Give a man a heart attack."

I take his face in my hands, palming his jaw, pulling his mouth to mine.

Cheers break out all over the restaurant. Wolf whistles rip through the air. All of a sudden, the crowd behind us has an accent, straight out of—

"Congratulations, darlin'." Harry pulls me into a hug as I huff a surprised sound.

Montana . . .

Louisa has Lawson in her hold. And that's when I see his brothers, Ruby, Addy, and Grace standing behind his parents.

Oh my god.

I spin around when Harry releases me. "Lawson Rawlins, what if I'd said no?"

He chuckles, breaking away from Louisa. A beat later, my face is cradled between his huge, warm hands. "Then I really would have something to atone for."

I gasp. He remembers *that*.

This man, my cowboy.

"As if you could ever say no to being my sister-in-law." Ruby slides an arm around my waist before Lawson releases me to her hug.

Holy hell in a hand basket.

Now tears glide down my face freely.

"Sister, actually. No degrees of separation in this family," Reed pipes up.

I chuckle and Ruby squeezes me before gravitating to her husband.

"Our last daughter, Harry. What do you think?" Louisa snuggles into Harry's side.

"I think our last captain has *finally* found her way home."

Sister.

Daughter.

Wife.

Lawson wraps around me from behind as I glance at the diamond on my ring finger, whispering, "Welcome to the ranks, Captain."

EPILOGUE
LAWSON
THREE YEARS LATER . . .

"**S**erenity House has the vote," Larry says.

Larry's the big man around here at Goldman Sachs, the one who calls the shots as far as philanthropic issues are concerned. He's one of our most senior employees and has a passion for all things women's issues, having three daughters of his own.

And one of the big reasons I took this job.

After days of researching which company's philanthropic efforts make the most impact and have the biggest budget for sponsorships, I applied for the top three. The universe must agree with my strategy, since I landed the job at Goldman Sachs.

I mean, I'm still helping people. But now I can do that and ensure bigger concerns like the safety of our women and children have the funding they need. At the rate my wife is expanding Serenity House and the services it provides, they're going to need it.

Carlie took over the House a year after we started. Serelle

handed over the reins, metaphorically, at least. She still makes her guest reappearances every few months. But Carlie is killing it as CEO, and Nadia is her new PR exec, having learned from the best. Rubes is busy running every event for the House, now four times a year.

The Christmas gala, the International Women's Day Luncheon, Summer Evening Under the Stars, and my favorite, the week-long women's retreat that takes place at R & R Ranch. Manuel is the lead guide, and he's adored by all as he delivers tough love in the safe space only he can provide for each guest to find themselves again.

We eventually took Carlson to court after multiple women stepped forward, and Carlie's payout went straight to Serenity's funding. My selfless damn wife never ceases to amaze me.

A knock on my office door pulls me from my reverie. I look to the door to see brown eyes light up over a sweet smile. "You ready, Cowboy?"

"Yep." Shutting the laptop closed, I lean back in my chair. "You?"

"Ah, well. Mills is going to freak out, but I think so?" She pads inside the office.

I rise from my seat and swipe up my phone, wallet and keys. "I can't wait to see her face."

"You're mean." She slides her arms around my neck, the bracelet the girls and Ma gave her with the little ships wheel and my damn name engraved on the back of it jingles, when I meet her in the middle of my office.

"Not mean. Excited."

She raises one elegant brow. "Lawson Rawlins, stop teasing her."

I mean, she has a point; I've been leaving baby hints everywhere every time Millie comes over. The odd parenting book. A rattle I picked up from the shit-and-glitter shop, as Carlie calls it. I slide a hand to her belly. "I'm not teasing her, Mrs. Rawlins. Just giving her hints. She's old . . ."

The shit-eating grin wrapping my face hardly falters when she slaps my shoulder hard.

"Mills may be many things, but old ain't one of them."

I know thinking about Millie getting older scares Carlie. And I guess at one point that little old lady was all she had. I understand, I do.

"Come on, stop procrastinating, or I'll install a car seat in the Chevy and insist on chauffeuring her and Henry everywhere they want to go."

"You're just cruel. You know that, right?"

"You love me."

"I hate you."

"Not anymore, Princess."

I kiss her. Hard. Deep—longingly so.

Fuck me. The thought that our child is growing in her belly fills my chest with warmth. Another version of this incredible woman is more than the world deserves.

She pushes her palms to my chest and breaks the contact. Her bottom lip worries its way between her teeth.

I press my forehead to hers. "Tell me, baby."

"What if I can't do both?" she breathes.

I slide my arms around her waist. "I have a plan for that."

"You do?"

"Uh huh."

"What is it?"

"Nope, you're going to have to wait and see."

"Ugh, tell me already."

I smile, pecking a kiss on her lips. "That's my line, Princess."

Millie sits on the sofa, holding Henry's hand, her worried gaze alternating between us. Carlie smiles, but she's nervous. So I dig into her bag and pull out the ultrasound picture. The small apartment that used to be mine and is now Millie and Henry's looks much cozier than it did when I lived here.

Carlie takes the image from my hand and passes it to Millie.

"Huh, will you look at that, Hen. They're having a baked bean?"

He chuckles and shakes his head. "I think it's a baby, my love."

She holds the picture back, squinting. "Ah, so it is." She places the sonograph on the coffee table.

Carlie's face falls. "You're not excited?"

"Oh honey, I am. But, once again, you're the last to know about this."

"What?" Carlie glances at me.

I hold my hands up in defense. "I didn't breathe a word."

Well, apart from the clues . . .

"He didn't have to, sweetheart. I've known you so long, I can read every expression, every little gesture. There's no secrets between us."

Now Millie's smile wobbles. "Congratulations, my girl."

Carlie huffs a strangled laugh, wrapping her arms around

Millie. Henry holds them both. In this moment, they are more like her parents than either her uninterested mother or her absent father ever were.

I mouth 'thank you' to Millie.

She takes my hand, squeezing it. "You are welcome, my boy."

I chuckle and fold my arms around the three of them, as if they will fit. As if I can accommodate my entire world in one hug.

I'll be trying my hardest to keep every single person in this little apartment safe and loved for as long as possible.

Save, I have something to atone for.

Luckily, I did once. Because without the sentiment that gnawed at me, propelling me to work at Serenity, the fine line we walked between hate and love never would have been traveled.

I, for one, am glad for every step we took along the way.

"I hate you," Carlie insisted repeatedly when we first met.

And life took those three little words and twisted them until they sounded like 'I love you.'

"Laws? You okay?" Carlie's looking at me, and I realize the expression that must be etched over my face. So I school it to the reverence I have for this fiery little woman and say . . .

"Yes ma'am."

THREE YEARS LATER . . .

Need to see daddy Lawson and his girls? Grab the Extended Epilogue here!
https://bookhip.com/KPQVRGF

Continue the series with Burning Love and our hot as hell firefighter, Miles Hammond.

<u>Need more cowboys? Head to Rosewood Ranch to meet Lawson's three brothers.</u>

To make a difference in the world keep turning the page to find out how readings this book helps!

HOW IT WORKS . . .

Every eBook read in this series helps, with **ALL royalties** for each book in the series going to charities picked by readers!

>>>

WHICH CHARITIES? AND CAN I PICK?

Each month, the royalty report will be tallied and a poll will be created for readers in our reader group (all are welcome) to choose their charity of choice for each book.

Info around this will be in the back of each book so you never lose it. You can also suggest charities by commenting on the poll post or emailing me!

>>>

JOIN, VOTE & MAKE A DIFFERENCE!

ACKNOWLEDGMENTS

Lawson and Carlie's book was such a joy to write! Laws is such a favorite, and for good reason. He has the biggest . . . heart 😄. And Carlie is pure fire in every aspect of her life. She's literally #girlbossgoals. For me at least, anyway . . . And just who Serenity House needed at the helm.

As always, thanks to my editors, Lindsey and Zainab. Your input and guidance is always wanted and appreciated.

To every *ARC reader* who volunteered to read this book, thank you!!

And to **every reader**! Just by enjoying this spicy, heartfelt story and turning the pages you have contributed to a positive difference for woman all over the world! So, don't forget to join the group and put in your vote!

Til next time beautiful . . .

Alex xx

P.S Here is the link in case you need it -
https://www.facebook.com/groups/24719317007675361

ABOUT THE AUTHOR

Alexandra Banks is a romantic at heart, and an optimist down to her very bones. Her love for everything romance sees her writing HEAs all day long.

But don't be fooled, there will be angst along the way, possibly heartbreak. But her fierce heroines can handle just about anything!

For more heartwarming reads, follow her on socials and join the mailing list so you never miss another heart throb!

www.ingramcontent.com/pod-product-compliance
Lightning Source LLC
Chambersburg PA
CBHW010343170726
48283CB00009B/2944